PLAN D

SIMON URBAN

PLAN D

Translated from the German by Katy Derbyshire

Harvill *Secker*

LONDON

Published by Harvill Secker 2013

2 4 6 8 10 9 7 5 3 1

Copyright © Schöffling & Co. Verlagsbuchhandlung GmbH 2011
English translation copyright © Katy Derbyshire 2013

Simon Urban has asserted his right under the Copyright,
Designs and Patents Act 1988 to be identified as the author of this work

First published with the title *Plan D* by Schöffling & Co. in Germany in 2011

First published in Great Britain in 2013 by
HARVILL SECKER,
Random House
20 Vauxhall Bridge Road
London SW1V 2SA

www.randomhouse.co.uk

Addresses for companies within The Random House Group Limited
can be found at: www.randomhouse.co.uk/offices.htm

The Random House Group Limited Reg. No. 954009

A CIP catalogue record for this book is available from the British Library

ISBN 9781846556920 (hardback)
ISBN 9781846556937 (trade paperback)

The translation of this work was supported by a grant from the Goethe-Institut
which is funded by the German Ministry of Foreign Affairs

GOETHE
INSTITUT

The Random House Group Limited supports the Forest Stewardship Council (FSC®),
the leading international forest certification organisation. Our books carrying the FSC label
are printed on FSC® certified paper. FSC is the only forest certification scheme endorsed
by the leading environmental organisations, including Greenpeace. Our paper procurement

For my parents
In memory of Günter Schabowski

Those who cannot remember the past
are condemned to repeat it.
GEORGE SANTAYANA

WEDNESDAY 19 OCTOBER 2011

1

WEGENER UNDID THE FLIES OF HIS CORDS, pulled out his penis with two fingers and relaxed. There was absolute silence for a few seconds and then hot urine splashed on to the dry leaves, coming in spasms; one gush dried up and then came the next, swelling into a steaming arc and then dwindling again. Wegener adjusted his legs wider, counting along. For the tenth, the eleventh, for the twelfth time the thin jet built itself up and shrank away, suddenly interrupted, and then there were only drips.

If you have to leave the crime scene, at least don't come back with piss on your shoes, Früchtl always used to say – and then never managed it himself. Nobody would have noticed his shoes if he hadn't said anything beforehand.

Wegener leaned his head back. Stared up into the night. The metal cladding on the pipeline glinted in the moonlight, a silvery strip vanishing between the trees on either side. That strip would glint on and on if you followed it, if you kept the same distance from the pipe and let the moonlight hit the metal at the right angle, through a blurred labyrinth of oak trunks and the concrete pillars of the pipeline viaduct, on and on for kilometres over the rustling leaf-strewn ground to the sector border.

This pipe is still lighting the way to the West, thought Wegener. This pipe is the big fat Ariadne's thread of socialism. He couldn't help laughing. The men at the top would sway their heads on their shoulders and say: Superficially, perhaps, but if you look closely you're sure to notice that this pipe is in fact lighting the way to the East, deep into the Socialist Union, into the Urals, all the way to Siberia even, and that's a crucial difference – it's only the gas that goes West, nothing else.

Wegener shook his penis, pushed it back into his trousers and zipped up the fly. In the depths of the forest, the forensics team's lights flared up, glistening spots dissected by tree trunks, more and more of them, quickly melding into one big spot towards which he was now heading half-blind as if towards the light at the end of a dark tunnel, stumbling over branches and shrubs until it was light enough for a glance down at his shoes: two stains on the right, one on the left.

Lienecke and his team had set up eight spotlights, four on either side of the pipeline, which was no longer glinting silvery but looked mottled and mossy, the largest of the many shabby supply channels slicing East Germany into ever thinner strips. Behind the fluttering tape, the man from the Energy Ministry and his security officers had long since petrified into bored, gawping spectators. Next to them, the generator droned on its trailer, red cables snaking like tracks of dried blood up the hill through the fallen leaves. Lienecke was handing out boxes full of rubbish bags. His assistants began raking leaves and tipping them in the sacks with the diligence of ants, as if the Politburo had just banned dried leaves with immediate effect.

As always when he watched Lienecke and his team at work – diving, climbing, digging, taping, scraping, bagging, sorting, sweeping, scratching – Wegener was glad he had nothing to do with their jigsaw puzzles, glad he could rely on these people who had realized early enough that fortune and misfortune depended on a drop of sweat, sperm or urine on a shoe and that inexhaustible patience was a rare gift which could get you a long way, especially in the German Democratic Republic.

None of the assistants talked as they worked. Lienecke said nothing either. There was only the drone of the generator and the rustling of the leaves. Now and then a branch cracked. The six stolidly rummaging men in their white overalls looked to Wegener like strangely com-posed animals in a laborious but fruitless search for food. This forensics species communicated via invisible signals, marked out their patch telepathically, possessed a secret choreography, stalked across the forest floor like a lethargic population of albino storks in synchronized slow motion, all in a row, one step per minute.

Wegener turned to the two uniformed men leaning against their Phobos and smoking, showing not the slightest appreciation for Lienecke's leisurely ballet. The People's Policemen gazed into the darkness, presumably envying their colleagues who had driven back to HQ more than an hour ago with the hunter and his two drooling mutts, drawing on wonky cigarettes, their noses inverted chimneys blowing the smoke downwards, although the smoke was not to be fooled and rose skywards undeterred.

Wegener squatted down. He grabbed a handful of dry leaves. It hadn't rained here for days. Maybe even for weeks. The leaf-collectors could hardly reckon on tyre tracks. Footprints were even less likely.

All that remained was the eternal hope of unthinkingly spat out chewing gum, paint marks on oak bark, scraps of paper slipped through holes in trouser pockets. Wegener stood up again and leaned against a tree trunk. His watch said quarter past nine. With a bit of luck they'd start packing up here at eleven. Without, some time between one and two.

A detective is distrustful twenty-four hours a day, Früchtl had said, and a distrustful detective stays until it's all over. A distrustful detective distrusts his colleagues, forensics and the murder victim, because he's distruster number 1. First and foremost, a distrustful detective distrusts himself. The only thing you can trust in is God, Früchtl had said, and you can't even trust in Him in this country.

Lienecke's crew was gradually nearing the pipeline. Bulging sacks piled up next to the generator. The bare forest floor was a wrinkly brown skin rife with rooty veins and holes but bereft of chewing gum and scraps of paper. Lienecke raised his right hand. His men nodded.

These are the pictures that will run around my head in a hamster wheel when I'm ninety, thought Wegener, on a permanent loop in my retirement home bed, once even the last of my synapses have given up the ghost and the saliva drips onto the sheets in threads. While the others are tormented by fever dreams of gorse scrubs and gammon steaks and their old Free German Youth buddies, I'll see two smoking PPs by a floodlit island in the leaves, on which the Köpenick chapter of the Ku Klux Klan performs slow-motion dancing, stalking, rustling while a dead man dangles in the background. And the nurse will say: 'There there, Mr Wegener!' and stroke her gloved hand across my last few grey hairs, almost tenderly, as if her hand didn't have a glove on at all. 'It's all over now, Mr Wegener, that was back then, your forest, your island in the leaves, your ballet, your dead man, the chubby PPs, the man from the Energy Ministry. That's all behind you now, it played a role in your life for seven or ten days, maybe even a leading role, but not after that. Never, ever again.'

Wegener noticed the tiredness suddenly grabbing hold of him. Wrapping itself stiflingly around his head, a foam mat as thick as a kerbstone, dampening everything, swallowing everything up. He wished he could have slipped right down the rough tree trunk into the dry leaves, curled up and asked Lienecke to turn off the lights, right now, all eight of them.

One of the PPs gave a grunt. Wegener turned around.

Two bright dots flickered across the forest path at a distance, coming closer.

Lienecke raised his head, nodded and looked down again.

His assistants abandoned their digging and delving and adjusted the angle of the front spotlights. One after another, the cones of light shifted towards the pipeline, illuminating a sombre open-air stage: let the show begin. The long, gleaming Phobos Prius came into view. Its oval radiator grille sparkled. Above the car the corpse suddenly shone too. Dissected from the shadow of the gas pipeline, it stood out glaringly against the forest's black, a limp marionette floating on a single string. This dead man's turning his back on us all, thought Wegener. He may be hanging on a rope but that doesn't mean he wants anything to do with the police. His secret's all his. He's got no time for nicotine-addicted PPs, Lienecke's leaf-collecting robots, a dog-tired detective. No one here is interested in the others. Everyone here has his own job staked out: hanging, smoking, staring, searching.

For a second, Wegener was conscious of the element of the bizarre that every crime scene had about it, the unreal combination of stopped time and automated activity, the objectification of a human being, the enforced, random community in which none of those present had ever been interested. The coincidence that ended up with one of them hanging and the others digging, a coincidence that could easily have been arranged the other way around.

In the present combination I'm a Hauptmann with the People's Police, thought Wegener, and the skinny old man strung up over there with the expensive coat, silk tie, gold watch and knotted-together shoelaces is the victim. Seventy-five or eighty years' life ended beneath the Main Pipeline North by the shores of the Müggelsee lake, for whatever reason, and the whole drama starts up again – the investigation factory, the questions, the lies, the hunches. There are only ever five possible answers: natural causes, accidental death, suicide, manslaughter, murder. One outcome is just as little use as the next, every result comes too late, only ever satisfying bureaucrats' ambitions and dulling relatives' pain but remaining forever inconsequential.

By this time the bouncing rays of light on the forest path had transformed into two headlamps which swept down the slight slope, glided through the hollow and turned in a dazzling arc. The exhaust pipe wheezed. A Wartburg Aktivist, thought Wegener, old but well looked after. The car came to a halt by the generator. The wheezing died down. The ministry delegation gaped. Two aluminium tail fins shimmered, a cloud of rapeseed oil drifted over, that familiar overheated deep-fried stench, and then the headlights went out, the interior light went on, a blond-haired man dug about inside a bag, put something in it, opened the car door, clambered out, greeted the gawping spectators, slammed the door and walked up to Wegener.

'Dr Sascha Jocicz,' he said with a slightly breathless voice. 'Forensic Medicine Mitte, duty pathologist.'

'Martin Wegener, Köpenick CID,' said Wegener and had to endure a long, painful handshake.

'Colonel Wegener?'

'Captain, Doctor.'

The doctor didn't smile while squashing strangers' hands on the job, so Wegener didn't smile either. Jocicz released him and viewed the pipeline, the dead man, the gleaming Prius, the bags of leaves. His eyes wandered from right to left across the scene, then back again from left to right. Scanning it in, thought Wegener. Jocicz turned around, strode to his Wartburg, snappily opened the lid of the boot, snappily extracted a large metal briefcase, snappily slammed the lid of the boot, checked his hair in the back window and ran a tender hand across his parting.

The man consists almost entirely of straight edges, thought Wegener, a square skull with a square chin. Below that, square shoulders. Legs like steel struts underneath his trousers, presumably. Muscled girders for marching extra snappily.

'Who's rattling so late through the night and the wind?' Lienecke ducked through beneath the crime scene tape.

'Ah, the Goethe of the forensics department.' Jocicz held his hand out to Lienecke and both men grabbed hold without moving a muscle in their faces.

'Evening, Ulf.'

'Evening, Sascha.'

Wegener wondered who was pressing harder, Ulf or Sascha.

'Problems with the starter motor?' Lienecke liberated his hand to scratch his head. The pathologist had won.

'They can't get it right. Or not with the winter production

series. It's the second one I've had this year. The pinion keeps on breaking.'

'How much is a starter for a Wartburg?'

'Too much. But I hear the new Agitator is a whole different matter.' Jocicz snapped open his metal case and pulled out a white protective suit.

'You know someone who drives an Agitator?' asked Wegener, looking up at the sky. A strong wind had caught the tops of the trees. The whole forest started rustling.

'I even know someone who drives a Phobos Datscha.'

'Me too,' said Lienecke. 'Chairman Moss.'

Jocicz smiled a square smile and climbed into his suit.

'What are you expecting of the gas consultations with West Germany, Hauptmann Wegener? My mother always says all politicians are criminals. A detective like you ought to have a feeling in his water for that kind of thing.'

'Your mother's probably right,' said Wegener. 'One thing's for sure – no one's going to get arrested in the end.'

'You're right there.'

'Lafontaine will stuff his face with sausages in Weimar,' said Lienecke, 'while they spend twelve hours arguing over the price of gas, and then he'll go home again. In his VW Phaeton with heated seats and a working starter.'

'Twelve hours isn't nearly enough.' Wegener looked over at the dead man now moving slightly in the wind. The rustling in the treetops had grown stronger. Leaves floated through the floodlight like huge golden snowflakes. 'Who can eat more sausages? Lafontaine or Chairman Moss?'

'Take a look at Chairman M, the human marsupial. He can beat anyone hands down at sausage-scoffing.'

'That's a six-month stretch right there, Sascha.'

'I said human marsupial, not bacon-belly. Human marsupial only gets you three months.'

Wegener turned and stared out at the darkness, suddenly getting the feeling someone else was there, someone with his eye on him, observing everything. Someone leaning on an oak tree with night-vision goggles and a shotgun microphone. Someone who'd have a lot to tell about what had happened here over the past few hours, and who only wished the search crew would finally end its pointless hunt for clues that didn't exist, because they'd all been removed long ago. So that the observer of the observers could go home at last too.

I can smell you, thought Wegener, you spies, behind your bushes and walls and masquerades. If there's one thing I can count on it's my nose, and you stink, brothers, down from the attics, up from the cellars, out from behind the rubbish skips. I can sniff out your cigarette butts, your bugs, your telephoto lenses, your self-assurance – that most of all.

Wegener was still staring.

Lienecke and the square-edged pathologist were looking at him. Nobody said anything.

Rustling of leaves and droning of the generator, nothing else. Whoever had been standing there now withdrew, soundless, invisible. This would be the moment to kick the PPs in the pants, thought Wegener, then run into the forest with torches until the fleeing shadow might detach itself from some tree trunk, the shadow you never caught anyway but at least you'd know it was really out there.

One of Lienecke's men called out, bent down, kneeling in the dead leaves. Lienecke put on his glasses and climbed over the fluttering tape.

'German forests,' Jocicz said, 'are a source of joy precisely up to the moment when you have to comb them for fingerprints.'

Wegener stepped up to the tape. 'Mind if I take a look at your work from close up?'

'Were you apprenticed to Josef Früchtl?'

'Thankfully, yes.'

'Then I can't say no, can I?'

'No,' said Wegener, 'you can't.'

Jocicz plucked at his protective suit. 'There's another one of these in the case.'

Now the four spotlights on the other side of the pipeline were adjusted as well. The dead man was suddenly backlit, the pipe a dirty bulge of bent metal, welding seams and fat bolt nuts. Awoken by the sudden daylight, moths circled on the air, alive once more. Tomorrow the cold autumn will send you plummeting from the branches in your sleep, thought Wegener as he clambered into the much too large plastic suit. The PPs turned away, smoking on into the darkness.

Jocicz was waiting by the tape. He smiled at the sight of a detective wrapped in cling film, making his square face a little rounder. Jocicz strode off, Wegener following him across the cleared ground, in a semicircle around the right-hand concrete pillar supporting the pipeline. With every step, a little more of the hanged man came into view, now turning hesitantly to his visitors until he finally showed a wrinkled waxy face, a bent beak of a nose, bushy brows, white beard.

Jocicz stopped in front of the dead man and shone his torch down him centimetre by centimetre. Pushed up the trouser legs and examined the pale, hairy calves. Pressed the thumbs of his gloves into the pallid flesh. Photographed the slightly curled hands, the discoloured fingernails, the joints. Eyed the worn-out shoes with their laces tied together, photographed them and said nothing. His movements had lost all their snappiness. Like a cat, he slunk around the limp body, made notes, climbed on a ladder, fingered the back of the corpse's head, the grey hair, the astounded face, shone his torch into the dead eyes and came down again.

Wegener watched. By the time Jocicz was done the silhouettes of the two PPs were sitting motionless in the car, chins on their chests. The group from the ministry was caught up in discussion. Lienecke's men had cleared the complete inner cordoned ring of leaves. One of them was loading the sacks onto two covered trailers, the others walking through the woods behind the tape barrier with hand-held lamps. Drunken outsized fireflies, they wouldn't find anything as long as they weren't supposed to find anything.

'If you wouldn't mind.' Jocicz had unpacked his friendliest voice. Wegener tried to muster up an interested face despite his tiredness. 'You did want to get close up.'

Jocicz pushed the folding ladder slightly closer to the pipeline, climbed up on the right-hand row of steps and made a gesture of invitation to follow him on the left-hand side. Wegener tugged a pair of gloves out of a pocket in his protective suit, pulled them on and tested the ladder for balance.

'Perfectly safe,' Jocicz called from above.

'A distrustful detective checks the ladder,' said Wegener more to himself than anything else, and climbed up until the dead man's back was forty centimetres away from his face. Now he could see the dark ring eaten into the long neck by the rope. Below them the Phobos Prius waited like a hearse that had been ordered too soon. Two dents in the black roof.

Jocicz looked over the hanging man's shoulder, his hands feeling, his rubber fingers climbing up the taut rope, clenching into a fist, pulling short and hard on it.

Wegener looked Jocicz straight in the eye. Jocicz held his gaze.

'An execution,' said Wegener.

'That's what it looks like,' said Jocicz.

'Or a staged execution.'

'That's possible too.'

'When?'

'About forty-eight hours ago,' said Jocicz. 'Probably slightly less. Cause of death not strangulation but a broken neck. They put him on the roof of the car and drove off, a metre and a half's drop: exitus.'

'OK.'

'Shoelaces tied together and a hangman's knot with eight turns, Hauptmann Wegener. A good chance of the shit hitting the fan.'

'So I noticed.'

'And the clothes look like he's a bigwig.'

'Absolutely.'

Jocicz ran a hand through his hair. A small yellow leaf that had caught in his parting floated down. Wegener noticed that the body smelled. Of sweat, of dull mould and the gradual onset of decay.

'What are you going to do now?'

Wegener clutched the cold crosspieces of the ladder with both hands. 'Investigate. I'm the investigating officer.'

'An investigating officer who can't arrest anyone.'

'That doesn't matter, nobody ever gets arrested anyway,' said Wegener and climbed slowly back down the ladder.

THURSDAY 20 OCTOBER 2011

2

WEGENER OPENED HIS EYES, CLOSED THEM AGAIN, opened them again. The fan was stuck to the ceiling above him like a round insect with three fat, flat legs. The lazy creature never moved a muscle, never had moved a muscle, presumably never would move a muscle. Perhaps it wasn't even connected up. Wegener tried to remember whether Karolina had ever got the fan to whirr, in some hot summer or other, to conjure up a bit of a movie atmosphere. He couldn't think of any occasion. The thing had always just hung dead and cast a slowly migrating shadow across the ceiling. A contorted spider's shadow.

He felt for his Minsk on the bedside table, pressed the menu button and held the luminous display right in front of his nose: 10:49. One missed call, 09:53, *W. B. Office*. Borgs had now been waiting an hour for him to call back, two hundred photos of the crime scene spread out in front of him, the witness statement from Hunter Whatshisname in his head, his paunch filled to bursting with the staunch determination that had seen him sweeping files off the desks of his department whenever political tornadoes appeared on the horizon for the past eighteen years. The Borgsian sweeping-off practice was fine by him in this case, Wegener noted.

He turned onto his stomach, pressed his face into the pillow, pulled the cover over his head and calculated how long this whole pipeline thing was likely to keep him busy: realistically, eight hours.

By then C5 would have taken over and slammed a security level on it: classified documents, over and out. Or it'd go straight to Normannenstrasse: State Security, Internal Department. Jocicz could hand over the post-mortem, Lienecke the evidence, he could be rid of the weeks of puzzling, the interrogation of passers-by, horse-riders, mushroom-pickers, pipeline security guards, the arguments with the Energy Ministry over investigations in the restricted zone and all the rest of it. All he'd get instead was a non-disclosure agreement under Special Investigation Status III, a thin yellow sheet of paper with a whole lot of small-print threats ranging from demotion to dismissal to Bautzen special prison. Then everyone who'd been there last night could sign on the dotted line that they didn't want to either lose their jobs or be sentenced to imprisonment for betraying official secrets and would therefore *in future speak or otherwise communicate with no one – including with related persons/spouses and/or the colleagues involved in the aforementioned investigation – on the subject of the aforementioned investigative stages or all accompanying circumstances.*

The part about *otherwise communicating* always made Wegener think of smoke signals. Perhaps because of the Red Indian camps Tobias Kirchhoff had used to organize every summer for the Free German Youth somewhere up in Mecklenburg.

Wegener imagined Jocicz, Lienecke and the forensic guys in a circle around a smoking campfire in Neustrelitz, each of them clutching a blanket in an attempt to *otherwise communicate* about the man hanging from the pipeline. Jocicz wrote on the evening sky with clouds of smoke: Believe me, men, shoelaces tied together, the hangman's knot tied eight times – it was them, without a doubt, for God's sake. And Lienecke, waving his blanket: No doubt about it, we found nothing in the leaves, not the slightest clue, and precisely that is the clue, they're the only ones who work so neatly! And all the forensics guys with synchronized fanning movements like a Greek chorus: Not the slightest clue, that's the clue!

Wegener tossed his cover aside, got up with a groan, opened the window a crack and shuffled into the bathroom. The last functioning ceiling lamp sent its sparse light down towards the washbasin. The toilet and bathtub were left behind in green-tiled darkness.

On top of the bathroom cabinet gleamed Karolina's old deodorant spray, a glittering salmon-pink phallus labelled *Action*.

The last piece of action in our relationship, Karolina had said at some point, and Wegener had replied: First of all, that was a really bad pun, and second at least this Action never runs out, it waits for you your whole life long, piled up on the shelves of the Konsum supermarket, produced with great solidarity by the Cosmetics and Care Combine. Karolina: Which you've never even heard of. Wegener: I prefer to smell like a man. Karolina: I can smell that.

And now he'd been incapable of throwing away an ugly spray can that had been lurking salmon-pink in his bathroom for the past year. That shone every morning in the spotlight of the semi-invalid lamp like a has-been singer on the Eisenhüttenstadt open-air stage belting out that old chestnut about the pain of loss that makes all of us the same.

Wegener propped himself against the basin with both hands and looked in the mirror at a face that had been his for fifty-six years.

Despite its beakish nose, receding fair hair and slightly too rounded cheeks, this face of his sometimes appeared good-looking to him. Not today. Today that visage, checked a hundred thousand times, looked lacking in contours, random, out of proportion, rendered ridiculous by red lines across it left behind by the folds of his sheet, a crumpled map marked with a few won and a lot of lost battles. Hauptmann Hanging Cheeks.

Nothing for Karolina to miss, thought Wegener and knew he'd thought the opposite just as often, in front of the same mirror with the same sheet folds across his forehead.

He turned the spray can around so that he couldn't read the word *Action* any more and turned on the radio. Jan 'The Smooch' Hermann, announced the perma-grinning presenter's voice, the king of the GDR's soft-rock swingers, and his new song 'No Doubt Time Hates Love'. A series of interchangeable chords set in.

Don't forget, said Früchtl's voice in his head, *men are like wooden floorboards, they get more beautiful as they age. Women are like wooden floorboards under a leaky roof, they get worse and worse until it all falls through.*

How I miss your verbal derailments, thought Wegener.

Under the steaming hot shower he attempted to ignore Jan 'The Smooch' Hermann's wailing and imagined the conversation the men from C5 would soon be having with him, including all the obligatory walking on eggshells.

The suspicion that the pipeline murder had not been a private matter dangled as conspicuously in mid-air as the neon Goldkrone ad at Alexanderplatz, the monstrous fear that must never be thought was now spelled out in metre-high neon-lit capitals, flashing green and red, impossible to ignore. So the gentlemen would hunch on Borgs' blue-upholstered office chairs with carefully controlled

funereal faces and reel off instructions learned by rote, driven by
the gnawing fear of actually emitting a comprehensible sentence. The
language of speechlessness, communication skills à la East Germany.
And they'd all keep peeking over at Borgs. And Borgs would sit
enthroned in his window nook like a well-fed friar, his hands folded
over his pot belly, apparently sleeping but at least permanently mute.

Wegener had experienced Borgs in this kind of competence pickle
twice before, on both occasions cases of 'acts in preparation for
attempted escape from the republic'. On both occasions curtailed by
'accidental death prior to implementation'.

On both occasions, Borgs had transmogrified into a silent monk
in the meetings with the special departments, letting the men in grey
suits do the talking, listening to the helpless ticker-tape sentences
and intricate insinuations and saying nothing. Nameless colonels
provided the C5 men with investigation findings, handed over
reports and slammed the files shut. Ancient games played according
to rules that had never been changed. In the end Borgs had ushered
the whole lot of them out with nothing but his friendly bulldog
expression. Without having barked a single word.

Walter, you've bitten your tongue to the top of the career ladder,
thought Wegener and turned off the hot water. Keeping your trap
shut is the true art of running a police department. Then he spotted
the tick on his right calf. A small black ball that had just taken the
first and last shower of its parasitic life.

The shabby chessboard of the police headquarters corridors still
always seduced Wegener into adjusting the length of his steps to the
pattern. He tried to put the tips of his feet down exactly on the edge
of a square, which led to a familiar problem – steps the length of
one square were too short, steps across two squares were too long.

The alternatives were mincing or striding. Wegener felt like striding. How often did you get an investigation where you could pass the buck to the specialists on the very first day?

With extended steps, he marched up to Borgs' outer office and celebrated the first victory of the day: the tip of his left shoe landed exactly on the line of the last square and touched the door at the same time. *Touché.*

Christa Gerdes didn't go to the effort of looking up from her monitor, preferring to hammer numbers into her old Robotron Kappa with enough emphasis to make her fur hat of a hairdo sway in time, merely folding out a gaunt arm briefly to form a wrinkled signpost straight ahead. *Women are like wooden floorboards under a leaky roof,* Wegener heard Früchtl murmur, knocked at the open door and saw instantly that he'd been right: the desk in the window alcove was sown with photos of the pipeline, the forest floor, the rope, the dented car roof and a face that looked somehow more alive in the yellowish light of the reading lamp than it had a few hours ago in the city forest.

Wegener took a deep breath and stepped into the boss's den, the darkroom, the smokehouse. Whatever they called this yellowed room it was all true, and no meeting in here ever lasted longer than fifteen minutes.

'Martin.' Borgs squashed out the stump of his cigarillo in a small cardboard tray. Annoyance over the pipeline murder was written all over his round face, a truckload of hassle was headed straight for his department just when everything could have been so good, a quiet October morning completely free of old men killed by bizarre ritual methods. 'Only four weeks to go till the consultations, Martin. And then this.'

'We seem to need the hard currency from the gas pretty urgently –'

Wegener closed the door behind him and pointed at the steaming cardboard tray – 'if we're even running out of ashtrays now.'

'Good old Christa,' Borgs said proudly and sank back into his chair. 'When she breaks things it's always the important ones.'

'A woman of consequence.'

'What do you think?' Borgs folded his hands in front of his pot belly.

'About hard currency or our man here?'

'How about a link between the two?'

Wegener dragged one of the blue-upholstered chairs up to the desk and sat down. 'It all looks as if we've got a problem.'

'Let's hope it's not us who has the problem.' Borgs ran his eyes across the photos. 'But they'll have a fit in the ministry at Werderscher Markt when they hear the whole story, believe you me.'

'Have you informed C5?'

'All in good time. I've only had it on my desk a couple of hours, haven't I? And I wanted to talk to you first.'

'Openly?'

'From man to man. As you can see.' Borgs lit up a new cigarillo, took a puff and heaved his short, fat legs onto the left-hand corner of his desk. A penny-shaped hole in each sole.

Wegener took off his coat and hung it over the back of his chair.

'Let's see what we've got,' said Borgs, smacking his lips and blowing a mouthful of smoke at the ceiling. 'One deceased male, about eighty. Cause of death: broken neck, hanged from the Main Pipeline North close to the sector border. Suicide ruled out. A crime scene as clean as a mermaid's backside.'

'Can't get cleaner than that,' said Wegener.

'Any cleaner is absolutely impossible,' Borgs confirmed. 'And slap-bang in the middle of this all-encompassing cleanliness someone leaves leads that clearly say old Stasi cadre have wiped out a supposed traitor. Shoelaces tied together, eightfold hangman's knot. That's how the Stasi got rid of their own. Last happened about two decades ago, in the course of the Revitalization of our beloved GDR. Allegedly. No one knows. Just one of those things everyone says when it suits them, behind closed doors. Right. And in a month's time Oskar Lafontaine's coming over to rescue our bankrupt old wreck of a state. Provided the wreck of a state behaves itself. Only right now it looks like the wreck of a state's been a pretty bad boy. What kind of a circus is this, Martin? Who's taking the piss here?'

Wegener fanned cigarillo smoke away from his face. 'Those traitor murders, are they just rumours or did they really happen?'

'Don't ask me.' Borgs shrugged his broad shoulders. 'I've never met anyone who knows. But it doesn't matter. The signs speak their own language either way.'

'Shoelaces tied together: You can't run away from us. I get that. But the hangman's knot?'

'Eight ties.' Borgs held up eight short, fat fingers through the smoke. 'The 8th of February 1950. Founding date of the Ministry for State Security. Call it a reminder of the old ideals, if you like. Of the tradition of brotherhood.'

'They were sick madmen.'

'Dangerous sick madmen.'

Wegener coughed. 'Two possibilities. Our man was with the Stasi, botched something up and they wanted to get rid of him. And make an example of him at the same time. A signal to insiders, if you like. So they revitalize the old method so that everyone in the Stasi knows: This is what happens when you go behind our backs.'

'Bullshit.' Borgs shook his head. 'The man's eighty if he's a day!

And even if the secret service does still knock people off, which it can't afford to do under the international agreements, then not like that. And not four weeks before the consultations. One proven violation of the rule-of-law criteria and all the lights go out over here. What's your second possibility?'

'Someone's trying to finger the Stasi by warming up their old methods.'

Borgs smacked his lips, puffed on his cigarillo, smacked his lips again. 'If I wanted to pin something on the Stasi it'd have to go public, I'd need a scandal. How's that supposed to work? Who's going to kick up a fuss? C5 will be taking over tonight. Special Investigation Status. Nothing will get out. And I can't imagine Uwe Speckmann running straight to the seven-thirty news with the story.'

'Now that would be a surprise.'

Wegener got up, drew the heavy curtain aside slightly and opened the old double window. Cold air blew into the room, replacing the stench of smoke with the stench of fat. Down on Lechner Allee, a white Phobos II Universal was battling with a parking space, the driver's bald head poking out of the side window, turning first right and then left, from here an indecisive, skin-coloured bulge. In the middle of the bulge was a plaster. The Universal paused at an angle, gave up and sped off.

'Maybe it was the men from back then,' said Wegener.

'What d'you mean, the men from back then?'

'Old-school cadre. The ones they say did all that in '89 and '90. Men who were in action back in Stangier's days. Then comes Revitalization, their good old Heinrich takes early retirement, Moss takes the hot seat, Speckmann takes over from Erich Mielke, they get the boot during the reforms and the New Direction. But there's still some kind of score they have to settle.'

'Possible in theory,' grunted Borgs. 'But twenty-one years is a bloody long time to wait. Why now?'

'Maybe our shoelace man had a really good hiding place.'

Borgs looked unhappy. 'And they still go to all that trouble setting the scene? Who's it supposed to scare nowadays?'

'Other traitors from back then. No idea. Maybe they only did it for the principle. But it's all pointless as long as we don't know whether our old man was with the Stasi or not.'

'We need to know who our old man is in the first place.'

Wegener sat down again. 'And what if it's just about the pipeline? The consultations?'

'I was thinking that too. Russian Mafiosi. Some crazy old guy who didn't pay his bribes. But the Russians do things differently.'

'The Russian method.'

'For example. What do you make of the dented car roof?'

'Improvisation. Or another symbol, one only insiders can understand. But why did they take the licence plates away with them?'

'No idea.' Borgs slid his legs off the edge of the desk. 'There's one thing that's important: very soon now, Werderscher Markt will be looking very closely at the whole thing. And the Central Committee will stick its nose in personally too. And for us, that means we do exactly what we're supposed to do. Work to rule. I don't have to give Kallweit even more of a target just because he wants to wangle more powers for the secret services.'

'That's me off the case then.'

'Almost.' Borgs the surly bulldog mutated into Borgs the wily bulldog. 'They found an envelope in the dead man's coat last night. They're still looking for prints.'

The wily bulldog shoved all the photos aside, ran his finger across his desktop and stopped at a note. 'The envelope's addressed by hand to one Emil Fischer, just the name, no address, no stamp, nothing. Inside was a sheet of paper, a computer printout. Text: *Dear neighbours, dear comrades, we're having a birthday celebration on Saturday, 22.10.2011. We hope its not too noisy.* No apostrophe in its. *Yours faithfuly,* faithfully with a single L, *M. Radecker, I. Dedelow, 16th floor.*'

'Then Fischer could be our man,' said Wegener.

'Or one of the birthday boys who didn't manage to put the envelope in Fischer's letter box.'

'True.'

'Maybe someone just broke into Fischer's letter box, we don't know. Christa's looked them up, there's only one combination of Radecker, Dedelow and Fischer registered in Berlin. At 32, Ludwig-Renn-Strasse.'

Borgs heaved himself out of his seat, waddled to the window, shut it and pulled the curtain straight. 'You take care of this thing today, maybe you can get an ID on him, a couple of comments from the neighbours, then we won't be completely empty-handed. And I'd like a detailed report, please, in tip-top form.'

'Tomorrow evening?'

'Tomorrow morning at the latest. Then we'll go on a work to rule until they take the case out of our hands. I'll get right on to the gentlemen. And if they want to see you too, Martin, and I assume they will, let me give you a little tip.'

'Keep shtum,' said Wegener.

'Learn from Borgs – learn to win.' The bulldog collapsed satisfied into its seat.

3

VOSS HAD A SMELL ABOUT HIM. Up to now, Wegener had only heard that Voss had a smell about him, and now he smelled it. Voss had a smell about him of unwashed Elasta ribbed vests made by the Sigmund Jähn Publicly Owned Company, of untipped Karo cigarettes, of onions, garlic, dental tartar, of obtrusive concern for exact observation of traffic regulations and of something else that Wegener couldn't identify. Perhaps a last, sad vestige of Florena Sport Deodorant, which had lost the battle against butyric acid, tobacco and various vegetables from the Allium family days ago and was now attempting to evaporate with as little fuss as possible.

'Sorry about the Navodobro, sir. Sieberg sat on it by accident, and no display can take that.'

'I'm sure we'll find the place without it.'

Voss leaned forward as he steered the squad car. His large-pored turnip nose almost on the dashboard, both hands clutching the steering wheel, his eyes screwed up in permanent dim anticipation of malign catastrophe. The seams of his grey police trousers cut into the fat Vossian thighs with the mercilessness of all East German uniform textiles and laced up the Vossian genitalia into a tennis ball-sized lump.

Wegener felt a cold shudder running down his back. It might be weeks before be got that abnormally round genital bulge out of his head. A bulge like that might come to you in your dreams. A bulge like that might even speak to you in your dreams. If that bulge starts telling me stories every night, thought Wegener, I'll jump off the top of the EastSide onto Alexanderplatz.

'Not again!' Voss cast a dark glare at the rows of phenoplast vehicles driving along Liebknecht Ring, keeping to the speed limit, respecting minimum distances. 'There! On the bridge pillar! Have you noticed what they've started scrawling everywhere?'

Wegener looked at Voss.

'*All PPs drive Phobos TTs!*' Voss snorted a few droplets of saliva at the windscreen. 'What the hell else? What else are we supposed to drive, eh? Maseratis? They should have sprayed it when the Trabi was done away with, the dickheads, at least it would've been new back then!'

Wegener tried in vain to wind his window down a little. The handle was broken off directly above the crank.

'And everyone else drives a Phobos as well!' said Voss. 'Apart from the couple of anoraks who can't bear to get rid of their Trabants. What they ought to write is: *Even* PPs drive Phobos TTs!'

'Voss, you go ahead and spray that across all the walls in Köpenick if you like,' said Wegener. 'Just don't get caught.'

'I've never got caught.' Voss put his left hand between his legs, plucking at the fabric with his forefinger and thumb.

Wegener looked out of the window. The first tower blocks appeared behind the birches rushing past, becoming more frequent, growing into an army of high-rises, an unsorted brigade of boxes. On the right were the gappy teeth of a construction site fence, behind it wasteland, heaps of earth, old tyres.

The sun stayed hidden behind thin scraps of cloud, shining murkily as if through frosted glass. Yellow birch leaves mottled the cracked asphalt, dots in flux, arranged in new patterns over and over by the wind. Then the road took a sharp left turn and the stack of buildings that was Marzahn was suddenly closer than he'd thought, appearing broad, chunky and white in front of the grey sky, a wall towering for miles along the horizon.

Voss groaned.

Wegener tried not to look, guessing he was still occupied with his hand in the groin of his trousers. Voss the Hoss, Borgs had said, he stinks like a horse but he'll gallop wherever you want.

'It was a school friend of my brother-in-law, you know,' sighed Voss, 'who blessed us with the Phobos. The name, I mean.'

Wegener carried on staring at the growing backdrop of Marzahn. One more glance at Voss the Hoss with his hand down his pants would spoil the whole day before it had even begun properly.

'It was a kind of a talent contest at the time. A competition. Did you know that, sir?'

Wegener shook his head.

'They didn't want a new Trabi, you know, everything was supposed to be different after Revitalization. Or at least have a different name. You could send in suggestions. This school friend of my brother-in-law . . . ' Voss sounded suddenly relieved. When Wegener looked over he had both hands back on the steering wheel. '. . . he looked up Mars in an encyclopaedia. The red planet, you get it, the star of socialism, if you like.'

Wegener took his notepad out of his coat pocket and opened up the page with Christa Gerdes' sketch on it. Green felt-tip arrows snaked through blue biro blocks to a black cross: 32, Ludwig-Renn-Strasse.

'I'm really sorry about the Navodobro,' said Voss.

Wegener rotated the drawing ninety degrees. 'No problem.'

'Landsberger Allee. Allee der Kosmonauten on the right.'

'Left,' said Wegener. 'On to Raoul-Wallenberg-Strasse.'

'Speaking of cosmonauts,' said Voss and put his foot down too far. 'This school friend, right, he came across a satellite of Mars in the encyclopaedia, flying around up there somewhere, and that satellite's called Phobos. And Trabant's another word for satellite, isn't it, so he sent in Phobos as his suggestion, with the explanation that if you call the new plastic car Phobos TT then it'd be a Trabant – but not a Trabant. That's what the TT stands for – Trabant Mark Two. But it's definitely socialist. 'Cause it spends its whole life circling the planet Mars.'

'Take the fourth right onto Paul-Dessau-Strasse.'

'Paul Dessau, Paul Dessau, Paul Dessau,' said Voss, driving slower with every Paul Dessau, his forehead up to the windscreen, his chin on the steering wheel.

'Over there, by the stop sign.'

'Yessir.'

The sun was suddenly back again, reflected from the opened windows of the tower block, a glaring spot of light leaping from pane to pane, skipping cheerfully alongside the police car down Raoul-Wallenberg-Strasse. A hundred thousand wives airing a hundred thousand kitchens, thought Wegener, getting rid of the smell of pea soup, solyanka soup, frozen schnitzel, and then they fetch the Rondo coffee out of the cupboard, make a brew, turn on DFF 5, Inka Bause's

'Talk Tough': *You better lose some weight or I'm applying to leave the country! Hey, you ex-West German – stop going on about the good old West! If they'd had Mondos condoms back then you'd never have been born!*

'Paul Dessau,' said Voss with relief and turned right into the residential area.

'Ludwig-Renn-Strasse is the second left. Number 32.'

'Ludwig Renn, Ludwig Renn, Ludwig Renn . . .' Voss wound to the left, counted down the house numbers, slowed almost to a halt, put on his right indicator, stopped in the parking lane and panted. A bean-shaped print shone on the windscreen where his forehead had been touching it.

Wegener opened the passenger's door and took a deep breath of fresh air. So this was how good it could smell in Marzahn: of autumn, of mown grass and only a tiny hint of deep-frying.

'I've put on twenty kilos since we've had to use rapeseed oil instead of petrol,' said Voss as he squeezed himself out of the car. 'Every time I get in the car I get a craving for chips with mayonnaise. This job gets you addicted, sir, absolutely addicted, but you can bet no one at head office is going to give me permission to go to a diet clinic!'

'You've got big bones.' Wegener slammed his door.

Ludwig-Renn-Strasse was composed of a handful of crumbling high-rises, decrepit Trabis, recycling bins for bottles, and yellow trees. A fat woman in tracksuit bottoms stood on a litter-strewn patch of grass, as motionless as a monument against sport. Two small black dogs scampered around her, led in unpredictable loops through the grass by their noses. One of the dogs crouched down with its legs apart, peed and stared.

Paint peeled from the cladding of the balconies. The last

geraniums shone out in a window box; on the next balcony the first Christmas lights flashed, a reindeer sleigh loaded with presents that would never come. Weeds grew between the lopsided paving stones. Would I rather live here or hang dead from a pipeline? Wegener wondered.

'Used to be a nice area,' said Voss, 'round about Revitalization. Look at it now – all old Trabis and maybe a Lada, max.'

'Number 32,' said Wegener and looked at the sketch.

'Probably one of those two over there.'

Voss the Hoss tramped over to the nearest street sign and gesticulated with his front hooves towards the right-hand tower. Wegener walked across the grass, counting the floors of the high-rise. He lost count somewhere in the middle and came to eighteen storeys on his second attempt. Manfred Radecker and Ines Dedelow lived on the sixteenth floor. So Fischer's flat was almost certainly somewhere in the top third. The expensive coat, the gold watch, the silk tie – nothing about the body went with this address. His worn-out old shoes at the most.

By the time Wegener got to the front door Voss was leaning over a wide panel of doorbells and reading out names to himself. Almost half of the name spaces were empty. Wegener leaned back. Red-toned prefab concrete sheets towered up to the sky. One sheet per storey, eighteen sheets in total. The balconies clad with corrugated metal that must have been white at some point. Now rust ate away at the cladding from the screwholes.

'R. Brose, Reinke, I. Holzmüller, they're all here,' said Voss, bending even further. 'M. Bussmann, Gert Herzog, E. Fischer – there he is, eighteenth floor.'

'Dead people always live at the top,' said Wegener and rang the bell.

Voss fumbled a tissue out of his uniform jacket, unfolded it and blew his nose.

Wegener rang the bell for *E. Fischer* again. Nothing. Then he rang *Radecker/Dedelow*. Again, nothing happened.

'They're all at work,' said Voss.

'Or in the Köpenick morgue.' Wegener pressed the bells next to Fischer for *Weber* and *A. Zauritz*.

The intercom crackled. 'Hello?' Voss called.

'Hello?' exclaimed a woman's voice.

'People's Police! If you wouldn't mind opening the door, please!'

'Only if you're in a good mood!'

'At this point, we're still in a good mood.'

'In you come then,' warbled the woman's voice. A weak buzzing droned from the speaker. Wegener pushed the door open.

The corridor smelled of soup. Dirty yellow plastered walls. The floor consisted of grey PVC squares with the edges curling upwards like old slices of cheese. Brightly coloured graffiti was scrawled across the metal lift doors:

Unemployed hero!

That's me, phenoplast-face

Ballack is bollocks

Ballack's the dog's bollocks!

'You can write your PP slogan here too,' said Wegener, taking one more deep breath and following Voss into the lift cubicle.

The lift made snapping sounds as it moved. Some of the storeys lit up as red numbers in a scratched display space, others were withheld. There were even more scribbles on the pale green plastic walls, some of them smudged into grey stains by solvent.

'*Everyone drives a Trabi, except for Moss, he drives a Benz,*' Voss read out. 'Here's one: *At least Adolf could build autobahns.*'

'They could be right there.' Wegener took his Minsk out of his coat pocket, turned off the ringtone and put it away again.

'Here!' Voss groped at the ceiling of the lift. '*All PPs drive Phobos TTs!* But over there it says everyone drives a Trabi except for Moss. They've got no idea, these idiots, they don't even know what's the matter with them here.'

The snapping sounds slowed down and the lift stopped with such a jerk that Wegener held onto the wall for support. An 18 lit up in the display. A dramatic bell rang. The metal doors slid aside, granting a view of a grubby corridor and a skinny woman. The woman was leaning against her open front door, smoking. Behind her was a pigsty full of junk.

'No smoking in here!' the woman called out with a grin. Greasy, reddish strands of hair drooped over her face like a sad rug. Her teeth reminded Wegener of the building-site fence.

'Apart from you, obviously,' Voss noted.

'Well spotted. I'm waiting for a fire to start so the cute fire brigade hunks will come round to see me.'

'Will the police do for you?'

'Sure, honey, you can do for me any time.' She laughed like a pneumatic drill, lifted up her flowery dressing gown and exposed a wilted leg with a dark blue bruise on the thigh.

Voss opened his mouth and closed it again.

'Do you know Emil Fischer?' asked Wegener. 'He's one of your neighbours here on the 18th floor.'

'*Bien sûr,*' said the skinny woman. 'Comrade Fischer's my only neighbour – everyone else has gone, gone for good. They didn't want to live next door to such a pretty young thing, as you can imagine, eh?'

'And you are . . . ?'

'Whatever you like, old man.'

'Do you know Emil Fischer?'

'Not at all, he's never here. I've only ever seen him a couple of times. I went round the other day to borrow a pound of butter, d'you want to know what for?'

'For your hair?' said Voss.

'I haven't got any more down there,' whispered the skinny woman, contorting her collapsed face into a facade of ironic regret.

'Do you want us to take you down the station?!' The Hoss was losing his temper.

'Believe me, you don't want me down your station, I promise you that. Anywhere but your bloody station!'

Wegener extracted the photo from his inside pocket, took three steps towards the skinny woman and held the print under her nose. A scent of schnapps wafted out of the flat. The building-site fence smile was wiped off her face.

'Do you live all alone on the 18th floor now, ma'am?'

'Looks like it,' breathed the woman, clutching hold of the door-frame for support. 'What have you done to him . . . ? You bastards! You've shot my last neighbour!'

'Which one is Emil Fischer's flat?'

'I'm not telling you nothing, you dirty cops, you wankers, you Nazi swine! You're the ones that shot him!'

Wegener turned away and walked along the dimly lit corridor. Thirty metres of bare, grubby corridor tunnel. A neon tube buzzed but stayed absolutely dark, another flashed on every three seconds, going out again with a slight click. The short flicker of light faded in cracks in the walls and then out again. On the floor were chunks of plaster, tangled balls of dust, stains that disappeared in the darkness, came back again, disappeared.

Wegener kept to the middle of the corridor. Waited for the next flicker for his next step. Stopped when it was dark. In the background, Voss was ordering the skinny woman inside her flat. The skinny woman yowled. Voss raised his voice.

Wegener opened up his Minsk and shone the display on the name signs by the doorbells. Two doors with no names. Above the third doorbell was a length of tape, on which someone had written the letters *We* in ballpoint pen, the rest torn off. In front of the fourth door was a large piece of plaster. Wegener held up his display: from the ceiling hung spiderwebs with dead mosquitoes suspended in them, dark water stains.

Three doors with no names. Then a strip of tape, this time with a complete name in red felt-tip: E. FISCHER. Wegener took the magnetic card for the police station car park out of his wallet, held his Minsk directly above the door's lock and attempted to insert the card between the lock and the frame. He got a couple of centimetres in, then no more. There was something blocking the way. Wegener pressed harder and the plastic bent. He pulled the card out of the slit in the door and tried slightly further down.

At the other end of the corridor, Voss and the woman had disappeared into her flat. Wegener bent down and inspected the lock. No signs of a break-in, not even a scratch. The barrel had a new cover on it. One of Lienecke's men would have to take a look at it.

The skinny woman's laugh echoed along the corridor and collapsed abruptly. The Hoss came trotting up, waving something in his right hand.

'Sir! She's got a spare key!'

Voss stopped under the winking neon tube, his face now an ominously flickering, flesh-coloured smiley. 'He gave it to her a year ago so she could water the plants.'

'With schnapps?'

'She swears she never helped herself to anything.'

Wegener shook his head, inserted the key into the lock and turned it twice, then pushed the door open with his elbow. Dazzling brightness. Two large windows, no curtains.

Voss huffed with disappointment as if he'd been expecting a penthouse rather than a prefab flat.

Wegener skimmed the one-room apartment with his eyes. In the left-hand corner was an old sofa bed, folded out and made up, the orangey-brown duvet neatly folded in half. To the right of the door was a kitchen area with a cooker and a fridge; next to the sink a pile of plates, cups, two glasses containing cutlery, Sonja coffee filters, a bottle of Lumikor cleaning fluid.

In front of the window a kitchen table with two folding chairs, on the windowsill several flowerpots with roses growing in them. The plants looked as perfect as if they'd just been bought. In the back right-hand corner, two walls separated off a small bathroom. Through the open door, Wegener could see a rosé toilet with a matching rug around it. The whole flat had the same grey PVC flooring as the corridor, albeit thoroughly cleaned. A few paler squares in the kitchen area had obviously been replaced.

'What do you think, Voss?'

'It looks like a showroom apartment: the socialist bedsitter in 1970. I couldn't live in a place like this.'

'I'm guessing E. Fischer saw it the same way,' said Wegener. 'No curtains, no pictures, no carpet, no tablecloth, no books, no shelves. Not even a wardrobe. But roses in pots.'

'Second home,' said Voss. 'Perhaps he lives somewhere else and only comes to Berlin every now and then.'

'Or he lives in Berlin and only comes here every now and then.'

Voss took off his cap. 'A mistress?'

'Maybe. But she'd have to be a very undemanding mistress if he rents a place like this. Looks more like emergency accommodation to me, in case push comes to shove. A hiding place. A hiding place with roses, not bad.'

'To hide from who?'

'Maybe from his murderers.'

'What happened to him then?'

'The case is probably level three by now. Thank your lucky stars I'm keeping you out of it. That way you won't have to sign anything later on.'

Voss nodded and put his hat back on.

'You wait here for the forensics team,' said Wegener. 'As soon as Ulf Lienecke gets here you can deal with the neighbours. There aren't many of them. Perhaps someone's seen Fischer in company, perhaps someone had a chat with him in the lift. Then can you get in touch with the property manager and get everything they've got on him.'

Voss dug about in his trouser pocket for the car keys.

'I'll take the train,' said Wegener. 'Then I can open the window.'

4

THE S7 JUDDERED, STUTTERED, JERKED, then suddenly sped off as if it had been held in a firm grip from behind and had just broken free with the last of its strength. The glass cube of Friedrichstrasse station receded, rain slapping against the scratched panes. The train hissed across its iron viaduct towards Alexanderplatz, constantly at eye level with the city's third storeys. Soot-blackened tenement facades passed by, grubby stucco, crumbling brick walls, heavy curtains behind brittle old window frames, stone guttering patched up with plastic and wire and long since just as leaky as before. Between the tenement buildings were lit-up multi-storey printers' typecases, made up of countless square segments in which the authorities collected Robotron populations, rubber plants and office staff.

Wegener felt cold.

The heating wasn't working, or wasn't switched on yet; perhaps the penny-pinchers at the public transport authority had been hoping for a mild October. The rain turned into light hail, click-clacking on the metal roof, stones of ice crawling diagonally across the window-panes leaving thin trails of water behind them.

The train leaned into a curve to turn right, a glowing comet's tail in the dark vale of buildings. Above the roofs, the silver sphere of the television tower appeared in the evening sky like a gigantic Christmas bauble. Lights played on the wet asphalt of Karl-Liebknecht-Strasse, refracting in the wandering raindrops on the carriage windows. Wegener suddenly had the feeling he could smell lebkuchen or mulled wine with cinnamon. Christmas grabbed hold of him with the vehemence of memories abruptly triggered, by a scent, a taste, by something you had not the slightest inkling of only a second before.

The train braked as abruptly as it had moved off. A piercing screech under the sheet-metal flooring. Standstill. The doors hissed for longer than they took to open.

Wegener got off the train, took the stairs to the ground floor and tried to get the Christmas associations out of his mind, all the remnants of the mother-and-father world he kept successfully pushing away, which kept coming successfully back again, the grievous loss that slithered along behind him on the downhill paths of memory and would crash into the back of his head on Christmas Eve at the latest.

When he pushed open the station's huge swinging doors, Alexanderplatz smelled of Phobos fat, thank goodness, rather than of chestnuts roasting on an open fire. A month and a half from now, mulled wine, stodgy stollen cake, candyfloss and dreary celebrations would get the upper hand.

The employees in the Berolina-Haus were still building socialism at quarter past seven in the evening; lights were on in almost all the windows. Wegener flipped up his collar and ran alongside the raised train tracks towards the glowing sandstone hulk, trying to ignore the increasing scent of bratwurst, dodging several puddles the size of dining tables on Dircksenstrasse and cursing: fifty-six years old and you still don't have an umbrella!

By the time he reached the glass canopy of the Berolina-Haus he was wet through. Next to the massive golden gateway of the main entrance shone the showy brass plaque with its endless engraving: *Ministry of Energy Export and Transit Industry of the German Democratic Republic. Departments I–IV, VII – Sub-Departments A–H.* Beneath that the state insignia.

Wegener walked up to the guard formation and handed over his ID chip-card. The card was inserted into a Borska mobile scanner dangling from a sergeant's belt. The scanner buzzed, two red lights went out, two green lights flashed. An obese chump of a guard shone a hand-held xenon lamp in Wegener's face, compared the chip-card face with the one in front of him, and looked satisfied enough. 'Welcome to the Ministry of Energy Export and Transit Industry, Hauptmann Wegener.'

'And I thought you'd be giving me a nice firm feel between my legs.'

'A sensory check isn't necessary for officers of the People's Police service after positive inspection of the service ID document and visual identification, sir.'

Wegener checked the remains of his hairdo in the reflective metal of the ministry's brass plaque and entered the reception hall. Warmth, vanilla air freshener, Rachmaninov. Piano concerto no. 3. He'd been here twice with Karolina, a couple of years ago when she'd applied for the post of assistant to some section head, been rejected, invited to another interview and rejected again. The transit business is getting so important they're bound to call me again some time, Karolina had claimed after the second rejection, and had done nothing but wait. Six months later she had the job.

Our victim fits in perfectly here, thought Wegener. This is where that suit, that watch, that tie belong. He strode across to the elegant walnut counter and placed his police ID card on the polished surface. 'I'd like to see Ms Karolina Enders, please.'

The receptionist raised two imaginary eyebrows and tapped at her Nanotchev keyboard with a deliberate lack of haste. Patterned fingernails: sun, moon and stars. Wegener put his ID away again, leaned against the counter and felt like he was on the other side of the Wall.

The hall of the Berolina-Haus was nothing less than an orgy. An orgy of brass and marble. A brash boast of a room for the energy-crazed EU sub-negotiators – look at what the GDR has to offer, and you're all gagging for it. Peace to the cottages, bring on the palaces. Ceiling lamps, wall lights, standing ashtrays, the signs for the individual departments – everything that could possibly be made of metal was shiny and golden. The floor was pale stone. Swathes of red carpet marked out paths across the spotless white, crossing in the middle of the hall, flowing up curved flights of stairs on either side to the first floor. A giant flatscreen covered in diagrams, stock market curves, flashing numbers. Energy prices from London to Beijing.

Seated on a suite of dark leather cubes, two young men in suits laughed, one showing the other something on his Minsk. Short-cropped hair. Pale, flattened faces. Russian gas boys, thought Wegener, and heard the receptionist telling Karolina over the phone that a Mr Wagner was here. Or something like that.

A tall white-haired man greeted the young Russians. The man couldn't bear to let go of his guests' hands. The smaller Russian said something that made all three of them grin. 'Lafontaine!' the white-haired man exclaimed. Now they were laughing out loud. The smaller

Russian attempted to pat the tall white-haired man on the shoulder but couldn't reach quite that high.

The receptionist gave a polite cough. Wegener turned around. 'Ms Enders will be down in a minute. Please take a seat.'

Wegener nodded, turned on his heel and went over to the seats. The white-haired man and his Russians passed him, all three smelling of tobacco, aftershave and avarice. 'We're very optimistic,' said the white-haired man, 'and Mr Jost is too, of course.' One of the Russians answered in German, something Wegener didn't understand. *Herr Jost* was mentioned, and a word that sounded something like *enda*. Perhaps he meant Enders.

Wegener sat down on the leather couch and tried to imagine Karolina sitting around at conferences with these Russian milksops, wearing an expensive suit and a genuine-looking artificial smile, a thousand snippets of information and target figures in her head, just turned thirty-five, still in the body of a twenty-year-old and the first half of the ministry career ladder already climbed, her eyes set firmly on the second half. A few years ago she'd have found the idea bizarre. A few years ago she'd have said: Making money's fine, but leave me out of the international state business stuff. International state business wasn't only about money; it was about power too. And everything to do with power ends up costing you your neck at some point, in this country. If you value your neck you should keep out of it – for life.

'I'm innocent, Mr Police Officer!' Karolina had emerged from one of the lifts and was making no attempt to conceal her surprise. A surprised face had never looked prettier. No face had ever looked prettier.

'I remember differently,' said Wegener, instantly regretting it. Every word he uttered now would have an unbearable hint of the past about

it, every sentence would point backwards, becoming a figment of
back then, a rip in time gone out of control. Wegener wondered what
was worse – that he couldn't stop himself or that Karolina didn't even
notice. She radiated confidence. She kissed him on the cheek, as
distant as if he was a child with an infectious disease. Sat down on
the sofa, leaving two spaces between them.

'Good choice of music for a foyer,' said Wegener.

'Thanks. I'll let them know.' Karolina took her Minsk out of her
skirt pocket and pressed two buttons in rapid succession. Mute.

'New telephone?'

'M7.'

'Oh, you're with the Stasi now, are you?'

Karolina was instantly somewhat offended. Her narrow mouth a
line across her freckled face that didn't know where to go. Her
eyebrows a double portion of childish affront. Her rust-red hair even
shorter than last time. A flat hat of a hairstyle that still looked good,
like everything about Karolina. Women wear their hair short because
they know men want women to wear their hair long, thought Wegener
and said, 'The assistant to a section head at the Ministry of Energy
Export and Transit Industry of the German Democratic Republic
could do with a bit more sense of humour. Humour's good for
business.'

The contours of Karolina's mouth softened. 'I meant to tell you
over a mulled wine. How was I to know you'd just turn up here out
of the blue?'

A few seconds' silence.

'You look so happy. Are you pregnant or have you been fired?'

Karolina laughed. 'Promoted.'

Wegener didn't know how to react, and he saw that Karolina
noticed that he didn't know how to react.

'So what do I call you now?'

'Section head in the Ministry of Energy Export and Transit Industry of the German Democratic Republic. Or gas whore. Whichever you prefer.'

'I'll take the gas whore.'

'Good choice.'

'Which section?'

'Central Europe. Section 1.'

'Sounds good.' Wegener attempted a charming smile, sensing it was a failure. 'Fancy a currywurst?'

'I'd love one. But all hell's loose here, what with the consultations coming up.' Karolina pulled a long-suffering face and raised her hands. No new ring.

'Ah yes, the consultations,' said Wegener. 'Maybe I can spare your place here a bit of trouble. With regard to those consultations.'

All signs of childishness vanished from Karolina's face. 'What kind of trouble?'

Wegener looked around. The moon-faced receptionist was on the telephone. The white-haired man and his Russian boys had disappeared. 'Is this place bugged?'

'I hope not. Why?'

'The answer will cost you a currywurst, conglomerate career woman.'

Karolina reached into her skirt pocket and pulled out a crumpled ten-mark note. 'All right, we're both fast eaters.'

Karolina put on more salt. Her double portion of currywurst was steaming on its cardboard tray. She'd already bombarded it with black pepper and Pikanta curry spice mix, and now she shook the salt cellar with a hand gesture that made Wegener feel wistful. He pulled the standing-level table further under the awning from which the rain was flowing down on all sides, slightly closer to the heating soldier. Karolina followed the table, the salt cellar still in motion. Jan 'The Smooch' Hermann was singing about time and love again from a tinny loudspeaker.

Wegener smiled. 'Have you seen a doctor about that?'

'Because I don't like tasteless food?'

'Because you use up the spice contingent of an average socialist household. All four people.'

'I work hard enough for four people, too.' Karolina skewered several slices of sausage on her wooden fork and they disappeared into her mouth.

'It got you a promotion, though.'

Karolina chewed and swallowed. 'That and the fact that we started up new sections. The West's getting greedier by the day. And we have to deliver more by the day.'

'And you earn more by the day.'

'That's the way it is when one state has something and the other ones don't.'

'Except we haven't really got anything either.' Wegener took a glug of his beer. 'The gas belongs to the Russians.'

'The Russians have the gas, and we have the land it has to be transported across. And the West wants conservative energy. Just sun and wind aren't quite enough in the long run.'

'How long have we got?'

Karolina shrugged and skewered her next load of sausage. 'Twenty or thirty years. Maybe fifty. Nobody ever said the transit fees would finance us until communist nirvana. But you know what it'd be like here without them. Dark as a dungeon.'

Wegener bit a chunk off his bratwurst and rinsed it down with beer. 'And Mr Chancellor is your Superman-next-door.'

Karolina smiled. 'Lafontaine's good for sales.'

'Because he makes sure you get new delivery contracts.'

'Because our Western brothers and sisters voted for a chancellor last year who doesn't consider the socialist idea a crime against humanity per se. Chairman M's delighted. Great rapprochement between the German brother states. The whole idea of the consultations is down to Lafontaine. With a double benefit: lower gas prices over there, higher transit fees over here.'

'I'm almost as delighted as Chairman M.'

'Martin, did you come just to discuss inter-German relations?'

'Maybe. How are they going then?'

'Difficult. Still.'

Wegener rested his elbows on the table and looked Karolina in the eye. 'I've got a murder case on my desk. Since yesterday evening. But presumably not for much longer.'

Karolina chewed, gave him a questioning look, and resumed chewing.

'Presumably C5 will take over tonight. Or someone else.'

'Why?'

'Let's not go into that.'

'What kind of a murder is it?'

'My victim's called Emil Fischer. Or at least that's what he called himself.'

Karolina took a swig of Wegener's beer. 'And what's it got to do with the ministry?'

'The man was hanged from one of your pipelines.'

Karolina put the bottle down, her wooden fork sinking to the table.

'It was all very quick,' said Wegener. 'He didn't suffer.'

'How reassuring. Which pipeline was it?'

'Main Pipeline North.'

Karolina released an audible breath and took another large swig of beer. 'Does the ministry know about it?'

'Of course. We can't conduct investigations in the restricted zone without informing your lot. They sent a team out to the crime scene, but they couldn't help us either.'

'And now you're wondering . . . ?'

'I can't help wondering whether the case has something to do with your lot. With the consultations.'

'Shit.' Karolina took a pack of Duett out of her coat pocket. 'Do they bug currywurst stalls?'

Wegener bit into his sausage and chewed. 'Don't worry, only the good ones get bugged.'

'Why are you telling me all this?'

'Because I'll be signing a form any day now that says I'm not allowed to say or ask anything about this matter for the rest of my life, unless I want to lose my badly paid job.'

'Since when has it made you sad when C5 takes over a case from you?'

'I'm not sad, I'm happy. This is the kind of shit that's only good for burning your fingers.'

'And that's why you're rolling up your sleeves and plunging right into it by activating a private contact?'

'Purely out of curiosity.'

'Maybe you just wanted to see me again?'

Wegener didn't respond for a moment.

'I don't trust C5,' he said.

'You don't trust anyone,' said Karolina.

'Yes I do. You.' Wegener took the photo out of his inside pocket and put it on the table. Karolina ignored the picture, looking him straight in the eyes.

'Martin,' she said. 'Don't get yourself in trouble.'

He pushed the photo further towards her. 'Our victim's about eighty. Nice suit, expensive watch. Might even have driven a Prius. Let's just assume his death has something do with the gas business. Then he might well have worked at your ministry. And he wasn't cleaning the pipelines, that's for sure. You know the place inside out. And you're the only person I know who knows the place inside out.'

'I don't know the whole place inside out,' said Karolina. 'The whole place is a monster, and it's getting bigger every day.'

'But you do know the well-dressed, long-standing management people, if you're a half-decent gas whore.'

Karolina sighed, picked up the photo and held it up in front of her face. Her fingernails were painted rust-red. Matching her hair colour. Matching her handbag.

Wegener felt shocked. He'd only just noticed, beneath a dripping awning on Alexanderplatz, in the dim light of Wurst Wilfried's run-down, pale blue sausage and chips van, alongside a glowing heating soldier, that Karolina wasn't the same person as a year ago. Perhaps it was the ministry people who'd changed her. Or her career progress. Perhaps you had to coordinate your fingernails and handbag with your hair, as a section head. Perhaps you got promoted if you wore socialist colours particularly often. Karolina was tougher, cooler, more perfect than she used to be. Karolina was more successful. Karolina was even more beautiful. Karolina was further away than ever. And yet just as close as ever.

Wegener turned away from her and went to the sales hatch to fetch another beer. When he got back to the table the photo was face-down on the yellow waxed tablecloth.

Karolina chewed.

Wegener drank.

'Afraid not. I'm pretty sure I'd have noticed him if he'd worked at the ministry.'

'Because of his age?'

'More the distinctive beard.'

'OK.' Wegener couldn't help feeling a slight sense of disappointment, awakening somewhere in his guts and now coming slowly to the surface. Karolina's memory was one of her sharpest weapons. If she didn't recognize the old man then she really hadn't ever seen him. That made a simple link to the consultations unlikely.

Karolina stared at her currywurst, pushing the end of a sausage around the cardboard tray with her wooden fork. Then she looked up at him. 'Now what?'

'I go to Old Father Borgs tomorrow. He gives me a non-disclosure agreement due to special investigation status whatever-it-is, and I'm off the case.'

Karolina skewered the last piece of sausage. 'It's probably better that way.'

'Absolutely.' Wegener took a swig of his beer again.

'The whole thing makes me kind of nervous.' Karolina sounded anxious. Her cheeks were burning, the heating soldier reflected in her brown eyes as a glowing orange dot; there was a smudge of curry ketchup in the left corner of her mouth. Wegener had to force himself not to pick up a napkin and wipe the sauce off.

'Why are you so sure C5 will take over the case?'

Wegener shrugged.

'Martin, I know that look. I want to know what's going on.'

'Knowing that might be dangerous.'

'No more dangerous than doing gas business with hormone-infused, cocaine-crazed Russian teenagers.'

Wegener smiled.

'Come on.' Karolina looked him in the eye. 'You know what we swore to each other. And we swore that our separation wouldn't change that either.'

'It'll never change anything.' Wegener noticed that he still couldn't utter the word separation. 'Radical trust in radical times.'

'Radical trust in radical times,' Karolina repeated, taking his hand. 'So?'

Wegener turned around. They were alone here. Wurst Wilfried was sorting beer bottles somewhere in the background, glass clinking against glass. The neon Goldkrone ad on the television tower was flashing in a wet blur, the EastSide Hotel rearing into the darkness like a giant glittery gherkin, a currency cock standing to attention, a daily reminder of the boundless potency of the market economy. The plasma mega-poster on the front facade was showing an advert for the new Phobos Flux convertible car, *Now with integrated Navodo-bro and extra port for Musikus-VI and other MP3 players: the new Flux convertible from Phobos – and at last there's no more roof over your head*. A couple of men ran towards the station through the dense curtain of hail, bent over, their collars drawn halfway over their heads. Water dripped off the awning onto the pavement. Two slices of sausage were floating in a dark puddle like oversized bait.

'The dead man's shoelaces were tied together,' said Wegener. 'He was hanged by an executioner's noose. Knotted eight times.'

Karolina lost control of her facial muscles.

'You wanted to know.'

'Martin!' Karolina stared at him in disbelief. 'You've almost been suspended once already!'

'This is nothing to do with Früchtl! Nothing at all!' Wegener realized he'd been speaking too loudly.

'So why have you just mentioned him?'

'Because I know what you're thinking.'

'Oh yes? And what am I thinking?'

'Früchtl was . . . a tragic case. An exceptional situation.'

'Oh yes? And that's why I found you running around our flat like a madman back then, is it, throwing everything that wasn't nailed down and shouting and ranting for hours on end?'

'I didn't shout and rant for hours on end.'

'*This bloody system's eaten up my best friend and there's nothing I can do!* Martin, I can still hear your every word of it, every single word!'

'Don't you worry, so can I.'

'And now what?'

Wegener wanted to put the photo away but realized he didn't have a hand free. Karolina was holding one of them in her manicured ministry fingers; the other was clutching the collar of his coat together as if he had to face a Siberian snowstorm.

'Now what, Martin?'

Wegener tried to force himself to relax. 'All I'm talking about here is facts. Shoelaces tied together, a rope with eight knots. That's how we found the body. That's all.'

Karolina was squeezing his hand so tightly now that it hurt. 'Promise me you won't get drawn into anything this time. Promise me, please!'

'You think I want to get involved in a political—'

'Promise me, Martin!'

Wegener pressed her hand back. There was astonishing strength in Karolina's delicate fingers. Her heating-soldier eyes skewered him like one of Wilfried's broiled chickens, her hand and his hand cramped brutally together. A little more pressure and their bones would start cracking and splintering.

'Being close to you can get painful,' Karolina pressed on, attempting a smile.

'And to you,' said Wegener. 'All right. I promise.'

'OK.' She relaxed her grip.

All was silent for a few minutes. The trains must have halted deferentially in the middle of their route. The station shone silent and abandoned. Wilfried had stopped rattling his bottles. Only the rain couldn't help hailing down onto the asphalt as before.

Their hands held each other tenderly now, with hesitant stroking fingers; they fit perfectly together, thought Wegener, it's as if our hands were still together, an inseparable couple, only the rest of us had to split up because I'm so weak-headed, weak-bodied, because I lose control of everything, but as long as hands can't let go of each other there must be hope for detectives and gas whores, there must be – even in this land without hope.

'You know what it'd mean if word got out,' Karolina said at last, clearing her throat. 'For the consultations.' She let go of his hand.

Wegener nodded. He could see the woman of the past changing back to the other one: the saleswoman, the politician, the career woman.

'In four weeks, we have a unique opportunity for détente between the two Germanies.' Now Karolina was a lecturer summing up the overall political picture in her ministry section. 'Everything depends on it: the realignment of our energy contracts, currency, jobs – maybe even opening the borders. Strictly adhering to the EU's constitutional criteria. If anyone starts to think the Stasi's killing people, if anyone gets wind of it in West Germany, it'll all be over. The end of the rapprochement policy. All for nothing.'

'Who's going to find out?' Wegener tried to find a credibly reassuring tone, but felt he sounded more like credibly depressed. 'No one's even going to find out about it here.'

'Let's hope not.'

'And if it does get out,' Wegener said, putting the last piece of sausage in his mouth, 'then that's obviously just the way they wanted it.'

Karolina stared. 'Who on earth would want that?'

'The Stasi,' said Wegener, chewing. 'Do you know what goes on behind the scenes over there?' He swallowed his liquefied sausage. 'Do you really believe they didn't regroup after Revitalization? Only better than before? Smaller? Less obvious? The Stasi's not the pruned-down, legal, harmless security service the Central Committee's always talking about. I've seen strange things over the past few years.'

'Now you're back to Früchtl again.'

Wegener felt the anger coming back. '*You're* the one going back to him! I'm talking about my everyday work. There are cases where the Stasi dictates the investigation outcome. Cases they just take away from us. Endless surveillance orders, unauthorized wiretaps, dubious security levels.'

'But that's how every Western domestic intelligence agency works too.' Karolina sounded as if she was trying to convince herself as well. 'Hans-Walter Moss cleared the place out back then with Uwe Speckmann, he still crows about it to every human-rights activist in the northern hemisphere. There's not much else left of Revitalization – breaking up and restructuring the Stasi might be his only historical achievement! I hardly think he can afford to put something like that at stake. Never mind the fact that the secret service legislation is one of the prerequisites for the consultations.'

'And who keeps a check on it? Who monitors it?'

'Oh, Martin.'

'I'm sorry, but do you really trust a head of state who'll have you bugged without a judge's permission if need be?' Wegener noticed he was losing his grip on the conversation. 'A man who barricades you into your own country? You trust him?'

Wurst Wilfried's fat head appeared in the van's sales hatch, rotated to the left, then right, then disappeared again.

'That's a different matter.' Karolina's surly mouth was back again. 'He kept his word in 1990 and opened the borders. What would you have done if your people were running away from you, at a rate of ten thousand a day? You'd have closed the Wall again too, otherwise your own party would have given you the elbow. And you do need power if you want to make real changes.'

'*His* people!' Wegener picked up his cardboard tray and threw it in the bin. He wondered whether Karolina really believed what she was saying. Whether a person could change so much in such a relatively short time. Whether the job at the ministry really had put her on the other side.

Karolina lit a cigarette.

'I never said the Stasi committed this murder,' said Wegener. 'I presume they're not that stupid. All I said was that there might be people who don't want the West to gain more influence. For the borders to open again. There are some people who have it pretty good here.'

'If I remember rightly, they used to say shoelaces tied together were a punishment for traitors,' said Karolina. 'In the old days, I mean.'

'Yes.' Wegener knew what was coming next. 'They were. So they said.'

'So why would the Stasi kill a traitor, twenty-two years after Revitalization, four weeks before the consultations? A traitor who's supposed to have betrayed what, exactly?'

'I told you, they probably have nothing to do with it.'

'Was the hanged man with the Stasi?'

'I don't know.'

'The consultations have to be a success,' said Karolina. 'At all costs. That's the only way. The only way to change anything here. Rapprochement means reforms, and reforms mean we'll one day be attractive for all the West Germans fed up with self-service capitalism, greedy managers and incompetent bankers and criminal funds. Then even more of them will come over to us. And then Moss can open up again, because nobody will be going anywhere any more.'

'Maybe he'll have to build the Wall higher. We'll be so popular, the whole of West Germany will want to move over here.'

'Your sarcasm will only make you lose more hair.'

'Honestly, you sound like you're talking to Lafontaine,' said Wegener, wiping the ketchup from the corner of Karolina's mouth with his paper napkin.

'Maybe I will.' Karolina drew her head back. 'I'm going to be at the consultations. The sub-negotiators need first-hand information.'

'They need pretty girls, that's all.'

'They can have them.' Karolina picked up her handbag. She kissed Wegener half-heartedly on the cheek, left, right, left, as if they were outside a Parisian street café rather than an old wurst van on Alexanderplatz.

'Will you take care of my gas bills for me?'

'As soon as you're an upright socialist.' She smiled, then she turned away and left.

Wegener watched her go, saw her scurrying away, a perfect arse in perfect motion. His hand lay alone on the yellow waxed tablecloth, a tough, spat-out leftover that Wilfried would clear away in a moment, chuck in the pig-bin. The hail drifted into rain. Wegener got another beer.

5

A HUNDRED THOUSAND BRIGHT DOTS MELDED INTO ONE BERLIN, spreading out, sprawling at the edges. There was not one spot where the city wasn't. Streets curved into strings of fairy lights, criss-crossing, producing a confusing map, an asymmetrical spiderweb growing paler on the margins and drifting off in the distance. Karl-Marx-Allee and Unter den Linden formed stubborn, yellowish straight lines. Tiny sprinkles modelled the boxy high-rise world of Marzahn on the horizon; next door were the piles of West Berlin office buildings, slim shoeboxes simply plonked down on the spot and still almost entirely lit up.

The sharply focused, electrified pointillism hinted everywhere at contours, superimposing rows of houses, squares and towers, outlining gaps, threading train lines through the hazy city, raising them from underground and then immersing them again. Cupolas raised their heads out of the night, Gendarmenmarkt, the New Synagogue, the giant cathedral, shiny bumps on a never-ending, dark body. The Palace of the Republic shimmered honey-coloured, a straight-edged treasure chest, the pillars of its dome of light rising steeply upwards and getting lost somewhere in the fog. The half-built monster carcass of the Metropol Palais on Friedrichstrasse was flooded by batteries of spotlights.

Right through the middle of the picture ran the long, gleaming scar of the sector border, dividing everything according to compass points, beating its way through everywhere, ripping the thin spider-web into halves, jagged, ruthless, lit up like a long, thin playing field, the length of a city, for whatever triumphs and defeats might come along.

Wegener turned in circles above the monstrous metropolis. Wegener was going round in circles. Wegener noticed his head revolving. Circles were the Wegenerian movement, circles were guaranteed to lead nowhere, but at least got you back to the beginning in the end. If I'm the beginning, thought Wegener, then maybe turning in circles will take me to me.

Below him, long strings of rain were falling on Alexanderplatz. The wurst stall he'd been to with Karolina was nothing but a dot. The lights went out in the Berolina-Haus. A train crept out of its semicircular cavern into the night like a tired snake and disappeared car by car behind the EastSide phallus. On the mega-poster, the *Economic Words of the Day for 20 October 2011* shone out in burgundy letters:

FORTUNE IS BLIND

Marcus Tullius Cicero

Wegener imagined the two Russian gas boys. They'd be sitting in some bar in Prenzlauer Berg. Maybe in United Brewers or the Dynamic Growth. Or right opposite in the EastSide, the sole enclave of capitalism in the whole of the Socialist Union, in the erect big-wigs' bunker that East Germans never got to see from the inside, only snapping up morsels of gossip about orgies, drugs and million-mark business dinners. Russian gas boys lived by the West German rules, thought Wegener. They'd be holed up over there right now with vodka and whores. Or vodka and gas whores. He tried not to think about whether Karolina had to sleep with the gas boys to lubricate the sleazy contracts. He didn't want to know if she ended up underneath one of those coked-up milksops for every deal, those idiots who thought East Berlin was their own private brothel, sighing a broken *Endas!* into Karolina's ear as they shot their loads. He forbade himself from wondering whether Karolina had screwed her section head to make it to section head. Whether it was part of her job description to wangle the best contractual conditions for her nation out of some arseholes in bed. Where she'd got the West German coat, the West German handbag, the West German boots. Whether her energy corporation lovers asked her to cut out all the labels, or Karolina herself had got that careful.

Wegener drank the last of his Radeberger, waved at the waiter and indicated his empty glass. The waiter nodded and strutted off to the bar. His fat arse wobbled in his black trousers.

The sphere at the top of the TV Tower went on slowly rotating, Wegener and his table moving eastward at a snail's pace. In a quarter of an hour the border would be out of view, then he'd have it all behind him, invisible, the other Berlin, the eternal unreal temptation, the EastSide, the Kaufhaus des Ostens, Wilfried's wurst van and Karolina, wherever she was right now, wherever she was taking off her West German boots and West German tights to redo the rust-red nail varnish on her toes.

His Minsk lit up, the display flashed *W. B. Office calling*. Wegener hesitated a few seconds and then picked up.

'Where are you?'

'Alexanderplatz,' said Wegener. 'At the TV Tower.'

'We're all done here.' Borgs sounded relaxed. 'Half of C5 came round, Kallweit as well, of course. We had a lovely chat.'

'And soon you'll all be off on holiday together to the Crimea,' said Wegener. 'Chewing on caviar in the sauna.'

'Fighting Crimean crime.' Borgs cleared his throat the way he always cleared his throat when he thought he'd made a joke. 'To be brief: C5 see the matter similarly. They even think it's possible it was some private act of revenge by ex-agents that got out of control. But they don't know anything definite.'

'I said something like that myself earlier.'

'Theory two: our man was making a bit on the side in the big energy business – bribery, corruption, something like that. It wouldn't be a surprise, what with all the money changing hands.'

'Hm.'

'At any rate their knees are really knocking over the consultations, as expected. The case is definitely going over to them. Hold on a minute, I've got Kallweit on my Minsk . . . '

The Pilsner approached. Wegener pushed his empty glass across the table. The waiter picked it up like a birthday present he'd never asked for and put the fresh beer down. The bill was stuck to the wet foot of the glass: *7 small Radebergers @ 2.60 Marks. Total: 18.20 Marks. Wishing you a wonderful East Berlin evening – from your team at The Fairview Terrace – the restaurant in the Television Tower.* Wegener swigged at the beer.

'Right, I'm back,' said Borgs. 'What are you drinking?'

'Radeberger.'

Borgs smacked his lips in envy. 'Fischer's flat?'

'Looks like an empty roost. Voss called earlier – the neighbours had nothing to say either. A couple of them saw Fischer in the lift every now and then, they said hello and that was it. No one knew him any more than that. Hardly very neighbourly.'

'O neighbours, in spirit we're brothers,' quoted Borgs, 'Let socialism be our guide, And think how we'll help one another, When we march strong and tall side by side.'

'Well, C5 can take care of the brothers in spirit now.' Wegener took out his wallet from his coat pocket. 'Bully for us. Fortune is blind, as I've just read.'

'We criminal investigators hang like hungry babies from Fortune's dry dugs, Martin. You'll get a yellow slip tomorrow. Sign on the dotted line and it's all wrapped up.'

'Fischer didn't work at the Energy Ministry, by the way.'

There was a few seconds' silence on the line.

'Says your ex.'

'I thought I'd ask someone I'd get an honest answer from for a change.'

Another few seconds' silence.

'Leave that out of your report.' Borgs sounded more serious now. 'None of that lot need to know you've been flashing photos around.'

'Don't worry, I'm happy to leave all the work to them.'

'See you tomorrow.' Borgs hung up.

Wegener looked at the Minsk screen, on which the elements of the Telemedia logo came together as a 3-D animation, only to come apart again instantly. He clicked into his address book and pressed Dial. Two rings before she picked up.

'Martin.' Karolina sounded tired.

'Are you in bed?'

'I was in the bath. Now I'm lying on the sofa and falling asleep with Volker Braun.'

'Serves him right,' said Wegener, looking out of the window. Berolina-Haus, the EastSide and the Kaufhaus des Ostens had disappeared. It was still raining.

'Did you forget something?' Karolina was making an effort to sound interested.

'Yes.' Wegener noticed the waiter watching him. 'The Russian gas boys you deal with – do you get to know them personally?'

'What do you mean, personally?' Karolina suddenly sounded wide awake.

Well, well, said Früchtl in the back of his mind, *that gave her a shock.*

'The question is: can you get the measure of them?'

'You mean are they dangerous?'

'Right. What kind of people are they? Have they ever threatened your people?'

Karolina stopped short. 'You think they've got something to do with your case?'

'I just think your business is the best business our state's doing right now. And I'm wondering what happens to someone who gets in the way, for whatever reason.'

'Your dead man.'

Clever girl, said Früchtl.

Wegener watched the waiter. He had poured himself a beer and heaved his fat behind onto a bar stool. The two cheeks of his arse flopped down on either side of the seat. 'All right, he may not have worked for the ministry, but he might have been from customs, from the pipeline conglomerate, some office that maybe puts a hand out when the euros flow to Moscow via East Berlin.'

No response from Karolina.

'Or does that kind of thing not happen?'

'I can't really tell, Martin.' Karolina sounded as if she was apologizing for something. 'I negotiate energy contracts, I don't write dissertations on the Russian gas mafia.'

'But you do have a personal opinion,' said Wegener.

'One of them was very pushy, right at the beginning. He kept asking me to dinner. At some point I agreed so he'd leave me alone.'

Früchtl laughed out loud.

'Where did you go?'

Karolina hesitated. 'To the EastSide.'

Wegener smiled. 'And how much is a gram of coke there?'

'Ho ho ho.'

'Did he make any trouble?'

'He got angry when I didn't want to go up to his room. The Russians are no different to other men in that respect. But he didn't threaten to string me up from a pipeline.'

'And what about in business? Has there ever been any pressure?' Wegener took a twenty-mark note out of his wallet.

Karolina hesitated. 'Last year there was a row about adjustments to the transit fees, although they're fixed in the transfer agreements. That got a bit nasty, and a few threats were made, of course. But on the energy policy level. Raising gas customs for the SU. Greater attention to the Asian market. And putting the brake on supplies, of course.'

'Of course,' said Wegener.

'I don't know what goes on a couple of stages higher. I don't know who holds their hands out there or not. And I don't want to know.'

Wegener imagined how Karolina looked right then. Her eyes tired. Her mouth opened slightly so that you could see her large canines. Lips moist. A warm, languid angel.

Perhaps she's naked too, said Früchtl, *she's just got out of the bathtub, hasn't she, and while you're talking to her, Martin, she's stroking one hand through her red pubes and . . .*

'So: you don't think they'd go that far.'

'To be honest, no. They're all out for money and German women, but they're not murderers. At least not the ones I know. I still won't go to dinner with one of them ever again, though.'

'That's what I wanted to know,' said Wegener.

'Why are you so interested anyway?'

'I don't know either. Old habits die hard.'

'You made me a promise.'

'And I've kept it. I'll be off the case first thing in the morning.'

'Good. Then I can sleep well.'

'Nothing you told me will be in my report.'

'I assume not.'

'You're a good gas whore, Karo.'

'I'm always good for you.' Silence.

'I wish I was with you now.'

That same old mistake you keep on making, said Früchtl.

'Go to bed, Martin.' There was a quiet beep.

Karolina has hung up.

Wegener stared at the twenty-mark note on the table in front of him, adorned with the national poet's crumpled face. He felt as rough as Goethe looked.

FRIDAY 21 OCTOBER 2011

6

THE SIREN WAILED THE PEOPLE OFF THE ROAD, two alternating notes each trying to out-shrill the other. Children were tugged aside, cars pressed themselves to the kerbs. The bearded chauffeur put his foot on the accelerator. The car thrust forward, the speed needle jerked, the engine growled above the siren. Ulbricht-Allee blurred into a greyish-brown mush of houses which was now getting a good stir, only the odd object rising to the surface for a fraction of a second, a bright blue headscarf, an old man with five dogs on leads, a drunk coming out of a bar on a corner, propping himself up on a short man with horn-rimmed glasses.

The Phobos Universal turned the corner. Wegener hung onto the ceiling handle with one hand, keeping his other on the headrest in front of him while everything lurched to the left, the bearded man hugging his steering wheel and bracing himself against the centrifugal force. The tyres whined. Wegener felt like he was about to pull the handle out of the car's ceiling. Then suddenly another straight stretch of road. The Universal threw itself in the other direction, righted itself, Wegener slammed against the door, the bearded driver jerked the steering wheel around, dodged a beige Lada with eyes showing no fear in the rear-view mirror, the gaze of a hara-kiri pilot.

Wegener noticed the plastic handle slipping out of his grip. He fell sideways onto the back seat, his nose drilling into the musty brown-grey-greenish padding, and he smelled cigarettes, plastic, perfume, unaired bedrooms. Voss must have spent some time in the vehicle. The bearded driver put the car in the wrong gear and put his foot down. Changed lanes. Someone hooted.

Wegener wondered whether he ought to sit up, and stayed down. He turned on his back. Stretched out as best he could. Countless tiny holes in the cream artificial leather of the ceiling padding. The colour shaded into a saturated shade of nicotine yellow towards the rear half. Grey protective covers over the headrests. The thin heating wires of the rear window lined a colourless sky with occasional treetops brushing through the picture, electricity cables, pedestrian bridges, traffic lights that the bearded driver ignored. Wegener couldn't help remembering how he'd squashed himself as a child onto the miniature back seat of the pale blue Trabant named Hannibal, his legs folded in on themselves, whenever his parents and he had driven to the Baltic or the forests of Thuringia or on their two trips to Prague. Lying down had been the optimum travelling position.

You didn't see anyone, and no one saw you. No passers-by, no other drivers, not even IFA truck drivers. And especially not your parents. They'd be entrenched behind the backrests of their front seats, driving every journey as a couple, reading street signs as a couple, making overtaking decisions as a couple, deciding together when and how loudly to hoot, warning each other of driving up too close to the car in front, of complicated curves, of possible mist in moor regions, not even turning around once between Berlin and Bolt-enhagen as long as all was quiet at the back.

In those days the Trabant had seemed to Wegener like a bed with a roof and windows, like a bed permanently travelling beneath grey or blue or cloudy skies, protected from rain and snow, overheated, opaque, steering itself on alternating surfaces, which you could guess at: tar, gravel, sand, field paths, pocked car parks, the concrete slabs of the motorway. More than forty years had passed since then. Every single back seat had got too small for him and his parents had finally arrived together at the Weissensee cemetery after all their shared journeys, in an ivy-covered double grave where they presumably decided mutually on what to do with all that dull eternity, which memories were worth being revived over and over again, what they could safely forget, who ought to be prayed for and how often and whether his father really still had to recite his Sunday speeches on his glory days in the Peter Hacks Mechanically Separated Meat Combine even after his death and the closure of the Peter Hacks Mechanically Separated Meat Combine and, if so, whether he couldn't at least shorten them a little.

Now all that Wegener could fit along back seats was his torso; there was no room for his legs any more. And instead of his father there was a hectic bearded man behind the steering wheel, the car didn't sway to and fro, it vibrated, and they weren't on their way to the Baltic coast but to the former Reichsbank building on Werder-scher Markt, in the fastest vehicle in the whole Socialist Unity Party car pool, complete with sirens and flashing lights, an hour before his shift started and with no explanation whatsoever. Wegener made a resolution to stop by the graveyard as soon as possible and cut back the ivy. You'll forget us once we've gone, his mother had said, you're an only child, you'll forget to extend the lease at the graveyard, one day you'll turn up at the cemetery and there'll be strangers in our grave. Maybe the Fingerhuts from next door, Wegener had said, and his mother replied: If that happens I'll come to you as an apparition!

Wegener stayed lying down and thought of his parents, of their photo albums with the dated and fastidiously labelled holiday pictures, of the days and weeks of his life he'd spent lying on Hannibal's back seat, a carefree traveller always under the same childish delusion that all this would never end, that it would go on like this for ever, remain an existence free from pain and loss, cheerful and not the slightest bit lonely.

The car braked sharply and the siren wound down with a howl, disappointed that it was all over already. The driver looked in the rear-view mirror and saw an empty back seat, then asked after the *Herr Hauptmann* with laboriously controlled confusion in his voice, as if the *Herr Hauptmann* might have slid out of the car somewhere along the crazed journey.

Wegener picked himself up, banished his parents to the back of his mind and clambered out of the door that the relieved driver held open for him. Ahead of him stood the huge Nazi block, stern and omnipotent with its hinted-at pillars, long, humdrum rows of windows and ribbed eaves, an inconspicuous giant, threatening but not directly brutal, restrained and yet still very much present – the Central Committee couldn't have found a better home for itself, thought Wegener.

A five-metre-high iron egg flaunted itself on the right-hand edge of the building, filled with lettering bound in a wreath, SOCIALIST UNITY PARTY OF GERMANY, in the middle two hard hands shaking: squared lines of fingers so abstract a logo that they transmuted into a confusing grid, prison bars shifted out of shape. Rust-tinted water had run down the hands and the letters, a dark tearstain on the pale countenance of the wall. Next to the wide staircase to the main entrance a granite pillar protruded from the cobblestones, upon it ex-Chairman Stangier's stony head, gazing sternly through horn-rimmed spectacles. Pigeon-shit on his nose.

Wegener nodded to the chauffeur, walked past the two hulk-shaped uniformed guards from the personal security squad, ascended the stairs – another two black-clad hulks who let him pass in silence, no Borska scanner necessary here – a bronze door and behind it the reception hall, cold and empty. Walls made of polished granite, bronze lift doors, a despotic suite of genuine leather armchairs that looked like they'd swallow up anyone who tried sitting on them, a lifeless large-screen TV, and nothing more.

The lift doors opened without a sound, giving way to a young man with a carefully maintained tan.

So that's what they look like – our East German high-flyers, Wegener noted. A healthy skin tone, the only class distinction in a classless society. If they let you out you get a tan and dark gelled hair, you turn into a melatonin marvel in pinstripes with black designer glasses, and the only worn-out thing about you is your smile.

'Hauptmann Wegener?'

'Good morning.'

'Right, good morning!' The tanned young man had soft hands that could exert a decent amount of pressure. 'Schmiechen, Under-secretary of State for Operative Cooperation in the Extended Central Committee of the GDR.'

'That's a long job title.'

'It is, isn't it?' Schmiechen dimmed his smile. 'Hauptmann Wegener, there's trouble on the horizon. Come with me, please.'

'Trouble for me? I'd rather go, in that case.'

'What? No, trouble for all of us.' A soft hand propelled Wegener into the waiting lift. Dark wood panels, a bronze handrail. No mirrors. The doors closed, the cubicle buzzed upwards and then stopped, the doors opened, the tanned undersecretary marched silently down a wide corridor, Wegener sticking to his side, two more security hulks giving them friendly nods this time, all accompanied by the scent of furniture polish and a Rondo coffee-vending machine. Large-format oil paintings showed workers at machinery, small and large cogs interlocking, clenched fists, red flags, determined expressions, eyes looking upwards, a yellow field landscape with long chimneys rising to the sky. The auspicious smoke of production that must once have escaped from them was painted over in a strong blue. The fresh, smoke-shaped patches of sky glistened on the matte canvas.

'What kind of trouble, Mr Schmiechen?'

'The worst kind.' Schmiechen stopped outside a high door above which bronze letters were mounted on the walnut panels: WORLD HALL. 'Make sure your telephone doesn't go off in here.'

Wegener took his Minsk out of his trouser pocket, unlocked the keylock and clicked on the post symbol. *U. Lienecke has sent you a TM*, then the text message ran across the screen: *Time for another trip to the crime scene this morning? E ministry putting on pressure to open up restricted zone. Best, U.* Wegener pressed *Response Option: I have received your message and will call back later* and switched off the ringtone. 'And what is the worst kind of trouble?'

'International trouble. Money trouble. To do with the case you took on yesterday.'

'The case I'm passing on today.'

Schmiechen's brown hand was already on the door handle. 'Take my advice – don't let the whole thing unsettle you. It's unusual for you, this kind of thing, and they know that. Right, let's go.'

The door swung open without a sound.

A gym, thought Wegener, a gym devoid of gymnasts where you're allowed to smoke, with huge, glittering chandeliers and a long table in the middle, dark suits with synchronized turning heads on top, twenty expressionless circular faces, creaking parquet with pale square inlets, the ceiling a suspended Hades of beams and broad skylights, the never-ending walk to the never-ending conference table, an invader on an eternal advance, thoroughly inspected, precisely categorized, his mind read long before he gets there, the soft, tanned hand on his back pushing him onwards with friendly determination, all the way to the centre of the table where there were two empty seats, and opposite them: Borgs and Kallweit.

Wegener sniffed the air. He was up against a wall of male sweat and cigarette fumes.

Smells like a politicians' changing room, said Früchtl.

Kallweit nodded. The dark rings under his eyes looked like a burglar's mask in a comic. Someone had barricaded Borgs into a white shirt. Something in his bulldog face winked.

There was a fair-haired man with frameless glasses at the right end of the table, a chubby bald head at the left end. Behind the bald head, a map of the world covered the entire wall: grey sea, dark grey continents. The Socialist Union, China, North Korea, Greece and Cuba shone out in gold.

'People's Police Captain Martin Wegener,' said Schmiechen as if presenting an invention that he wasn't quite sure worked.

'Martin *Alfons* Wegener,' added the fair-haired man via ceiling loudspeaker, in a metallic voice. Curved microphone antennae grew out of the table in front of every seat.

'Colonel-General Heribert Steinkühler,' Schmiechen explained in a low voice, 'First Deputy Minister of State Security.'

'Do take a seat, Mr Wegener.' Steinkühler shuffled a few papers, sucking on his cigarette at short intervals. The glowing tip pulsated like a small, hot animal.

Wegener sat down.

Schmiechen sat down next to him.

On the table were half-full ashtrays and small collections of lemonade bottles: Bioneer Soda, rhubarb and fruits-of-the-forest flavours. The kinds you couldn't get in any branch of Delikat.

'Wegener: the name comes from Wagner, the wheelmaker.' A dark voice, just as metallic. Schmiechen nodded to the right. The bald-headed man in front of the map. On top of the bald head lay a few very lonely, very dark strands of hair. 'In other words, the inventor of the wheel. The man who gets things moving.'

'Dr Wolfgang Münzer,' whispered Schmiechen. 'People's Commissioner for Domestic Issues on the Central Committee.'

Steinkühler was still sorting through his papers.

Wegener inspected the rest of the troop. The suits were sitting at the table as stiffly as if the Central Committee had propped up a row of shop-window dummies to make the group look larger. Fifteen facial quarries. None of the quarries showed the slightest sign of emotion. None of the men noted anything down. None of them moved a muscle. None of them touched the Bioneer Soda. Half of them were smoking, that was all. Nameless bureaucrats you couldn't commit to memory because they stayed as silent as Borgs. One with a receding hairline, one with a moustache, three with mousy hair. One with slightly longer mousy hair, one slightly younger with large ears and a wart by his nose. These mugs would be forgotten in a couple of hours, unrecognizable, subsumed in the mass of East Berlin faces.

Don't let them spot any emotions, said Früchtl: *show these blow-up dolls you're a hard man.*

Wegener: Since when have I been a hard man?

Früchtl: *I thought you'd fall for it.*

'Comrade Wegener.' Steinkühler took an artificial pause and removed his glasses. 'We've asked you here on a matter that is not merely tangential to the national security of the German Democratic Republic, but of direct concern. Everything we are about to discuss with you is subject to military classification. That means we're dealing with state secrets here. It's important to me that you're absolutely aware of that.' Steinkühler stared at Wegener along the length of the table. He smiled. A set of gold crowns smiled along with him.

'I'm aware of . . . '

'Please speak into the microphone.'

'I'm aware of the importance of classified information.' And that's what I'll sound like once all your smoking gives me throat cancer, thought Wegener, with a Robotron robot voice, a talking tin can.

'Yesterday we received the title story of the forthcoming edition of the West German news magazine *Der Spiegel*,' said Münzer. 'Not yet final, not yet complete, as of the afternoon of 20 October.' The map behind him darkened, two projectors switched on with a whirr beneath the gym ceiling and a highly enlarged black-and-white fax sheet appeared: a hammer and compasses flag, bloodstained, complete with the headline *STASI MURDERING AGAIN. How an obstinate secret service is gambling away Europe's energy future.*

'In the article, a man whose name is not revealed claims to have witnessed a murder this past Sunday, which was allegedly committed on the orders of the State Security. In East Berlin.' Münzer scratched his double chin. 'The murder in question is the case you've been working on since Wednesday evening, to no great avail.'

At last, said Früchtl, *a funny arsehole. Funny arseholes are rare on the ground.*

Wegener tried not to react. Steinkühler was still watching him. The gold crowns had vanished.

'According to your investigations, the victim is a certain Emil Fischer of 32, Ludwig-Renn-Strasse in Berlin-Marzahn.' Münzer reached for a water glass and took a sip. A tinny gurgle glugged out of the speakers. Then he put the glass down so carefully that there was no sound to be heard. 'You assumed correctly that this address was a front. The *Spiegel* informer now claims that the victim was in reality a certain Albert Hoffmann. Does that name mean anything to you?'

Wegener shook his head.

The projector's picture changed, now showing a black-and-white group photo of Hans-Walter Moss with dark hair, thinner than he was now, surrounded by old men. The picture changed again to an enlarged section: Moss grinning like a shark in a school of sprats, close to his side a grey-haired man looking earnestly at the camera.

Münzer folded his arms. 'Professor Albert Hoffmann is or was a political scientist, holding a chair in Heidelberg from 1977 on. In 1983 he emigrated from West Germany to the GDR on the grounds of his political convictions. During the Revitalization years he was on the advisory staff of the Chairman of the State Council.'

'A very clever man.' Steinkühler's voice. 'I met him out in Wandlitz once. In the old days, of course.'

Münzer flicked through his papers. 'This new *Spiegel* contains all sorts of useful information. Photos of the crime scene. Photos of the body, albeit blacked out. It's a proper investigative magazine. Solving the case while our detective is still freshening up his private contacts at the Ministry of Energy Exports.'

Kallweit shook his head as sadly as if Münzer had just been singing one of Jan 'The Smooch' Hermann's songs of sorrow.

Whoever told them about my meeting with Karolina, Wegener thought, they needn't have bothered. They know anyway because they know everything, because every eye and every ear in this country is their eye and their ear, I Spy With My Little Eye, the all-new improved omnipresent version.

Ask them if Hoffmann's your victim, said Früchtl.

Wegener bent to the microphone. 'And is Hoffmann the victim?'

Münzer looked at him.

One of the suits sneezed. Nobody blessed him for the rest of his life with the Stasi.

'We can't yet be absolutely certain,' said Steinkühler. 'But there are a number of positive indications.'

'We're assuming he is for the moment,' said Münzer.

Steinkühler's teeth sparkled again. 'You see, Comrade Wegener, for twenty years the imperialist journalists have been trying to, let's say, discredit the State Security's employees and the institution itself. That's not difficult, of course, given the past history the apparatus does have. What they deliberately ignore is that we're a completely new institution, in terms of personnel and our legal foundation, with a drastically altered, in fact also drastically reduced mission. A domestic intelligence service just like West Germany, Britain and the USA have always had. Did you know that according to our internal estimates about 250 agents of the West German Federal Intelligence Service are working undercover in GDR state institutions?'

Wegener shook his head.

Don't, said Früchtl: *don't move: even a shake of the head or a nod count as full sentences in here. Take a look at Borgs, that fat little pillar of salt, he's doing it just right!*

'It's true though, Inspector. Even if it doesn't fit with the image the people in the West like to have of us. All of us in this room know:

today's State Security is an absolutely harmless organ. Smaller and more strictly regulated than most comparable institutions.'

Wegener nodded. Früchtl groaned.

'We also know that the intelligence services always come up against the boundaries of legality in their practical work, always have to, I must emphasize, and in the USA much more often than anywhere else, by the way. But that doesn't include murdering one of our own country's citizens. The old Mielke system has been out of existence for more than twenty years. The *Spiegel* is spinning a yarn, and come Monday it'll be printing a yarn.'

Obedient coughs of laughter from the suits.

'We'd already considered the fact that the murder might be an attempt to pin the blame on the State Security,' said Wegener. 'Until now there'd been no public attention, though.'

Don't take my advice then, said Früchtl and went off in a huff, diffusing through the map of the world to smoke one of his reeking cigars in the fresh air.

'There'll be plenty of that come Monday, thanks to the *Spiegel*,' said Münzer. 'Claus Kleber refuses to call off delivery of the magazine. Not exactly all quiet on the western front, as they say.'

Low murmurs from the suits.

'The Chairman of the State Council spoke to Federal Chancellor Lafontaine on the telephone last night,' said Steinkühler. 'You'll be aware, Comrade Wegener, that the resumption of talks between the two Germanies has been linked to so-called rule-of-law criteria since the Schäuble era. The Federal Republic, incidentally, keeps a keen eye out to make sure that other countries fulfil these criteria, while flouting them itself whenever it wishes. Nevertheless, these criteria include the anchoring of the State Security as a domestic intelligence service operating within the constitution in the 1994 Berlin Accords.

And operating within the constitution obviously rules out murder as a means of defending the German Democratic Republic.'

'Come on, Wegener, ask the question at last!' clanged Münzer's voice. An angry god grouching at his dimwit creation from on high. 'I've been waiting since you arrived!'

'Why am I here?'

'Presumably because you were on duty the day before yesterday,' said Münzer with a wave of one small, fat hand at the other end of the table. 'Now comes the interesting part.'

Steinkühler took off his glasses and cleaned them meticulously on a white handkerchief. 'Lafontaine is favourably disposed to the GDR. Despite that, he had to inform the Chairman of the State Council yesterday that the consultations cannot take place until the Hoffmann matter is cleared up without a trace of doubt. Because, and this is a quote, *it is impossible to explain to the West German public and the country's allies that the Federal Republic is concluding billion-mark deals with a country that may have violated international human-rights conventions.* To say nothing of the fact that Hoffmann was originally a West German citizen.

'Now, you know better than I do, Comrade Wegener, that a People's Police investigation can take months, sometimes even years. We don't have that kind of time. Let me remind you once again of the importance of confidentiality in your profession before I tell you that we urgently require a realignment of the energy agreements and the resulting liquid funds, for budgetary reasons. More urgently than you think. Should we be forced to relinquish the currency involved, we'd face drastic changes to our society.'

Wegener nodded. The men in dark suits lowered their eyes. Kallweit studied the grain of the wooden tabletop. Borgs stared towards Cuba. The projectors switched themselves off.

'Under these circumstances the State Security, being confronted with such an absurd accusation, cannot carry out its own investigations, of course. West Germany would never accept that. I regret to say that means our country's elite civil servants will have to rely on others to prove their innocence. The State Council Chairman and the Minister of State Security have therefore suggested an unconventional compromise to the Federal Chancellor.'

For a moment even Steinkühler himself looked rather incredulous. 'This compromise is also an impressive affirmation of the State Security. West German police officers will accompany the investigations on the Hoffmann case. To guarantee the independence and objectivity of the investigation process and a comprehensive exchange of ideas with the Lafontaine government.'

'Accompany or accomplish?' Wegener asked into the microphone. Münzer grinned.

'The main concern at the moment is cooperation. Jurisdiction issues are not at the forefront.' Steinkühler lit a new cigarette. 'This morning the Federal Chancellery informed the State Council Chairman's office that they'd accepted the proposal. Albeit in conjunction with the announcement that all previous agreements between the FRG and the GDR will be regarded as null and void, should the outcome of the investigations suggest the State Security was involved in the Hoffmann case. To put it plainly: the consultations are at stake.'

'In other words,' said Münzer, 'the country's economic future depends on Hoffmann's real murderers being found. You didn't expect that, did you, Wegener?'

'I'm still coming to terms with the compromise,' said Wegener. 'An East–West German investigation. Just like that.'

'Lafontaine has no interest in the consultations failing. He promised his industrial magnates energy security and price stability before the election. Without the prospect of concluding supply contracts with the GDR, he probably wouldn't have won the elections at all.' Steinkühler was still rubbing away at his glasses. 'And when it comes to our side, Comrade Inspector, and I'm saying this as the deputy head of the East German domestic intelligence service, so almost as a witness in your case, if you like . . . '

Loud murmurs of laughter from the suits.

' . . . there is no Hoffmann file in our offices, no Operation Hoffmann, not even an observation order. Otherwise we wouldn't put our economic future in the hands of a police investigation.'

'To put that another way,' Münzer fumbled at his microphone, 'even the compromise itself proves our innocence. We certainly wouldn't make a trading contract with a volume of more than seventy billion marks dependent on the outcome of a criminal investigation if we didn't already know what that outcome was going to be.'

'The investigations will establish that the State Security has nothing to do with the case,' said Steinkühler. 'It's a good opportunity to make it perfectly clear to the last vestiges of capitalism that our system is more constitutional than theirs. And the energy agreements will remain valid. That's the target to be reached in full.'

Nobody said a word.

Kallweit looked around the table with his deeply melancholy face. His fleshy lower lip hung even lower than usual. The dark bags under his eyes looked as if they'd been painted on. 'Ask us how you can help us, Wegener.'

'How can I help you?'

'The Chancellery gave us a name this morning,' grunted Kallweit, visibly pleased to hear his voice coming out of the speakers as well now. 'The man they're sending us is called Richard Brendel. I assume you've heard that name.'

'The head of some West Berlin special unit.'

'A celebrity,' said Kallweit. 'One of the best men they have over there. He'll be working with you.'

Wegener knew Kallweit was expecting awe rather than thirst at that moment, so he reached for a bottle of rhubarb Bioneer Soda and screwed off the lid, a picture of calm.

I'd have gone for fruits-of-the-forest, said Früchtl.

'To be perfectly honest, Wegener, we have no choice but to leave the matter up to you.' Kallweit suddenly looked even more depressed. 'As you can imagine, this wouldn't have happened under normal circumstances. The case wouldn't stay with the People's Police, and certainly not in your hands.'

'Ah yes, there was one more thing . . . ' Steinkühler assumed a thoughtful pose and flicked through his papers. 'The disciplinary procedure.'

'Which was abandoned,' said Wegener and drank. A strong, slightly artificial rhubarb flavour. A tiny bit too sweet.

'Which nevertheless showed that you and your former superior, a certain Major Josef Früchtl, tend to cross jurisdiction boundaries.'

Correct, Gout-face, said Früchtl, *that's exactly what we used to do.*

Kallweit cast a meaningful sideways glance at Münzer, and one at Steinkühler. 'Now, the Federal Chancellery and Richard Brendel expressly demanded that the People's Police officer working on the case from the outset is not withdrawn. As if we—'

'In any case, you're still on it for the time being.' Münzer's voice was drowned out by a sharp burst of feedback. 'You've got Brendel to thank for that. Down to brass tacks: you report to Borgs and Kallweit. Brendel reports directly to the Chancellery. I'll be in contact with the Chancellery and the party leadership on our side. Any information passed on to third parties and you'll be up for breaching state secrets the very same day.'

Wegener noticed he was getting hot. His shirt was sticking to his back. A drop of sweat ran down his chest, across his belly, tickling, only halted by the waistband of his trousers. Perhaps it was Borgs who'd told them about Karolina. Perhaps it was their spies. I've probably been under observation for the past two days, thought Wegener, from the point when we found the body. You people know more than I ever will, you're backstage, you're shifting the scenery, you're the directors here. I'm the one stumbling across the boards. But, my dear mustachioed, receding-hairlined, mousy, warty, bug-infested friends, I can stumble in unforeseen directions.

'Any questions?'

'Who is Brendel bringing along? Pathologists? Forensics? Or is that all down to us?'

'That's not clear yet. Presumably he'll have someone from the Federal Intelligence Service with him. Then we'll have 251 FIS-men in the country. We're aiming to keep Ulf Lienecke on the case. Brendel's role will be more that of an advisor.'

Wegener looked into Steinkühler's pale blue eyes. 'If you'll forgive me saying so, Comrade Colonel-General – you know the evidence situation and our leads and suspicions, as absurd as they may be.'

Steinkühler feigned curiosity.

'So if this is supposed to be an investigation strictly by the book, and that's what it'll have to be with this Richard Brendel tagging along and with the whole political backdrop, then the State Security won't just have witness status, it'll automatically be under investigation.'

One of the suits choked. Kallweit stared at the ceiling as if Almighty God had finally revealed His plans for the coming nuclear Armageddon to him.

Steinkühler put his glasses back on. 'Your chance to be glad about something, Comrade Hauptmann!' His gold crowns shone out. 'Now you're finally officially allowed to poke your nose into things that are none of your business. You're the first People's Policeman in this history of the German Democratic Republic to investigate the State Security. But – and this may be your personal drop of bitterness at the end of the day – not the first to investigate the State Security *successfully.*'

Wegener smiled.

Borgs scratched his double chin.

The old dog's managed to keep his trap shut again, said Früchtl.

7

THE OPERA SINGER'S VOICE CLIMBED HIGHER AND HIGHER. There appeared to be no end to the musical scale for her. The orchestra was panting for breath. The vocals threatened to shake them off entirely. Lienecke steered his way through ankle-deep autumn leaves, clutching an imaginary steering wheel, walking out a detour around an oak tree to reach the police barrier, then ducked beneath the white tape and took a few steps to the hollow where the mobile generator had been standing thirty hours ago.

The singer rejoiced.

Lienecke stopped in his tracks, opened a door made of thin air and closed it again. He strode a few metres up the hill to the beat of kettle drums, picking up speed, chasing after an invisible escapee, running now, catching up, grabbing the invisible man, jostling, clutching hold, holding him firm and then manoeuvring him back to the crime scene.

The sun splashed bright stains onto the forest floor and the dead leaves around the barrier glowed in countless shades of red, yellow and brown, making a bright and yet monochrome carpet. Violins soared, picked up their theme, varied it, repeated themselves. To powerful brass chords, Lienecke shoved his imaginary prisoner to the left, past the concrete pillar of the viaduct, under the dirty pipeline tube to where the Prius had been.

The singer started in again. Her voice grieved around in minor realms, fretted, lamented and accused. The violins sobbed in solidarity while the wind blew new leaves down from the treetops, driving them along before it, sprinkling the half-bare forest floor and covering it up again spot by spot. Lienecke climbed, shoved, pulled as the singer found her way back to her old strength and began to kick up a fuss, suddenly singing against an inescapable fate, getting even louder, Lienecke changed roles at the flick of a switch: now he was Hoffmann having a noose put around his neck, then he was the hangman plying the noose, then Hoffmann again, the orchestra droning on with all its instruments, rising to a threatening crescendo, arching, the woman's voice sailing above, long since contorted into a scream as Lienecke pulled the noose closed and became his own victim, tugging at it with his right hand, his face a mask of horror as the singer squealed.

Wegener pulled the earphones out of his ears. Instantly, the only sound was the wind in the trees.

'We can retrace their movements this far.' Lienecke came back to the police barrier. 'From the hollow over there, back, moved the car, drove it forward, the man was hanged, and exit left.'

'You make it look so nice.' Wegener pressed the Stop button on his music player and wound the two ends of the cable around the aluminium casing until he could tuck the earplugs into the bundle.

Lienecke tugged down the zip of his checked jacket. 'I'm sweating here even without committing a murder.'

'You were on your own. There were two of them.'

'They get the man to come here under some false pretence. A handover, a meeting, whatever. Then the victim realizes the danger and makes a run for it, they catch him, a short struggle – that's where the bruises come from – one of the buttons comes off the victim's coat and lands in Q4.'

'When did you find the button?'

'Yesterday. In leaf sack number twenty-four.' Lienecke took a piece of paper out of his jacket pocket and unfolded a sketch, drawn by hand, fastidious, to scale: a tight grid of squares showing the road through the forest, the slightly curving pipeline, the Prius, markings and notes. 'He didn't get far. Eighty metres.'

'He was an old man.'

'An old man caught in a trap.'

'They tie the rope around his neck,' said Wegener, 'and they somehow get him to stand on the roof of the car. Probably with a gun. And then they drive off.'

Lienecke's index finger slid across the grid towards the hollow.

'This is where we found the leaves with engine oil on them.'

'Can they have been blown over there?'

'No.' Lienecke looked up from his sketch. 'Then we wouldn't have found several leaves with oil stains all in one place. If we draw a straight line from the hollow towards the pipeline, where would we come out?'

'They turned on the lights,' said Wegener.

'That's what I think.' Lienecke wiped his moist forehead with the back of his hand. 'The car was parked so that they lit up the pipe with their full beam. We could probably work out exactly where, down to a few metres. But there's no point – not a single print.'

'And on the path?'

'Dried leaves and the ground's as hard as rock. The meteor-
ologists say it hasn't rained properly for about three weeks. We've
got a few semi-prints, but you know what it's like – good old
socialist unity car tyres. Looks like all summer tyres or M+S. And
then the forester came zooming over them as well. We might as
well forget it.'

'So all we've got's a few drops of oil.'

'We've got nothing. Phobos engine oil, used by an estimated six
million citizens, is hardly a major lead.'

'Maybe it isn't Phobos oil.'

'Martin, don't kid yourself. You know as well as I do what'll come
out of the tests.'

'Ulf, you're the eternal voice of doom.'

Lienecke shrugged. 'They were being careful. And forests are very
forgiving crime scenes. We'll go through the leaves again but I
wouldn't get your hopes up. Either Jocicz scrapes together a bit of
DNA or you can start praying for a confession.'

'Praying's for people who blame someone else when they mess up.'
Wegener looked Lienecke in the eye. 'Be honest, what do you think
of all this mess? No useful leads. And then the nonsense with the
shoelaces and the noose.'

Lienecke folded up his sketch. 'Hard to say. It's not my first murder
with a sparse evidence situation.'

'But it is your first murder with secret service symbolism.'

'I think the old cadre theory's not bad at all. It sounds a bit over
the top at first, but a murder's always the result of too much or too
little emotion. And when Moss started his Revitalization in 1990 and
fetched Uwe Speckmann over to the East that did split the Stasi in
two, that's a fact. He had to chuck out the whole Mielke generation
to get at the democratic currency. And in their place, a few young

opportunists suddenly had unforeseen career chances with the State Security.'

'Hundreds of people lose their job every day, and they don't go strangling anyone.'

Lienecke presented a regretful smile. 'But not with the Stasi, Martin. They were the elite, they had a private subscription to privileges and benefits. It was written into their contracts that they'd never fall on their faces for their whole lives. And then along comes Chairman M and gives them all the boot. Some young whipper-snappers climb the career ladder, make it big even though they've never done anything to earn it. And the powerful men of yesteryear are suddenly inglorious benefits claimants.'

Wegener nodded. 'All right. I understand. Maybe the rats did bite each other to death in all the confusion back in 1990. Maybe they did tie shoelaces together back then. But maybe that's just another Revitalization conspiracy theory. In any case Hoffmann's much too old to have been a newcomer back then, a cuckoo in Moss and Speckmann's feathered nest.'

Wegener pressed the music player into Lienecke's palm. 'Who's that woman in your earphones?'

'Forget women, ask me about the specifications. Robotron Musikus M VI, 120-gigabyte memory. The first batch is sold out already. What shall we do with the crime scene now? Release it again?'

Wegener looked at the white plastic tape stretching from tree to tree into the forest. 'What radius have we got in the outer ring?'

'Eight hundred metres.'

'And when does the ministry want it released?'

'As soon as possible. The undersecretary's putting pressure on us because the spot's in the middle of the restricted zone. I'd say we can get two more days out of them before there's trouble. But then you want to question the ministry people too, don't you?'

'And you mean they'd be more cooperative if we give them their beloved forest back first.'

'It's up to you. We've been through everywhere. We've got seventy-eight sacks of leaves from the inner ring. I sent another thirteen people across here this morning. We're not going to find anything more here, I can promise you that.'

Wegener clicked on his Minsk. 'Two-thirty. Richard Brendel's coming around five. Let's just walk the outer radius one more time, for the record. That'll make me feel better.'

'I love getting paid to go for walks,' said Lienecke, turning around and striding off.

Wegener lashed his scarf tight, knotted the ends together and took his black gloves out of his coat pockets, one of the presents from Karolina that never wore out only because they permanently reminded him of the merciless past. Never give leather gifts in relationships, thought Wegener, leather outlives every love. It's best to give things with close sell-by dates – meat, fish, butter, eggs, milk, they make nice surprises for birthdays and anniversaries, perhaps flowers are all right as well, but not the kind you can dry and hang up. Reject all presents made of stone, wood, metal, glass, porcelain, horn and animal hide. There's nothing as reliable as getting dumped, and then suddenly the stuff turns into torture instruments that recite their little lines every day: Look at me, I'm still here, but she isn't.

Lienecke had a fifty-metre head start, his checked back, lowered head and pale trouser legs striding purposefully in a south-easterly direction, disappearing for a few seconds behind tree trunks and popping up again, not turning round.

Wegener tried to catch up but couldn't. He was wading through a rustling cloud of leaves. His shoes were moving somewhere beneath the yellow-brown surface like brainwashed moles, every step triggering an eruption that penetrated the surface, two hard-working underground warriors on Mission Forest Crossing at the height of mega-autumn. Wegener steered around mossy tree stumps and broken-off branches. He had the feeling his feet were sinking in deeper and deeper; he'd soon be up to his middle in this crackling covering, a slow downfall, no firm ground under his feet, only a yellow rustling carpet and dark trunks blocking out the horizon.

A lone bird grumbled in its tree.

Wegener turned around. Lienecke's forensics Phobos and the pipeline had vanished from view. The fluttering tape led deeper and deeper into the forest's isolation, in which Lienecke's burly checked figure had long since turned into a mystic Scottish dwarf unwaveringly following his trail. Keeping strictly to the white barrier, from oak to oak to oak, all reaching their plucked branches reproachfully to the blue sky, last leaves still sticking it out on the twigs, not wanting to be driven out of their home height, clawing stubbornly to the bark.

In front of Wegener, the brightly coloured ground rose and fell in gentle waves, which made him feel he could walk on water. The situation seemed as unreal as the meeting earlier at Werderscher Markt, his conversation with Steinkühler, who had previously been just a name to him, a Stasi spectre never to be seen, one of the men you asked yourself what they did when they sat down at their desks in the morning, assuming that they and their desks actually existed. The meeting had been nothing less than a minefield. Goldmine Steinkühler and his bald-headed companion Münzer had long since tapped all the others, wired them up and programmed them, the whole squad of suits, a whole load of Stasi spear-carriers left in the dark themselves.

Not one of them knew the truth, they had only been given a tiny hors d'oeuvre of information. None of the really important things were said in the World Hall, only behind padded office doors, tête-à-tête in twos, or maybe threes at the most. And Steinkühler was holding the reins. Alternatively: even Steinkühler was just a puppet on a string who didn't know everything. The whole republic-wide secrecy administration must be incredibly hard work for people like Moss and Speckmann. They only dealt with people who knew less than they did. They had to keep an overview of who knew what. And who knew what other people knew. And who knew what other people didn't know. An information labyrinth. Could Moss be certain that Speckmann wasn't having him watched? Could Speckmann assume that Steinkühler wasn't eavesdropping on him on Moss's orders? Was there anyone in this country who wasn't being watched by someone else?

One thing's for sure, thought Wegener – they know everything about me. Who I eat currywurst with, who I don't sleep with any more, what me and my dick get up to under the shower. The number of my trips to the cinema, tyre changes, toilet cleaner purchases, recycled bottles, haemorrhoids. Wegener realized he didn't care any more. Presumably you just came to terms with it one day that you were known by people you didn't know yourself. That you were basically living the life of a celebrity. And maybe the whole external knowledge thing wasn't that much of a drama, provided you just gave up looking for proof that the Stasi had abducted a friend of yours and perhaps even killed him. In other words, if you had nothing to fear except for the secretly public nature of your private life.

In West Germany, TV personalities got themselves freighted off to the jungle and filmed shagging each other, the proletariat got to live in a Portakabin on 24-hour camera, all the kids put their photos on the internet, their home-made pornos, their daily grainy masturbation sessions. Scanners undressed travellers at the airport, the entire country was under CCTV surveillance, every taxi, every underground train, every market square. State security was on the up everywhere; just not in the GDR. Everywhere there was unbridled observation, watching, registration, sometimes above board, sometimes unofficially.

People have always had an exhibitionist and a voyeuristic side to them, thought Wegener, and now they can live them both out with no inhibitions. One lot under the diktat of socialism, the others under the diktat of their technical possibilities.

He conjured up a picture of Steinkühler. He was sitting in his seat high above East Berlin. Facing a wall of monitors. A walking man flickered on all the screens, filmed by satellite from above at an acute angle, sometimes slightly obscured by tangles of branches but still constantly visible because three lenses had him in their sights at the same time. All the screens beamed in autumn-leaf yellow, immersing Steinkühler's grey office landscape in a sunny light, making his face appear slightly tanned, turning him into a holidaymaker on the island of Rügen, on the beach at midday in weather fit for a king, his crowns flashing more golden than ever. Steinkühler doesn't cast a shadow. Steinkühler sits mutely in front of his wall full of Wegeners and forest and watches the dark figure battling through the leaves, a mono- tonous programme that he knows the ending to already. Which is why Steinkühler shows no sign of surprise when the figure on his screens suddenly gets his left foot caught, circles his arms – look out for rooty stumbling blocks, they're lying in wait everywhere – and all the tumbling man can do is raise his hands to his head as he trips over and then he's lying face down in the leaves.

No pain, just rustling. Moisture and all of a sudden the smell of earth and decay. Nothing hurt. Wegener opened his eyes. Directly in front of his face was a large, red-brown stain. Thin veins ran exactly parallel to the dark, fissured ends of the leaves. The mouldy smell grew more intense. There was something moist sticking to his cheek.

Wegener drew in a breath, saw Hoffmann's neck in his mind's eye again, the stretched white flesh with the violet notch from the rope, the matted hair, behind it Jocicz's square face, his yellow rubber-encased fingers, the eight knots, the shabby Hoffmann shoes, close together, united by tied laces into a hanging heel-click. There was nothing to find in these pictures, nothing that triggered a realization, nothing that took him any further. Laces, rope, oil drips – they were the facts, out of which Lienecke might wrest a few more inconsequential facts, with a little luck, but not a motive, not a clue that led to a name or an address.

These things would lead to nowhere, they'd been placed, planted, thought up, the whole thing was a professional job by men who knew exactly what they were doing. And those men were hard to find. Wegener wondered how Früchtl would see this absurd situation: a murder by the Stasi rulebook of 1989, a Colonel-General Steinkühler as a witness, an imported celebrity detective as a chaperone. Früchtl would have started by sitting down and ordering meatloaf, with three fried eggs and chips with mayonnaise, he'd have gulped it all down and then presumably warned him to be mistrustful, as ever. Not to trust Steinkühler, Münzer, Kallweit, Borgs, Lienecke or Brendel.

Wegener knew perfectly well he was being drawn into something where everyone had better cards than he did, where everyone had plenty of back doors and scapegoats, everyone else but him. Brendel was untouchable. Steinkühler and Münzer knew things that would protect them. Kallweit could put the blame on Borgs. If the worst came to the worst, Borgs would shovel the shit one level down. And on that level lay Hauptmann Hanging Cheeks, face-down in the crackling leaves, the transience of all earthly things in his nose.

Of course I'd start by ordering meatloaf, said Früchtl's voice, *with three fried eggs and chips and mayonnaise, and gulp it all down. Of course I'd warn you to be mistrustful. And of course they've got you fucked with this job, Martin. Who wants to get drawn into a special investigation where you get a shit-load of trouble if you find anything out and a shit-load of trouble if you don't find anything out? But remember, getting fucked can be a good thing, even if it's your own state that's using you against your will, because everything that happens to you in life is just as much disadvantage as advantage; even when you get raped it's all about trying to enjoy it. At least you've had sex for a change. And you're not going to shut up anyway,* said Früchtl, *you've always just been pretending to be over it, over me, over us, over the whole crock of shit, so at least be honest enough to use this opportunity, find out what you've always wanted to know. You've never been closer to the truth and who knows, maybe the whole thing will lead you to me in the end.*

Nothing leads to you, said Wegener. If you start looking for you, you come up against glass walls, you bite into granite, collide with ramparts of solidified silence. I don't know what they did with you but I'll say one thing for them, they certainly did it thoroughly. Dictatorships are tiring, Josef, there's probably nothing as tiring as dictatorships, honestly, you lose even your last will to get up on your feet. All you want to do is stay down. If you stay lying down, Josef, no one can knock you down any more.

Wegener didn't get the feeling that Früchtl was listening. His Minsk rang. He rolled over onto his back and found his pocket was empty. The sound was coming from the carpet of leaves. He fumbled for the ringing, picked up first a stone and then the phone: *Karolina Office calling.*

'Wegener speaking.' He sank back into the leaves.

'I've just been called into Braun's office.'

'That's what you get for falling asleep over his poems.'

'Dr Hans-Jörg Braun. My section head.'

'I assume . . . '

'They grilled me about our relationship, Martin!'

'You're having a relationship with your section head?'

'About *our* relationship! Oh, you're such a . . . '

'We're having a relationship? At last!'

' . . . a stupid arse-hat!' Karolina couldn't help laughing.

'I haven't the faintest idea what an arse-hat is.'

'Take a look in the mirror.'

You guys are listening, thought Wegener. Steinkühler in front of his wall of monitors. Smiling autumn-leaf yellow. A headset on his head. His fingers wandering across a Nanotchev keyboard. The mountain range of voice curves rising and falling in a diagram. A live recording.

'He asked me why I'm getting visits from the police, why a visit with official ID. I told him you were just messing about, they're all uptight here because of the consultations and—'

'Not on the phone.'

'What?'

'Not on the phone.'

'Why not on the phone? Where are you anyway?'

'I'm lying in the forest by the Müggelsee. You should try it some time, it's very relaxing.'

'You're taking the piss.'

'I'll be in touch, OK?'

'OK. And next time you turn up here, keep your ID to yourself.'

'Or else?'

There was a beep. She'd hung up.

Wegener exhaled. Above him, pale clouds crept across a grey surface, in front of them black bars of branches. The smell of decay had grown fainter. Now there was an added note of fungus. Common stinkhorn. Then the Minsk display lit up: *Karolina Enders sent you a TM: Or else I'll have your gas cut off. K.*

Wegener clicked on Response Option: *I will contact you as soon as I return from vacation* and then on Send.

Lienecke's face appeared on the horizon. 'Out of condition, Herr Hauptmann?'

Wegener reached out a hand. 'Yeah, I'm single.'

'That's all your own fault,' said Lienecke, 'so no complaining. The government has entrusted you with the future of the Holy Land, but you go falling over at the first opportunity.'

Wegener let him pull him up and patted half the forest floor off his coat. Lienecke was back in motion. 'I still can't believe you actually talked to Steinkühler. Or at least to one of his doppelgängers.'

'You don't need a doppelgänger if no one knows what you look like.'

'Another great way to save money.'

'Is it much further?'

'We're about halfway.'

They spent fifteen minutes in a mute crocodile, stubbornly following the tape, feeling like two degenerate horses that didn't dare to escape from their ridiculous plastic-fenced paddock, spotting no leads, no evidence, no chance to achieve anything at all. Then they approached the forest road from the other side, the Phobos appeared, the stained pipeline turned up, and they found themselves exactly where they had started out.

'We're going round in circles,' said Lienecke.

'But at least we know we're going round in circles.' Wegener leaned against an oak tree. He felt the same wave of tiredness as yesterday and the day before. A pail of viscous exhaustion tipped out over his head, plastering him all over, sticking heavy to his limbs. He could already envision the well-rested, luscious Richard Brendel. A sunbed-brown cop who jogged every morning and got it up every evening. A salad freak whose wife indulged her organic food obsession in the Kaufhaus des Westens food hall and had a crisis after three days with no sushi. Wegener imagined Brendel as wide awake. Sleepless and totally independent of sleep. There was no other way to get to be head of the West Berlin standing special commission, the top crime fighter in the biggest shithole in West Germany. He had to admit the guy had balls. Accompanying a highly politicized investigation in East Berlin without any real competence had to be a sign of either acute megalomania or a taste for tough challenges.

'If you were the Stasi,' said Wegener.

Lienecke looked amazed. 'Yes?'

'And you had to get rid of someone, in a hurry. What would you do?'

'So I wouldn't get caught?'

'Right.'

'I'd do it in some way that no one would seriously believe I'd done it.'

'And how?'

'By making everything look like I'd done it.'

Wegener nodded. 'That's just what I'd do too.'

8

HOFFMANN'S PROFESSORIAL BRAIN WAS A GREYISH LUMP in an oval metal dish. Delicate furrows ran through the firm matter, their irregularity producing a regular pattern. Wegener was reminded of the first and only scallops he'd ever eaten, at a New Year's reception for police management staff hosted by the city mayor to mark the first ever time they'd met the crime statistics targets. Borgs had passed his personal invitation on to him, because Borgs was ill in bed with the traditional Borgsian flu, and told him if no one from the murder squad turned up the vice squad would eat up all the smoked pork, and the smoked pork was delivered straight from the Molotov and therefore discharged of any suspicion of inferior quality; in other words, innocent. And no man should miss an opportunity for innocent meat.

The Molotov girls served the scallops in scallop shells, fried in butter, seasoned with lemon, salt and pepper, and on the side celeriac and mascarpone mash, pear and mango chutney and crispy bacon rashers.

For the first time in his life, Wegener had thought about the culinary dimensions of escaping to the West. The fact that there were edible things in the world that were denied to people in certain regions, and that the people in the denied regions knew that these edible things were available in plenty in other regions of the world – it was that fact that made the East Germans tantamount to animals. Lower forms of life kept in cages, relying on fodder tossed to them through the bars of the Iron Curtain. And scallops, celeriac and mascarpone mash, pear and mango chutney or crispy bacon rashers were not usually on the menu in the socialist zoo.

Before that New Year's reception, Wegener had never flirted with a woman to get at her seafood. The young, dark-haired Molotov nymph with her perfectly rounded spheres of breasts laced high on her chest must have had an eye for his immense appetite, for she had popped up unrequested at his table on every round of the town hall, delivering a plate and a smile – first the complete portion including accompaniments, then only scallops in shells, then only scallops – a confident, force-feeding Lolita, her almond eyes full of sex and ridicule. The contest was long since under way, the duel with his own stomach – how many more portions would he manage? – and at the eleventh, really the very last one, her inevitable question: What are you going to do with all that protein?

Molotov Magdalena. Mussels Magdalena. Moon-eyed Magdalena. More, more, more Magdalena. With a gaze that saw effortlessly through clothing, that frisked his stuffed male body, traced the curves, pierced all the way into his guts, where the seafood proteins were just being digested, broken down, processed into virility – available only three hours later by the way, Captain. The girl liked her heroes full. Wegener noticed he liked girls who liked their heroes full.

That evening he'd caught a glimpse of paradise: Magdalena's

gazes, a never-ending swinging of the door to the kitchen, an excess
of alcohol, breasts and fat, while the squad heads alongside him had
eaten like digestive organs on legs, showing up in full dress uniform
for camouflage's sake. The smoked pork of previous years had given
way to the tenderest beef brisket and mildest horseradish cream sauce,
the uniformed stomachs had shredded their slices of beef with knives
and forks instead of cutting them, dragging the chunks to and fro
through the smooth sauce, their heads bent low over the mayor's
Meissen porcelain so as not to lose a single drop of cream en route
to their mouths, so as to imbibe every single free-of-charge calorie,
eating in reserve, savouring in reserve and leaving as little as possible
for the others.

Later, during the *relaxing part of the evening*, Wegener had swayed
on one of the extremely un-relaxing chairs, knocking back one Solo-
tov vodka after another, with the warm feeling in his belly of having
made up for half a century of scallop-free existence in just under two
hours, with the warm feeling in his pants of soon making up for more
than four years of monogamy over several hours, with the warm
feeling in his head of not having to think of Karolina because of all
the vodka, for all the police stomachs turned up to the New Year's
reception *without partners* sat dully on their chairs, belching, swig-
ging Blue Curaçao and spending the entire evening picking fibres of
beef out of their dentures. *You're the only men in Berlin who put
morals first and then food.* Mayor Modrow had mangled a Brecht
quote, harvesting a limp burst of un-ironic applause.

All that was three years ago, and the memory of the firm cylinders
of scallop still tasted so nutty that a professorial brain on a weighing
scale could kiss it awake in a matter of seconds. Back then Wegener
had thought it a clever formula to gauge the condition of a state by
the eating behaviour of its police force, and he still did now.

'Gorgeous, eh?' Jocicz sounded like he was talking about a woman. Lienecke gave a half-hearted nod.

Wegener's eyes wandered around the old pump-house. The room had four-metre-high tiled walls and a well-preserved tiled floor. Long windows with cast-iron bars sliced the last remains of daylight into grey rectangles. Beneath the windows were old transformer cases, next to the two mortuary slabs two huge black-varnished monsters of machines with giant engine blocks, with thick and thin tubes growing out of them into the ground and the walls like iron tentacles. Behind the pumps shimmered the metal casings of metre-long switch panels with countless rows of buttons, lights and controls.

For Wegener, this backdrop morphed into the interior of a spaceship, a mixture of the command HQ, engine room and the sickbay of the ancient socialist starship *Walter Ulbricht*. Jocicz was the ship's doctor in his white coat, on the clean metal sheet was one of the aliens who had fallen in the Battle of Köpenick: a thin, pale body with a violet necklace of bruises and his chest folded open, emptied out from the larynx to the pubis, with a crumpled face that had been rolled down from the bare skull like a saggy, skin-coloured sock, so that the hooked nose now seemed to be sniffing at its own exposed windpipe.

'This place was supposed to be a provisional solution four years ago,' said Jocicz, following Wegener's gaze around the machine room. 'The building works in Schönhausen have been going on since then, and by now it looks worse there than before they started. This little treasure here was the most state-of-the-art pumping station in Europe back in 1901. That's the kind of thing we were once capable of. Now it's a provisional morgue.'

'But presumably the provisional morgue with the best atmosphere in the whole of the Socialist Union,' said Lienecke.

'In the aesthetic and the olfactory sense.' Jocicz nodded. 'No matter how much formalin you spill in here you can still smell the oil and pump grease.'

Wegener sniffed the air. Jocicz was right. Through the stench of formaldehyde, the SS *Walter Ulbricht* really did smell slightly of lost eras, of mustachioed engineers, golden yellow lubricant grease, dirty cotton rags, diesel and handmade cast-iron technology. It could only be a matter of minutes before the commander entered the room, examined the disembowelled alien with satisfaction, flicked a few switches and gave the order for take-off into the depths of the cosmos, all set to bring the joys of the planned economy to starving extraterrestrial cultures.

'Life in the GDR can be pretty exciting, eh, Captain?' Jocicz winked. 'You're standing next to a corpse in a pump station, waiting for the Superman of West Berlin.'

Wegener turned around. 'Do you know Brendel?'

Jocicz shook his head. 'Never met him, never heard of him. But he seems to be a big cheese next door.'

'Apparently so,' said Wegener. 'No one knows any more than that.'

'Just for the rest of the case . . . ' Jocicz straightened a trolley of dissecting equipment. 'Are you heading this investigation, I mean in the operative sense, or is our new boy in charge from now on?'

Wegener looked at Jocicz. 'Would you behave differently towards me if I wasn't leading this investigation in five minutes' time, Doctor?'

Jocicz thought for a moment and gave a square smile. 'That's one of those questions it's probably better not to answer.'

'Probably. For the time being Brendel and I will be leading the investigation jointly. If anything changes we'll let you know.'

Two bright specks of light brushed across the windows and cast contorted white squares on the old tiles for a second.

'Here we go,' said Lienecke.

Outside, tyres crunched on the gravel, no other sound. No engine vibrations, no rattling, no roaring. Lienecke climbed onto one of the old transformer boxes.

'Can you see anything?' Jocicz had obviously had the same idea with the transformer boxes and didn't want to be the second one to climb up.

'Mercedes S-600,' said Lienecke, not even trying to hide the awe in his voice. 'Say what you like about capitalists, but they certainly have plenty of legroom.'

Wordlessly, Jocicz climbed onto the box next to Lienecke. Wegener hesitated, then climbed up as well.

On the forecourt stood a shiny black tank. Two pointy triangles of gleaming glass as headlamps. The long flanks of the limousine gave off a metallic shimmer, the Mercedes symbol sparkled above the massive radiator grille. No one was visible behind the dark windows.

'Have fun with our potholed roads,' said Wegener.

'Air suspension,' murmured Lienecke, 'infrared night-vision assistant, 120 metres visibility range, pre-safe brakes, Distronic Plus with radar cruise control, fatigue recognition, 272 horsepower. And you can't hear anything. Nothing at all.'

'You never stop surprising me.'

'Take a look at *su.greenwithenvy.gdr*.'

'That'd be the perfect car for the Stasi,' said Jocicz.

'I think they like to travel unnoticed.' Wegener climbed down from the transformer box. 'Ulf, if Brendel sees you drooling at the window like that he'll have you washing his car tomorrow.'

'And you know what?' Lienecke was still staring out. 'I'd do it at a snap. Including the interior.'

'Me too.' Jocicz jumped down to the tiled floor and positioned himself at the slab. He obviously felt safer close to his corpse. 'If I got to drive it.'

'I can't believe every task-force head has a fat-cat car like that over there!' Lienecke turned around and spread his arms in resignation. 'What do the real fat cats drive?'

'Look at the registration number,' said Wegener, 'F–BG 38. It's a Federal Border Guard car.'

'F–BG 38,' aped Lienecke, 'It's *Flipping Brendel's Gas-guzzler*! Why should the Federal Border Guard drive an S-Class Mercedes?'

'Why does the circus artiste lick her own pussy?'

'You tell me.'

'Because she can.'

Outside, four car doors slurped shut one after another. Footsteps on the gravel. A muted laugh. Borgs, thought Wegener – *El Silencio*. He can laugh every now and then; laughter has no meaning. Non-committal. If the Hoffmann case goes wrong, if it really goes belly-up, then even Borgs might have to open his mouth at some point. But not to laugh.

By the time the heavy wooden door opened with a slight squeak and revealed Kallweit's important occasion face, Lienecke was leaning casually against one of the pumps, looking for all the world as if he'd never been interested in cars. Jocicz was standing to attention at the mortuary slab.

'Gentlemen – here come the reinforcements.' Kallweit made a hand gesture like the quiz show host of the Collective Winnings Gala when he unveiled the main prize of the week, a brand-new Phobos Flux GL II with electric phenoplast convertible hood in Florena Cosmetics blue.

After Kallweit came Borgs, giving a silent nod around the room, then a tall, slim man with grey hair appeared. A pretty-boy, thought Wegener, a couple of years older than me but still several classes better-looking, an actor playing the inspector, a man who gets the job because he looks the part. The slim man surveyed the scene. A pale blue stare swept across the room, oscillating calmly between Lienecke, Jocicz, Wegener, the corpse, and back again. Not friendly, but not unfriendly either.

Although Wegener had been seeing naked dead people on mortuary slabs for twenty-three years, the pale, sawn-open Hoffmann suddenly seemed robbed of his dignity. As if Brendel were some other life form. As if it were a gross betrayal to present one of your own men to this other life form, so pale and sawn open. Although Hoffmann even came from Heidelberg originally, so he was one of them. Wegener ran his eyes over the sharp hipbones, the wizened penis nestling in a grey pubic den like a perished naked mole rat, the long foreskin that thickened at the tip into a colourless, fleshy knob.

'Richard Brendel,' said the slim man, taking large strides towards the slab and instantly becoming a conqueror, an initiator, a well-mannered man who had taken the first step while all the others had stood around instead of welcoming their guest. One–nil to him.

We've only just kicked off and the West's ahead already, thought Wegener and asked himself whether Jocicz's handshake was still as firm as the day before yesterday or if he saved his energy for his East German colleagues.

Brendel's eau de toilette got to him before the man himself did. A heavy, saccharine scent slightly reminiscent of sweet-shops. A touch of liquorice. A hint of rose. A bit of sherbet. Wegener noticed simultaneously that he liked the smell and that he found it annoying that he liked it. Then their hands gripped one another, a normal, firm handshake, a brief glance into the blue, blue eyes. Brendel's mouth smiled a subtle smile. Or his mouth was shaped in such a way that it looked subtly smiling from close up. You had to look up to the mouth's owner. He was at least one metre eighty-five, if not one ninety. His features were a good-looking fortress that might be concealing anything at all. Capitalism didn't just have more legroom – it smelled better too.

The second man now shaking hands around the room looked like an intellectual thug. A sturdy body, shaven head, rimless glasses. No subtle smile; he was expressionlessly earnest. Or a tad condescending. Or, thought Wegener, you just read condescension into a West German face like this because that's what you expect to find.

'Dr Christian Kayser, our liaison officer at the Federal Intelligence Service,' said Brendel. Kayser stayed as motionless as if he still had to get used to his title himself. His rimless glasses reflected the spotlights over the mortuary slab.

So that's him, thought Wegener, the 251st FIS man in the German Democratic Republic.

Kallweit strutted to the middle of the room. A cockerel about to get high on his own pathos.

'Gentlemen, unusual circumstances have always called for unusual measures.' Kallweit put on a concentrating face, acting as if he hadn't spent hours mulling over his speech in advance. 'This is certainly the most unusual measure in my time in office. But it's not only consensually agreed by the Chairman of our State Council and the Chancellery in Bonn, and thus the first police investigation in the history of our two states in which West German officers can work independently on GDR territory, but it's also – as I'm sure we've all realized by now – of the greatest political import. The outcome of this matter may influence the course of the German–German consultations, and in the worst case it may bring grave economic consequences for the GDR – and for the FRG.'

Kallweit looked over at the dead man, the others following suit. There he is, the cause of our grave economic consequences for the GDR and the FRG, thought Wegener, a cold skeleton with an outsourced lump of brain. What once went on in that lump may change the course of history. Or it already has changed it. And now things are playing out.

'So on behalf of Minister Speckmann and Colonel-General Steinkühler, who at this moment are informing Chairman Moss of the next steps, I'd also like to point out that we're practically representing pan-German interests in the coming operation.' Kallweit arched his back and a slight paunch curved beneath his long, black coat. 'West Germany is reliant on the Russian gas, we're reliant on the transit fees. It's as simple as that. What we have to do now is make sure the contracts can be signed. Wegener, Brendel – go ahead.'

Brendel gestured in Wegener's direction as if giving him the floor.

'I'll give you a brief rundown,' said Wegener and turned to the slab. 'At the moment we're assuming that this is the body of Albert Hoffmann. So far we haven't found any witnesses who knew Hoffmann well enough in recent years to identify him. There's a team searching Hoffmann's flat right now and they've found genetic material, the DNA test is on the way. So we'll have to put up with 99 per cent for the time being. Hoffmann was found dead forty-three hours ago, hanged from the Main Pipeline North in the Köpenick forest. That's about ten kilometres before the Potsdam Hand.'

'The Main Pipeline North divides into five smaller pipelines at Potsdam,' Kallweit explained. 'The East Berliners call it the Potsdam Hand because—'

Brendel and Kayser nodded.

'Dr Jocicz estimates the time of death as two days before he was found,' said Wegener. 'That would be Monday, the 17th of October, around late afternoon.'

'Between 3 and 5 p.m.' Jocicz looked around the room. 'I'm afraid I can't be any more precise than that.'

'There was a Phobos Prius at the crime scene. The killers apparently forced Hoffmann to climb on the roof, using the Prius as a trapdoor, if you like. Both registration plates were removed but the exact same model is registered to Hoffmann, so we're assuming it's his car. If that's the case he'd have driven to the forest himself. Which suggests he knew the killers.'

Brendel and Kayser nodded.

'There's barely any evidence, I'm afraid. We've got the button, which clearly comes from Hoffmann's coat. And we've got a few drops of engine oil – that's all.'

'Analysis?'

'In the lab. Now for the things that make the case tricky.'

Wegener looked at Kallweit. 'The hanging, the shoelaces, the eight knots in the noose. The murder method fits in with a legend about alleged internal punishments for Stasi traitors at the time of Revitalization. We have nothing to confirm this assumption, I have to add. But the signal's still clear enough. Hoffmann was supposed to be branded a traitor.'

'Was Hoffmann with the Stasi?' Kayser's glasses glimmered.

'Not according to Colonel-General Steinkühler.'

Kayser smiled.

'As we all know, our current information is that next Monday's *Spiegel* cover story will deal with Hoffmann's murder.' Wegener tried to ignore Kayser's smile. 'It quotes a source who claims to have witnessed the killing as a member of the State Security. The informer asserts his personal innocence and accuses the State Security. He also has photos of the crime scene – that means either he really was there or he knows one or several individuals who were there. We also know that Hoffmann had rented a one-room flat in Marzahn under the name of Emil Fischer. We haven't yet established how long for, or for what purpose.'

'Anything in the flat?'

'Nothing at all,' said Wegener. 'Just a bolt-hole for sleeping in occasionally.'

'Two colleagues from the Hamburg Crime Squad are on the *Spiegel* case,' said Brendel, 'but we can't expect much out of them, what with our source protection legislation. So we've got three key questions: Was Hoffmann with the Stasi, perhaps as an unofficial informant? If not, why did the killers lay that trail? And who's the *Spiegel* source, how did he get the material, why did he go public with it? It's about public opinion, not money. There are plenty of institutions that pay much better than the *Spiegel*.'

Just like you always imagine West Germans, thought Wegener, always thinking about money.

Kallweit stretched. 'What's your first impression?'

'Just a speculation,' said Brendel, 'but if we assume that the killers want to sabotage the consultations, they've achieved what they wanted as things stand. So whoever hired them could be from any-where where they'd profit from high gas prices in Western Europe.'

'Plenty of people would profit from that.' Kallweit looked down and sucked in his stomach. 'The OPEC states and the other gas sup-pliers. For example in the Middle East. And in West Germany the alternative energy companies. If the gas price goes up, so does the pressure to maintain the subsidies for solar and wind power.'

Brendel's eyes felt their way along the dead body. 'The hanging, the shoelaces. It looks like a lot of things, but not like a professional job with an international economic background. And our intelligence services haven't got anything so far that takes us vaguely in that direction. Right, Christian?'

The bald man stood as if turned to stone, his hands behind his back. 'The Chancellery has given us the green light, so I can officially inform you that the Federal Intelligence Service has no information justifying suspicions towards oil states or other countries with relevant natural resources. Which doesn't mean that no such indications exist. It's just extremely unlikely.'

'Everything brings us back to one question,' said Wegener. 'Why Hoffmann? Twenty-one years ago he was on the advisory staff to the State Council Chairman. It'd be a major coincidence if his death had nothing to do with that.'

'Belated punishment for a traitor,' said Brendel, 'whether he was with the Stasi or not. That's what the picture tells us. They want us to think someone called him to account. What was the man doing for the past quarter of a century?'

'Leading a double life.' Wegener leaned against the glossy black metal of the pump. 'That's all we know.'

'Then it's time we took a closer look at him. Do we know his real address?'

'We found out this morning,' said Wegener. 'Greifenhagener Strasse. Prenzlauer Berg district. The three of us will go over there later.'

'The forensics team's been there for six hours now,' said Lienecke, 'so they're probably nearly finished.'

Kallweit gave a polite cough. 'Gentlemen, there's one thing we have to bear in mind. The State Council Chairman would certainly inform Colonel-General Steinkühler if he had any idea of how Albert Hoffmann's death had anything to do with—'

Kayser's smile struck Kallweit dumb. There was a sudden silence in the pump-house. Jocicz coughed.

Kallweit walked across the room as if looking for the end of his sentence, took a sidestep and stopped at the slab. In his black coat he became a priest about to administer the last rites to the gleaming corpse. 'We can only make very careful enquiries in that direction. To be honest I don't think it's necessary at all, Hauptmann Wegener.'

Muted orchestral music. Brendel rummaged in his coat pockets. The music grew louder. 'My son put it on my phone yesterday.' Brendel grinned. 'In preparation for my stint abroad, so to speak.'

He's even better looking when he grins, thought Wegener. Lienecke and Jocicz exchanged glances.

Brendel had located his mobile phone in the inside pocket and picked up. The music was interrupted.

Kayser raised his eyebrows in an unstated question.

'The title song to an old East German detective series,' said Lienecke. '*The Invisible Cross-hairs*. He's come prepared.'

Kayser dropped his eyebrows again. 'Not something I need to know.'

'Not necessarily,' said Lienecke. 'East German culture.'

Brendel listened, said thanks and then hung up. 'We've found a former colleague of Hoffmann's from his time in the West. Doctor Werner Blühdorn. Still lives in Heidelberg but he's supposed to be giving a presentation at the Humboldt University on the 24th.'

'What a coincidence,' said Kayser.

Borgs had stood up from his transformer box. 'Mr Jocicz, could you please explain the pathological findings to our colleagues from West Germany. Your corpse is getting warm.'

Not bad, thought Wegener – a whole twenty words.

9

TWILIT BERLIN TOOK ITS CUE FROM BORGS and kept its trap shut, busy as always but not saying a word, all its grumpy rattles and squeaks shut out by armoured doors and windows: *S-Guard special security enhancements*. Tiny leather labels stitched into the panelling.

Wegener leaned forward and stared over Kayser's shoulder at the tachometer: a saffron-yellow backlit semicircle, the last number at the bottom right 340. The last number on a Phobos circular tachometer, banally lit from above, was 170. Exactly half. The highest speed that a Phobos ever got to was another 10 to 20 km/h below that, depending on the load. Wegener sank back against the pale leather padding of the back seat. The bad joke came to mind that the Phobos had left plenty of VWs behind it on West German autobahns. When it sped past them on the back of a Mercedes tow-truck.

'By the way, shall I turn the seat heater on, Hauptmann Wegener?' Brendel half turned to the back. 'The leather's a bit cold.'

Wegener wondered for two seconds whether the question could be serious. Brendel looked as if he meant it.

'But only to make Ulf Lienecke jealous.'

'I'll turn it on to 3. Give me a shout if it's too warm.'

Wegener made a sound of agreement and asked himself whether anyone could possibly admit having an overheated backside to a West German police officer. It probably wasn't a feasible proposition.

Brendel braked the car gently and came to a stop. Just as at the traffic lights earlier, people stopped to stare, ogling, looking as if the Wall had just tipped over. Some of them stood open-mouthed with amazement. The driver of an ancient Wartburg apparently hadn't believed his rear-view mirror, had got out of his car and was standing aghast in front of the shiny bonnet. The Mercedes symbol was a hairline cross aiming at his genitals. The faces of passers-by betrayed enthusiasm, horror, malice. An elderly man turned his back on them.

Brendel and Kayser were silent.

Wegener realized he was ashamed. Ashamed of these oglers who surrounded the car at every junction, betraying their country. People with the poverty of their state, its inability to produce the highest-quality goods and genuine bling, inscribed on their faces the instant they saw a Benz. With their envy curdling into crude childlike expressions. With their minds suddenly readable. And Wegener realized that, despite his shame, he wished Karolina were at these traffic lights. Karolina ought to see him on the back seat of this FIS special security state chariot, ought to see his face emerging behind the descending tinted window, ought to stare at him, incredulous and admiring as he leaned back casually amidst so much luxury.

The electrically lit ashtrays shimmered in red-brown walnut wood. Buttons and knobs glowed in the same saffron yellow as the tachometer and all the dashboard instruments. There were screens mounted in the headrests of the front seats. Dimmable reading lamps in the padded ceiling, leather-bound armrests, silvery trim. Karolina ought to see him like this. As a first-class investigator on a national-level special assignment. With a slightly warmed backside. Driven by a sweetshop-scented special inspector from West Berlin – the best-chauffeured man in the GDR for this half an hour. No Central Council member in his Volvo was a match for an S-Guard-S-Class, no other person in the country could keep up with this saffron-yellow, silvery, leathery, warm-arsed S-situation.

Brendel's muscle car can be our wedding car, thought Wegener, Karolina and him in white and black, Früchtl turns up again as my best man, all driving through Berlin in this enormous Mercedes. Where did thoughts like that come from, what triggered them? Früchtl beeps the horn, Karolina has tears running down her cheeks, the people throw flowers, Hauptmann Hanging-Cheeks has got his true love back again, there is such a thing as good news, congratulations from Chairman M: Dear Martin, our wedding gift to you and your delightful gas whore is permission to emigrate. You know what they say about redheads: rusty roof – damp cellar, give her one for me while you're at it, but make sure it's from behind the way us tough old dogs like it, eh?

Why can't you just stop loving Karo? said Früchtl. *Why can't you just stop it after all this time?*

Don't tell me that, Josef, tell it to my love.

Your love's deaf in both ears.

Beg your pardon?

The traffic lights switched to green.

'Can you get a Minsk here without a contract?' Brendel curved around the Wartburg. The driver was still standing in the road.

Wegener leaned forwards. 'You can, but they're bloody expensive.

Otherwise with a twelve-month minimum contract. With Telemedien POC. If you're a citizen. If you're not – no idea.'

Brendel had to dodge a parking delivery van, swerving to the left and then back again. The Mercedes got back in lane as if there had been no evasive steering. 'You wouldn't happen to have an old M5 lying around? An M6 costs more than an iPhone in the West now.'

'Afraid not. But I can ask around at the office.'

Kayser turned around. 'Is it just a rumour, Hauptmann Wegener, that the GDR has such a significant head start in the mobile telecommunications sector because it's all Stasi technology?'

'It's not a rumour,' said Wegener. 'I'm told the State Security uses telephones that are two generations further on than anything on the market right now. They're supposed to have an M9 in operation.'

'With bugging function?' asked Kayser.

Brendel's head fell slightly towards his chest.

'With bugging function and automatic scent sample collection,' said Wegener. 'But don't worry, the scent sample function only works with East Germans.'

'What model have you got?' asked Brendel.

'An M5. The proletariat doesn't get anything above an M5 or M6 over here. The rest ends up on your side of the border.'

'So we subsidize the evolution of socialist secret services technology with our hard-earned wages,' said Kayser. 'That's what I call beating capitalism with its own weapons.'

'Seeing as our HQ just supported the production of imperialist warships by installing a new Thyssen lift, you're more than welcome to buy our telephones.'

Brendel turned around slightly. 'So if anyone offers you an M5 in the next few days and they're interested in euros . . .'

Wegener nodded. 'I see you've already got a Navodobro, though.'

'Kallweit got it for us from your stock. Our navigation system only works with GPS signals, not GLONASS.'

'Something completely different: What are your bourgeois terrorists up to nowadays?' asked Kayser. 'I used to come across them now and then.'

'No idea.' Wegener looked out of the window. 'Is the West German press interested in them then?'

'Not really. But I always read internal reports.'

'What terrorists?' asked Brendel.

'They call themselves the Bürger Brigade,' said Kayser, 'after some guy called Alexander Bürger who nobody knows.'

'Never heard of them. What do they get up to?'

'Write threatening letters,' said Wegener, 'and that's about it.'

'That makes them writers, not terrorists.'

Kayser clicked his tongue. 'Aren't all writers terrorists? They want to change the world but they're too cowardly to pick up a gun.'

'There aren't any political writers any more.' Brendel indicated left and turned off. 'They're all desperately seeking the right words to plague other people with their sensitivities, and they hate history because they have no stories of their own to tell.'

'To answer your question: the State Security presumably has the Bürger people under control,' said Wegener. 'The Stasi's not as slimmed down as they like to say.'

'Speaking of the Stasi,' said Brendel. An arrow flashed up on the Navodobro screen, *150 metres, destination distance 11 kilometres, arrival time 19:36.* 'I didn't want to ask Kallweit directly, but it'd be good to know what security level we can access files up to. I got the feeling he didn't know himself yet.' Brendel went down a gear. The car took the bend. 'We've got that meeting tomorrow morning with a Major-General . . . '

'Wischinsky,' said Kayser.

' . . . Borgs called it *a meeting* anyway. Hauptmann Wegener, we're going to have to treat the State Security as a suspect. You realize that?'

'I realize that.' Wegener noticed the leather seats were getting unpleasantly warm. 'You can imagine that's not exactly all in a day's work for an inspector with the People's Police.'

'I can well imagine,' said Kayser. 'Presumably not one of your favourite tasks either.'

'Depends how much career potential you have left to mess up and how fast you want to get rid of it.'

Well, you've certainly done that already, said Früchtl.

'If the worst comes to the worst we can put our heads on the line,' said Brendel. 'But are the gentlemen prepared for the interrogation to go the other way around this time?'

Wegener slid to and fro on the hot leather. 'Steinkühler put it like this earlier today: I was going to go down in history as the first police-man in history to investigate the State Security, but not the first policeman to investigate the State Security *successfully*.'

'Steinkühler's wrong about at least one thing,' said Brendel, turning off the seat heater. 'There are three of us policemen investigating the State Security.'

It was almost dark by the time the Mercedes turned onto Greifenhagener Strasse. Alongside the brick tower of the Gethsemane Church glowed a last violet strip of sunset, shrinking further behind the roofs with every minute. The high windows of the nineteenth-century buildings were dingy yellowish rectangles, showing sections of sideboards, bookshelves, pictures and old-fashioned wallpaper. Antique chandeliers, candles and wonky lampshades gave off a dim light. Brendel stopped in a no-parking zone in front of a dented Phobos

Universal, rummaged in the glove compartment for a plastic-coated Parking Permission sign, jammed it behind the windscreen, seemed to remember suddenly where he was and put the plastic card away again.

'A class enemy in a no-parking zone,' said Kayser as he heaved himself out of his seat. 'You don't see that every day.'

The central locking system made all the indicators on the car flash twice. Cars and walls were steeped in cheerful orange for seconds, a colour that Wegener found strangely unfitting. He felt the cold air on his backside. All that was left of the sunset was glowing rooftops, behind which all of Germany seemed to be ablaze.

'What number?'

'51.'

'I chose a good parking spot then. Right opposite.'

Hoffmann's building stuck out above the others in the road by two storeys, a seven-floor late-nineteenth-century house with rusty balcony railings, greyed stucco and a broad double bowfront. Wegener pulled his Minsk out of his coat pocket, clicked into the *TM* list and checked the address. Number 51, seventh floor. No light in any of the top-floor windows. Wegener counted again.

Brendel looked around. 'Wrong house number?'

'No, but it's all dark up there. And according to Lienecke the forensics team ought to be still there.'

'Maybe Hoffmann didn't pay his electricity bill,' said Kayser. 'Our first motive for the murder on the gas pipeline.'

Wegener went up five worn steps. The front door was open. In the corridor a PP was leaning against the wall playing something on his Minsk. He put it away with clumsy haste when he saw Wegener and poked one index finger into the air: 'Seventh floor on the left, sir.'

'So we were right after all,' said Brendel. 'Dead people always live on the top floor.'

'In the East and the West,' said Wegener, taking a deep breath and starting to climb an enormously creaky staircase. Brendel and Kayser creaked after him. On the second floor they ran into forensics men, four bored faces in white full-body suits, boxes and files clutched to their chests.

The door to Hoffmann's flat was open. In the hall was a chaos of cardboard boxes, shouted orders and questions; every now and then camera flashes. The obligatory greasy-haired computer expert was lugging a Robotron Sigma and a medium-sized Nanotchev Omikron out of the flat and greeted them with a grunt. They could still smell his sweaty shirt once he was out-groaning the stairs on the sixth floor.

Wegener kept an eye out for Frank Stein but all he could find was bent, white figures putting their stuff away.

'The ground's safe, gentlemen. You're welcome to enter.'

Wegener turned around. Stein was standing behind him, the door to the guest toilet now open.

'If the police are using the murder victim's toilet the evidence must be pretty much secured,' said Wegener.

'Almost done.' Stein nodded. His thick hair was plastered to his skull, looking like the cap of a Mephistopheles costume that he hadn't taken off since carnival season. The steely glasses frames had slipped down to the thin tip of his nose, and a grey suit hung loose on his teenager's body. He was well aware that his workmates called him Frankenstein, and his workmates were well aware that Frank-enstein was well aware of it. It's inevitable, that nickname, Stein used to say, and he was sure his father, a cheeky bugger from Cottbus, had chosen the combination of first name and surname out of pure malice, having always wanted a voluptuous daughter and not a skinny criminologist of a son.

'Report or tour of the flat?'

'First the tour, then the report.'

Frankenstein performed a slight bow and then strolled through an obstacle course of cardboard boxes, crates and washing baskets full of papers into a high-ceilinged room. Bookshelves lined all the walls up to the very top.

'A library!' Frankenstein spread his arms and turned in a circle like a tipsy anorexic ballerina. Not a hair on his head moved. 'The whole flat is one big library! Take a look at this!' The ballerina whirled through a white double-door into the next room. 'He even blocked out the windows. All of the windows facing the road and all but three at the back.'

Wegener, Brendel and Kayser looked around, exchanged glances and then followed Stein, who was already one room further on.

'What we have here, you won't believe it, is nine rooms like this, nine rooms full of books and eight of them without windows. At first we thought there was no end to it – you walk into a flat and you're in a parallel universe! A parallel universe library!' Now Stein was a home owner unable to get a grip on his wealth. 'But that's where we were wrong, gentlemen, everything's perfectly normal here, we're still in Prenzlauer Berg. The explanation is: first of all, the building goes back a lot further than you'd expect from the front, it's some kind of gigantic house, and secondly our man's had two flats knocked together.'

Stein strolled onwards. The next room was twice the size of the four before it. Two nineteenth-century salons melded together, two identical chandeliers suspended from identical stucco rosettes. A pale line of new floorboards ran along the middle of the room.

Wegener did a pirouette of his own. Endless rows of shelves, closed by dark cabinet doors at the bottom, and above them, forced into fastidiously precise order, the brightly coloured load of thousands of book spines. Worn folios were stored behind glass doors and the gold-embossed leather spines of collected works and encyclopaedias glistened black, brown and red.

Most of the volumes had a bouquet of bookmarks sprouting from them, turning the books into respectable punks with luminous paper hairstyles. In the middle of the room was an antique leather-bound desk. Opposite the desk was the first window Wegener had seen in the flat, a huge glass arch divided into two large wings. Through the arch, you could keep watch on the night sky over East Berlin: the glittering sphere on top of the television tower, the EastSide, the cathedral dome, the Palace of the Republic with its pillars of light.

Kayser planted himself mutely in front of the view. Hands behind his back, his face an astounded reflection of the panes.

Wegener walked up to one of the shelves, leaned forward and read: Altvater, Mahnkopf: *The Boundaries of Globalization*. Bredow, Brocke: *Crisis and Protest*. Mathias Jopp: *Dimensions of Peace*. A hardback collected edition of OSCE yearbooks from 1982 to 2010.

'Do you still have living space allocations over here?' Brendel was suddenly standing next to Wegener. 'I mean, in the GDR?'

'We're in the neighbours' flat now,' called Stein. 'It's all in the same order but the other way around!'

Wegener shook his head. 'No need for that after '91. The population went down from sixteen million to fourteen and a half, and that was the end of the housing shortage.'

The two of them followed Frankenstein into the next room.

'Then it's perfectly normal for a retired politics professor to live in a 250-square-metre library. Full of the latest West German publications.'

'I'm afraid that's never going to be normal over here. Not even if there were only a million of us left.'

For a brief moment Brendel looked as if he wanted to say something in reply, but he didn't.

Wegener slowed his pace. 'You're wondering who a man has to blackmail in the GDR to get hold of a flat like this.'

Brendel nodded. 'That's what I'm wondering. And you obviously are too. How about the Chairman of the State Council?'

'Or it could be the Secretary-General. Or the Deputy Chairman of the State Council. Or the Chairman of the Council of Ministers. To name a few.'

'Millard?' Brendel frowned. 'I always thought the Council of Ministers was just for decoration.'

'Even Hermann Millard must have enough power to get someone a flat like this.'

'Enough power to get someone hanged?'

Wegener looked Brendel in the blue eyes. 'You can ask our Major-General Wischinsky that tomorrow morning.'

'But then he won't get me an M9.'

'Maybe he would, though – so he can bug you.'

'This is the end of the library!' called Frankenstein.

Wegener and Brendel entered a crowded room that obviously had to store everything there hadn't been space for in the other nine rooms: a double bed, two wardrobes, a small dining table with two chairs, a TV and a two-seater sofa by a white marble mantelpiece. Outside the window were seven flowerpots with roses growing in them.

'Not bad, eh?' Frankenstein was as happy as if he'd be moving into Hoffmann's flat next week.

'Not bad at all,' said Brendel and extended his hand. 'Richard Brendel, West Berlin Crime Squad.'

Frankenstein puffed up his cheeks. 'Sorry, of course. Stein, Frank Stein, Frankenstein. People's Police. East Berlin People's Police. Welcome to the other side of the anti-capitalist protective rampart, Mr Brendel.'

'Frank, give us the low-down,' said Wegener and turned around. Kayser was nowhere to be seen.

Stein pushed his glasses up his nose. 'Right: in the library rooms we've got nothing special, nothing under UV light, no relevant evidence on the floorboards. The whole flat must have been cleaned in the past three or four days, and cleaned thoroughly. Bucket and dried floor-cloth in the kitchen, traces of scouring fluid in the sink, et cetera.'

'Hoffmann's cleaning lady?' Wegener ran a finger along the mantelpiece. No dust.

'We're questioning the neighbours but I think it's pretty likely to be the cleaning lady either way. Certainly there hasn't been a professional here trying to get rid of evidence. There are dirty plates in the dishwasher indicating at least two people. Two fish knives, two forks, two white wine glasses, two sherry glasses and so on. Unless Hoffmann was in the habit of eating off two plates at the same time.'

'Used dishes?' asked Brendel. 'Even though someone's cleaned the place?'

'Put in the dishwasher but it was only a quarter full. So we're looking for an economically minded cleaning lady who'd rather put up with a bit of a smell than waste publicly owned energy reserves.'

'Fingerprints?'

Stein went over to a cardboard box containing several plastic bags and reached into it. 'As far as we can establish, we've got prints from three different people in the kitchen and the living room. If we have to search the library book by book we'll be stuck here until the next Revitalization. I'd like to avoid that if there's no urgent need.'

'Three people,' said Wegener. 'That means Hoffmann, the cleaning lady, if she exists, and who else?'

'And maybe this pretty little thing here.' Stein put a framed photo down on the dining table.

Wegener and Brendel leaned over the picture. A young blonde on a beach. The woman was smiling at the camera, wearing a red towel wrapped around her chest, holding the towel up with one hand. In the background were a few blurry people in bright blue water.

Früchtl would have said *passed with distinction*, thought Wegener, strictly according to his National People's Army grading system for female beauty, and Früchtl would've been right, there was no other option but *passed with distinction*. The girl was a looker all right.

'How old is she?' asked Brendel.

'Mid to late twenties,' said Kayser. Despite the creaky floorboards Wegener hadn't heard him coming in.

'Frank Stein, Frankenstein.'

'Christian Kayser.'

'Condoms in the drawer of the bedside table.' Stein cleared his throat. 'Lots of condoms. Apart from that a whip, handcuffs, battery-powered dildos and an, er – erectile dysfunction treatment.'

'An er erectile dysfunction treatment?' Kayser grinned. 'What kind?'

'It's called Upright. An East German product. I'm told it's very effective.'

'A happy old man.'

'Anything else to do with the woman?' Brendel picked up the photo.

Stein pulled a notebook out of his trouser pocket and flicked through it: 'One open box of tampons, a second toothbrush and deodorant in the bathroom. Florena Action.'

Wegener coughed.

'A bit of underwear in one of the drawers in the right-hand wardrobe. Bras, knickers, socks, tights. All very good quality.'

Wegener pointed at the photo. 'We'll need copies as soon as possible. What do you mean, very good quality?'

Stein cast an embarrassed glance at Brendel and Kayser. 'I mean West German goods. If you ask me.'

'It's not that great quality,' said Brendel. 'I'm always getting holes in my socks.'

A constable knocked at the open door and nodded a greeting.

'Weigt, what's up?'

'Sorry – Frank, if you've got a mo, come downstairs for a minute, it's worth it.'

'Why?'

'I don't want to bother you.'

'You're not.'

The policeman presented a row of wonky teeth. 'Some fat-cat West German's parked in the no-parking zone. A Benz, a mother of a car. We've ordered the tow-truck, I just don't know if they'll have space for the thing on the back.'

'Forget it,' said Kayser, 'the thing only just fits on the auto train to Sylt. But if you want to give it a try anyway, watch out for the rear bumper, that's where the sensors and cameras are for the automatic parking aid. They probably cost about the same as your boss's annual wages.'

The policeman froze.

'Hoffmann's mistress?' Kayser pointed at the photo. 'Or what else? A whore doesn't hand out framed photos.'

'It's not his wife, that's for sure,' said Brendel. 'There's exactly what a woman needs in the flat to sleep with him now and then. No more and no less.'

'She needs socks to sleep with him?'

'Old men,' said Brendel. 'They like to try out odd things.'

Wegener contemplated the roses. 'Frank, have you got anything with a possible link to the murder date? Any sign of an appointment?'

Stein shook his head helplessly. 'There are baskets full of files and stuff here, as you can see. Then two computers, a Sigma and a relatively new Omikron KC. The only things on his desk were bills and books. We're going to have to search through it all.'

'OK, then concentrate on three areas when you go through it.' Wegener waited for Frankenstein to find his pencil. 'One: everything to do with the woman in the photo – name, address, love letters, whatever. Find the cleaning lady, she'll tell you who she is. We need that quickly.'

Stein scribbled. The only sound for ten seconds was the pencil lead scratching against the pad. The frozen PP left the room without a word. The floorboards creaked.

'Two: is there any indication that Hoffmann was being blackmailed or blackmailing someone else? Locker keys, large sums of cash or other valuable items, contracts for bank accounts and so on. And in connection with that: is there any indication that Hoffmann had anything to do with the consultations or maybe even with the transit business?'

Frankenstein scribbled. 'Three?'

'Where should we put Hoffmann on the political scale? What side was he on? What was his position, what did he publish? And in fact: what was he doing since Revitalization?'

'Anything else?'

'Contacts in the West,' said Brendel. 'Someone obviously sent him at least bras and knickers for his girlfriend.'

'Contacts in the West, of course,' repeated Stein, still scribbling. 'And then: why the double life as Emil Fischer in Marzahn?'

'I nearly forgot . . . ' Stein rummaged around in the box and pulled out a small plastic bag. 'We've got something on that. It was on the floor under the desk.'

Brendel took the bag and held it under the desk lamp. 'An ID card?'

'A work ID,' said Stein, looking through a folder. 'To be precise, a work ID for a gardener. Issued to one Emil Fischer of 32, Ludwig-Renn-Strasse in Berlin Marzahn.'

'A work ID for a gardener?' said Kayser. 'What gardener needs an ID?'

'It's a security ID,' said Stein. 'Access permission to some restricted zone or other. There was a copy of an official confirmation from the State Security attached – hold on, confirming that . . . ' Stein fished a folded sheet of paper in a plastic sheath out of his folder ' . . . that *the bearer of this identity card, comrade Emil Fischer, has been successfully subjected to the police and secret service regulation tests in accordance with sections 123 and 124 of the control legislation by State Security Central Department VII (protection of persons and properties) for the purpose of access permission to national special security zone B–W–I. Valid until*, then there's a date stamp . . .' Stein turned the page. '*Issued 17.9.2006, Petty Officer Stefan Kröcher, CD VII.*'

'He's a bit of an all-rounder, our professor,' said Kayser. 'A library, a model girlfriend and green fingers on top.'

'And a broken neck.' Brendel handed the ID card back to Stein. 'What is this special security zone B–W–1?'

Stein shrugged. 'No idea. But it sounds like one of the most important special security zones we've got.'

10

MAJOR MEATLOAF LOOKS BETTER WITH EVERY MONTH in retirement, I'd be thinking now, thought Wegener. Major Meatloaf is obviously still spending most of his leisure time outside, catching the last autumn rays. The sun doesn't stop at the Iron Curtain, even though it knows all too well how unashamedly good old men look with a bit of an old-man tan. Provided they have snow-white hair. Even better if they have not only snow-white hair but green eyes as well. As green as the eyes of Major Meatloaf, who'd be just strolling through the Schusterjungen pub, saying hello to people at every turn, who'd order a large Bürgerbräu from the large, bearded landlord by indicating a pint-jug-sized space between two flat hands, who'd then discover his observer, smile, come closer and collapse with a groan on one of the battered pub chairs. There he was, there he wasn't, good old chronically obese Josef Früchtl. Now he mentally asked one of his three favourite stupid opening gambit questions, today: *Where's your hair got to? Gone West?*

Special assignment, said Wegener.

Your hair's on a secret mission. And you have to stay at home.

We all have to stay at home.

If you gotta go, you gotta go, said Früchtl as he took off his coat, *even if it's your hairstyle. How are you?*

Fine. Or at least same as usual.

Fine or same as usual? There's a difference.

Not for you, not the way you look.

Thanks for the compliment.

The landlord came puffing over and plonked a large, foam-spilling beer jug down on the table. 'Cheers, Captain. Meatloaf?'

'I'll have the meatloaf,' said Wegener. 'With two fried eggs, please.'

'Chips or fried potatoes, Captain?'

'Chips. And extra mayonnaise.'

The landlord obviously hadn't expected anything else, wiping his sleeves across his wet forehead and steamrollering towards the kitchen.

Food is eroticism for the elderly, said Früchtl.

You were saying that twenty years ago.

And I was right. Twenty years ago I was fifty-five. D'you think that's young?

Certainly too young to put women on the shelf for good.

Früchtl shook his head sadly. *You never learn, Martin, do you? I was talking about eroticism, not sex. Food is eroticism for the elderly. Sex is sex for the elderly. What are the ladies in your life up to?*

Working on their careers.

Is that all?

Meeting Russian gas boys and negotiating contracts. Saving the fatherland.

Your ministerial concubine. Still stuck on her?

Wegener pulled a face.

You ought to be glad it's all over.

Why?

Früchtl raised his hands in indignation. *Because relationships between successful women and unsuccessful men end in suicide or impotence!* Your *suicide* or your *impotence!*

And I have to take life lessons from an old granddad who finds meatloaf erotic.

Not just meatloaf, murmured Früchtl with a longing gaze at the kitchen door. *Chips with mayonnaise too. But don't tell anyone. Women aim upwards, Martin. Women always want a man they can look up to. If women climb up the ladder, men have to climb even higher. To keep the gap equal. If they can't keep up with the climbing they get replaced. Or in the language of East Germany: women only want men who've brown-nosed a few more arses than they have.*

The opinion of a pathological sexist who slept through forty years of emancipation because he was too busy re-enacting his affairs' working relationships.

Früchtl grinned. *The opinion of a pathological sexist who never got told anything else by the proudest, most successful and most intelligent – or as you'd say: most emancipated – women in their weak moments, when they're most honest.*

Wegener groaned.

Martin, how's a woman supposed to feel protected by a guy with less money in his account than she has?

I've got a firearms licence.

A firearms licence! Früchtl pulled a face as if he'd spotted a litter of puppy dogs chasing their own tails. *What use is a firearms licence? An undersecretary of state in the Energy Ministry doesn't need a firearms licence. He takes out his M7 and calls someone and then he gets a table in a private room at the Molotov or a Phobos Datscha with air conditioning and a trailer coupling or an invitation to a fisting party on Rügen where they insert real bananas – the Latin American ones and not your crappy little Euro ones.*

Wegener drank the last mouthful of his beer and twisted the empty glass in his hand. So tell me what to do then, Professor of Women's Studies.

There's nothing to tell, said Früchtl. *Only time can tell, and time's passing though our beautiful half a country. I've never heard of a heartbreak that lasted longer than eight and a half years.*

Only seven and a half to go, then.

Früchtl nodded so earnestly that it wiped the grin off Wegener's face. Nobody said anything for one full minute.

Then Früchtl changed the subject: *How's your top-secret case?*

My dear Josef, this top-secret case is extra-top-secret. This time I didn't just sign a yellow paper, I had to sign a red paper too.

Früchtl frowned. He turned in both directions. There was nobody at the neighbouring tables.

Did you know they have red papers too?

No.

Well they do. A nice shade of red. Like your old Lada.

Früchtl raised his eyebrows in respect. *And now you're loafing around here eating my favourite food instead of working?*

Our West German investigators are in the EastSide, telephone conference with Bonn. No entry for inspectors.

Do you cut the yolk open?

I don't have to take on all your strange habits, Josef.

There's nothing better in the whole world than warm, runny egg yolk. It's got a texture a bit like blood.

Wegener raised his empty glass and waited to catch the landlord's eye.

Früchtl said nothing.

Wegener said nothing.

The landlord was pulling a wheat beer with one hand, the other hand holding the remote control for the TV enthroned on a shelf above the toilet door. There was the sound of white noise. In the white noise someone said *Robotron office equipment factory Ernst Thälmann POC and Robotron sensory electronics Otto Schön POC registered an export increase of 6 per cent*, white noise, *attributed to the rise in sales of the portable midi-computer Nanotchev Omikron KC 2.0 in West and South Europe*, white noise. Fragments of a newsreader appeared with long skin-coloured extensions flickering from the sides of his head, his whole skull transformed into a pair of concertinaed bellows; someone was pushing the newsreader's face through an egg-slicer, the strips of face said *aiming in future for the development of the Nanotchev Rho and the sound player Musikus M06 in Robotron microelectronics Wilhelm Pieck POC. And now for sport*, white noise, snowfall, then the picture calmed down and the words *Aktuelle Kamera* formed, the slices flowed together into a round head, and under the head was the name *Axel Kaspar*.

The landlord turned the sound off. Michael Ballack carried several cones across a training pitch in the training camp on Hiddensee. Matthias Sammer gave instructions from the trainer's bench, his mouth moving silently.

Ballack made an unhappy face and complained to Sammer about something. Cut to the training pitch from above. The players were running across an artificially green-looking piece of grass in white shirts, twisting their torsos left, right, left. Now Sammer's bad teeth spoke to the camera.

Remember Hulvershorn? asked Früchtl.

Wegener shook his head.

A hulk of a woman, three cubic metres of pure police. Everyone called her Berlin's Miss Piggy because she had such a porky face. She was with the Mitte unit for years. Nothing and no one could shake her. She's been paralysed on one side for two years, had a stroke. I visited her the other day – she's sharing a room with two drooling vegetables in a run-down joint in Pankow and had tears in her eyes because her bum was itching like billy-o.

The landlord brought a new beer and changed the channel. Speed skating.

Went to the bog that lunchtime, poor thing, and the nurse didn't wipe her off properly. So now good old Hulvershorn's lying in bed with her itchy arse for what feels like decades, ringing and ringing the bell, and nobody comes. She can't scratch it, she can't reach!

Wegener leaned back.

So I go and look for someone – no one around. Not in the whole place. The end of the story is: I go and get the AIDS gloves out of the trolley and wipe Berlin's Miss Piggy's crack for her. Früchtl shrugged his shoulders. *That's when I realized: you gotta get out of here. This is no country for old people.*

It's no country for young people.

Maybe. But you can reach your own arse. Hulvershorn can't. What the Prenzlauer Berg rowdies and the Stasi and two divorces didn't manage over forty years, the Pankow Comrades' Care Home cracked in two hours: reduced Berlin's Miss Piggy to tears.

So you thought you'd just bugger off, said Wegener. Because you're scared of an itchy bum.

Everyone's got their own good reason to bugger off, Martin. Being scared of an itchy bum wouldn't be the worst one. This whole state is a burning ruin just before a tropical storm. The only thing they produce on a global level here is injustice.

I know, said Wegener, I'm part of the production chain.

Some people get disappeared too, because they're an itch, an itch on the state's arse. At some point along comes the big hand and scratches, and if you're unlucky it scratches you right off. Nothing's changed in the slightest over the past twenty years when it comes to the state-administered correlation between itching and scratching.

What did you find out, Josef? What did they do to you?

When I was fourteen they threw the family next door out of the house, down the stairs. I was just coming home from Youth Service, in my brown shirt with my black neckerchief that looked like a cut-off swallow's tail.

Josef . . .

He fell down hard, the neighbour, he was bleeding, he was getting kicked, but he smiled at me as I walked past, and later I always thought perhaps that was his last smile, and he gave it to a fourteen-year-old Hitler Youth. Let that Hitler Youth see what to do with a leftover smile that lasts a lifetime.

Listen, Josef . . .

It all started over again after '45. You know, Martin, I was always in the thick of things, always on the front line, and you can say in retrospect: It was all wrong. But you'd have been the same as us. Everyone would have been the same as us. Too bad we were the unlucky ones who had to be us, day in, day out, no conditional tense. The Germans purchased a worldwide patent for opportunism in the twentieth century and—

Would you give me a break with your after-the-war-stories for once, said Wegener, surprised at how vehement he sounded. I want to know what they did to you! Not in 1945, in 2010!

Früchtl just smiled.

Into the silence, the landlord delivered a slice of meatloaf as thick as the police handbook with a crown of steaming fried eggs, wishing him the best of luck.

Wegener looked at the empty chair on the opposite side of the table. Then he cut open the egg yolk.

SATURDAY 22 OCTOBER 2011

11

WE'RE BOTH GOING GREY, NORMANNENSTRASSE AND ME, thought Wegener. We're degenerating slowly but surely – but we're keeping upright whatever happens.

A year ago Stasi HQ had already seemed more monstrously drained of colour than any other building in Berlin, and now wind and weather and pollution had worked on the headquarters at number 1, Normannenstrasse to make it an even more unreal monolith. Huge and skulking, the block rose into the drizzling sky over the length of a football pitch, the two wings rendering it the barracks of an invisible army, a mutated detention room swelled larger and larger by an invincible secret service megalomania until the whole borough, the whole country had become its backyard, easily observed at any time out of ten thousand windows with wooden frames mouldering away and scattering dandruff made of tiny nicotine-coloured varnish chips on the concrete wasteland outside the main entrance.

Like a sponge, the rough plaster of the facade had swallowed everything up for decades – the dirt from the Trabant engines, the soot from the brown coal heaters, the fat from the Phobos fumes. It had donned a greasy coat, East Berlin camouflage that no one could escape, worn by all the official Stasi employees: indefinable, lustreless, nondescript; *Stasi-coloured*, thought Wegener.

The uniformed man in the miniature guard's hut looked over at him every ten seconds, stared ahead again, looked over, stared ahead, expressionless and undecided as to whether to leave his ridiculous Wendy house in the drizzle to play at authority and bark in the required manner at the man who'd been lurking around the grounds for ten minutes: Papers! Visitor's pass! Appointment slip!

It was raining a year ago too, Wegener remembered. A short conversation in an almost empty room, three chairs, a table, a lamp and nothing else, just two men: one talking, the other silent. In front of him file MW–B 1101–IV/2010 (PPB), which was kept more assiduously than a love-struck fourteen-year-old's diary. 'The Stasi is my Eckermann' – that song had come to mind right in the middle of it all and he had to pull himself together to stop himself humming the tune. That evening he'd tracked down the old Wolf Biermann record and chanted along and drowned his sorrows in Blue Curaçao.

Maybe it drizzles all year round on Normannenstrasse. Rain from a cloud full of rage and sorrow over what you got to hear when you bugged your compatriots. Eavesdroppers never hear good of themselves, said Wegener under his breath, twisting his new umbrella by the handle so that the rain sprayed off it. He suddenly thought of Karolina. Perhaps because she had always made fun of him for never having an umbrella. He took his Minsk out of his coat pocket and put it back again. A minute later he took it out again and dialled.

You've reached the Ministry of Energy Export and Transit Industry of the German Democratic Republic, said a syrupy woman's voice, and Wegener thought: I haven't reached anything yet, I've got to get past you first, you plastic gatekeeper. *Departments one to four and seven and subsections A to H, the direct line of,* then there was a pause. *Karolina Enders*, said Karolina's voice in not half as friendly a tone as the syrupy woman, then came another pause and a long-drawn-out beep. Wegener hung up.

By the time the Mercedes drew up a few minutes later the rain had stopped. Shallow puddles on the concrete slabs of the courtyard reflected bright patches of sky. Wegener closed his umbrella. The Wendy house inhabitant hastily flicked through his clipboard in search of notice of a visit from some West German minister that he'd missed.

'Can we park here?' Brendel had already got out of the car – black suit, white shirt, red tie. 'Good morning, by the way.'

'There's certainly plenty of space,' said Wegener. 'Morning.'

Kayser climbed out of the passenger seat with a groan, greeting Wegener with a raised hand and tipping his head back to admire the building. 'Nice paint job.'

Also wearing a suit and tie, Wegener noted and wondered what the gentlemen thought of his cords and wool coat. Presumably: typical People's Police.

Brendel grabbed a briefcase from the back seat. 'Do you know the place well?'

'I'd rather not.'

Brendel gave him a conspiratorial smile as Kayser held a pile of papers under the uniformed man's nose. The man nodded, spoke into a telephone and nodded again. A neck mechanism activated whenever he's dealing with FIS people or his own superiors, thought Wegener, looking at the wall of honeycomb concrete that blocked the view of the glass entrance from the courtyard and supported the projecting roof above it. He tried to imagine Erich Mielke being chauffeured beneath this roof back in the day, in a black Volvo with chrome trim and red leather. He didn't manage it.

Revitalization was twenty-two years ago now. Wegener was amazed when he worked it out in his head. The Revitalization regime had long since become history itself, all the old powers-that-be had faded into obscurity, Erich Mielke and Heinrich Stangier were nothing but cardboard cut-outs, historical jesters in an antique chamber of horrors who had been forced to vacate their seats before their worthy successors pulled them out from under them, but there was no need for them to bear a grudge because their successors would go through exactly the same thing themselves one fine day, secretly stabbed in the back in the good old German Democratic way.

A second uniformed man appeared to take over from the first one. The first one tipped his peaked cap towards the Mercedes and stomped to the main entrance. Kayser followed him, imitating his military gait, and turned around with a grin.

As Wegener entered the foyer behind Brendel, his nose was instantly welcomed on board the Stasi time machine: dust, PVC, scouring powder, stale air, civil servants, air freshener, files. An olfactory grey that would still be wafting around the building in a hundred years' time. Wegener recognized the square red marble pillars, the gallery on the first floor, the coat of arms with the flag and bayonet, the rubber plants, Marx's bearded head and torso protruding from a block of bronze. There he was, good old Karl, only the rump left over and still too heavy to throw away.

'Incredible,' said Kayser. 'No one's going to believe me back at the office in Pullach.'

The uniformed man spoke briefly to the lump of dough on reception and then scurried onwards. Kayser stayed right behind him, turning a stumbled circle as he walked, not wanting to miss one rubber plant, one bust, one single photo.

Secret-service tourism, thought Wegener, noticing that the reception lump was also on the phone now. The whole building would know they were here in less than three minutes.

A dark marble staircase led up to the first floor, then to the second and the third. The uniformed man and Brendel proved their fitness; Kayser and Wegener were panting. The windows in the stairwell afforded a free view of even more grey concrete blocks, complex annexes and outhouses, narrow bridges over courtyards and beyond them an endless landscape of flat roofs. Stasi City.

'Incredible,' said Kayser.

'No one's going to believe you back at the office in Pullach,' said Brendel.

On the fourth floor they turned left into a corridor, fifty metres later came a security point, two more uniformed men, a thorough ID inspection, briefcase search, body search, a metal detector switched off, another fifty metres of corridor, now carpeted instead of PVC, then a right turn past countless doors, not one name tag outside them.

The corridor ended in a spacious anteroom with two desks, behind which sat bespectacled young men almost impossible to distinguish from their papers, surrounded by piles of files and Nanotchev models that Wegener had never seen before. In a padded wall was a padded door, the next room even larger, wood panelling, flag, Speckmann's portrait, a snooker table-sized piece of 1970s furniture, and behind it, in a black leather seat, sat the owner of a ladies' hair salon with its own back-room solarium.

'Major-General Renate Wischinsky,' grunted the uniformed man with a vacant look, clicked his heels and marched out of the room.

The padded door fell silently closed.

The hairdresser stood up. Her flat face must have been the result of a collaboration between a stonemason and a saddler. Carved viewing slits and a slot of a mouth, a scrawny nose hump, a hard square of chin, all covered in a layer of tanned kid leather dyed the colour of the wall panels. On her head was a bouquet of bleached hair that trailed down to her shoulders.

Wegener was gobsmacked.

Kayser took care of the introductions. Wischinsky nodded in recognition of her guests' names and ranks, keeping her mouth slot closed, and sat down again. The snooker table kept anyone who might have the bizarre idea of shaking hands with Renate at a distance. Once Kayser was finished Wischinsky gave an economical gesture, presenting three wooden visitors' chairs without cushions.

'To get straight to the point,' said Brendel even as he sat down, 'I assume you've been informed of the facts in the Hoffmann case.'

'That's correct,' said Wischinsky.

I bet you cut bread with your voice for tea, thought Wegener.

Brendel nodded. 'Allow me to ask a direct question.'

The corners of Wischinsky's mouth shifted two millimetres upwards.

Brendel got even more friendly. 'How do you evaluate the modus operandi of the killing?'

'Naïve amateurism,' said Wischinsky.

That pleased Kayser. 'So the State Security did amateurish work during Revitalization?'

'The State Security has never done amateurish work.'

'That's news to me.'

'You're a liaison officer, am I right?'

'Correct.'

'No wonder you haven't got any further than that.'

'Great,' said Kayser, 'I love cheeky Stasi women.'

'So who did do amateurish work?' asked Brendel.

'The amateurs were old cadres operating on their own accord.' Wischinsky looked from one to the other. 'Men who believed the GDR ought not to evolve. Men who didn't accept that Heinrich Stangier wanted to take well-earned retirement and Hans-Walter Moss placed more weight on professional skills than old contacts when choosing his secret-service officers. Those men were no longer employed by the State Security and therefore not acting on its orders.'

'When they . . . ?' Kayser leaned forward slightly.

'When they attacked the successors appointed by Moss.'

'So those murders really did happen.'

'There were seven cases and one attempt. The perpetrators were apprehended and sentenced in an internal procedure. Most of them are dead now, a few of them are still behind bars.'

'That's all?'

'That's all. I was the assistant to the prosecuting counsel in 1993. So you won't find anyone here in the building who can give you more precise information on the events than me.'

'That's why we're talking to you today.'

'Exactly.'

Kayser and Brendel fell silent. Wegener couldn't tell if it was a deliberate tactic or out of surprise.

'You think the State Security is involved in the Hoffmann case,' said Wischinsky. 'All I can tell you is: I'm unaware of either a killer or a motive.'

'Was Hoffmann with the State Security?' asked Wegener.

'No.'

'Not even unofficially?'

'No means no, Inspector Wegener.'

'They why would someone want to kill him in that way?'

'You're the investigator.'

'Do you have a file on Hoffmann?' Wegener crossed his legs.

Wischinsky eyed him like something edible for two long seconds. 'There is a file, which was operative on an irregular basis from 1985 on, over a period of six years. The last entry is dated 23.11.1991.'

'There was no further operation from then on?' asked Kayser.

'Not even an internal memo proposing opening a new operation,' Wischinsky declared, deliberately slowly. 'Hoffmann had resigned from his position on the advisory staff to the State Council Chairman on that date and held no further official or unofficial offices.'

'That was the time when the Wall was closed again,' said Brendel. 'Did Hoffmann have anything to do with that?'

'I suspect you're overestimating the influence of a political advisor,' said Wischinsky. 'The State Council Chairman has about forty of Hoffmann's kind. Specializing in all kinds of areas.'

'Why did Hoffmann give in only two years after Revitalization?' asked Kayser.

Wischinsky's tanned facial hide twitched. 'Giving in is your interpretation. Hoffmann was around sixty at the time. He was tired.'

'Most people work longer than that.'

'If it bothers you that the Federal Republic is constantly raising the retirement age, perhaps you should think about relocating here,' said Wischinsky with an inscrutable grimace.

That was a smile, thought Wegener.

'Political advisors are often active to a great age,' Brendel commented soberly. 'But there's no need to beat about the bush, Major-General. We'd like a copy of the Hoffmann file.'

'Aha, would you now?' Wischinsky gave an understanding nod. 'I'm afraid I'll have to disappoint you.'

'Oh dear,' said Kayser. 'Men hate it when women disappoint them.'

Wegener looked at his watch. Minute five of the conversation: time to play the gender card.

'I'm sure you're used to it, Mr Kayser. And incidentally the file is a level-one classified document.'

Kayser mimed amazement.

'The person under observation was in direct contact with members of the government.' Now Wischinsky was a nursery teacher explaining the Ministry of State Security to children from West Germany. 'Level-one files are not permitted to be copied. Never, if you get my meaning.'

'We'd be happy to view the file here on the premises,' said Brendel.

Wischinsky's eye slits grew a fraction narrower. 'The file isn't on the premises. Colonel Steinkühler requested it. He wants to take a thorough look at it.'

Kayser tittered as if he'd heard a joke that you only get once you're already laughing. He slapped his thigh and shook his head. The titter grew a little more grating. A thick vein stood out on his bald skull.

Brendel and Wischinsky stared each other out. The tittering faded away rather slowly.

'You know what I find so funny?' A slightly crazed grin contorted Kayser's red face. 'We shove billions of euros in fraternal subsidies up the arse of this desolate dictatorship every year, and when we come over and want to help you wipe the shit away because you can't even do that on your own, you pull up your pants double-quick so no one gets a look at your bum.'

Hulvershorn would be glad of so much dedication to hygiene, thought Wegener.

'Major-General, we're investigating a murder.' Brendel sounded even friendlier than before. 'I'm sure you understand we have to ascertain whether the matter has anything to do with Hoffmann's former activities.'

Wischinsky nodded yet again. 'You see, Mr Brendel, even if I had the documents here in my desk I wouldn't be allowed to give them to you without betraying state secrets. Place an application to view the file – everything else is up to Colonel-General Steinkühler and Minister Speckmann.'

Kayser stared at the ceiling.

'You've obviously read the papers thoroughly,' said Brendel. 'In your opinion, was there any information in them that might be relevant to our investigations?'

Wischinsky considered for a moment. She obviously thought the question was a trap. 'Let's just say it was rather dull reading. And that's not often the case with level-one files.'

Wegener cleared his throat. 'Perhaps you could bring yourself to give us a little more detail. It must be in your interest too for us to find Hoffmann's murderer. The West German press is bound to put the blame on your institution. The circumstances do suggest it. Perhaps one of your people wants to damage the State Security. Someone not acting on orders.'

'There are no orders here to kill GDR citizens.'

'But there is, as you know, a source in Hamburg who claims to have witnessed Hoffmann's murder and to be a State Security employee,' said Wegener. 'And who has provided a whole lot of insider information.'

'Alleged insider information about your murder case perhaps, but not insider information about the State Security.' Wischinsky leaned back in her seat. The leather creaked. 'Nobody believes the story about the bloodthirsty GDR secret service. The *Spiegel* is writing its very own Hitler diaries.'

'Is one of your employees missing?'

'The only thing missing around here is Mr Kayser's manners. Since we don't have a current file on Hoffmann, there aren't any employees involved for me to look for. You do understand me, don't you?' Wischinsky looked around the room to underline her question. 'And for your information: contrary to rumours, 99 per cent of the employees of the Ministry of State Security are office staff and not professional killers. We have an armed special unit that I won't reveal the size of. Every one of those gentlemen is on German Democratic Republic soil, and if they do take action then it's not to string up old men and tie their shoelaces together.'

'And someone who worked for the Stasi before Revitalization?' asked Brendel. 'Perhaps a former informant?'

Wischinsky made another attempt at a smile. 'We're talking about 90,000 full-time employees and more than 180,000 unofficial employees, Mr Brendel. Large amounts of files were destroyed during the Revitalization process. Only 15 per cent of the rest is in digital form. How are we supposed to find someone like that, in your opinion?'

'Now listen,' Kayser was getting louder now. 'Come Monday morning, all the West German media will be reporting a Stasi murder, the consultations are as good as cancelled and your socialist paradise will be bankrupt by next spring, including its comfortable retirement conditions. How about a little bit of patriotism, Renate?'

Any minute now her leather skin's going to split, thought Wegener, to start tearing and peeling off, Major-General Renate will grab at her collar like in a spy movie, tug the brown mask and the trailing wig right off her head, and underneath there'll be a haggard, toothless old man's skull with a thin fuzz of hair and saliva round his mouth – Erich Mielke.

'If I see things correctly,' said Wischinsky at freezing temperature, 'what we have here is three special investigators with a dead man whose murder is a cack-handed citation of an illegal practice by subversive elements that has only been known of in rumours for the past twenty-two years. Three special investigators who furthermore don't actually believe in a killer from the ranks of the State Security because there's not even the slightest motive, and who also have absolutely no idea of how to find such a killer even if he did exist. I'm required to cooperate with you in this exceptional situation, gentlemen, but I am not required either to provide you with secret-service documents you are not entitled to access, nor to suggest that you carry out a search for mysterious murdering ex-agents in strictly confidential ex-agent files that don't exist. If you want my advice: do your jobs and do them well. Is there anything else we need to discuss?'

What a silence, thought Wegener. These old padded walls still work well enough. They make soundproof islands, spaces as silent as the grave in the middle of all Berlin's screeching, moaning and groaning, sound-free zones where thoughts can bounce off each other like chain mail in a head-on collision, maximum contrary forces. Seeing as it was so quiet, he put Fischer's gardener ID down on the snooker table. There was a slight slap as the plastic card flopped onto the wood.

Wischinsky reached for the ID and inspected it. Her eye slits expanded by a millimetre.

'Can you tell us which property this document refers to?' asked Wegener in a friendly tone. The leather mask assumed an expression he hadn't previously thought possible. Something between disbelief and realization, something that couldn't be concealed even in a carved stone face.

'Where did you get this from?'

'I'm assuming you can tell us what the abbreviation stands for, Major-General?'

'Berlin Wandlitz, special security zone 1.' Wischinsky raised her eyes and looked at Brendel. 'This document entitles the bearer to enter the government quarter.'

'You mentioned you were required to cooperate with us,' said Kayser. 'What specific form does that cooperation take?'

Renate had lost her bearings now. The second sign of emotion in one minute, Wegener noted: confusion.

'Release of documents up to classification level three,' Wischinsky ran down the list: 'naming of non-confidential sources, implementation of intelligence measures.'

'Bugging operations?' asked Brendel.

Wischinsky lowered the ID card and put it down on the table in front of her. 'Acoustic residential monitoring and observation of persons.'

'Then we'll contact your office if we need anything. I'd like to ask you neither to communicate the measures we request internally nor to document them.'

'That can be done,' said Wischinsky in a wooden voice. Her leathery head was still in Wandlitz.

Brendel and Kayser stood up.

Wischinsky remained seated. 'I'll have a copy made of the ID card for you.'

'Sorry,' said Kayser and grabbed the card off the desk with an athletic swoop, 'but the ID is an exhibit in a bilateral special investigation and subject to level-A classification. Level-A documents are not permitted to be copied. Ever.'

Wischinsky's mouth slot trembled. For a second, her right hand seemed to be feeling for an alarm button or a machine gun or a

Russian nuclear missile, then she clenched her fist so hard that white knuckles stood out under her overly tanned sunbed skin.

'We're looking forward to working with you. Have a nice day,' said Brendel.

Kayser and the ID card were already outside.

Two new uniformed men were waiting outside the padded door to take them on a guided tour back to the main entrance. One of them walked ahead, the other at the rear. When they stepped out into the courtyard, about twenty men in Stasi-coloured suits were taking turns to pose by the Mercedes bonnet, photographing each other with their Minsk cameras.

Then there was a bang.

12

'MAYBE IT WAS A GAS LEAK,' said Borgs.

The crumbling tiled walls of Karl-Marx-Allee moved past Wegener with their pompous boulevard chandeliers that had always reminded him of Nazi lanterns, beneath them blank faces on the wide pavement, talking into their phones, staring, afraid. The black cloud of smoke had now risen so high that it appeared above the flat roofs, an expanding, giant sneering face, ragged at the sides from the wind.

Brendel stopped at a red light.

'The walls certainly trembled in Normannenstrasse,' said Wegener, holding his Minsk to his ear as he pressed the walnut electric window button. The car windows glided up but Borgs' response was still drowned out; the oncoming traffic had washed along the next wave of fire engines. A panicked choir of sirens raised its volume to the pain threshold.

Brendel shouted something to Kayser, and Kayser shouted something back.

Outside, everyone was holding their ears. Dim sunlight suffused the junction with cold light while passers-by crossed the road using 9/11-style gestures, their gazes raised to the sky. For the first time, no one took any notice of the Mercedes.

Feels like the Apocalypse, thought Wegener with a glance at his Minsk. The display indicated the call to Borgs but he couldn't hear anything. For a few seconds he had the feeling he was nothing but a spectator now. As if all this had nothing more to do with him. Emigration application filed, authorized, and he'd be off across the border any day now, never to return. Karolina, her iron lack of interest in him, the last ruins of socialism, all the state, official and private lies, all left behind, forgotten, terminated, for ever.

One last guided tour around the Wild East: the lunch queue outside the Yeltsin, everyone in the line holding telephones to their ears despite the noise. Stone statues on the roofs of the decaying workers' palaces like rows of deep-frozen marksmen, behind them the mushrooming black cloud, looking as if it would have the whole of Berlin in its grip in an hour's time, swathed, blacked out for ever. It'd be no great loss: rusting Phoboses by the side of the road, the kiosk awning with the faded Club-Cola logo; the Buletta snack bar with its Wart-Burger ad showing two overblown meat patties with faces smiling at each other from between their halves of bread roll, the yellow B of Buletta lying on its back, a cheap copy of the Western world's Golden Arches. Someone had sprayed GDR on the tiled wall next to it, declaring the middle letter dead with a black cross.

'Hello?' Wegener yelled into his Minsk, noticing too late how ridiculously helpless he must sound.

Brendel moved off again. The sirens had turned a corner in the background. *The connection to Borgs' mobile was interrupted.*

Kayser turned his questioning face to the back seat.

'An explosion at the Palace,' said Wegener.

Kayser nodded as if he'd been expecting just that. 'And?'

'Gas leak. They suspect.'

'Ah, good old gas.' Kayser turned to face the front again.

Karolina, thought Wegener – she has appointments in the Palace of the Republic now and then. He clicked into his call lists and pressed Dial. The display flashed *Network disruption*.

New sirens came closer, patrol cars dashed past, behind them personnel carriers, then another squad car.

Brendel caught Wegener's eye in the rear-view mirror. 'Perhaps it's not quite the right moment to pay a visit to Wandlitz.'

'Or perhaps it's just right. There's not much else we can do.'

'He's right there,' noted Kayser. 'Thanks to that fascist prune of a major. She may have plenty of material in her beloved files but she didn't have a clue about the Wandlitz thing.'

'At least we know that the ID's real,' said Brendel. 'Or a first-class forgery.'

Wegener stared out of the window. An anthill gone mad after someone had stamped on it by accident, put the boot in right in the middle. A thought crept up on him, coming closer, exerting its presence: Hoffmann's ID forger. If you had him – you could get him to make a West German passport. And a police ID, West Berlin Crime Squad. And if he doesn't fancy it I've got him by the balls, thought Wegener: forging official documents in the Hoffmann case, supporting enemies of the state, go directly to Bautzen jail, do not pass Go. So he will fancy it. He'll forge whatever I want, just for me. Brendel gets hold of the blank documents we need through his connections. And once the murder job's done it'll be three officers going back to the West, not two. At some old border crossing point in the wilds of Thuringia. One with old, faulty cameras. Come in as a duo, go out as a trio. The East German export nation living up to its name.

'How's old Borgs nowadays? Still smoking like Eisenhüttenstadt, is he?' Karl-Heinz Meffert slid his feet across the white gravel of a well-kept garage forecourt, grinning like a horse. 'He used to get his tobacco from Cuba back in the day. Who knows which of the eunuchs he's got by the balls! Harr-harr!'

'Still smoking and coughing his heart out,' Wegener confirmed.

'Good stuff, though,' said Brendel. 'I had a try.'

Meffert's horsy grin turned into a camel grin. 'And smoking's gone out the window over in your West, hasn't it, banned everywhere and all that, right? Sic transit, tobacco epicureans, sic transit!'

'You can still do it in private. That's about it, though.'

'Give me a dictatorship of the proletariat any day, none of your dictatorship of the protectorate.' Meffert had stopped outside a double garage, fished a key ring fit for a very busy prison guard out of his jacket pocket and unlocked it. 'You'll love this, you're gonna lose your lunch in a minute, wait and see!'

The right-hand door of the garage opened without the slightest squeak.

A popemobile, an accident-damaged vehicle, thought Wegener. Or a four-seater lawnmower.

Meffert scratched his polished skull. 'Take a seat in a genuine state secret, gentlemen. With a name like Kayser you'd better sit at the front. And the other two at the back, please.'

'A buggy?' asked Brendel in slight bewilderment. 'From Trabant?'

Meffert folded himself behind the wheel. 'Never heard of a buggy. We just call it *our Golf.*' He turned the ignition key and the engine came to life with a rattle. 'Get it?'

Wegener sat down on the back seat next to Brendel. Soft artificial leather padding, no seatbelts. The exhaust roared. Meffert had turned halfway round in his driving seat, put his arm around the passenger seat and was steering the golf buggy backwards out of the garage with bared teeth. A smell of bad eggs mingled with Brendel's sweet-shop perfume.

'This doesn't run on sunflower oil, does it?'

'The last diesel engine in the GDR,' called Meffert. 'Well, almost!'

Kayser smiled. For the first time, thought Wegener. Not an arrogant twist, not a smug gesture, not a superior symbol. So that's what Mr Kayser from the FIS looks like when he's happy. Maybe because he's allowed to sit at the front. Or because Meffert's got his arm around the seat. A pair of smirking lovebirds, East and West. Neither of them have any hair but they're joyfully united, perched on a motorized hatbox.

'They knocked everything down round here, back in '92. The whole Wandlitz ghetto. All they left was the trees.' Meffert cranked the steering wheel with his right hand and drew a circle in the air with the left. 'Five times the space, built everything new, bigger houses, bigger grounds and a golf course round the back. At the boss's request.'

'Eighteen holes, I assume,' said Brendel.

'Good God, no. Nine!' Meffert switched to forward gear, put his foot down and tore across the courtyard so fast he sprayed white gravel. 'We're in the GDR, there's enough holes here already. Get it?'

Wegener leaned forward. 'Chairman M plays golf?'

'He tries.' Meffert turned onto an asphalt road after the last garage. 'He has official visitors here from abroad, thought they might like to play a few rounds. And to make sure they don't spend all day hiking around and have a bit of time left for saving socialism, he put in an order for this little beauty.'

'Moss himself?' asked Kayser.

'Chairman M himself,' Meffert confirmed. 'It's a prototype.'

'So does Chairman M ever drive his prototype?' asked Kayser.

'No, I have to drive him!' Meffert's camel grin blossomed again as he slowed down and headed for a mini-roundabout. In the middle of the circle were withered rose beds. There was well-kept parkland wherever you looked: old weeping beeches, linden trees and willows on cropped lawns. Rabbits hopped about, their ears alert. Professional eavesdroppers, thought Wegener. Stasi pets. Hidden all over Wandlitz to listen in on the government. You're not safe anywhere in this country, least of all where you'd expect it. The distrustful investigator distrusts Wandlitz, Früchtl would have said. And the rabbits.

'How long have you been in the job?'

'Twenty-three years and five months,' said Meffert without having to think about it, and turned into the first road off the roundabout. 'Two years on the main gate, guard duty. Then individual property guarding. After Revitalization I trained up to security desk officer, then deputy security director for the national special security zone B–W–1, then security director for the national special security zone B–W–1.'

'That's what I call a career,' said Kayser.

'You mean a Stasi career,' said Meffert and fluffed the gear change. The gearbox screeched and the buggy juddered before it was in the right gear.

Now Brendel leaned forward. 'The head of security is Moss's golf caddy?'

Meffert gave a barking laugh. 'They're our weekly meetings, Mr

Brendel! That's when we sort out all the stuff to do with the colony here. Fresh air, no one to listen and no one to bother us. The boss practises his drive in between. And then we send someone over to the bunker. Get it?'

'I bet it's fun chugging around in this little beauty,' said Kayser. 'It's got a lot going for it.'

'You're telling me!' Meffert's head bobbed up and down. 'Trabant de luxe. Better suspension than any Phobos, better seats, better engine.'

'And better roads,' said Wegener.

The first villas were hidden behind treetops, hedges and cast-iron fences. Black-glazed roof tiles and white fractions of facades peeked through the leafy walls. Surveillance cameras at all the gateposts. Spirals of barbed wire on top of the fences.

'The East looks a lot like the West, doesn't it?'

'Sometimes the West looks a lot like the East as well.'

'Harr-Harr!' Meffert turned onto a broad, tree-lined avenue. Old oaks faced each other. Large patches of shade on the smooth asphalt. Not a single pothole, noted Wegener, leaning back against the padded headrest. Above him, the trees reached their knotty branches out to one another, crossing their heavy wood, hundreds of hands with skinny fingers extended across the tarred border, growing into a dark roof punctuated by bright spots. Meffert accelerated and the spots blurred, the leafy canopy grew even.

A sudden thin screech of tyres. Muted engine roars.

Wegener and Brendel turned at the same time.

Something was flying after them from the end of the avenue, approaching them, flashing as it was hit by the spots of light. The roaring increased at split-second speed, turning into the staring radiator face of a fat black Volvo, four, five, six black Volvos racing past as if pulled on a string, contorted reflections of the buggy and the oak trunks in the tinted windows, six identical snapshots in time, and then the cars had disappeared into the shadows of the trees, no longer visible: stealth limousines. Only the roaring of the engines remained on the air as if an old Tupolev was hovering above them. Somewhere far ahead burned red stains of brake lights. Tyre screeches. The roaring died away.

No one said anything.

Hoffmann the bunny rabbit, thought Wegener as the wind tousled his hair. What was Hoffmann the bunny rabbit listening to in Wandlitz, behind the hedges he pruned as Emil Fischer? What had he eavesdropped on, mowing lawns and watering flowers while the fat cats drank their fat-cat coffee on their fat-cat patios or fat-cat whisky in their fat-cat libraries? What had he picked up on, and had it cost him his wrinkled neck?

As Wegener turned his head Brendel's blue eyes were looking at him, looking through him, directly and with no sense of shame. For one or two seconds, four eyes were locked in conversation, two blue and two greyish green, on the artificial leather-padded back seat of the only East German golf buggy in the world, where soon Moss and Lafontaine might be sitting and staring at each other with just as much fraternal alienation. Wegener looked back up at the leafy roof, not knowing what he'd just read in the blue of Brendel's eyes.

At the end of the avenue, Meffert braked and turned off the road onto the lawn, curving around a pond with dense reed banks, driving past a group of oaks and down a hill. The buggy jolted over roots, rumbled on, all of them bouncing on their seats, and then they were at the bottom. A field the size of a sports ground opened up. Far at the back gleamed a cream-white villa.

'That temple over there,' Meffert called out, 'that's the Moss residence! We just call it *Duncarin*! Get it?'

Then he put his foot right down on the accelerator. The buggy jerked forward and shot out into the empty space. Kayser held onto the side bar with both hands, a powerful gust whistled through the open car, Wegener ducked down and Brendel tried to rein in his fluttering tie. The tachometer needle climbed to 50 and then 60 km/h.

'And that's where the Volvos just went?' yelled Brendel. 'To Moss?'

Meffert was using only his right hand to steer. The airstream seemed to make his grin even broader. 'Interior Ministry, Foreign Ministry, security, escort vehicles. I know so many registration numbers by heart you wouldn't believe it! My whole noggin's all full of registration numbers! I keep thinking of going on that game show with Wolfgang Lippert! Wanna bet I can . . . '

'Something must be up!' Kayser yelled against the whistling.

The needle was now at 70 km/h.

'Questions like that are for the head gardener! Get it? Harr-Harr!' Meffert took his foot abruptly off the accelerator and slammed on the brake, sending Brendel and Wegener sliding against the front seats. Meffert turned the steering wheel and headed for a patch of birch trees.

The buggy picked up speed again. Wegener saw Kayser doubling over. The Kayserian fists clutched at the side bar. The birches came closer, Meffert not braking but accelerating even more, getting faster and faster, holding the wheel in place with one hand, sitting as if frozen, aiming, steering, swishing precisely between two greyish-white birch trunks.

Kayser slowly righted himself.

Wegener noticed his heart was racing.

' . . . Wanna bet I could identify all the registration numbers of the passenger vehicles authorized for Wandlitz by the first three digits?' yelled Meffert and laughed a lonely laugh.

The narrow track led through the dense birch wood, snaking gently to the left and then the right, leaving the trees behind it and ending on the first golf course Wegener had ever seen. Lush green lawns, cropped like the grey crown around Kayser's bald head. Hills, ponds, a bunker. Nobody was playing.

Meffert taxied the buggy onto a green where two men were standing around in olive-green work clothes. A red-haired man with an angular face was talking to a younger man. He pointed to the sky and then grabbed at the air with both hands as if kneading a floating lump of dough. Then he spotted the buggy and made a brisk arm movement. The younger man nodded and withdrew in some disappointment.

'Anton Dörnen,' said Meffert and stopped the car. 'Gardening security officer for special security zone B–W–1.' Meffert showed his teeth. 'Just kidding. There's no such job just yet.'

'Harr-Harr,' said Kayser.

Dörnen had taken a few steps towards the buggy. He was in his mid-forties, Wegener guessed. An honest, hard face. A thin ginger moustache that you only saw when he was standing right in front of you.

Meffert waited for them all to get out of the buggy.

'Anton, we've got a large muster in today. Mr Kayser from the Federal Intelligence Service of the Federal Republic of Germany, Mr Brendel from the West Berlin Crime Squad, and Mr Wegener, Berlin People's Police. They've come about Emil.'

Dörnen distributed firm handshakes, then folded his arms behind his broad back with soldierly discipline and looked around at them all in restrained expectation.

'I don't know any more myself yet,' said Meffert in Dörnen's direction, removing a silver case from his trouser pocket and taking out a cigarillo. 'Thought we'd just deal with it together. I don't know Emil as well as you do.'

Dörnen nodded.

Wegener turned down Meffert's offer of a cigarillo with a shake of his head. 'Mr Dörnen, how long has Emil Fischer been working here in Wandlitz?'

'I've been here since 2003,' said Dörnen in a bass voice, 'and Emil was already there then. I'd say since the end of the nineties. We've got the exact date in the files.'

'End of the nineties is about right,' said Meffert.

'Isn't an eighty-year-old man a bit too old for a job like this?'

'Not at all,' said Dörnen. 'Emil's as fit as a fiddle. Our rose expert. Breeds them himself. I don't know anyone with more experience than him.'

'His work here is hardly any physical effort,' Meffert explained. 'He loves his job, gets out and meets people, has something to do. We value older people's labour in the GDR.'

'At the top of the state too, unfortunately,' said Kayser.

'And what kind of a person is Fischer?' asked Brendel.

'A good man,' said Dörnen. 'Reliable, friendly and clever. We call him the Professor.'

Wegener nodded. 'This might seem an odd question, but have you ever thought something might not be quite right about this Emil Fischer?'

Dörnen looked as if his nine greens had just wilted. 'No.'

'No unusual incidents in all the years?'

'We were pretty surprised when he didn't turn up to work four days ago and didn't call in sick. We haven't been able to get hold of

him since then. It's not like Emil at all.' Dörnen gazed at his lawn. 'I
assume he's gone over the Wall?'

'Why do you assume that?'

'It's pretty obvious.'

'No, it's not obvious to me at all.'

Dörnen's tough face looked as if it wanted to smile. 'So the gentlemen from the West have just come over for a round of golf, have
they?'

'Do your gardeners often climb over the Wall?' asked Kayser.

'Depends which wall you mean.'

Meffert barked a short laugh and thumped Kayser on the back.
'Wandlitz for dummies, lesson one: the GDR has three walls. One on
the inner-German border – you know that one well enough – one
around the Wandlitz special security zone, and one around *Duncarin*.
Right now we're behind the second wall, as we like to say.'

'It'd be kind of you to tell us what's happened to Emil,' said
Dörnen. 'We're worried about him.'

'He's dead,' said Kayser.

Dörnen's face hardened even more.

He had no idea, thought Wegener. He had a cuckoo's egg in his
nest for nine years and he thinks his Emil's skipped the republic.

'Mr Meffert, how strict are the screenings before you let someone
work in Wandlitz?' asked Brendel.

'Stricter than anywhere else.' Meffert blew out a cloud of smoke.
'Criminal record check, two independent psychological reports,
political assessment meeting, detailed biography check and a check on
friends and relatives. Intelligence reports if they have anything. That's
how we do it now. Used to be not quite so thorough. So now what?'

'Not much,' said Kayser. 'But maybe we'd better talk about it in
your office.'

Meffert shrugged, sucked at his cigarillo and blew out the fumes. 'If we really have a leak here I'll take the responsibility. And the department heads will be informed anyway.'

Brendel watched the smoke blowing away. 'All right. Emil Fischer was working here under a false name. He was leading a double life.'

Silence.

'I assume he wasn't employed full time?'

'Two or three days a week,' said Dörnen. His tough face showed not the slightest sign of emotion. 'From March to October every year.'

'Did he have access to particularly sensitive areas? Did his job bring him into contact with members of the government?'

'No, not at all.' Dörnen shook his head. 'I mean, he worked all over the colony. But he was pruning the roses, not talking.'

'He must have had contact with someone,' said Wegener. 'He managed to get in here with a false identity. He spent years working here as a gardener, and it won't have been just for his love of roses.'

'What was his real name?' asked Meffert.

'We're keeping that to ourselves for the time being,' said Brendel. 'But to get back to my colleague Mr Wegener's question – what might Fischer have wanted here?'

Meffert tapped ash onto the green. 'Don't think someone can work here as a gardener or a chef or whatever you like and then wander around as he pleases, peering into the ministers' windows and searching their desks if the back door happens to be open. It doesn't work that way round here.'

'How does it work, then?'

'There are duty rosters with specific deployment areas and schedules. If someone's supposed to cut the semi-rough on the golf course for three hours in the morning and mows Undersecretary Kant's lawn instead he gets the boot.'

'But you can't keep an eye on every single person all the time.'

'All the workers in the colony carry a GLONASS tracker with a personalized signal. We always know where our people are at any given time.'

'A valued tradition in the GDR,' said Kayser. 'So that means we can see from your duty rosters what Emil Fischer was up to over the past six months.'

'You can see what he was up to over the past ten years,' said Dörnen. 'Which deployment sections, which times. We don't delete anything. This is a national special security zone.'

'Are there any residents in the government quarter who were regular customers, if you like?' asked Wegener. 'Who only wanted their roses watered by Fischer and no one else?'

'Most of them never meet the person who looks after their garden. They leave at seven in the morning and don't get back till late.'

'But most of their wives stay at home, don't they?'

'Dr Wanser,' said Dörnen. 'Emil was often at Dr Wanser's. He hasn't got a wife.'

'We're sorry to hear that,' said Kayser. 'What did Dr Wanser have for our Emil, then?'

'Confetti, Fair Play and Helmut Schmidt,' said Dörnen.

'I'm guessing at roses,' said Brendel. 'Otherwise I'd ask if you've been drinking.'

'And of course Sweet Mielke and Stangier's Pride. Fischer's own breeds.'

'Who is this Wanser?'

'Dr Gert Wanser,' said Meffert. 'Dietmar Dath's right-hand man.'

'Minister of Culture,' Wegener explained.

'Aha.' Kayser looked disappointed. 'And can we talk to this Dr Wanser?'

Meffert threw his cigarillo towards the edge of the woods and blew the last of the smoke through his yellowish teeth. 'He's been in Bulgaria with Dath for two days. Some kind of literary tour.'

'But can we contact him?' asked Brendel.

'Via the ministry,' said Meffert. 'They must have telephones by now in Bulgaria. So what do the police think Fischer was after? Was he planning an assassination?'

'No.' Brendel leaned against the buggy. 'He wouldn't have had to spend ten years digging in the dirt for that. And I assume even Fischer wouldn't have got bombs or weapons in here, would he?'

Meffert smiled. 'I assume not. So what then? Espionage?'

'We don't know yet,' said Wegener. 'Maybe he was just procuring information for his own purposes. Or he had a passionate interest in literary tours.'

'Why did you immediately think of assassination?' asked Kayser.

Meffert scrutinized their faces. 'Because of the explosion, of course.'

Kayser put on an innocent face. 'But it was just a gas leak.'

Meffert looked at him. 'Right. And the six Volvos just now, they were the customer service team from Gazprom.'

13

I WAS A NAZI, FRÜCHTL HAD SAID with a heavy tongue numbed by Goldkrone brandy, slumped low in his green chair, *then I was a communist, I was young, what else was I supposed to be back then but a Nazi, a communist, a fascist socialist. And now I'm a citizen. An old citizen detained behind walls, all right, but a citizen. If they could localize that Nazi-communist-citizen experience in some way, extract it, siphon it off from the brainstem, transform it into a serum that you could inject newborn babies with*, Früchtl had said, *a quick jab in the back of the head, then I wouldn't have lived my messed-up life for nothing, then there'd be an end to the never-ending wrong tracks every young generation takes, with their ideological signposts that always point right and left and never straight ahead. At least then my own changing sides and changing direction and Hitler salutes and Stalin kisses would have served some purpose, wouldn't have been for nothing*, Früchtl had said, *Josef's service to humanity for the production of a cure for the goddamn plague of Redundant Political*

Generational Idiocy. Then all the great loss might have a tiny point to it. Oh, childhood! Oh youth! Oh manhood! Oh prime of my life! Oh miserable pile of shit! Früchtl had yelled.

His own generation had bowed and scraped as long as they'd been supple enough to bow and scrape to someone, long and hard until they'd all got hunchbacks and now half his comrades were long dead, killed by the great leaders and the great pretenders of the dead century, the crappiest century in human memory, while the other half had gone stiff, frozen in bent-backed humility, permanently bent and twisted by the hideous spirit of subservience, crooked and timid and crowded into the GDR.

If only they could find the ideology spot in the brain, the place where political delusion is consolidated, and if they could inject my experience serum right there, Früchtl had shouted, *wisdom by the vial that instantly caramelizes in your skull to sticky understanding, to permanent insight, if they had that sweet spot to immediately siphon off what you'd learned, to copy it, to immunize the human race – then we'd invent ourselves a race of citizens, politically centred from the cradle to the grave, the first intelligent creation, immune to any kind of extremist influence. God messed it up: Früchtl tries to put it right. Logically thinking, that understanding ought to be neither in the right half nor the left half of the brain, but precisely in the middle.*

'I was a Nazi, then I was a communist,' said Wegener, raised the beer bottle to his lips and drank. A year and a half ago the Minsk didn't yet have a Dictaphone function, or he'd have recorded Major Meatloaf every time he spoke, the old man would have leapt in at the touch of a button with his explanations, given impromptu People's Chamber speeches and slung mud at fascists and socialists alike for hours on end without taking a breath, while his housekeeper Erna

Bock stood at the stove in one of her flowery aprons, stirring, simmering, sieving, sizzling, seasoning, night after night the only listener
to one of the greatest speakers in the GDR, plenum, people and television audience in a single flowered entity.

What a burden, thought Wegener. Erna Bock had borne that
burden with the same pride with which she wore her flower-patterned
aprons. On Sundays Wegener had been her replacement burden-
bearer, a second listener, an assistant cook, another mouth to feed.

All of a sudden he noticed how much he missed those hours in
Früchtl's nicotine-stained little house. How he missed the speeches,
the smell of meat in the pan, the flowery aprons. He didn't have a
single recording of the accusatory, dark, ironic voice from the green
armchair. All he'd have had to do was take along the recording unit
from the station. Just one time. If only he hadn't been too stupid to
realize the present was something like happiness. If only he didn't
make the same dumb mistake over and over again of thinking
everything he loved would last for ever, because his imagination had
no scope for a really brutal loss, for reasons of self-protection alone.

I'm not the kind of guy who sits in a graveyard with a bottle of
beer, thought Wegener, and look at me now – sitting in a graveyard
with a bottle of beer, in front of my parents' ivy-covered grave, and
not as a belated death vigil but because Karolina lives round the
corner, only two streets away, and because the graveyard's always
been a simple excuse to be close to her. As if the old birds had chosen
their double grave in Weissensee to save him time and effort for evermore. A practical combination mourning station: he could cry tears
here in one go for Father, Mother, Früchtl and Karolina.

Wegener wondered what Brendel would think if he saw him here.
Brendel, who'd come within a hair's breadth of wrapping Leatherface
Wischinsky round his little finger on the strength of his charm and

his sweetshop perfume. Who'd wheedled copies of all the duty rosters and personnel documents out of Meffert with a smile. Who'd never be unfriendly in the course of this investigation, not to anybody, even if they snapped off his Mercedes symbol in Prenzlauer Berg. Who didn't let anyone know what he thought of this crumbling country, the fat-cat colony of Wandlitz, the old trousers of his East Berlin colleague.

Wegener realized there was nothing you could do but idolize Richard Brendel, if your name was Martin Wegener. Anything other than pure admiration was totally impossible in the face of such a height difference. Brendel had so much going for him in the superiority stakes: rank, West German origin, stature, sweetshop perfume and a slim-cut movie-star face with built-in blue eyes. And as a bonus a company car that made all of East Berlin jealous. Not including all the other things he didn't know about yet. The man was sure to be a perfect cook. Married to a brunette bombshell gallery-owner. Musically talented – played the piano. Or at least volleyball.

And then there was Wegener: East German, a head shorter, less hair, less of a career, a broken-down Wartburg Aktivist, no piano, no parents, no Früchtl and no wife. All he had was cord trousers. If I still had Karolina, thought Wegener. If beautiful K-k-k-karolina was still waiting for me outside the k-k-k-kitchen door, or the police station door, which she never did, but if she did do it now, wearing those clothes from our currywurst date, then it wouldn't matter that my life now consists mainly of *less* and *no*. Karolina would outweigh all Brendel's possessions.

A beautiful woman had always been the joker that won every trick. With a beautiful woman by your side, sparse hair became an intellectual look, lack of career became nonconformity, having no car became environmentally conscious, East German cords became cult clothing. With Karolina by his side, Brendel's happy life would be a clichéd painted backdrop. A malign boomerang that would come back and hit him on the head. Suddenly all the success and status symbols would only make it painfully clear that Brendel didn't have a Karolina of his own.

Just like I haven't got a Karolina of my own, thought Wegener, which might not be so awful if there hadn't been a time when I did have a Karolina of my own. The fact that I once had Karolina and don't any more is like getting the last man on earth hooked on the last reserves of alcohol in the world.

His Minsk rang.

Telepathy. Brendel or Karolina. Or both. A conference call on the subject of hair loss and inferiority complexes. Wegener took the telephone out of his trouser pocket.

'Frank?'

'This mountain range of documents!' Stein sounded tearful. 'This ocean of papers! I'll still be reading Hoffmann's essays and electricity bills when socialism develops into communism!'

'It must be a lot then.'

'I'm turning into a political scientist. If I understand it rightly, Hoffmann advocates a mixed form of GDR and Federal Republic. Crazy, eh? The best of both worlds, a mixture of West and East, if you like. And he calls it, hold on, he calls it: Posteri ... bugger ... '

'He calls it what?'

'Po-steri-ta-tism.'

'I was a Nazi, then I was a communist,' said Wegener.

'You were what?'

'Is it any use to us?' Wegener drank a mouthful of beer.

'This Posteri-crap? Who knows. But maybe one of the ring binders.' Rustling paper. 'I found this this morning, copies of a land register entry. Hoffmann owns two apartment buildings in Heidelberg, which he rents out. That's where the money comes from. Apart from that, he seems to have a holiday hut in Mecklenburg.'

Wegener drank another mouthful and let his eyes wander across the graveyard. The gathering dusk had swallowed up all colour. Only two rows of red plastic grave candles glimmered on either side of the main path. A stunted runway, thought Wegener, for emigrating souls. His parents' grave was dark.

'Martin?'

'I guess we'd better go over there then, to the holiday hut. Anything on the Hoffmann-equals-Fischer front?'

Frankenstein's voice grew a pinch more cheerful. 'Not a line, nothing. Apart from the ID card you've already got.'

'Did Brendel talk to you?'

'He came in with the Wandlitz information. Doesn't look all that hopeful either, eh?'

'This Dr Wanser,' said Wegener, 'it'd be good if you'd take a look at him. He probably knows as little as the rest of them. When it comes to Hoffmann, that lot out there are living in cloud cuckoo land.'

'Right, I'm on Wanser's case. Meeting at half eight tomorrow morning. Kallweit rescheduled an hour earlier.'

'Another great weekend.'

'You're telling me. I still won't be through with the papers by then, though, I'll tell you that right now.'

'And the explosion? Gas leak?'

'No one knows anything. C5 are tackling it personally, so it's silence all round. Oh, before I forget, we found a few love letters at Hoffmann's flat that'd blow your hat off. Fifty per cent heartache, 50 per cent politics.'

'From the young beauty?'

'No, they're ancient. They're from twenty-five years ago. Signed with initials: M. T.'

'*No Doubt Time Hates Love.*'

'Mon commandant,' said Frankenstein military-style, 'it's back to work for me. See you tomorrow.'

'Half eight.'

''Fraid so.'

Wegener got up from his bench, threw the empty beer bottle in a waste basket and tried to imagine the rotting remains of his parents really lying two metres below him in the cold ground. At least someone had trimmed their ivy. Perhaps a relative of Eduard Wickensack, 1912–1993, who was buried next to them. Or the chain-smoking son of the graveyard gardener Dierssen.

Next summer I'll plant things here, thought Wegener, I'll plant a bed as flowery as Erna Bock's aprons. A bed of aprons.

Then he walked along the candlelit runway towards the western exit.

Standing outside Karolina's beige nineteenth-century tenement building on Colombetstrasse five minutes later, Wegener wished he'd drunk five beers and not just one. Even acts of desperation got more difficult the longer ago the relationship was. The first couple of times at the beginning, he'd managed to play the mortally wounded drunken love-sick loser and ring at her front door without feeling shame. At some point that shame had crept up on him and never gone away again. Now the shame was here he couldn't ring the bell any more. No matter how much he'd had to drink. His nightly act of compulsion had degenerated into a plan. Something considered. Something including numerous ulterior motives. Self-pity, jealousy, anger and of course hope for a weak moment that might lead to a spontaneous shag, if you helped it along with a bottle of Red Riding Hood Ladies' Choice sparkling wine.

His voyeur's shop-doorway hiding place was as dark and empty as ever.

There was a light on in Karolina's flat.

The last stage of a relationship is observing the other party, thought Wegener, counting lit-up windows, being outside while the other party's inside. Only watching now. Or listening. Sitting in without making an appearance. Perhaps it was an occupational hazard for detectives. Or perhaps only for East German detectives. Obsessive observation. Living out a love you mustn't present to the other party any more. Because it isn't presentable any more. A love you may only present to yourself. Maybe a love like this isn't love at all any more, thought Wegener, maybe a love like this is just about wallowing in your own suffering.

He took his Minsk out of his pocket and dialled. She picked up after the fourth ring.

'Martin, I can't talk right now.'

'That's a shame. Otherwise I'd have come by.'

'I'm sorry.'

'Me too.'

'Where are you?'

'In the graveyard, and you?'

'At the ministry.'

Früchtl groaned inside his brain, the groan of a man being horribly tortured, who's just had next week's torture schedule explained to him in detail.

Wegener felt his heart skip a beat. The lit-up window. Karolina never forgot to turn the light off when she left the house. For a second he thought he'd seen a shadow. A shadow moving behind the net curtain. Much taller than a woman's shadow. More like a tall man's shadow. A Brendel-shaped shadow.

'Martin?'

'I thought you'd have Saturday night off at least.'

'The consultations. I've got a thousand things to sort out.'

'Are you getting my gas cut off?'

Karolina didn't laugh. 'I'll call you tomorrow. Or was there anything important?'

'I just wanted to know if you were in the Palace today and I have to nurse you for the rest of my life.'

That'd be the ideal solution, said Früchtl, *then you can look at her as long as you like, she can't get away, you get to dress her and undress her and get a sniff at all her orifices, all her glands, it's all there on a plate for you, a defenceless, body-temperature, organic scented blow-up doll made of soft white flesh.*

'Bad luck, I'm all in one piece.' Three seconds' silence. 'We'll talk tomorrow, OK?'

'Sleep well. When you get home.'

'You too.'

He hung up, put the phone in his pocket and felt his wobbly legs, a heart going crazy, bright fog in a heavy head. He sat down on the kerb. Weeds between the paving stones. A squashed Duett cigarette packet. Four of six street lamps were lit. A Lada turned the corner and roared past. Brendel, thought Wegener, holding his nose with one hand. What if Karolina's visitor was Brendel? That wasn't possible, of course. They didn't even know each other, couldn't possibly. No chance for them to meet. And anyway, the car would be here somewhere. Or maybe not, deliberately. Brendel would hardly be stupid enough to park his Mercedes right outside her house.

Wegener wondered whether the absence of the Mercedes could be assessed as a strong enough indication of Brendel's presence in Karolina's flat. It all fitted together too well. Brendel in his dark suit and sand-coloured trench coat. Her in her neat two-piecer. Both perfect. Immaculate. Of a beauty that couldn't be overlooked. That you had to devote yourself to whether you wanted to or not. Multiplied by the couple effect. The two of them next to each other: hand in hand. Smiling. Exponential charisma. The Prince of Benz and his Rose Red. A love without borders.

Wegener smiled, although he hardly felt like smiling. Then he saw the two red dots. Two smokers in a Phobos right outside Karolina's front door.

His trouser pocket rang. He leaned back slightly and pulled the telephone out again. Number withheld.

'Hello?'

On the other end of the line breathing in, breathing out. 'Mr Wegener?'

'Who is this?'

'I have to talk to you.'

'You already are.'

'In person.'

'Aha. What about?'

'Not on the telephone.'

The men in the Phobos flicked their cigarette ends out of the open windows. Wegener lowered his voice.

'I don't care who you are. But I would like to know what this is all about.' He got up and crossed the road towards the Phobos.

'It's about Hoffmann. Is that enough for you?'

'That's enough.' Wegener walked faster. 'When?' The engine started.

'I'll be in touch.'

'Don't you want to tell me—'

'Don't bother getting the call tracked, I'm calling from a phone box.'

Wegener started running but the Phobos was already moving, picking up speed, zooming out of Colombetstrasse. Two brake lights and then it was round the corner. The caller had hung up. The light was on in Karolina's living room. The smell of old cooking fat on the cool evening air.

SUNDAY 23 OCTOBER 2011

14

MARX IS SIPPING COCA-COLA THROUGH A RED AND WHITE *striped straw. He closes his eyes in contentment and offers Engels a glug. Engels takes the Coke and hands Marx half of his Quarter Pounder in exchange. The two men smile. Now Engels is drinking Coke as Marx bites into Engels' burger. The orangey-yellow slice of processed Cheddar melts on the hot all-beef patty. The special sauce drips, the pickles sweat. Marx licks his fingers happily.*

A scene that might be found equally absurd, repulsive or even blasphemous in the German Democratic Republic and the Federal Republic of Germany. And a scene that sums up what divides the two halves of Germany: our clichés of two competing systems, whose antagonisms have dictated the events of world history over the past hundred years and have always been regarded as irreconcilable competitors for the favour of the ideology-crazed masses, as earthly derivatives of heaven or hell, depending on the interpretation of the opposite camp.

Although communism of pure faith issued its own death certifi-
cate with the erosion of the Soviet Union in the 1990s, and
although predatory capitalism is on the brink of lethal collapse
following the global financial crisis, our view of this dogmatic
dualism has not altered in the slightest. To this day, the market
economy and socialism form the thesis and antithesis for which
no one is prepared to come up with a synthesis. Marx and Engels
are not to be allowed to enjoy a Quarter Pounder until the end of
their days.

'Enjoy a what?' Kallweit gaped at Frankenstein.

'A big hamburger.'

'Yum.' Kayser smacked his chops. 'A nice big beef patty.' He licked
his lips.

An ox with a faint inkling of its impending slaughter, thought
Wegener, slowly getting scared of ending up as a nice big all-beef
patty on a sesame-seed bun.

'That's the introduction to *Justice in Excess*,' said Frankenstein,
holding up a blue book with a library sticker on it and reading the
subtitle off the dust jacket: '*How we can overcome the war of the
systems.*'

'And Hoffmann wrote it?' Kallweit asked.

Frankenstein nodded. 'Chapter one's about how so-called degenerate mixed forms of capitalism and communism in China and Vietnam
are no use as models for Germany, because these systems are entirely
based on corruption and—'

'Yeah, yeah.' Kallweit waved an impatient hand. 'When did this
nonsense come out?'

'Two years ago. Published by Aufbau-Verlag, East Berlin. The book
was Hoffmann's last publication – according to the library it's

something like a summary and a reworking of his texts on Posteritatism from the seventies and eighties.'

'Po-what?'

'Posteritatism,' said a proud Frankenstein.

'So?'

'I think what we have to realize is that Hoffmann was, if you like,
a friend of both political systems. And that made him an enemy of
both political systems too.'

Kallweit still had the facial expression of an ox. 'And that means?'

'That means we can't set any limits when it comes to the motive,'
said Brendel. 'If we're even dealing with a politically motivated
murder in the first place.'

Kallweit sighed. 'Not good. Carry on.'

Frankenstein pulled sheets of handwritten notes out of a transparent plastic cover.

'The short version, please,' said Kallweit with a glance at his watch,
'I've got another twenty-four minutes.' He tapped his crooked finger
on the copy of the *Public Eye* on the table in front of him. The Palace
of the Republic took up six columns on the front page, a black hole
gaping in the middle of its golden facade: a mouth wide open with
shock. Inside the mouth leered crooked steel girders, the soot-
blackened state crest dangling above.

'Right, the short version,' said Frankenstein. 'The door-to-door inter-
views on Greifenhagener Strasse were as good as useless. They did know
Hoffmann at least, but everyone described him as, I quote, *friendly and
reserved*. Since he moved in – that was in 2009 – he's been seen several
times in the company of a young woman. Hand in hand.' Frankenstein
inserted a dramatic pause. 'But there are no indications as to the girl's
identity. They did at least confirm that Hoffmann has a cleaning lady.
Comes every Monday, apparently. So we'll wait for her tomorrow.'

'Financial situation?' asked Kallweit.

'Two apartment buildings in Heidelberg, fully let. Minus all the outgoings, that adds up to about 5,000 euros a month coming over from West Germany. Compared to that his GDR pension looks pretty modest, about 1,400 marks. Emil Fischer earned an average of 450 marks a month for his rose-pruning. He didn't go to Wandlitz in the winter.'

'That income must have covered his living standards, no problem,' said Wegener. 'So he was financially independent.'

Kallweit's oxen eyes scanned the assembled parties. 'Emil Fischer's flat in Marzahn was rented?'

'Yes,' said Brendel. 'I presume a rented flat made the security check for Wandlitz easier back then.'

Kallweit rubbed his eyes with his crooked index fingers. 'Are there any colleagues from when he was active in politics?'

Frankenstein lowered the papers. 'The Interior Ministry couldn't give us any names. All we've got so far is his former Heidelberg colleague, a Doctor Werner Blühdorn. Luckily enough, he's coming to give a talk at the Humboldt University the day after tomorrow, and we'll talk to him after that. What we haven't got is someone from Hoffmann's stint on Moss's advisory staff.'

Kallweit shook his head so hard his jowls wobbled. 'Have you told those idiots how important the matter is?'

'Hoffmann was a kind of external consultant back then,' said Frankenstein. 'He wasn't sitting in the ministry all day.'

Karolina doesn't sit in the ministry all day either, thought Wegener, but she says she does, and instead she sits at home and tells me she's sitting in the ministry. So who knows where Hoffmann really used to sit.

'That's what makes it so difficult,' Frankenstein continued. 'His secretary and his liaison man to the Politburo aren't alive any more. And the files are stored in some basement somewhere.'

'I can't believe there's no one out there who knows this Hoffmann guy! He wasn't Deutsch Mark, the ghost of the national bank!'

'I'm afraid that's what it looks like right now.'

'And Moss?' Kallweit only seemed to notice what he'd just said with a few seconds' delay. He pressed his index fingers to his eyelids and rubbed them.

'We need your permission for that,' said Wegener.

Kallweit rubbed his eyes so hard he seemed to want to go blind as soon as possible. 'What a crock of shit! I can't believe this!'

'Wandlitz,' said Brendel. 'Dr Wanser.'

Frankenstein took another sheet of paper out of the cover. 'I got hold of Wanser this morning. Undersecretary of State in the Culture Ministry. At first he was shocked by Hoffmann's death and then even more shocked when he heard that his personal rose surgeon had sneaked into the government quarter under a false name. Couldn't think why. Never doubted Emil Fischer's identity in all the years.'

Kallweit stared at the ceiling and folded his hands.

'He might have been planning an assassination attempt,' said Brendel, 'or he was spying. Those are the two conceivable possibilities. Our problem is there's nothing to corroborate either of the two options.'

Kallweit closed his eyes. He's praying, thought Wegener. To St Egon, to give him patience in these troubled times of gas explosions in government buildings and fake gardeners. And to send him a fast solution to the investigation, with a couple of nice photos for the front page of the *Public Eye*. Let the successorship to the Deputy Minister of the Interior soon be mine. Amen.

Kallweit unfolded his hands and rubbed his eyes for the third time.

'He must have kept his distance from Hans-Walter Moss. He'd have recognized him. From the old days.'

'Hoffmann used to have a moustache,' said Wegener. 'He shaved it off for Wandlitz. And he wore glasses, he had longer hair than before, a worker's uniform. It wasn't a spectacular disguise but it was enough.'

'He wasn't interested in Moss at all.' Brendel flapped open a small notebook. 'We've got his personnel files. According to the records, Hoffmann refused to switch to the team that looks after the top politicians' private gardens, five years ago. That would've been his opportunity if he'd been in it to get at Moss.'

'Elite gardeners,' grunted Kallweit, spitting a few droplets of saliva on the battered Palace of the Republic. 'He works there a whole eleven years and does nothing but prune roses. Doesn't want to get close to Moss. Obviously doesn't want to get close to anyone. What do the other gardeners say in Wandlitz?'

'I've called them all in,' said Frankenstein. 'I'll deal with them this afternoon. They've already been questioned internally though, with no outcome. It may sound a bit absurd, but maybe Hoffmann really just wanted to work there. At the heart of power. Maybe he had withdrawal symptoms after he left politics.'

'Possibly,' said Wegener. 'His reasons weren't necessarily illegal. Maybe he liked digging in the earth next to the people he used to sit around conference tables with. Maybe that was his way of giving them the finger.'

Kallweit opened his mouth and closed it again.

'And maybe he heard something while he was at it,' said Wegener. 'By accident. Walked past an open window and witnessed a conversation he shouldn't have heard under any circumstances. Or someone just thought he'd heard something.'

'We don't have the slightest indication of that.' Kallweit shook his head. 'What on earth do you think he overheard, Wegener?'

'For instance something to do with the consultations. Bribery, siphoning off gas along the way – how should I know?'

'Rubbish.'

'We mustn't rule it out,' said Brendel. 'Not until we know what Hoffmann was up to in Wandlitz.'

'Then don't rule it out, if you insist, but that point stays classified!' Kallweit looked at Wegener. 'I don't want it down in writing any- where, I don't want it mentioned verbally, not to anyone, I don't want it even hinted at!'

'Whatever you say.'

'Has Borgs been in touch with the Energy Ministry yet?'

Frankenstein looked at his watch. 'He's just arrived there.'

'We've got just under thirteen minutes left,' said Kayser. 'I'll just present what my intelligence people have for us.'

Kallweit nodded with great resignation, as if someone was about to read out his own private surveillance reports.

Kayser opened up a leather folder piled high with faxes and computer printouts. 'To start with the things we can safely ignore: We have – here comes a bit of bureaucratic jargon – *no credible indications that interest groups or special forces of oil-producing countries or other relevant states are currently performing oper- ations* which might be linked to our case. For several reasons. First of all the volume of gas currently transported to Western Europe via the GDR is ultimately relatively small. And secondly they wouldn't be so indiscreet.'

'You mean they wouldn't murder Hoffmann to harm the consult- ations,' said Wegener.

'They certainly wouldn't hand photos of the body and dubious witness statements over to the press. Those kind of operations always avoid public attention by all means necessary, they never go actively looking for it.'

'So what would an influential oil state do, let's say? If it wanted to prevent the consultations from taking place?' asked Kallweit.

'Political pressure, bribery, blackmail, corruption,' said Kayser. 'Certainly in some cases bodily harm or murder, but not publicly staged like this.'

'So that's all the wild conspiracy theories out of the window. At least we're getting somewhere.'

'At least almost all of them. The Federal Criminal Police Office gave us a nod on GreenFAC. They've been making waves in the past few years.'

Kallweit's face was a droopy question mark.

'GreenFAC is a consortium of alternative Western European energy companies,' said Brendel. 'The market leader in West Germany and somewhere in the top ten worldwide. Solar cells, wind turbines, water power.'

'You're kidding me!' Kallweit spat a second volley at the *Public Eye*. 'A West German solar-cell manufacturer stringing people up from gas pipelines in the German Democratic Republic! If I present that to the Secretary-General as our main line of investigation this evening we might as well hang ourselves up right next to Hoffmann!'

'Let's stick to the facts,' said Kayser. 'One of GreenFAC's main shareholders is an investor from Munich, who the Office for the Protection of the Constitution rates as a stooge for the Albanian mafia. That means the company gets its money from people who are used to achieving their financial goals by illegal means.'

'So?' asked Kallweit.

'If the new transit agreements come about, Western Europe will be flooded with cheap gas for the next twenty years, and then no one's going to be buying geothermal heating and solar roof panels. And Lafontaine's also announced he plans to cut subsidies. So if we add it up over two decades, we're talking about billions of euros.'

'But why Albert Hoffmann of all people?'

Kayser made an obvious effort to sound patient. 'If they really want to make it look like the State Security's killed someone, they have to choose a victim who makes sense. And Albert Hoffmann's a hole-in-one in that respect. A political thinker, a West German, influential during Revitalization.'

Things started rattling inside Kallweit's skull. The machinery had been set in motion. Tiny cogs started turning by the millimetre, driving larger wheels, rust flaked off, steam exuded, hot air, thought Wegener, gradually finding its way through the countless hollow spaces, past limestone-encrusted channels, past blocked pipes, while the apparatus groaningly produced questions and conclusions, scrubbing them again, assembling them anew until the whole rhubarb eventually escaped from his mouth with the usual delay.

'Right, we've got this GreenFAC. A rather adventurous suspicion,' noted Kallweit. 'Other than that, we know that Hoffmann got himself into the government quarter but we don't know why. We don't have the slightest idea to explain it. There's an unidentified lady-friend. Plus a *Spiegel* source we can't get to. So we haven't got any witnesses whatsoever for anything. We haven't got a motive. We haven't got much, gentlemen.'

'There's another thing we haven't got,' said Brendel. 'Hoffmann's Stasi file. Because we're not allowed to see it.'

15

THE DEAD MAN SWAYED TO AND FRO. Perhaps someone had bumped into him. And now the momentum wasn't giving way, even though whoever had provided it was long gone.

Like a pendulum in a vacuum, the body swung from right to left in a repetitive motion, the legs close together, the hands on its trouser seams, a swaying plank of Hoffmann, sawn out of a single piece of wood and wrapped in a pale trench coat. Someone was throwing generous handfuls of dead leaves from the sky. Wegener walked through the yellow rain towards the swinging corpse. Once he'd reached the pipeline he saw Karolina. She was standing behind an oak trunk, staring at Hoffmann as if at a Wimbledon final. Her head followed the pendulum movements. Tears fell from her doe's eyes. Wegener took her in his arms. Karolina was frozen through.

I'm too hot, said Karolina.

You're lying, said Wegener.

And you always tell the truth, Martin.

Pull yourself together – radical trust in radical times! exclaimed Wegener. Then he saw it: the corpse was naked under the trench coat. An erect penis protruded from between the two halves of coat. And the dead man wasn't called Hoffmann, of course. Hoffmann didn't wear a trench coat.

Post-mortem erection, said Karolina.

Yuck, said Wegener.

Rhythmic creaking, every time the corpse swung from one side to the other. The rope scraped against the cladding on the pipeline. Karolina gave off a slight sweetshop scent.

They've drilled a hole in my head and filled it with crushed lead, thought Wegener, just like the ribbed white egg that hung from Mother's old kitchen lamp as a weight, a defective, unhatched miscarriage in off-white porcelain.

Further along the forest path, an out-of-focus Brendel was shaking a barrier. He had grabbed it with both hands and was strangling it like a red and white striped snake so scared it was playing dead. Then he shook his head and left the beast in peace.

Wegener woke up.

He stretched. The dream ebbed away as slowly as crushed lead. His head grew lighter. The swaying corpse with the erection under its trench coat faded. Warm forest air wafted through the open driver's door into the Mercedes. The sun was shining. There was a smell of moss.

Brendel squatted down. He fished a set of keys out of a small plastic bag and fiddled around with something. After a minute or so he came back to the car.

'Locked. And none of them fits.'

Wegener yawned. He tried to sit upright on the warm leather seat. The back of his shirt was soaked with sweat.

Brendel turned the Navodobro touchscreen towards him and pressed the *Alternative Route* icon. The silhouette of an egg timer appeared. Pixels of digital sand trickled from the top half to the bottom half. Then the timer made a 180-degree turn and the pixels trickled back again.

Wegener tried and failed to suppress a second yawn. Brendel reached under his seat and returned with a silvery thermos flask in one hand, twisted off the lid, half filled it with steaming milky coffee and held it out to Wegener.

'We went to the Intershop yesterday,' said Brendel.

'What did you get – coffee and bananas?'

'Coffee and toilet paper. Kayser was having so much trouble on the toilet we decided to treat ourselves to twelve rolls of West European toilet paper.'

'You had to go to the foreign currency shop for toilet paper? Don't they have West German toilet paper in the EastSide?'

'They do at the EastSide. But not at police headquarters.'

'I see. And what's the place like apart from that? Cocaine orgies on the Steinway?'

'I wish. Quite a lot of Russians. Other than that, just your average hotel.'

Wegener took a sip. The coffee carried on brewing inside him, seeping hot down his gullet and forming a boiling spot in his stomach. It was impossible to say anything about the flavour now. There's no way for a German to talk about the amazing taste of real coffee to another German in the year 2011 without humiliating himself, thought Wegener. We're a nation of dwarves, 14.5 million midgets, a whole country full of shrunken Huns, we're all much too short for the Intershop and that's how we'll stay for evermore.

'But it's really scratchy, the stuff they give you here.' Brendel stared at the display. He was obviously rather troubled by the subject of toilet paper. The egg timer turned over. 'It doesn't have to be four-ply. But wood?'

'Old newspapers,' said Wegener, downed his coffee in one large gulp and gave Brendel the lid back. 'It's all old newspapers. The GDR wipes its collective bum on yesterday's propaganda. You see, the Politburo has no sense of irony.'

'The Politburo presumably has proper toilet paper.'

'They are professional arsewipes, after all.'

An exclamation mark flashed on the display: *No alternative route available.*

'A 3.4-kilometre walk,' said Brendel, getting out of his seat. He picked up his briefcase from the back seat and waited for Wegener to climb out of the car before pressing the remote key. The warning lights flashed and four door buttons vanished soundlessly into leather obscurity.

'If a hiker comes past and sees the car,' said Wegener, 'he'll think he's done a Rip Van Winkel and missed reunification.'

Brendel grinned. 'Would you be in favour of reunification?'

'I would. But the East Germans wouldn't stop complaining, even in prosperity. Take my word for it.'

'Because they don't really want the Wall to fall? Or because it wouldn't go fast enough for them?'

'Because they've taken complaining to new heights over the past sixty years. You can't just give it up. We're world complaining champions.'

'Maybe we'd better forget about reunification then.'

'Then we'll complain about you forgetting about it.'

Wegener ducked under the barrier. Brendel vaulted over it. His jacket hung over the arm he was carrying the briefcase with. His shirtsleeves rolled up, top three buttons undone. No tie today. The August look in October.

Brendel smiled a let's-go smile and then they walked side by side over a soft carpet of fir needles. The path was set lower than the forest, a winding trench in which an entire People's Army company could lie in ambush for Federal Armed Forces troops, if it ever did come to a fratricidal war. Ferns grew rank on the shady banks of the path; glimmering beetles fought their way across mountain ranges once pressed into the earth by tractor wheels. No sun in the narrow, pale blue section of sky.

They'll make a hiker of me yet, thought Wegener, envisioning the stretch of map on Brendel's laptop: an arrow marking the position of the holiday hut, all around it green forest areas with small black fir tree symbols, yellow squares of arable land, then the bold, criss-cross line dividing socialism from imperialism, which had reminded Wegener of the cut along Hoffmann's pale chest cavity. No more than forty kilometres to the border – everyone had instantly seen that: Brendel, Kayser, Frankenstein, he himself. With a bit of effort you could make it in one night.

Wegener thought of the picture-book hero Franjo the Fox, who had found a hole in the wire mesh version of the anti-capitalist protective rampart back when it was still called the anti-fascist pro-tective rampart. Franjo had crept through the hole with the jolly song 'I'll be blessed in the West' on his black foxy lips, which the juvenile reader could sing along to, thanks to the musical notes included on the page, only to go through a whole load of depressing experiences in the Federal Republic, with stingy imperialist fellow foxes who wouldn't share the geese they'd caught, with hens who launched themselves from their perches in desperation over their exploitation, and with Harry the Hunter, who wanted Franjo's fur to make a collar for the wife of the local Christian Democrat leader Kriegbaum. Emaciated but all the wiser, Franjo the Fox had set off home for paradise after a week of bitter revelations, singing 'Do what's best – don't go West', to the same tune as his previous hymn of self-delusion.

'If I had a backpack with me,' said Wegener, 'and I asked you to forget me here in the woods . . . '

Brendel looked ahead of his feet as he walked. His briefcase swayed. An elegant businessman in the middle of the East German provinces, thought Wegener. The only question is: what is he selling?

'Someone asked me in West Berlin to take them over to the East,' said Brendel. 'In the boot of my car. They said I wouldn't have to go through the checks with all my special permissions.'

Franjo the Fox, thought Wegener – they've got him on the other side too. And the special unit head's the hole in the wire fence.

'Then they checked me twice.' Brendel switched his jacket and briefcase to the other arm. 'Some want in, others want out. Typical Germans. It's all much more complicated than it ought to be.'

'But they say there are more and more who want in.'

'That's true right now. We've got an army of unemployed who can't imagine anything better than becoming co-owner of a whole country overnight. And there are the new anti-capitalists who come out in a rash when they hear the words bailout fund.'

'There's a cynical dimension to that development for inmates like me, as I'm sure you can imagine.'

Brendel nodded. 'It must seem absolutely absurd to you.'

'That pretty much hits the nail on the head.' Wegener took his Minsk out of his pocket. No reception. 'Good old Auntie GDR would never have dreamt the Westerners would start banging at the doors.'

'The GDR has the American banks to thank for that. And Lafontaine does too, by the way. If it hadn't been for the subprime mortgage crisis Roland Koch would still be the chef in the kitchen at Bonn. And now all of a sudden socialism's booming.'

'You know what's amazing about socialism? It's always in fashion where it's not practised.'

Brendel smiled a sarcastic smile. 'And you know what that means.'

'Of course, it means immortality. Marx and Engels will never go under, but they'll never be a success either. Communism is a semi-erect cock, my old boss used to say: it won't give up and it won't come either. A pretty bitter fate.'

'And what's your bitter fate?' Brendel's blue, blue eyes looked at Wegener with curiosity.

'My bitter fate is the bitter fate of all East Germans. Being in the wrong place at the wrong time. And now we're lifelong guinea pigs in the empirical levelling research group by the name of GDR. With toilet paper you can use to sand down your furniture, and a complete renunciation of any form of truth. I still think the most telling thing about socialism is that it's so incompatible with the truth.'

'Having no form of truth would mean you can't work as a policeman here, though,' said Brendel. He stopped suddenly in his tracks, took a couple of steps into the forest, put down his briefcase and draped his jacket over it. Then he knelt down in the ferns. His pale blue shirt tightened across his broad back. There was the flash of a small pocketknife. Brendel leaned forward, sawed and stood up again, reached for his case and returned, a large cep mushroom in his right hand. The brown cap was slightly flecked; beneath it the olive-yellow gills and a white, club-shaped foot with earth, pine needles and the remains of moss still clinging to it.

'It is possible to work here as a policeman,' said Wegener. 'If you can live with the conditions.'

'What do you mean?'

'Are there maggots in your mushroom?'

Brendel eyed his find critically. 'I'd have to cut it open to see. The foot looks fine. I'd say, no.'

'But you don't know for sure. Just like the people in this country. Maggots or not? Sometimes someone comes across as incorruptible, and then you hear second or third hand that he's an informer. But maybe that's not true either. Maybe someone's been spreading rumours about him. But on the other hand rumours can be true even if they're made up. And so on. You'll never be quite sure. There are no reliable indicators. All you can do is guess. And if you decide to trust someone, all it takes is a trifle to make you doubt him again. A rash comment. A joke. A single word. Sometimes not even a word. Not even a joke. You turn into a mistrusting machine.'

'Which you have to be anyway, as a detective.'

Wegener took the mushroom out of Brendel's hand and examined it. Firm flesh. The gills had only two small snail holes in them. The cap was intact. 'But *you* can leave your mistrust in the interrogation room. For you it's all over when you go home. Here, your whole life's an investigation, twenty-four hours a day. Here you suspect everyone. All the time.'

'You think the FRG's a country with only honest people in it?'

'I think the GDR's a country with no honest people in it.'

'Not one? Don't tell me that. What about you?'

Wegener smiled. 'I'm a man. Men are always dishonest.'

Brendel couldn't help laughing. 'I've never looked at it like that. But you're probably right. And aren't there any honest women either?'

'Yes, there is one.'

'Then you were lying just now.'

'I told you so.'

Brendel took the mushroom back, wiped earth and moss off the foot and put it in his jacket pocket.

They walked on side by side along the fir-needle padding. The mushroom cap stuck out of Brendel's pocket like a large, velvety bread roll. An invisible bird croaked from the dark treetops, two short, one long: ack-ack-aaaaack.

The path took a sharp bend to the left. Right, thought Wegener, the pipes aren't on the map.

Brendel stopped.

Fifty metres ahead of them, the long bulge of a pipeline traipsed through the forest. The northernmost finger of the Potsdam Hand, not quite as thick as the Main Pipeline North but still impressive. The haggard, bare pine trunks were a toothpick nursery with a serpent threaded through them, jacked up on A-shaped concrete pillars, an abstract Russian/East German art installation, with a soundtrack from a single speaker: ack-ack-aaaaack.

'I requested your personnel file before I came over,' said Brendel, walking slowly on. 'I had to decide who to work with on the ground. You were on the case from the beginning, that was a good start.'

'And then there's that nice disciplinary procedure.' Wegener walked round a large root. 'I'm a troublemaker on top of everything else.'

'I don't mean to question your competence,' said Brendel. 'Everything fitted together. An experienced policeman, the first on the crime scene, not in the Socialist Unity Party. It would've been tricky with a party member on my tail.'

'You might be right.'

'Do you ever feel the after-effects from back then?'

'We tend not to feel the effects at the station when we feel the after-effects, if you see what I mean. It's been all quiet for a while. Steinkühler mentioned it the other day so I'd understand why I was your chosen one.'

Brendel nodded. 'This might sound a bit over the top. But I really admire what you did.'

'You're right, it does sound over the top.'

'Standing up to the authorities in a country like the GDR isn't easily done.'

Wegener shrugged. 'It wasn't about standing up to the authorities for me. The times when people here tried to play at heroes are long gone now.'

'So no more heroes either.'

'We have to import our heroes. You should know.'

Brendel's free arm made an indefinable movement. 'What was it about then?'

'Let's just say it was about the truth.' Wegener looked at Brendel. A slightly damp forehead, a friendly gaze from blue eyes, the respectful expression of a man who still believed that a bad state automatically produced good people. Ahead of them, the pipeline crossed the forest path on two pillars like a futuristic gateway to another world. Newer metallic elements glinted silvery next to the old cladding. A metal ladder led up the right-hand pillar; on top were barbed wire and latticework with pointy crowns, behind them heavy screwed fasteners secured with steel claws.

'I was looking for a friend of mine,' said Wegener. 'The man who trained me, long before Revitalization. If there's anything I can do, then it was him I learned it from.'

Brendel did not react.

The pipeline gateway was above their heads now. On the underside of the pipe was a hoard of rusty screws, evenly distributed across the dark curve. Now Brendel stepped into the shade of the pipeline.

'Is your friend still missing?'

'Yes.'

'What's his name?'

'Josef Früchtl. Major, retired.'

I'll never get used to that ret., said Früchtl: *it looks like retarded or retrograde or retracted old detective.*

'What do you think happened to him?'

Wegener hesitated. It was hard to make out Brendel's face in the shade. 'Josef worked as a private investigator after he retired. He was offered a job a bit more than a year ago. Research. Something political. Someone commissioned him, he didn't tell me what it was about.' Wegener was the first to leave the shadow. 'It sounded like pretty hot stuff. But Josef wasn't the kind of man who was afraid of anything or anybody.'

That sounds better, said Früchtl: *ret. stands for retrained as a hero.*

I'm using the past tense, thought Wegener, I'm talking about the old man as if he was somewhere right here in the forest, buried metres deep and impossible to find for all eternity.

'And then he suddenly disappeared?'

'From one day to the next, without a trace. No one knew anything, no one knew the case, no one had heard or seen anything. So I strode into Normannenstrasse on some excuse or other and got myself locked in the building overnight.'

Brendel's face was stuck somewhere between horror and admiration. 'You locked yourself into the Stasi headquarters?'

'I spent the night in the basement, looking for the archive. Once I found it I couldn't get in. So I went through any old filing cabinets in any old offices. It turned out later they were the documents for the chauffeur service. They got a few nice snapshots: Hauptmann Wegener staring anxiously at the surveillance camera with night-vision function. They'd identified me before they even came to pick me up.'

'And that was that.'

'Disciplinary procedure, official warning, threat of immediate suspension with incontestable loss of my pension in the event of a repeat offence. It could have been worse, though.'

'You go looking for the truth, even at the highest personal risk. And you still say there's no truth in the GDR?'

'When I say that socialism's incompatible with the truth, I mean the public truth. The actual truth does still exist, of course it does.'

Wegener stepped on a fat fir cone, which pressed painfully against the sole of his shoe. 'The thing is, even if I had found anything on my stupid adventure – we can't just go running to the *Spiegel* and kick off a scandal over here. You can write a complaint to some internal department or other, which then sweeps the place clean. But the place never gets swept clean. The dirt's piled three metres high. The truth under socialism is the truth you have to keep to yourself.'

'An ineffectual truth.'

'As ineffectual as socialism.'

Ack-ack-aaaack, came a shriek through the fir trees, then something flapped off.

They stomped mutely along the ground, which was growing ever sandier. The pipeline was now a constant companion, staying close by them, taking brief detours but returning straight to the forest track, a loyal gas serpent that didn't want to be alone any more after hundreds of kilometres of Siberian waste. Wegener wondered whether it was a stupid coincidence that Hoffmann's hut was by the pipeline that he eventually got strung up from. According to Frankenstein, he'd owned the place for more than twenty years. The major pipeline construction wave had kicked in about fifteen years ago. So probably Hoffmann hadn't come to the pipeline, the pipeline had come to him.

We're a week too late, thought Wegener, the detective's good old space–time dilemma. You always have hundreds of questions for people who can't answer them any more. Before that you spend thirty, forty, fifty years living in one country, in the same city, sitting next to them on the underground or at a bar, you meet them in the queue for the cinema and in the station lavatory, all without knowing them, not realizing that one day you'll spend weeks and months reconstructing the life of that man drinking beer at the kiosk, that woman reading the paper on the park bench, that Romanian prostitute by the side of the road, after you'd have had all the time in the world to ask them any question you liked at the kiosk or on the park bench or by the side of the road, to find out their murder motives, the motives for their murders, to record them on tape, type them up, get the victims and the murderers to sign all the papers and file them away as a thoroughly solved case in a folder with the title *Cleared-up Future Crimes*.

His Minsk was still looking for a network. No call from Karolina that morning. Was Brendel with her last night after all? wondered Wegener. The West Berlin Crime Squad had got file MW–B–1101–IV/2010 (PPB) from the Stasi, so Brendel knew his life inside and out, so he knew Karolina's name as well, so he knew her address as well. Maybe they'd run a check on her in advance. Working in the ministry, she was the perfect source, easy enough to put under pressure. Brendel might have pumped her for information on her ex-partner's past, character, habits and weaknesses. The two of them meet before he even gets to see Brendel himself. They get on well. They like the look of each other. No wonder. And they come together with no strings attached. The best insurance policy against post-coital complications is still the 170-kilometre concrete affair-breaker that meanders right across the city. There'd be no risk. So they might as well take the risk.

'I might have got hold of something for you,' said Wegener. 'A colleague of mine is selling an M6.'

'I'd be very grateful to that colleague of yours.' Brendel combed the sides of the track with his eyes. 'How much?'

'Twenty kilos of Ritter Sport chocolate, Olympia flavour. In unmarked bars. Or a ton of toilet paper.'

Brendel grinned. 'I'll send it over.'

The path was sloping gradually uphill. Thicker fir trunks grew at greater distances with brownish yellow grass between them. Countless brambles were working on stifling the forest beneath a mesh of thorny tendrils.

'Would you really go over to the West, Martin?' Brendel's eyes were still fixed to the ground. 'If the opportunity arose?'

'You're always thinking about it. But the opportunity never arises. So you just don't know either way.'

'And your girlfriend?'

'She's working on her career.' Wegener noticed he was glowing. The coffee boiled up again, rising to his head, driving sweat onto his forehead. 'And she hasn't been my girlfriend for a year now. If girlfriend was ever the right word.'

'I skipped the private details in your file,' Brendel said quickly. 'All I know is, you were in a relationship at the time of the disciplinary procedure.'

I'm naked, thought Wegener. I'm wearing underpants, cord trousers, a shirt, socks and shoes, but I'm naked. I'm walking naked through the woods next to Benz-Brendel. I stand naked in a sad shop doorway at night and look up at Karolina's love nest that was once our love nest. I have to rescue my bankrupt state from going bank-rupt, naked. The clothed people like me naked best of all.

'Your ex-girlfriend.' Brendel hesitated. 'Is that the woman you trust, Wegener?'

'If you can see through me that well you ought to call me by my first name.'

'Then I feel really sorry for you about all that happened, Martin,' said Brendel.

'So do I.'

If he gives me a matey pat on the back after all this German–German male bonding, thought Wegener, I'll start weeping into his 350-euro shirt.

'Kayser hasn't seen your file, by the way.'

Wegener nodded. 'Thanks, Richard.'

'What for?'

'Thanks for telling me.'

The path forked at the end of the slope. The pipeline stuck with the left fork while the right-hand path vanished into bushy grass, bent and turned into a small clearing with a low, run-down house squat-ting in the middle.

The sun had suddenly remembered its job and appeared from some-where, transforming the clearing into a shabby imitation of a Scandinavian paradise. Crickets chirped. Dark red paint peeled from the wooden walls of the hut. Roof tiles coated with dried moss. Closed shutters that must once have been white. An old wood-chopping block rotted away by the front door. Once the slaughterhouse table, soon the victim, thought Wegener. The smell of resin came at him as strongly as if half the forest had just been chopped down.

'Nice place,' said Brendel. 'A bit lonely.'

'Perhaps that's just right for a lonely old man.'

'I can't put Hoffmann together in my head.' Brendel took the plastic bag of keys out of his pocket. 'This hut doesn't go with his flat. The flat doesn't go with the gardener's job. The gardener's job doesn't go with his political writing. The political writing doesn't go with a twenty-year-old lover. And the fact that the lover's missing doesn't go with anything.'

'And the pipeline,' said Wegener, 'what does that go with?'

Brendel turned towards the pipeline, looking at it for several seconds and then shaking his head. Then he took the key ring out of the bag, dodged a few bramble branches and fought his way across the clearing to the front door. Wegener stuck behind him.

A brigade of East German spiders must have been working off their own personal five-year plan on Hoffmann's holiday hut. The stained wooden walls were covered in glittering webs. Brendel picked out the oldest and longest key, poked it around in the lock and turned it. The key fitted. A bolt clicked. The door swung into the dark room with a slight squeak, as if just opened from the inside.

Musty air. A scent of plastic. The window shutters painted contorted lattices of light on the grey PVC floor. Wegener made out the shapes of seats, a wood-burning stove, the outlines of a cupboard. The back of the room was submerged in darkness. No one at home.

Brendel had opened up his briefcase and now took out two protective suits, gloves, plastic bags and a camera. I'm naked and I'm staying naked, thought Wegener as they climbed into the suits. And Brendel puts more on every day, gets more and more clothed, more and more protected; he not only has his impenetrable mask of a face, he has a growing wardrobe of costumes too: the constabulary costume, the comradely costume, the competence costume, the Karolina's cavalier costume.

'Was there a photo of her in the file?'

'Yes.'

Wegener felt an instant stab at Brendel knowing exactly what he'd been asking about. 'A good one?'

'I thought so.'

'Mourning the loss of a woman's hell, but mourning the loss of a beautiful woman's the medieval torture chamber of hell.'

'Mourning the loss of a dead woman's even worse, maybe. But sometimes it's easier, I'm sure.'

Wegener looked up.

Brendel zipped up his suit. 'When we call the forensics team we'll tell them to bring a pair of bolt-cutters. For the padlock on the barrier.'

'I'll let Frank know.'

'Martin, it's important to me that you believe me.' Brendel was still fiddling with his zip. Wegener pulled on a pair of gloves. 'I didn't read your surveillance reports. And I don't want you to think I read them.' Brendel's eyes caught Wegener's for a second, then they both turned away towards the path.

The juddering came closer, getting louder, birds screeched and a white Phobos II with red racing stripes appeared behind the trees, jolting up to the fork in the track and braking sharply.

Wegener and Brendel stood motionless.

The car stared at them with its round double headlights. The sun reflected off the front windscreen.

Then there was a crunching of gears. The reverse gear howled. The wheels spun. Dust gathered underneath the car and dispersed between the tree trunks in seconds, like a small beige mushroom cloud.

16

THE MECKLENBURG DIRT TASTED EARTHY AND BITTER, stinging in his eyes, turning into a dust-dry pump that sucked the air out of his lungs, creeping into every nook and cranny – his ears, his nose, every pore. Wegener saw Brendel's running white suit ahead of him, a bizarre mixture of an astronaut and an Olympic sprinter, the bent arms racing back and forth to the beat of his gait. He saw his own legs, two plastic sausages flying forwards and folding backwards, hammering alternately into the dull sandy ground like unfit clappers on a completely useless machine. The reverse gear of the fleeing Phobos screamed in his head, intensified to the shrillest of all sounds. Brendel's white suit moved in the growing dust cloud as if in a bubble of dirt: a long-distance runner on a desert planet, a space sheriff in a sandstorm, fighting desperately and yet with no chance of reaching the finishing line.

Wegener felt his stomach cramping, his lungs stinging, the white plastic sausages beneath his torso going numb with effort, those

wobbly tubes gambling away their last strength, growing lame, refus-
ing to work. Let the capitalist legs do overtime, you can bet these
East German thighs aren't going to, we've reached our daily target
and it's time to knock off now, we don't give a shit.

Brendel disappeared around the bend and Wegener slowed down.
Stopped and bent over. Realized he was losing his balance. His shoulder sank into the sandy track like it was a duvet, he felt fir needles
pricking his cheek, the resin scent was back all of a sudden, the ear-
splitting panting was his own ear-splitting panting, he wasn't breathing
air any more, he was breathing dirt, the dirt was inside him, in his
stomach, in his veins, he was completely saturated, a gasping Mecklenburg maggot just about to collapse.

Then it all came vomiting out of him. A big warm gush. And
another big warm gush. Wegener tasted milky coffee, stomach acid,
fir cones, sand, mushrooms, earth. A third gush rose up and splashed
out of his mouth, weaker this time, hitting his face, running stinking
down his chin.

He lay on his back and coughed. His eyes were watering. Or perhaps he was crying. From all the effort. From all the confinement.
From all the missing Karolina. I know this, thought Wegener, that I
have to be weak to get even weaker. That just a little bit of sadness
can trigger a big sadness. That I have to cry over something, anything,
so I can cry over Karolina. That I wish she'd see me lying here like
this, so weak, so lost, so misery-stricken, so I could at least get the
stale tenderness of pity, at least a regretful look that might bear a
certain resemblance to the loving, admiring look of the old days, that
I might confuse for a second with that old-days look even though it'd
really be only the degenerate, asocial cousin of that former loving
look, but I'd rather have the degenerate, asocial cousin than nothing
at all.

Wegener suddenly knew he'd never be with Karolina again. Perhaps he'd needed the cloud of dust to see clearly. It's all over, long since over, it'll never come back again, said the cloud. Karolina wouldn't ever think of you if *she* was lying on the ground gasping somewhere, said the cloud. You'd always think of her, but she wouldn't ever think of you. Karolina would think of someone else. And if there wasn't anyone else, at a pinch she'd think of nothing at all. Just so she wouldn't have to think of you.

You're dead, said the cloud, wake up and smell the coffee, you're dead to her. You know the truth really. You're the one who always wants to know the truth and you know this truth here, but you don't want to admit it so you don't care. Go ahead. But if you ignore the truth you don't have to know it. Then you don't give a shit about the truth. And if you don't give a shit about it you can leave it alone. Either you care about the truth or you don't. But then you're not allowed to make a distinction. Then you can't not care about the truth in private and care about the truth at work. The truth's the truth. The truth is the thing you can't change. The truth is the facts. It's your job to find out the facts. Even the facts where you're concerned. Close the Karolina Enders file, case concluded, the guilty party is the inspector himself, the witness is cleared of all responsibility for the failure of the relationship. There's no punishment for the guilty party, though. Having ruined the relationship all on his own and now lying crying and vomiting on a forest path in Mecklenburg-Western Pomerania is punishment enough.

At some point the dust cleared. At some point the coughing stopped. At some point Brendel was standing above him, a sandman merely shaking his head and saying nothing. Wegener felt as if the sandman had just beaten him.

* * *

'Hello?'

'Dr Braun?'

'Who's speaking please?'

'Martin Wegener, Köpenick People's Police, Criminal Investigation Department. Do you have a minute to spare for me?'

'Well, I've got two minutes. But not much more.'

'Dr Braun, I was in your building the other day . . . '

'Ms Enders' visitor.'

'That's right. I heard I caused a bit of a fuss.'

'Well, it was a visit with a police badge.'

'Old detective habit. It was just a private matter.'

'Ms Enders mentioned that. We had a little chat about it.'

'I hope I didn't cause any trouble.'

'Well, there was some confusion. We're in the middle of preparing for the consultations, and some of the staff seem to have overreacted slightly.'

'I can imagine.'

'Mr Borgs has straightened it all out. A colleague of yours. He came to see Dr Moss this morning.'

'Yes, on an investigative matter.'

'Well, that's all sorted out then. Mr Wegener – '

'Dr Braun, thanks for your time.'

'Goodbye.'

Wegener hung up. Karolina's boss was a stupid idiot, no doubt about it. Probably a double-chinned monster. An obese, over-correct energy bureaucrat. Maybe a Stasi informer. Maybe not. Maybe both Karolina's bosses were Stasi informers. Dr Braun and Dr Moss. And the first doctor didn't know what the second doctor was up to. Both doctors permanently working towards the same end and yet still up against each other. Doctoring around with their colleagues' private matters. Suspecting each other. Each hiding documents that the other doctor had to look for. Doing everything twice over. Thinking up red herrings and dead ends, each of them constantly being led in the wrong direction and leading the Stasi in the wrong direction with the other doctor's red herrings and dead ends, because they passed on everything unfiltered, because that meant a never-ending supply of half-truths and fictions ending up on the desks of some overworked Stasi agents who got contradictory information from a thousand sources, who had everything in the end, the facts and every conceivable fantastical variant on the facts, who were gold prospectors up to their necks in a river of information and had to watch out they weren't swept off their feet by all the tapes and copies and notes and photos and evaluations.

What a lot of hard graft, thought Wegener. What a hard-grafting state. A state with no proper toilet paper but hundreds of well-paid archivists of all that obsolete chaos.

There was a knock.

Wegener's office door was open before he had time to respond. In came a sweat-soaked shirt, Frankenstein peering out of the collar in torment. His cardboard Mephistopheles haircut had suffered severely over the past few hours.

'Nothing. We might as well forget it.'

Wegener put his legs up on his desk, realizing too late that he'd turned into an imitation of Borgs.

'If you'd at least got part of the registration number.' Frankenstein wiped a sleeve across his moist forehead. 'But just a white Phobos II, what am I supposed to do with that?'

'A white Phobos II with red racing stripes.'

'All right, with red racing stripes. By the time you two called in he was long past Rostock, dragging his racing stripes behind him.'

'I told you there was no phone reception.'

Frankenstein pulled a chair up to the desk and sat down. 'We've had another close look at the maps. There's another access road to the hut. From the other side, if you like. The Navo didn't show it because it's not a proper road, just an agricultural road.'

'And the track we parked on isn't an agricultural road, or what?'

'Don't ask me. The road, or whatever it is, splits into two. Pretty much in the middle of the bend is the hut. But the left-hand curve is an *agricultural road*, according to the map. And the right-hand one's called a *private access road*. The *private access road* is in the Navo, the *agricultural road* isn't. So the Phobos came via the agricultural road and that obviously doesn't have a barrier. Never mind, forget it. Lienecke just called, they've finished with the hut. Nothing there.'

'No surprises there, then.'

'It's not looking too good for us.'

'True.'

'I heard Brendel wants to leave. Now of all times.'

'Just for the day. He has to report back to Bonn. They called him in, there's nothing he can do.'

Frankenstein looked sceptical. 'Hoffmann would've made a good Speckmann. The perfect secret-monger. His workmates from Wandlitz refused to believe he wasn't a gardener and his name wasn't Emil.'

'Maybe he was really the head of the Stasi and his name really was Emil,' said Wegener. 'Anything's possible in this country. But that's the good thing over here: it never gets boring, things always take a turn for the unexpected.'

'Speaking of unexpected turns, have you taken a look at the explosion site? They must have very big gas pipes up at the Palace.'

'I was just going to head over there.'

Frankenstein moved towards the door. 'There's something else I want to ask you.'

'Go ahead. You don't usually ask for permission to ask me things.'

Frankenstein attempted to repair his damaged hairdo with one hand. 'Do you trust them?'

'Brendel and Kayser?'

'Yes.'

Wegener dropped his legs off the desk. 'Frank, I've pretty much given up trusting people. I don't even know how any more. I hear what they say, and it seems sensible and useful and all that, I have no reason to doubt either of them. But if you told me you were digging a tunnel and you'd be in the West by next month, I wouldn't tell either Brendel or Kayser. Just because you can never be 100 per cent sure. You know that and I know that.'

'But you'd give them 99 per cent.'

'89 per cent. Top marks. You wouldn't?'

Frankenstein had finished with his hair. 'I just noticed you were on first-name terms with Brendel.'

Wegener smiled. 'You think that's an expression of trust?'

'You don't?'

'No. I think it makes it easier to talk about breaching trust later on. It sounds better in the familiar form. *You fucked me over from the very beginning, Richard* doesn't sound as dumb as *You fucked me over from the very beginning, Mr Brendel.*'

'Well, at least your cynicism's still in good shape,' said Frankenstein as he left the room, closing the door behind him.

I'd tell you about the plan, Karolina, thought Wegener, if Frankie decided to dig his way over to West Berlin, I'd confess all to you if

I'd strung Fischer-Hoffmann up on his pipeline with my own two hands, I'd tell you everything, I'd even tell you that I still love you with no regard for the consequences, that I still think of you when I'm turning in, when I'm tossing off, when I'm frying up, because everything that makes me Martin Wegener was easier to bear with you than with anyone else. Against my will, against my intentions, against all my principles, I'd let you know that you can fall back on me your whole life long, like an old abandoned cardigan that was one day not good enough, that maybe really was a bit itchy and that's now waiting patiently at the bottom of a drawer. I'm your forget-me-not, my de-energized energy angel. The things we take our leave of get more and more beautiful as time goes by, they blossom in old age, that's their subtle trick, they're suddenly there again and instantly irresistible because they show you a familiar face in a world that seems like a new foreign country every day, they're a signal of the homeland, they offer an opportunity to go back in the midst of thousands of forwards, and your lifelong, personal stubborn cardigan is me, Karolina, and I promise you I'll always be that stubborn cardigan for you, I'll warm you when you need it and I'll keep going as best I can, but there's one thing you have to tell me so I can do it: Why did you lie to me yesterday for the first time ever?

Wegener picked up his Minsk, opened up a *TM*, wrote *I have to see you – radical trust in radical times* and pressed Send.

Then he stared at his office wall. There were two cracks in the wall. One crack ran from the top right to the bottom left. The other from the top left to the centre of the wall. Together, the two cracks formed a Y. He suddenly couldn't take his eyes off the Y. His eyes could rest on that Y, staring at that Y he could rest himself, forget the whole lot of them for a while, from Frankenstein to Braun, from

Brendel to Borgs, including the never-ending questions that other people asked him and he asked himself, that lifelong search for answers and then for new answers and then for even newer answers and so on and so forth.

When his Minsk vibrated to announce a *TM* a few minutes later, he savoured the feeling of not having to look and knowing the answer anyway.

17

WEGENER LISTENED INSIDE HIMSELF, checking whether he felt anything. Perhaps satisfaction. Or scorn. Or something as obscure as tickled national pride. But there was nothing there. Nothing hurt, pricked at him, formed anything tangible. He stared at the huge gold mirrored facade with the house-sized hole in it with the same emotionless gaze as at the Y-shaped crack in his office wall not long before.

The Technical Brigade floodlights cast dazzling dots upon the golden wall, long fragments of glass were carried away by black dwarves, brightly reflecting the brigade lights over and over as if they wanted to drive all of Berlin crazy with belated SOS signals. Tip-up trucks were piled high with chunks of concrete, scraps of mesh gratings and bent pipes. Remains of a titanic invalid. A crane swayed its bony arm high above the Palace of the Republic, crossing the bright pillars of the dome of light, which extended into the dark blue sky as if nothing had happened.

Wegener headed for the barrier and ducked into the mute crowd of gaffers, which had not grown smaller in the past thirty-six hours, and didn't shrink during the night either, surrounding the damaged Palace like a shocked sect around its defiled temple. There was a holy commandment of silence in the crowd. Everything had long since been said here, every line of the news reports quoted too often, everyone was all conjectured out and had nothing more to say. Wegener pushed his way past men and women of all ages, a representative delegation of the entire nation. If not a hole in the Wall then at least a hole in the Palace, and what a whopper too. *Guess the size of the crater*, silent fun for all the East German family, ideal for ages 9 to 99.

The old men were still wearing their ushankas, the old ladies head-scarves and woolly hats; anything as long as it covered their heads, covered their backs in case state bankruptcy did fall from the sky after all. The young generation still hadn't grown tired of pale imitation denim and fake baseball caps, all the punks looked just as stupid as thirty years ago with their misguided hedgehog haircuts, with their desperate desire not to look as bourgeois as their parents; nothing and no one had changed: studded leather jackets, white tennis socks in slip-ons and sandals, nylon dresses and plastic jackets with imitation fur collars. Wegener realized he was a fully paid up member of the gang. The representative of the cord trousers faction. There was no ignoring that any more, here and now. He'd got caught in his own trap by mingling with the crowd.

His cynicism was no use to him now, nor his police rank, nor his belief that he was infinitely superior to the dumb regime with its nanny state methods, its carrot contingents and stick committees. Nor his image of himself as a scornful observer, a critical, invulnerable mind that could never be caught out because he decided for himself what affected him and what didn't. The regime's lying to you, thought Wegener, your people are lying to you, you're lying to your-self. You're a lying son of a lie. You can't even trust Martin Wegener. You're like the tubby old lady in front of you, like the peach-fuzzed teenage rebel next to you, like the spotty, pointy-titted girl behind you – a cog in the machine, a nameless number, a ten-figure file code, a random inmate of a state-sized disempowerment prison, and there isn't really the slightest reason to see yourself as anything better, anything more independent.

Wegener suddenly saw that everyone standing here thought the same way as he did. That everyone took themselves out of the equa-tion, privately pronounced themselves a smiling outsider, a mental non-citizen who had escaped in their mind, swimming across the Spree or the Baltic and now living in the West, in Mindtown, Freedom County.

Everyone standing here, the entire republic, every single individual had long since made the break, had taken their leave of the fatherland, the homeland, the dream of a just society, everyone around him had gone West into mental exile a long time ago, had been walking around the potholed, greasy, grubby, crumbling streets of Berlin with their heads vacant, merely physically present, modern-day golems, dumb comrades on command with the only thing at the top of their hollow heads their fur hats, felt caps and headscarves. The country's empty, thought Wegener. We're a ghost state.

A man next to him had taken his Minsk out of his coat pocket and was holding it in front of himself at stomach level. It was an M7, Wegener noted, so the man or his wife must work for the Stasi, the government or Robotron Electronics. A loading progress bar filled the screen, then a still photo of Angelika Unterlauf's face appeared, twitched, opened its mouth and grinned motionlessly at the camera, and then the real-time transmission was loaded and started up at a low volume: *decided today to significantly simplify and accelerate the naturalization procedure for immigrants to the GDR from the Federal Republic of Germany . . .*

Unterlauf's head froze for a moment but her voice continued: *objective is to deal more quickly with the rising number of immigration applications, a spokesman for the Politburo commented. Assistance is to be provided for those West Germans who hope to enrich the GDR's socialist society with their labour, their solidarity and their ideas, to exchange nationality quickly and simply within the time limits. At the same time, the Politburo has both tightened the immigration selection process and raised the welcome payment for new citizens from West Germany from the current 850 marks to 1,000 marks as of 1 January 2012.*

Unterlauf's head twitched, wobbled and stood still: *applies to all citizens of the Federal Republic of Germany born from 1970 on who can prove either long-term involvement in left-wing politics – such as in the current case of the popular immigrant and political activist Horst Streicher – or a violation of their human dignity by the capitalist system. The next news programme is at 11:15 with Andrea Kiewel.*

The East German flag now fluttered on the display. The man in the coat didn't switch off. The first few bars of the national anthem sounded. Wegener looked up. The Technical Brigade had trained its floodlights on the Palace as the choir kicked in: *From the ruins risen newly.* Thin blue flashes from welding machines flickered out of the black explosion hole, steam rose, then a loud metallic screech, and the huge, soot-stained GDR coat of arms dropped away, dangling on thick steel cables below the arm of the crane as the man in the coat clicked the national anthem to full volume and the choir surged. *Triumph over bygone sorrow, can in unity be won* – the black garland of corn with the hammer and compasses floated in front of the floodlit golden wall, swaying slightly to and fro, then there was a jerk and the coat of arms rose slowly heavenwards, followed by the spotlights – *German youth, for whom the striving of our people is at one.*

Wegener noticed that the whole army of golems was now singing along, without exception, the entire Marx-Engels-Platz was rolling off Johannes R. Becher's lyrics, having long since drowned out the Minsk choir, belting out line after line into the darkness, bellowing after the hammer, compasses and corn as they rose ever higher, the old men, the punks, the lost souls, the winners in life, the pointy-titted girls, the spies, the spied-upon, all singing at the top of their lungs as they stared at the Berlin sky, where the coat of arms was now hanging between the pillars of the dome of light like a risen fire victim and was finally swung back metre by metre by the crane and vanished into the night.

A chill ran down Wegener's spine. He knew he'd never believed the gas leak story – *you are Germany's reviving, and over our Germany, there is radiant sun* – and now they were spreading the next huge lie right here and now and covering up the truth, and the entire obedient nation was standing like a bleating flock of sheep right in front of the shiny golden fibs and not noticing, just carrying on and walking on and singing on regardless as usual, just like me, thought Wegener, *and over our Germany, there is radiant sun, there is radiant sun . . .*

'You have a pretty unhealthy lifestyle.'

'Oh yeah?' Karolina didn't look particularly surprised. 'That currywurst on Thursday was your idea.'

'It was a double currywurst,' said Wegener.

'If you say so.'

'And now a large Wart-Burger with bacon and two small Branden-Burgers. That's no fault of mine.'

'Think yourself lucky I didn't take the special offer Magde-Burger as well.' Karolina turned to face the counter. 'If only they'd bring the damn stuff, I'm so hungry I'm falling off my chair. Anyway, there's fresh rocket on the Wart-Burger. Rocket's good for you.'

'The rocket's in the mayonnaise, probably one leaf per Wart-Burger, if not less.'

'Rubbish.' Karolina pointed at an illuminated ad showing an idealized burger in a bun resting on a bed of leaves. The top half of the bun had jolly cartoon eyes and two slices of cheese bent into a yellow smile. 'It says there: Get me now with fresh rocket!'

'With a little asterisk.'

'Martin, my little asterisk.' Karolina showed her immaculate white teeth. 'Just shut up, OK? What's the matter anyway?'

Wegener took a deep breath.

'Come on, out with it.'

'Let me just say first of all: I'm really sorry.'

'Carry on.'

'I went to the graveyard last night.'

'Yes?'

'I called you and you weren't at home.'

'Yes?'

Wegener felt himself blushing.

Karolina looked at him. 'You're kidding, right?'

'Kidding about what?'

'You saw there was a light on in my flat.'

Wegener evaded Karolina's eyes and examined the ad. The Wart-Burger beamed at him. Next to it hung a portrait of the Buletto founder S. Seifer. He was grinning even wider than his burger.

'I'm disappointed in you.'

'I'm sorry. I told you already.'

'Martin! I forgot to turn the living room light off in the morning! When you called I was sitting at my desk in the ministry! The taxi came at eleven, I got home at ten to twelve and saw that I'd left the light on all day. I know, I'm not setting a very good example for someone who works in the Energy Ministry. Any more questions?'

You absolute idiot, said Früchtl's voice.

How doubly beautiful she is when she gets really angry, thought Wegener. And I'm the number 1 mistruster, Josef, look what you've made of me.

You should be glad you're number 1 at anything, said Früchtl.

Karolina shook her head. 'And why should I have to explain anything to you anyway?'

'It was a coincidence, Karo. I have to go down your road to get to the station, and then there was a light in your window.'

Karolina stared at her plastic tray. Wegener took her hand.

'Have you kept your promise?' Karolina closed her eyes. She looked as if she already knew the answer.

'No,' said Wegener, 'I haven't, because I do everything wrong that I possibly can do wrong, because I have a bloody thankless job to do, and if I'm unlucky or politics rears its head or whatever, then things happen that I can't control.'

Karolina pursed her lips.

'Karo.'

'Martin. We're sitting here on a Sunday night in a Buletto restaurant, all because I forgot to turn the light off in my own flat. I'm worried about you. It's none of my business any more, but someone has to tell you: you've changed since Früchtl disappeared. You're seeing ghosts. I don't know how else to put it. Sometimes I think you're going paranoid.'

'Sometimes I think I already am.'

'Your irony doesn't help matters.'

'That was cynicism.'

'An East German who wins a round-the-world trip on West German TV, that's cynicism.'

'No, that's irony.'

'There's nothing worse,' said Karolina, 'than an uneducated know-all.'

'Don't be so hard on yourself, Karo.'

'Two Branden-Burgers, one Wart-Burger with cheese?' The bum-fluffed young man acted as if he hadn't heard anything.

'They're for me,' said Karolina. 'Is there fresh rocket on the Wart-Burger?'

'There's rocket in the mayonnaise.'

'Only in the mayonnaise?'

'It says so on all the posters.'

'What do you see over there on that stupid poster?'

Bum-fluff puffed out his chest. 'A cheese Wart-Burger in a salad decoration. But that's just a serving suggestion.'

'Then serve me the damn thing just like that.'

'I'm sorry, I can't do that.'

'So you mean *you're* suggesting to *me* that *I* serve this Wart-Burger like that *myself*?'

'The advertisement says—'

'Get me now with fresh rocket,' said Karolina. 'That's what it says.'

'The asterisked text explains that—'

'What does the asterisk explain, can you tell me that? I haven't got my electron microscope with me, I'm afraid.'

'That the cheese is analogue cheese,' said Wegener, 'that the meat is only 25 per cent beef, that the vegetable fats may contain traces of bacon, and that the buns are produced with sugar substitute products made in the socialist world. My money's on Cuba.'

Bum-fluff gave an unhappy nod.

'Oh, forget it.' Karolina waved a hand. 'But don't you dare tell me to enjoy my meal.'

Bum-fluff made like a banana and split.

'Looks like I'm not totally paranoid after all,' said Wegener.

'Semi-paranoid is even worse, you asterisk expert. What'll be next?' Karolina unwrapped one of the Branden-Burgers, eyed it sceptically and took a bite. 'Will you at least talk to me about it?'

'Who else can I talk to?'

Karolina chewed and swallowed. 'Of course the thing with Josef was a shock. It's absolutely normal for you to look for an explanation. But the explanation doesn't consist of a conspiracy behind every light left on by accident.'

'It's my job to spot conspiracies behind lights left on,' said Wegener.

'Then switch off your job mode after 6 p.m.'

'Right, I've got that lever on my back.'

'Josef gone and then our separation. All at the same time.' Karolina put the half-eaten burger back on the tray. 'You couldn't deal with it, Martin. You still can't deal with it.'

How tough she's got, thought Wegener, how radical, how pitiless.

I've always been into ice-cool Amazons, said Früchtl. *What could be more sexy than a victorious, brutally pretty alpha female for you to throw yourself on her mercy, Martin, to do what she will with you – rough you up, love you up, play you up, your own private dominatrix. The thrill of submission is incredibly undervalued, you know. How many generations have dreamt of finally being enslaved by a juicy young lady dictator instead of yet another dried-up old man of a tyrant . . .*

Josef. Please.

'It was easier for me. I had you to be stark raving mad at,' said Karolina.

'We both know who the guilty party is.'

'Post-traumatic stress disorder. Ever heard of it?'

'Sure. I wake up with it every morning.'

'You've lost your faith in your fellow human beings.' Karolina grabbed hold of his hair so hard it hurt. Her hand slipped down to his cheek, stroked him for ten seconds, then lowered to the table. 'That's what your problem is.'

Wegener felt this brutally tender Karolina touch stopping him in his tracks. He wanted to answer but he didn't know what.

Karolina looked him in the eye. 'Go and see a doctor.' Wegener stared at Karolina. 'I mean it. What's the last delusion that went through your head? I mean after you suspected I'd go to the effort of categorically lying to you about my whereabouts?'

'I never said you were lying to me.'

'Yes you did, of course you did.'

Wegener shrugged. Voices were raised at the sales counter. Bum-fluff was arguing with several agitated customers, who kept pointing at the special-offer monitors.

'More poor fools who fell for the rocket trick,' said Wegener.

'Don't change the subject,' said Karolina. 'Tell me. What else is going through your sick mind?'

Bum-fluff pressed frantically at a remote control until the burgers vanished from the screens and the evening news appeared, Michael Illner looking at the camera in confusion, to one side and back at the camera.

'If I tell you that you'll have me put away.'

'Martin.' Karolina shook her head. She picked up the remains of her Branden-Burger and put it in her mouth.

'I've just explained . . . '

Now pictures of the Palace of the Republic flickered across the screens. The sound was suddenly far too loud, far too hysterical. *The spokesman for the Berlin Police President officially stated that the explosion that caused considerable damage to the Palace of the Republic and the People's Chamber yesterday morning was not, as previously assumed, due to a defective gas valve, but an act of terrorism.*

Karolina choked. Coughing, she turned to the counter.

In early comments, members of the Politburo were overwhelmed and appalled by the idea that the terrorism that has plagued the imperialist world for years should now have spread to our republic.

Wegener had got up and was patting Karolina on the back. Her cough intensified, punctuated by frantic attempts to breathe, greedy, helpless gasps for air, a beautiful red fish torn cruelly on an invisible fishing line from the warm waters of the South Seas and suddenly finding herself on the rocky dry land of reality.

The Buletto customers streamed silently towards the monitors.

There has been no news as yet on any claims of responsibility. The Interior Ministry has imposed an immediate information blackout so as not to compromise the investigations. At an initial press conference, the police spokesman assured the press that the authorities responsible are doing all they can to clarify the background to this cowardly attack. The police have not yet answered the question of whether the so-called Bürger Brigade, an illegal grouping known for sending threatening letters in the past, may be involved in the bombing.

Karolina's coughing calmed down. She looked at Wegener out of wet eyes, then she retched, arched her back and vomited the Brandenburger in an elegant curve onto the black and white tiled Buletto floor. Chewed mixed meat product, mashed bun with Cuban sugar substitutes, chunks of analogue cheese, bacon fat and stomach acid splashed against the chair legs, the table legs and Wegener.

Wegener held onto Karolina from behind, stroking her head, kissing her scented helmet of hair as she spat, cramped up and spat again. A long thread of saliva dangled from her lips and swayed, unbroken, beneath her twitching face.

You're wrong, you bloody Mecklenburg dust cloud, thought Wegener, Karolina thinks of me when she vomits too, we both think of each other when we vomit, no matter if it's on agricultural roads or in fast-food restaurants, we stick together even when times are hard, even when living-room lights are left on and Früchtls vanish and Bürger bombs go off, not even a separation can separate us because we're Martin and Karolina, the socialist version of the classic couple that *has* to be unhappy because only frustrated emotions can get really major, because happy endings are boring to us, there's no tragedy to them, because it's not sensational sex or lifelong fidelity or marvellous matrimony that are the highest level of relationship-consciousness in this damn state, it's a shared past, the knowledge of what to expect, the avoidance of any further surprise, the security of knowing your future disappointments in advance.

'The last delusion that went through my sick mind,' Wegener whispered into the delightful little ear peeking out of the red hair directly in front of his mouth, 'the last delusion actually tried to persuade me that the explosion in the Palace was really a bomb . . .'

Karolina's retching had died down to a whimper.

MONDAY 24 OCTOBER 2011

18

BLÜHDORN'S BULKY FIGURE SLUMPED OVER THE LECTERN, his head sank onto his broad chest, the shiny round circle of skin on top of his semi-bald pate now staring into the lecture theatre like Cosmos-Kali, the eyeless alien from the Margon Mineral Water ad: a skin-coloured sphere with no sensory organs whatsoever, a grey, shorn garland around its non-existent face.

The imploring bearish voice leaking softly out of the ceiling speakers and filling the room like sticky acoustic syrup couldn't possibly come from this dramatic lump, who had just been yelling and shouting for the past hour, by the end as red as a lobster, dripping sweat and gesticulating wildly to the frozen student body who were getting smaller and smaller on their folding wooden seats.

. . . and that's why, my dear comrades, it's down to you. It's always been down to you for the past sixty years. We, the other, western Germany, we sinned against you, we took the wrong path, back then at a time when no one knew what was wrong and what was right.

You may judge us for that. But judge us with the open hearts of brothers and sisters who can forgive. Judge us as a family of one German people that stand by one another at the end of the day, no matter what has happened. Because there is no alternative to the family. Because there is no alternative to the German people. Because the loss of the German people would mean a total loss of everything for all of us. Never lose sight of the fact that it was a historical co-incidence that separated us into different camps. We could have been you – and you could have been us.

There's no changing the facts. We have no influence over the past, no matter how much we wish we had. But the future is in our hands with every second. In your hands! If you turn your backs on social-ism, then the desperation, the faith and the suffering of your fathers and grandfathers, mothers and grandmothers were for naught, then decades of socialist struggle were in vain, and believe me, even though I was fighting that battle on the other side of the border, I know how hard and self-sacrificing that struggle was for you and your families, what setbacks it brought with it, how much injustice and harassment you had to tolerate before Revitalization. And I know as well that you would have wished for faster changes over the past twenty years, more radical reforms, and that you are impatient and asking your-selves how much longer it will take before you can finally lead a life that offers all the freedoms we have allegedly enjoyed for so long in the West.

But don't be deceived. We Westerners are the true slaves of the last six decades, we are the nation that is not free, that is oppressed. We may be allowed to travel, we can buy whatever we want, of course, a third BMW, a seventh watch, a fiftieth pair of Italian shoes – but at what price?

Don't believe that the majority of the people you envy are happy.

Don't believe that these people lead a fulfilled life, on the Majorcan beaches and in the shopping malls and in front of their enormous televisions that are just as shallow as everything they show, 55-inch mirrors of their lost souls, filled to the brim with brainless puppets like Mario Barth and Tine Wittler and Carmen Nebel, with American trash, cheap fast-food TV that combines consumption and excretion into a simultaneous process, shallow distraction from their own exist-ence as human junk, the self-imposed precursor to the Matrix.

These television zombies are the slaves of capital, in a constant search for more and then even more, obediently desiring what the advertising industry tells them to desire, at the price of their own freedom, prisoners in a hamster wheel of status symbols and vicarious satisfaction.

They pile up debt, they are incapable of harnessing their greed, addicts and victims of superficiality, and that might all be acceptable, it might all fall under the autarchy of the individual who has a right to make himself unhappy, but, dear comrades: I have lived in that madhouse, not because I wanted that madhouse, but because I wanted to change it, and I have seen a thousand times over what capitalism does to people – it dulls their senses, it sucks out the pea-sized remains of their brains and puts possessions, the same tat over and over again, the crude god Mammon in place of what really counts. It kills all compassion, all consciousness of justice, every wish for true values, it even kills decency – and with that it ultimately kills the people themselves.

It's not the millionaire who helps his poverty-stricken neighbour, it's the poverty-stricken neighbour who helps the millionaire when in need. While the millionaires don't even help their own. Because they're all greedy, blind egomaniacs who want nothing more than to make love to the money slot of their cash machines. Because the suffering of the poor has long become abstract for the millionaires, too far off to understand: the cares of another species, the problems of an alien planet. Mammon makes individuals into brain-dead androids who consider the others brain-dead androids. Is there aught we hold in common with the greedy parasite, Who would lash us into serfdom and would crush us with his might? wrote Chaplin. There can only be solidarity for like with like. We may wish it were not so, but it is so and it will never be any other way.

And that is why we need socialism. Not because we are so averse to freedom that we would not grant all the idiots their idiocy, the waste of the only life they possess. Go ahead, we call to them with joy and hope, double-quick, drive yourselves out of your tiny minds, rob yourselves of your dignity, your future, your lives, you uncultured egomaniacs, you animals with a minimum of speech, you ridiculous collections of organs: the faster the intellectual precariat uses up its specialized cells, the faster death will come to release you all, kill you, turn you into tiny piles of biomass for us to use for more warmth than you gave your fellow human beings during your lifetime.

It is not out of pity that we fight for the poor souls, as the even poorer superstitious believers do, but because the stupidity of the stupid affects us all! Because that stupidity drills a hole in our German boat and drags us all down to the dark depths of a bestial, futile existence of no value. Because it makes the society we want to live in impossible. For that society is only possible as a whole or not at all, it can only exist with the participation of every single individual – or it is doomed to failure.

That's why we get involved. That's why we allow ourselves a value judgement on the lives of our fellow citizens, that's why we call for them to change their behaviour, that's why we have to face the con-sequences when they want to sabotage our project. Capitalism in

West Germany has produced hundreds of thousands – millions – of these homunculi. Their priests bear the names Oliver Geissen and Andy Borg, their saints are Tommy Hilfiger and Steve Jobs, their lives are free of care and therefore devoid of care for humanity, they fight only for themselves and their sinecures, they have never done anything for a fellow human being, they have never been humanists for a second.

All they want is to enjoy material benefits and be entertained as they do so, a chicken leg in their mouths and a mistress in their arms tickling their scrotum with a peacock feather, they are fat, tired animals, cocker spaniels in the land of Cockaigne, who would enable the next rule of Fascism at any time because the suffering of their own history has grown as alien to them in their comfortable degeneracy as they have become alienated from the origins of their race.

And there are those who have awoken. They have dragged themselves by their own hair out of the slime of dehumanization and idiocy, they have dared to open their eyes and to help others to open their eyes in turn. They have made the Swabian wheelchair-user Wolfgang Schäuble pack his doctored coffers and put him into a retirement home, they have voted for the old, new, honourable party and after years of effort finally made Oskar Lafontaine chancellor, a man who did not strive for that office out of pure will to power like all the others, not one of the vain, narcissistic men who want only to hear their own voice on the television and at party conferences, who have the image of their face plastered everywhere so that they can look themselves in the eye when they drive around the country, because they think their eyes are the most beautiful in the republic, because they can't get enough of their own visages.

Oskar Lafontaine, ladies and gentlemen, has remained a decent man. And that decent man has shaken the West Germans awake.

Firstly by sending out a signal through the realignment of the Social Democratic Party: the established powers will change nothing here! Then by involving the people in his politics, occupying autobahns and airports, blocking the infrastructure, mobilizing the masses, halving the banks, electrifying the political proletariat, pestering the government, forcing them to rethink, to breathe new life into the dried-up corpse of democracy – for thankfully we, the thinking workers and those who think like workers, are still in the majority, even in the West.

It was us who took Lafontaine from 2.6 per cent in 2003 to 18.3 per cent in 2007 to 33.1 per cent in 2011. It was us who took the first step towards overcoming capitalism; but, my dear comrades, it was only the first step. The road to our goal is endlessly long, the corruption in our republic is tougher than steel, the change of an established economic system is a long and difficult task with many setbacks, and it calls for all our perseverance. At the moment Lafontaine is still reliant on the coalition with Claudia Roth and her Jacks in the Green, blocking important decisions, emblazoning justice on their manifesto but struggling to keep their word when they ought to put it into action. Our progress is fragile.

And that's why you are so important. We in the West need a country to look up to. Lafontaine has to offer his people a shining example. On the stony path that lies before him, he has to be able to point a finger at your tenacity, he has to have the chance to ask the people in the West: You want to give up already, and your brothers and sisters in the East have kept going for sixty-two years? If you throw in the towel you will throw it for us too. Then all of Germany will throw socialism – and with it the life's work of generations of upright socialists and communists – into the waste disposal unit, and then the nay-sayers will crow even louder: 'The socialist idea does not work, you can see that it has failed, does the GDR still exist or not?'

You are our life insurance policy. And we are yours: via currency payments, transit agreements, economic aid. We need each other. And we can learn from each other. Let us continue improving socialism, let us wipe out the last mistakes, let us complete the historical task begun after World War Two – and that still means: never again Fascism, never again war, instead equal rights, social justice, peace and – at last, my dear comrades – at last true freedom!

Blühdorn raised his head and his fleshy red face stared out at the audience, who now began to clap hesitantly, then louder and louder until they were applauding with enthusiasm.

Wegener took a look at his Minsk, which was in front of him on the folded-down miniature desk. The display was lit up. *Frank Stein sent you a TM: Please call back! Met cleaning lady, girl in photo is Hoffmann's daughter: Marie Schütz!* The students' clapping got louder and louder. Then they rose to their feet, still applauding. A wild standing ovation broke out, flushing Blühdorn out of the lecture theatre and not stopping even when he'd gone.

Wegener looked over at Kayser. He was slumped on his folding seat with his mouth half open, snoring.

'Was it very painful for him?'

Blühdorn had taken off his soaked shirt and was sitting on a stool bare-chested. His belly was a bloated medicine ball that curved over his thighs. The dark hair on the ball grew together in the middle of his belly into a black seam, which crept down around his navel to his waistband. In the cold light of the meeting room, the man turned into a dripping gorilla, the fur on his back running riot over his shoulders like an unmowed lawn. Wegener saw tufts of nose-hair, tufts of ear-hair, tufts of finger-hair, a dark thicket that made him want to fire up a flamethrower to singe it all off. Sweat dripped from Blühdorn's forehead onto his elegant leather shoes and the grey lino floor.

'We're assuming he died instantly,' said Wegener. 'Like an execution. Just as brutal but just as quick too.'

Blühdorn nodded.

Wegener gave him a few seconds. 'The two of you were friends?'

Blühdorn simply kept nodding. 'We were. But that's a long time ago now.'

'Did you have a fight?' asked Kayser.

Blühdorn glanced up. His fleshy face looked amused. 'No, why? Albert emigrated to the GDR and I always admired him for that. We were in regular contact by post, even after Revitalization. Until Moss closed the Wall again. After that Albert isolated himself completely.'

'From you as well?'

'From everyone, as far as I know.'

'When did you last hear from him?'

Blühdorn shrugged a hairy shoulder. 'Probably a Christmas letter in 1991 or so. You can't find many people to tell you about Albert, am I right? I thought as much.'

'How would you describe him?'

The fleshy face smiled. 'Intelligent. Determined. Far-sighted. Cool-headed. Educated. Courageous. The most convinced socialist I've ever known. And the most convinced freedom fighter.'

'Maybe you should have married him,' said Kayser.

'We'd have looked like Laurel and Hardy,' Blühdorn smiled again. 'What's a West German officer like you doing behind the Wall?'

'What's a West German doctor doing here?'

'You'd know that if you'd stayed awake in my lecture.' Blühdorn wiped the sweat off his brow with his balled-up shirt. 'I've got eagle eyes, my good sir. I can even see the future.'

'You see socialism and you mistake it for the future,' said Kayser. 'There's a difference.'

Blühdorn struggled to his feet, stood as upright as he was able and waddled over to the table where his case was. 'Albert was the genius of Heidelberg. He couldn't just analyse politics in retrospect, they can all do that. Albert put a name to mistaken decisions before they were even made. As clear as day. And he was almost always right.'

'Because he was cleverer than the others?'

'He was certainly cleverer.' Blühdorn stuffed his sweat-soaked shirt in a plastic bag and took a clean one out of his case. 'But there were two other things he was, more importantly: a great humanist and a great strategist. Do you understand what I mean? That mixture? He knew what people wanted because he could think like them. And he knew what you had to do to give the people what they wanted, because he calculated on a multidimensional level and never disregarded anything just because it might not fit at first glance. He adapted his theory to the facts, not the facts to the theory. Until everything was right. You'll be a long time looking for another academic who's so true to himself.'

'Dr Blühdorn.' Kayser sat down on a shabby chair. 'If Albert Hoffmann had been an oracle he'd still be alive right now.'

'You think so? I'd reckoned with him dying much longer ago.'

Wegener took the now unoccupied stool.

Blühdorn's eyes searched the bare room for another chair but didn't find one. 'People who represent new political ideas always live dangerously in single-party dictatorships. Albert didn't come over here back then because he didn't have a comfortable enough life in the West, as you can well imagine. He wanted to get involved, get in on the act, prove his skills. He didn't want to practise follow-up political science any more, he didn't want to play the retrospective wise guy, he wanted praxis, progress, facts, he wanted to democratize socialism. In the years before Revitalization he was Hans-Walter Moss's closest political companion.'

'He was one of many advisors,' said Wegener.

Blühdorn's fleshy face grew scornful. 'Where do you get your information from, Inspector? From the State Security?'

'We wish,' said Kayser.

Wegener switched his Minsk to the dictate function and looked at the mountain of flesh. Blühdorn had heaved his considerable backside onto the table and was now enthroned there like Buddha. The clean shirt was still in his hand. This Buddha wasn't a man to bluff, you could see that. He knew he was their first real source.

'Is there anything else you want to know?' asked the source.

'How did Hoffmann get from a West German professor to an East German political strategist?'

'His publications on Posteritatism caused a huge wave of interest in the late seventies. Including in the GDR. Someone from Humboldt University recommended him to an undersecretary of state at the Politburo, he had a contact made, and Moss fetched him over here at the beginning of the eighties.'

'As a kind of special advisor?'

'Officially as a professor of Marxism-Leninism. Unofficially as his personal strategist, integrated into the advisory staff.'

'And what exactly was Hoffmann's job?'

'The future of the GDR. The future of socialism.'

'So what we're going through today,' said Kayser.

Blühdorn didn't bat an eyelid. 'You wouldn't recognize what we're going through today if Albert Hoffmann had still been advising Hans-Walter Moss after 1991.'

'So why did he give it up?' asked Wegener.

'Moss wasn't the right man for Hoffmann's visions. He went along with it to begin with. But then he ran out of courage and the politician came out in him. The never-ending fear for his power. No wonder – before Albert, Hans-Walter had only had inferior mentors.'

'What visions do you mean?'

Blühdorn raised his eyebrows. 'What visions? All the visions! Do you think Moss has ever had the slightest idea of how to get the GDR even a millimetre out of the shit creek that Ulbricht and Stangier and all the other brain-dead old codgers steered it into? Albert's most important project was opening up the Wall. I told you, he thought like the people. And he knew that socialism can never work if you lock the people in. You can lead a horse to water but you can't make it drink. How do you bring up your children? Do you threaten to ground them to make them eat their greens, or do you promise them an extra hour's TV? Those ancient cretins of East German politicians propagate a beatific, ultra-just state and then they shoot their own people in the back when they see things differently – what kind of historic crock of shit is that? How could any one of them assume for even a second that something like that would work for longer than an instant of history?

'Albert knew what image was all about, even in 1970. He knew that a new state model needs as good a reputation as possible to cover up its practical weaknesses, especially during its teething troubles. Even the name: German Democratic Republic! Countries that call themselves democratic never are – have you noticed that? In marketing terms, the GDR was light years behind the Third Reich. A lying, corrupt and unjust state, which didn't even have the imagination and far-sightedness to cover up its own crimes.'

'So it was Hoffmann's idea to open up the Wall in 1990?' asked an incredulous Wegener.

'Of course!' Blühdorn slid off the table and started putting on his tent-sized shirt. 'And he knew from the very beginning what it meant: a mass exodus to start with. Down from 16.67 million to 14.3 million, or less than 14 according to the toughest calculations.'

'And then Moss closed it up again because he got scared it was a belly flop,' said Kayser.

Blühdorn nodded, buttoning up his shirt in silence. He suddenly looked years older. The black fabric flopped around his meaty body like a Batman cape. The loudspeaker of socialism was suddenly no longer a muscleman, just a sad, furry bundle of lard, his medicine-ball belly bloated by failed political dreams that he couldn't digest.

Wegener wouldn't have believed it possible in the lecture theatre, but now he felt rather sorry for Blühdorn. He could put on a sterling show behind a lectern, he could play the class-war hero, carry a crowd on a wave of enthusiasm, but he himself was long since hollowed out and weak in the face of so much failure, stuffed with hundreds and thousands of wilted illusions.

'It would've been *the* historical chance,' said Blühdorn. His voice was surprisingly firm. 'Albert had written down the future for Moss and his Politburo, a 200-page manifesto. It was called *Plan D*. Open the borders, successively reduce the State Security, refrain from political restrictions and censorship, introduce real parliamentarianism. That's Posteritatism, that's what Albert worked on his whole life long: the social justice of communism coupled with the democratic, liberal and rule-of-law qualities of Western market economies. Sure, how's it supposed to work, who's going to finance it and so on – but that was exactly Albert's genius, his prophetism coupled with strategy, he'd have managed it if only history had given him the chance.

'Read *Plan D*, if the government hasn't thrown it away: investment in environmentally friendly technologies, recruitment of socialist-leaning scientists from the capitalist countries, development into a green welfare state over forty years, world leader in the production of electric drives, hydrogen drives, wind power, solar cells. Social justice through environmental justice, ecology plus economy – it wasn't the Greens who came up with that vision, it was Hoffmann! The GDR could be all that today. The Socialist Ecological Republic of Germany.'

'SERG,' said Kayser. 'Sounds like a Scandinavian brand of crispbread.'

Wegener cleared his throat. 'Do you have any idea who might have killed Hoffmann?'

Blühdorn looked from Kayser to Wegener to the tips of his shoes. Then he shook his fleshy head sadly.

'Can you think of a possible motive? Could the murder be related to Hoffmann's work for Moss in some way?'

'Twenty years later? I don't believe a word of what it says in the *Spiegel*. Nobody does in West Germany, by the way.'

'Stasi Murdering Again,' said Kayser.

'Ridiculous!' Blühdorn stuffed his shirt into his trousers. 'A cheap secret-agent movie. It might have gone like that in 1990, perhaps. It'd have surprised me then, but perhaps not quite as much as now.'

'Did Hoffmann have access to confidential information back then?'

'You mean he found out about something back then and they string him up for it now? Twenty years later? He'd have to have seen photos of Josef Ackermann buggering Moss with a Good Delivery gold bar for that.'

'So you've got no explanation for the murder,' Kayser noted.

'I think the same as what you're presumably thinking,' said Blühdorn. 'That Albert was up to something over the past twenty years that he didn't let on to anyone about. And this time he might have miscalculated, for the first time. He got caught out. I always knew the Playmaker couldn't keep still for so long.'

'The who?'

'The Playmaker.' Blühdorn fished a red tie out of his case. 'That was his nickname at Heidelberg, after he came over here. The puppeteer, you see? The man in the background pulling all the strings, the one who says what goes on. A sweeper who leaves the goal-scoring to the other players.'

'You were just talking about Hoffmann's plans to make the GDR into a model state for regenerative energies,' said Kayser. 'The former Vice-Chancellor of the University of Heidelberg, Professor Dr Granz, has been chairing the supervisory board at GreenFAC for over ten years. Hoffmann was hanged from a gas pipeline only a few weeks before the key consultations on securing West Germany's energy supply. What does that tell you?'

'That you have no idea.' Blühdorn had wound the tie around his collar and his chubby hands were tying a Windsor knot with no need for him to look. 'Or you wouldn't bother me with such stupid questions. Albert and Granz knew each other, of course. But when *Plan D* was written Granz was still a long way from a job in the energy industry. Maybe the two of them did have some contact during the past two decades. But Albert was a nobody in the GDR after '91. If Granz had asked him for help, what could Albert have done for him? He was retired.'

'Maybe sabotage pipelines,' said Kayser. 'GreenFAC will suffer major losses under the new transit agreements. And Hoffmann would obviously have preferred to see the GDR as a socialist safari park than a transit country for cheap Russian gas. That might make for an alliance.'

'Take that to the *Spiegel*, I bet they'd print it.' Blühdorn pulled his tie tight and reached for his case. 'My plane leaves at two, and before that I have to go through four body scanners to give the girls of East Berlin a look at my hairy balls. You need to hurry up with your questions.'

'I've only got one more.' Wegener switched off the dictation function and put his Minsk in his trouser pocket. 'Who else can give us more information about Hoffmann and his advisory work, apart from Moss?'

'The State Security.'

'Thanks a lot,' said Kayser, 'but Central Department VIII is drinking sangria out of buckets on a collective trip to Cuba. Anyone else?'

'Nobody I know. Get yourself an appointment with Egon, I'm sure he'll free up half an hour for his old hanged buddy.'

'What about Hoffmann's daughter?' asked Wegener.

Blühdorn froze. 'His daughter?'

'You didn't know he had a daughter?'

'What daughter?' Blühdorn looked pale all of a sudden. 'Who on earth is Albert supposed to have had a daughter with?'

'We don't know that either.'

Blühdorn shook his head. 'Rubbish. I don't believe it.'

'Wegener, show him the *TM*,' said Kayser.

'What's a *TM* supposed to prove?' Blühdorn looked angry now. 'You can leave your phone where it is. If Albert had a daughter I'd know about her.'

'Let's change the subject then,' said Kayser. 'Did Hoffmann have any political companions in the GDR that you know of? Friends? Relatives?'

Blühdorn stared at Kayser. 'Jesus, just get hold of his file! You can bet the Stasi had their eyes on him back then, it'll list every Tom, Dick and Harry Albert rang up from '83 to '91!'

'Great tip, thanks.'

Wegener's Minsk rang. Number withheld.

Kayser took a notebook out of his jacket pocket. 'Then we'd like your address in Heidelberg and all the phone numbers where we can get hold of you, Dr Blühdorn.'

'I'll give you my card.' Blühdorn sounded exhausted. The Minsk was still ringing.

Wegener pressed Answer. 'Hello?'

'Pankow, in one hour.'

'Where exactly?'

'Do you know the funny farm in Berlin-Buch?'

'I do.'

'Take the U85 road towards Blankenfelde, past the funny farm on your right, then after two kilometres you get to the Horst Sindermann Workshops for the Disabled POC, a brown prefab.'

'OK.'

'Directly after that there's a small turn-off on the right, with a sign saying *Universe Car Recycling.*'

'Right.'

'Follow the road and drive onto the premises, just keep going straight ahead and you'll automatically get to the scrap-metal press. I'll be waiting there.'

Blühdorn had handed Kayser a business card and picked up his case.

'I'm not coming alone,' said Wegener. 'An officer from West Germany will be with me.'

'Are you serious?'

'Absolutely.'

Kayser put the card away in his notebook.

'Good. That's perfect.'

'See you in an hour then,' said Wegener and hung up.

Blühdorn waved a hairy paw in farewell and then steamrollered out of the room.

'There he stomps,' said Kayser, 'back for a few more turns in his hamster wheel of status symbols.'

19

VOSS STEERED THE VOLVO MUTELY through the afternoon rush hour on Friedrichstrasse. Phoboses and Wartburgs crept along at walking pace, the deep-frying aroma from hundreds of juddering oil engines wafting through the jammed canyon between the buildings, a greasy smog turning East Berlin into the largest and most decrepit chip shop in the Socialist Union. Behind the windscreens were tough everyday faces, emptied heads, an army of traffic zombies changing gear, accelerating and braking.

On the leather back seat of the Volvo, Wegener felt like a member of the Politburo, to his left MP Kayser, behind the wheel the MP's chauffeur Voss; all that was missing was the motorcycle cavalcade and the two hammer-and-compasses flags on the bonnet. Through the tinted windows, the cracked turn-of-the-century facades with their open plaster wounds looked even gloomier than usual. So this is how the party leadership sees our country, thought Wegener: through dark glass that makes everything even worse than it already is. They ought to make the windows of bigwigs' cars rose-tinted, with a pretty contortion effect that raises the corners of pedestrians' mouths.

'There's no point in blaming ourselves,' said Kayser. 'The horse has bolted and been shot. None of us could have guessed that the cutie was his daughter; even Blühdorn didn't seem to know about her. And the two of them were obviously still the best of friends when she was born.'

'I'd say the horse has bolted and gone to ground,' said Wegener.

'Let's look at it like this: it wouldn't have happened if that bitch Wischinsky had let us have Hoffmann's file. She can get us Hoffmann's third cousin's glasses prescription at the touch of a button, if she wants to. But she doesn't.'

Wegener shrugged. 'I can hear Kallweit's ranting now. First we don't find out anything at all, and then it takes us days to sort out even the victim's basic family circumstances. He won't dare to go to the Central Committee with that, he'll lie awake at night and get a stomach ulcer or have half a heart attack, and it'll be all our fault.'

'If we're lucky he'll have a whole one. And what have we got coming now in Pankow?'

'Certainly a busybody, that's for sure. Maybe a busybody who knows something.'

'That'd be a real private Nuremberg Rally for me, with a torchlight parade and a speech from the Führer, if someone around here knew anything. I still don't understand why we have to drive out to the back of beyond for it, though.'

'Where does the FIS meet its anonymous informers? In the middle of Marienplatz in Munich?'

Kayser pressed several buttons on his phone and inserted a hands-free headset bud into his ear. 'This is Christian. Yes, I'll wait.'

Voss drove hooting past the gasping snake of cars curving from the Rosneft fuel station onto Jägerstrasse. A Vietnamese man was fly-posting at the edge of the road. *The Blockbuster of the East is here: Antonia Hiegemann and Peter Sodann in* RED REVENGE – *at a cinema near you from 28 October!* Someone hooted back. Two beer bellies were arguing at the front fuel pump, one with a canister in his hand, the other in sandals, over rapeseed oil for 32 pfennigs per litre. Voss scratched at his groin. At least he didn't smell today. Wegener closed his eyes. He didn't want to see any of it.

'Yes, Christian. Get Jens to send me a complete list of calls – mobile, landline, second mobile, work line, everything you've got – but never mind the crap with the judge's permission, we'll get that later if we need it. If they make trouble threaten them with the Chancellery. What? No, today.'

Wegener felt his Minsk vibrating in his trouser pocket. He pulled it out just far enough to see the display, which was switched to Mute – *Karolina Office calling* – then he pushed it back as deep as he could and closed his eyes. The vibration alarm tickled the inside of his left thigh.

'I know that too. No, I don't care. There's a guy sitting there, all he has to do is enter some number or other and then he gets a file, prints it out and faxes it to you. All done and dusted.'

Karolina, you're making my balls dance, thought Wegener. In the old days your hands did that trick, your dextrous, beautiful little hands with the elegant scratchy nails, and now you need a Minsk, a number combination and a couple of radio masts, but you can still do it.

'It's a matter of five minutes. And I want the guy to start right after lunch.'

You don't know anything about it, but we're having telephone sex right this minute, thought Wegener. Actually you ought to be talking to your boss about some transit agreement emergency plan crap, your thoughts are floating in the midst of an Uzbek natural gas supply, turning in circles, your mind's anywhere but on me, but your call is twitching only three centimetres away from my dick, you've got your ear right against my balls while I creep across Berlin on Swedish leather, and if I pressed the green button you'd hear how they're throbbing, how you're spurring them on, how you're kissing them awake, how they've missed you and your mouth, your stubborn Karolina tickle in my groin, we've missed it so much that words fail us.

'Right. Werner Blühdorn. Doctor. Grüner Weg 55, Heidelberg. I don't know. The last twelve months. And please go through them for calls to the GDR. Yes, to me. I'll call this evening about GreenFAC.'

Wegener pulled his coat over his lap so Kayser couldn't see his erection. The vibrating had stopped. From outside, Phobos engines juddered their chip-pan exhausts into the Volvo's ventilation. Voss had free rein now and speeded up, the car leaning into the curves and nobody speaking.

Kiddo, it was more personal in the old days, thought Wegener.

'Incredible.' Kayser grinned.

'What do you mean?'

'There's actually a sun in this state.'

Wegener looked out of the window. Low fields with hedges, bushes and fences. The occasional meadow planted with fruit trees, motionless horse silhouettes. In the background a toy tractor creeping across neatly combed earth. To go with it cloudless, ice-blue sky, a bright light that made green and brown and pale yellow possible. No grey, thought Wegener: that's unusual.

'You ought to wear more bright colours,' said a jolly Kayser. 'Not always that dark cord of yours.'

'Yes, dear,' said Wegener, 'perhaps you can send me over something elegant.'

'Give me your sizes and I will.'

'33 waist, 45 shoes. Easy to remember – very German numbers.'

Kayser grunted in agreement.

The road bent into a slight left curve, crossing a few hundred metres of sparse coniferous woods full of ferns and mossy rocks. Now the sun's rays caught the Volvo and broke through the windscreen, making the worn red leather shine bright and suddenly putting Wegener into an unexpected good mood, the atmosphere of an exciting excursion, a foolish impulse to sing out loud.

The asphalt road surface came to an end, giving way to an unpaved area full of potholes. Voss slowed down and taxied straight ahead to an open iron gate with eroded corrugated metal walls jutting into the landscape on either side of it.

'Wow,' said Kayser, leaning forward.

Behind the corrugated metal barrier, a skyline of piled Trabant corpses darkened the cheerful sky, a never-ending, roughly bricked phenoplast fortress rising and falling in square-edged waves, seemingly extending to the horizon and staring out at its visitors from a thousand blind headlight eyes. The mobile GDR of the first half of my life, thought Wegener, dumped here and forgotten for ever. Perhaps ours is here too, our beloved Hannibal, presumably right in the middle somewhere.

Voss drove through the gate and was now on the main boulevard of Wreck City. On either side, winding side roads engulfed by house-high blocks of junk branched off every fifty metres, snaking away and producing block by block a weather-beaten colony of Trabis,

constructed from decades of automotive output, dirt and rust concealing the remains of the faded pastel paint jobs that had coloured the
streets of East Germany for half a century: baby blue, linden green,
sand yellow, ochre.

'Do you know this place?' Kayser stared in amazement out of one
side window, then the other.

'No, never seen it,' said Wegener, 'never heard of it.'

Kayser turned and watched the barred gate getting smaller and
smaller in the rear window, turned back again, looked along the
perfectly straight main thoroughfare and shook his head in disbelief.
'They're all here. Absolutely all of them.'

'Sir,' said an unmoved Voss, 'there's no end to it.'

'There is an end,' said Wegener: 'everything comes to an end some
time, Voss, I'll bet you the new clothes Emperor Kayser's planning to
send me straight from the Bread & Butter fashion trade fair.'

'Yes, siree.' Kayser was still astounded.

After a kilometre or so they could tell Wegener was right, and
another five hundred metres ahead the boulevard ended in an enormous square, framed by wonky rust-heap walls. In the middle were
two monstrous scrap-metal presses, which seemed to have broken
down on their first day in action: a handful of cubed Trabis were
scattered around as if someone had been practising on the machines
and then given up again straight away. Maybe nobody knew how to
operate the things properly, thought Wegener, they got bought off the
Russians and put straight into retirement. Now young birch trees
grew up between the cubes, transforming the plaza into a strange
mausoleum for long-lost childhoods on long-forgotten back seats.

Voss stopped the Volvo indecisively in the middle of the square.
All three of them got out, looked around and took in the bizarre
backdrop. Kayser took photos on his phone. They must be eight or

nine metres high, these car-body walls, thought Wegener, if not more. He took his Minsk out of his pocket, clicked into Transnet, selected the location function and watched the satellite photo building up bit by bit: dark squares appeared, divided by pale lines, in the centre a circle marking the spot where the three of them were standing. Around them was the chaotic web of countless paths, link roads and cul-de-sacs. A scrap-metal Rome, photographed from far above but not one bit easier to grasp.

I ought to bring Karolina here, thought Wegener, and show her this monument to transience so all the dead Trabis remind her how little time we have left, how fast our daily lives in the now become a cruel yesterday while we're in free fall, the ground in sight, closing our eyes to the crash-landing.

A piercing sound burst the silence.

Voss gave a jerk and moved like a panicked Robotron robot that's just received several conflicting commands at once.

Kayser stood still, shielding his eyes from the sun with both hands and keeping a lookout.

Feedback, thought Wegener and turned in a circle looking for its source. The same sound as in the World Hall, just much louder.

The painful sound stopped as suddenly as it had started.

'Mr Wegener,' said a metallic voice via loudspeaker. 'Thank you for coming. The same goes for your companions.'

Wegener looked at Kayser. He nodded towards the right-hand scrap press.

'Where are you?' called Wegener.

'In the background for the moment,' said the loudspeaker voice. 'I wanted to speak to you in person but right now I don't intend to show myself. Hence the rather unusual situation. I hope you'll excuse me, but at least you can understand everything I have to say.'

'Why are you hiding?'

'There's no need to shout, I've installed a directional microphone.'

'Right. Why are you hiding?'

'To guarantee mutual independence. I'll permit myself to set out a few conditions. If you fulfil my conditions I'll cooperate with you, and if you don't I'll take my leave.'

'What's your name?'

A genuine laugh from the speakers. 'That's the least of our concerns at the moment.'

'You used to work here, didn't you?'

'Very good, Detective, that's right. That means you could spend days searching the premises and never find me.'

'I don't feel like looking for you,' called Wegener. 'What have you got to offer and what are your conditions?'

There was a click. Some kind of setting had been changed, and now the loudspeaker voice blared across the square from a different direction, sounding even tinnier: 'In return for my statement on the murder of Albert Hoffmann, I demand a personal witness protection programme. Safe conduct to the West. A simple, fair exchange, I think. So it's all the better that you've got a gentleman from the Federal Republic with you.'

Kayser moved towards Wegener. 'Either the guy's sick,' he said quietly, 'or we've hit the jackpot hiding in a rusty old Trabant.'

'I can't promise anyone witness protection,' said Wegener just as quietly, 'and certainly not a ticket to West Germany.'

'He's no idiot. Be honest with him, let's see what he comes up with.'

Wegener looked in the direction where the voice had last come from. One Trabant after another, all with the same sad radiator face. 'That's not easy,' he called. 'An emigration application can only be granted by the Central Committee after a State Security check; it's the result of a complicated procedure. We'd have to hear your statement first. How do you imagine that would work?'

'It's perfectly simple,' said the loudspeaker voice. 'Just ask your gentleman from the West to make a phone call. If I'm informed rightly, your current investigation has a certain significance for the future of both Germanies. I'm sure they'll be glad to make an exception.'

'But we can't sort it all out right now!'

'Oh, yes you can. The public prosecution office sends an LBVD by Virtual Post Procedure, ensuring me immunity from prosecution and adoption into the witness protection programme if I make a statement on the Hoffmann case. I receive the necessary emigration papers by the same route. And don't worry, you won't be helping a murderer escape – I haven't killed anyone.'

'If we're supposed to set such a complex process in motion, we need to know at least something about what you have to offer.'

Click. Back to the first loudspeaker: 'I can't tell you who exactly killed Hoffmann. But I do know what interest group is behind it. And I can tell you another important witness.'

'Who we'll have to find first of all.'

'He's easy enough to find, he's behind bars already.'

Wegener hesitated. 'Were you there when Hoffmann was murdered?'

'No. But I know the killers' context, as I said.'

'It's all a bit vague for a free ticket to paradise, don't you think?'

The voice from the speaker sounded amused. 'It's news to me that West Germany's paradise.'

'It's certainly more of a paradise than this junkyard.'

'Without my help, your investigations will still be going round in circles in ten years' time. With my help, you can clear up the matter in the foreseeable future. It's up to you to decide how much that's worth to you.'

'What would be the address for the LBVD?'

'It's very easy to remember, I set it up specially: lasthope@socialism. gdr. And just so you don't misinterpret the situation: you're being filmed by a video camera, which is streaming our conversation to a protected server, and a friend is monitoring the server. The LBVD will automatically be forwarded to that friend as well. If you decide to accept my conditions you ought to mean business, otherwise I'll make the whole lot of you into the next big Transnet scandal.'

Shade. The sun had disappeared behind a cloud.

'Bloody hi-tech,' said Kayser.

Wegener looked around. 'Call Brendel, tell him to make sure Bonn puts on the pressure at the highest level. That'll be quicker than if I try to get the bureaucracy moving over here through Borgs.'

'What's an LBVD?'

'A Legally Binding Virtual Document. An electronic certificate.'

Kayser nodded, dialled and strolled towards the boulevard with his phone up to his ear.

'You're trying,' the loudspeaker voice noted. 'Good.'

'We could have discussed all this on the telephone,' called Wegener. 'Why all the fuss?'

'I'm in a bit of a rush, Mr Wegener. This setting helps you to understand that time is humankind's most valuable asset. And junk-yards don't get listened in to, unlike telephone lines. Except by me.'

A loud click. The loudspeaker was off.

Kayser was standing on the boulevard, speaking into his phone as he checked out his surroundings. He walked over to the nearest block of cars, casually knocked on one of the phenoplast bonnets, listened to his telephone and spoke.

Voss leaned motionless against the Volvo.

A slight wind wafted through the ghost town, sending swarms of mustard-coloured chunks of foam chasing through the dirt, eternally durable remains of seat padding that now led exciting lives of their own. The sun was back again. Tiny fragments of glass flashed everywhere in the Trabant backdrop, as though someone had sprinkled sugar over this gigantic work of art. Wegener sat down on one of the scrap cubes and panned his eyes slowly across the towers of cars. Not the slightest motion.

After five minutes, Kayser came back and sat down next to him. 'We're in luck, Brendel's with them right now. The Chancellery's informed Moss's office, and they're contacting the Interior Ministry now. But Brendel needs a name to get an emigration application granted at high speed.'

A loud crackle. 'Have the LBVD made out for Ronny Gruber,' said the loudspeaker. 'Ronny with a Y.'

'He seems to have a good microphone.' Kayser shook his head and typed a text message into his phone.

'The game's on,' said Wegener loudly. 'I think you can come out now.'

'As soon as I get the LBVD.'

'How many Trabants are stored here?'

'Good question. Half a million, I'd say.'

'And are they going to be scrapped?'

'Not worth it. Look at this place as a symbol of our country, Detective Wegener, and then you'll be able to answer any further questions yourself.'

'If that's the case I'd say our country will still be standing in a hundred years.'

'Stangier quotes are always a blast,' said the loudspeaker voice with dry sarcasm. 'You're right, phenoplast never rusts, only the supporting structures. But I think you'll agree that it's not necessarily going to get any prettier around here.'

'Not unless you like it morbid.'

'I prefer it lively.'

'You're part of the Bürger Brigade,' said Wegener.

The voice laughed. 'It took a while for that penny to drop. The present tense is incorrect, though, otherwise we wouldn't be here.'

'Right. Past tense. You *were* part of it. And why did you leave?'

'Can't you guess why I'd want to leave these days?'

'Because of the bomb.'

'I don't think much of bombs. They tend to leave large holes in our understanding. I see the LBVD's just arrived. I'll check it and then come over to you.' A short screech of feedback and the loudspeakers were dead.

Voss was sitting in the Volvo with the door open, listening to the radio, and the wind wafted the latest hit across the square, *No doubt, time hates love . . . No doubt, my darling, I hate time . . . Today we're still two turtle doves, but tomorrow that's not worth a dime, but tomorrow that's not worth a dime . . .*

That bloody crooner's following me everywhere, thought Wegener. If I'd just fallen in love I wouldn't even hear the crap: even if I bought the CD and shoved it in my CD player not one sound would come out of the speakers, not one syllable, because happy people don't have an ear for kitschy misery like that, they can't even perceive it, it makes no impression on them, the stuff comes to nothing, echoes unheard, but as soon as you're suffering from the usual big female chill, loss of trust and thrill, from Karolina's lack of suffering, from her repulsive, inviolable satisfaction with things the way they've turned out and are set to stay for ever and ever, as soon as you join the club of the everyday unhappy, from that moment on a million glands are activated in your inner ear that attract all that musical cheese, that locate and amplify those pathos-laden dirges and brand the crappiest and most banal lines onto your brain, *No doubt, time hates love . . . No doubt, my darling, I hate time* – and all of a sudden those lines come across as irrefutable truths, like singalong philosophy.

The entire world, your own exorbitant misery, it all dissolves into some stupid rhyme, becomes explicable by some logical juvenile formula that brings tears to your eyes, the dumber the lyrics the stronger the tears flow, *Today we're still two turtle doves, but tomorrow that's not worth a dime, but tomorrow that's not worth a dime,* that's exactly the way it is, all of a sudden banality turns to realization, yes of course time hates love, it doesn't leave anything of love, it uses it all up, wears it down, implants the tiniest mutant emotions that go on dividing, spreading, running wild and changing love, hardening it, winding it up and making it curdle, making it something completely different to what it originally was, perhaps tolerance, perhaps numbness, perhaps indifference.

And suddenly Martin and Karolina, who sixteen months ago were skinny-dipping in the Wannsee Lake and then eating overripe strawberries on a tartan blanket, lying closely entwined on the grass, smelling the summer, smelling each other, touching, admiring each other, each thinking the other just as immortal as themselves, as that tender moment, as that scent of grass and smoke and the slowly drying beads of lake on their skin – suddenly these two, who did, really did, belong together like no one else ever belonged together, suddenly they've turned into a black and white picture postcard, a vague possibility that it might have been that way, on that day, at that hour, and even if it was that way it'll certainly never be like that again, and that's why time hates love, thought Wegener, and that's why I hate time, and that's why I'm humming along to this awful song and that's why Kayser's looking at me as if I'm one wreck short of a junkyard.

A low crunching sound.

The two men turned at the same moment.

A wiry young man wearing glasses and black clothes was walking towards them from the direction of the main boulevard. Wegener had to admit he'd thought the man was on the exact opposite side of the yard. The man was carrying a Nanotchev under one arm and gave a friendly nod.

'Thanks very much for all your efforts, and welcome to a historical moment in time. By far the fastest-granted emigration application in the history of the GDR, enabled by an efficient cooperation born of the spirit of understanding between East and West. You should be proud of yourselves, gentlemen.'

'The pleasure's all ours.'

'Ronny Gruber,' said the wiry man.

'Kayser,' said Kayser.

'Wegener,' said Wegener. No one extended a hand.

'The documents have really arrived.' Gruber lit a cigarette. There was a headset dangling around his neck. A short dark haircut, hard features. Fast-moving eyes behind square lenses. 'And they're real as well.'

Gruber inhaled deeply and blew out smoke. Then he sank down onto one of the cubes and leaned over, resting his thin arms on his thin thighs and breathing as if he'd just run a marathon.

'So?' asked Kayser.

Gruber closed his eyes. 'You want to hear my statement?'

'You'll be picked up by a special C5 unit in half an hour, to take you across the border before midnight. We don't want the whole country to know how easy it is to get out. So, let's get on with it.'

'The Bürger Brigade killed Hoffmann.'

A crow appeared in the sky, coming closer above the piles of scrap. It turned in three indecisive circles and then settled on a dented Trabant roof. From there, it eyeballed Voss as if he was a record-sized prey.

Oh Karo, thought Wegener, how I'd like to give you a good rogering by the Wannsee right now, with that unfaltering erection from earlier on, I'd make you a baby for us to bring up strictly by Früchtl's principles, a mini-citizen, far away from right-wing and left-wing lies and all this Stasi Brigade nonsense.

Wegener rubbed his eyes and forced himself to concentrate.

'Why?' asked Kayser.

'For two reasons. Hoffmann was in possession of highly explosive papers. State secrets. From his days on the advisory staff. That stuff must be incredibly important to Alexander Bürger, for some reason or other.'

'Did the killers get the papers from Hoffmann?'

'I can't answer that. I wasn't there by the Müggelsee.'

'And the witness you wanted to tell us about?'

'I'll send you a *TM* when I get to the West. Just a precautionary measure.'

Kayser sighed. 'What about the thing with the shoelaces?'

'That was just a sham. To pin the blame on the Stasi.'

'So it was all about preventing the consultations.'

'Right.' Gruber drew on his cigarette with his eyes closed. 'You could have thought of that yourselves, couldn't you?'

The crow decided Voss was one size too big for it and soared off.

'We'll wait for the C5 people now,' said Kayser, 'and we'll make sure you get a friendly reception. And just so you don't get bored during this part of the service, why don't you tell my colleague Mr Wegener a few details about the bomb in the Palace of the Republic? Have we got a deal?'

Gruber nodded.

Wegener watched the shreds of foam getting shoved around near his shoes. Every time he guessed what direction they'd be going in next, the wind made them do the opposite. Pale blue nail varnish – that's what Karolina had on her pretty little toes that day by the Wannsee. He heard Gruber talking as if from a distance.

20

EASTSIDE RESORT – THE WEST IN THE EAST. NUMBER 1 ALEXANDERPLATZ, BERLIN (E).

Wegener put the business card back down on the polished cherry-wood desk and reached for the contents list of the minibar – *2 cl Putin Vodka, only 9.20 euros/27.60 marks, 0.2 l Red Riding Hood Sparkling Wine medium dry, only 12.50 euros/37.50 marks, 0.33 l Radeberger Pilsner, only 7.40 euros/22.20 marks* – and then he laid the list aside and knelt down on the bright blue carpet, which was decorated every fifty centimetres with a golden yellow imitation of a royal crest, soft and mown short like the green of the Wandlitz golf course.

Wegener slumped onto his front. Buried both hands in the fluffy surface. Pressed one cheek firmly to the floor. Rubbed his face against the silky wool, to and fro. So that's how the East German girls felt when they got taken from behind in the Russian gas boys' and West German money men's penthouse suites. Humiliated and secure and fucked. Between cherry wood and brass. Shoved across the royal pile by a coked-up Russki or a blind-drunk Swabian. No risk of carpet burns thanks to the quality floor covering.

Wegener rolled onto his back. Almost more comfortable than his own bed. The ceiling was the creamiest-coloured of heavens, replete with white plaster mouldings and little light-bulb stars. Luxury lighting. Saffron-toned wallpaper. The same colour as the tachometer in a Mercedes: Egypt at sundown. A male voice in the corridor. The voice came nearer. I've never been so close to Egypt, thought Wegener and got to his feet.

The lock on the room door clicked and in came Kayser, his phone wedged between his ear and his shoulder. 'Maybe. And what did you tell him? Hmm. My wife would say the middle road is always deadly.' He waved a thin sheet of fax paper, pressed the fax into Wegener's hand and contorted his face into a wonky expression of triumph. 'In my suite, I get a pretty good signal up here. No, Richard flew over to Bonn this morning. Never mind. But I can have a look and see if there's anything lying around in his room.' Kayser shouldered open the connecting door to the next room and let it fall closed behind him with a bang. A plastic tag swayed from the brass handle: PLEASE DO NOT DISTURB, I'M DREAMING OF GLOBALIZATION.

Wegener scanned the fax:

O. T.: *Blühdorn, Werner; Grüner Weg 55, 69117 Heidelberg* (FRG)
O. P.: *24.10.10.–24.10.11.*
Foreign calls (selected: GDR) from landline:
Dt. Telekom; (Tel.: 06221–566 78 90; **Line owner:** *Ruprecht Karls University Heidelberg; Seminarstrasse 2, 69117 Heidelberg): Number 0*
Foreign calls (selected: GDR) from mobile network: O2–*Germany;*
(Tel.: 0176–13 22 487; Line owner: Blühdorn, Werner; Grüner Weg 55, 69117 Heidelberg): Number 0

Foreign calls (selected: GDR) from landline: *Dt. Telekom; (Tel.: 02171–334 23 00; Line owner: Blühdorn, Werner; Hoeningsweg 1, Leverkusen-Opladen): Number 4*

Itemized calls:
0037 / 0182 356 6 24 / 24.10.11. / 13:02 (24.73 euro)
0037 / 0182 356 6 24 / 24.08.09. / 3:52 (2.87 euro)
0037 / 590 560 0 / 23.08.09. / 14:08 (12.54 euro)
0037 / 0182 356 6 24 / 23.08.09. / 1:24 (1.09 euro)
0037 / 0182 356 6 24 / 22.08.09. / 2:56 (2.23 euro)

Line owner of itemized numbers called:
Tel. 0037 / 590 560 0 (fn) – Humboldt University, East Berlin; Unter den Linden 6, 1012 Berlin (East); (A-Tr.: Vice Chancellor's Office, Humboldt University, East Berlin)
Tel. 0037 / 0182 356 66 24(M) – Schütz, Marie; Ludwig-Renn-Strasse 32, 1046 Berlin (East)

My dear Marie Schütz, thought Wegener, if Uncle Blühdorn called you today at 13:02, five minutes after he told us he knew nothing about a daughter of Albert Hoffmann's, then there's a 99 per cent probability you're the Playmaker's baby.

He tapped the number into his Minsk. A dull dialling melody. A loud crackle. A computer-generated voice: *The subscriber of the number 0-1-8-2-3-5-6-6-6-2-4 is not available at the moment, you can ...* Wegener hung up. He copied the number into the *TM* section and wrote:

Dear Frau Schütz, I'd like to get hold of you before the State Security does. Best regards, Hauptmann Martin Wegener, People's Police Berlin, Köpenick CID

Then he pressed Send. The grainy envelope fluttered across his display, revolving 180 degrees as if it had been blown by a gust of wind, and vanished off the bottom of the screen. A line of text was overlaid: *Your message has been successfully sent to '01823566624'! Greetings from your Telemedia POC team.*

Wegener got up, shuffled across the cotton-wool carpet to the minibar, took the mini bottle of Red Riding Hood sparkling wine out of the cooler, tore off the thin skin of aluminium foil and unscrewed the cap. Then he reached for a glass from the shiny cherry-wood shelf next to the shiny cherry-wood desk, poured the foaming wine into it, fished the pack of Ültje peanuts out of the glass dish, kicked the door of the minibar closed with one foot, shuffled ten metres to the wall of sand-coloured curtains and drew the shiny material aside with two hefty tugs: a single window from floor to ceiling, soundproof double-glazing and below that Berlin, Alexanderplatz, an endless ocean of civilization in greyish-blue dusk, an urban oceanic trench with prefab reefs and concrete cliffs, full of schools of Phoboses, darting forward fitfully and then stopping, then darting on again, always in search of the fish in front of them with their glowing fourfold eyes, seeking out an asphalt road through the darkness. You aimless idiots, thought Wegener, you think you can move freely but if you take a single wrong turn you'll smash up against the glass wall of your aquarium.

Then he drank. The icy, bubbly wine scratched his throat, refreshing him, making him wide awake, fizzling out to a breath of scented steam. Wegener leaned his forehead against the cold windowpane and stared down. So that's how they felt, the West German businessmen, the EastSide foreigners for whom it was all just a trip to the zoo, dictatourism with the romantic kick of a safeguarded adventure – charge the danger to my credit card, one night in jail, honey, wish me luck. The detached house in Frankfurt, the yacht in Hamburg, the Porsche in Munich, the loft kitchen in Düsseldorf – it all looked much more attractive from East Berlin; the distance was a magnifying glass, making their possessions properly visible.

It was only the detachment that gave their own wealth a really impressive volume: returning home to all those assets was suddenly the most valuable thing of all. They could savour all they'd achieved in a new light now that they'd missed it for a day or so, the distance had brought them closer to it now they knew that no one in the whole of East Germany had a detached house, a yacht, a Porsche or a loft kitchen to call their own, that they possessed more than an entire nation, that back in Düsseldorf you could be the loft-kitchen king of the GDR, that it was only socialism that could give them back their joy in capitalism.

Wegener opened the second wine bottle, stuffed the salty Ültje nuts in his mouth and gave a patronizing smile down at the Alexanderplatz aquarium. For a couple of minutes he was Hard-Currency Helmut, a West German businessman, an industrialist, a steel trader or a chocolate-factory owner, enjoying the prospect of going home to the Federal Republic and therefore the view of the Democratic Republic, suddenly able to admire its exotic capital city, to value its shabby hugeness, its tasteless giganticness, moved by its anonymity and disfigurement, by its crusted-over scars, by the omnipresent patina of rust, moss, dirt and grease, breathing its scrappy delights through the double glazing of the EastSide facade, hearing the morbid heartbeat of screeching trains, rattling engines and the dull silence of television-tower-deep dives into the dark recesses of a crumbling metropolis, tasting the oily Phobos exhaust fumes between the crumbs of peanuts, even smelling the citrus-dust-floor-polish charm of the Stasi HQ entrance, the freshly mown grass of Marzahn, Karolina's artificial-flower Action deodorant.

Wegener smelled his whole country, the fusty mildew of the perspiring old buildings, the awkwardness of the frustrated youths, the self-destruction of the opposition activists, the porosity of the half-baked production units and Publicly Owned Companies, the self-aggrandizement of the state's self-presentation, the bitter-almond frustration of former fighters, the overpriced, soured West German cream in the Intershops, the iron mistrust of a people under surveillance, the greasy plastic jackets and fur collars of the old, the faint scent of Nautik soap, the resinous, cotton-reinforced phenoplast of the Phoboses, the nutty intimate cleansing lotion Yvette.

He smelled smoked pork, grilled chicken, Russian solyanka soup, Bino stock cubes, meat in aspic, potato dumplings, bottled peas, carrots and asparagus, Hungarian stewed peppers, the moist feet of young women in tan Esala nylon pantyhose, the fungus between their toes, the wet of their hairy armpits and fannies, he smelled the lardy bumcracks of the Politburo, the bland, stale omnipotence of the snoopers, the treacherous security of the workers and peasants, the verdigris of all the corroding bronze Lenins, the black-and-white pigeon droppings on the Palace of the Republic: he smelled the inevitable end that was coming slowly closer and yet was still so far away.

Wegener raised the miniature bottle to his lips, drank it in one, dropped it on the soft carpet and imagined for one moment what it would be like to jump down to Alexanderplatz from this height, a stylish head-first dive from the sixty-metre EastSide board, past the plasma mega-poster –

MAKING CAPITALISM OUT OF SOCIALISM IS LIKE MAKING EGGS
OUT OF AN OMELETTE

Margaret Thatcher

– past the lit-up Goldkrone sign, so at least the last advert in his life
would be for brandy, and then a continuous descent, the former
human being transformed into a pile of flesh and bones the moment
he hit the ground, gone for all time, one of those who didn't want to
play along any more and plunged to the depths of the city, the horrified
Wurst-Wilfried as his spectator, blood and brains no longer just in
his sausages but now also on his checked apron, on the glowing wires
of his hissing heating soldier, on his pale blue bistro van – covering
it all from top to bottom.

'My people believed Gruber.'

Wegener turned around. He watched Kayser's gaze slip down
from his face onto the peanut crumbs on his chin, the empty wine
glass in his hand, the Red Riding Hood bottle on the floor. 'I don't
know what to believe any more,' Wegener said.

'Me neither,' said Kayser. 'I'm getting the Federal Criminal Police
Office to run him through their computers, they've got all the data
from the state offices too.' He pressed a button on a remote control
and the flatscreen on the wall came to life, with a white-bearded
Sandman puppet flying above a pipeline in his plastic spaceship,
following the tube through an endless forest, smiling a frozen smile
inside his round transparent dome. Cotton-wool clouds against a blue
studio sky.

'I wonder how he'll like it in the West,' said Wegener.

'I wonder if he'll get there in one piece,' said Kayser, 'or in lots of
little ones.'

'Anything new on GreenFAC?'

'Small fry.' Kayser waved a piece of paper. 'It looks like they wanted to put pressure on the Chancellery in the run-up to the consultations. The biggest fish is Marie Hoffmann's number. So good old Dr Blühdorn really did lie to us, that cheeky lardarse. He not only knows the daughter, he goes and calls her up and all.'

'Marie Schütz,' said Wegener. 'Not Hoffmann. Maybe her mother's maiden name. Or she's married.'

'Have you tried her yet?'

'Mailbox. I sent her a *TM*.'

Kayser sat down on the bed. 'When Richard gets here in a moment I've got to go and see Stasi-Steinkühler with him. You know that, don't you?'

'I do now. What for?'

'I think it's about file access issues. They didn't tell us anything specific.'

'Then you can cable your bosses where we've hidden our state gold reserves.'

'We know that already. And you're meeting Borgs?'

Wegener nodded. 'Did Richard lose his wife?'

'Yes. But I don't know anything more than that. Must be a long time ago.'

'Have you got a wife, Kayser?'

Kayser didn't look surprised. 'I used to have one.'

'And?'

'Didn't work out. I traded her in for a self-cleaning wall-mounted electric cunt with real hair.'

'You're lucky people over there in the West.'

The Sandman had landed on a pier on the Baltic coast, climbed out of his transparent bubble, and now jumped off the pier into the water. He was gone for a moment, drowned, no air left in his wooden lungs, and then he popped up again out of the cellophane sea and gave a cheery wave at the camera.

21

'MERRY CHRISTMAS,' SAID THE BIG FAT POLICE SPIDER Borgs, who had squished himself into a tiny armchair in the corner of the foyer, with the back of his head against the windows so that he had a good eye on the whole of his web. At some point a CID man can't sit any differently, thought Wegener, at some point you start always sitting with your back to the glass wall, you always have to be the one who sees everyone and is seen by no one, on guard duty your whole life long, and in front of you on the wobbly coffee table a plate of—

'Green cabbage!' Borgs spooned a portion into his mouth and munched, chewed and swallowed.

Wegener looked around. The whole of the Cinema International was decorated with fir branches and fairy lights, there was a four-metre Christmas tree between the doors to the large hall, complete with a golden set of hammer-and-compasses on the top and oversized bullet casings hanging from its branches. In front of the tree were white felt snow and an ancient sleigh surrounded by rough cloth sacks with brightly wrapped parcels spilling out of them. Bored students in red-and-white camouflage outfits were attempting to attach bullet-hole stickers to the slanted wood of the wall panelling.

'*Red Revenge*,' said Borgs. 'The premiere's on the 28th. Thirty million marks' production costs. The GDR is a force to be reckoned with, Martin.'

'If you say so.'

Wegener pulled up another armchair and sat down. 'Are you going to see the film?'

Borgs' fat hands rubbed his pot belly. 'Any time a failed female politician hunts down Santa Claus, I'll be there. Especially if you've got Peter Sodann playing Santa and getting beheaded in the end with a rusty sickle from Stalin's private collection. Mind you, the *Neues Deutschland* writes –' Borgs the magician produced a previously invisible newspaper, which had obviously been jammed between his hip and the side of his seat, flicked through it, raised his index finger – '*Antonia Hiegemann drives the Coca-Cola-coloured symbol of capitalism to insanity through an orgiastic Kalashnikov concerto, although she would no doubt have managed the same feat without the use of weapons, merely with the aid of her merciless thespian talent, which could hold its own against any reindeer sleigh in the woodenness stakes.* And you'd think politicians were the born actors!'

'They are, they're just bad actors.' Wegener had opened up the special menu: Christmas stollen cake, goose drumsticks, hot sausages, potato salad, cinnamon star cookies, Silesian white pudding with lebkuchen gravy.

'Two mulled wines!' Borgs announced to a young, mousy-faced waitress squeezing her way behind him. The girl turned around, gave a harassed nod and dashed off to the bar. 'I feel a bit sorry for him, poor old St Nick. Everyone's always mean to fatties. I'm like his civilian doppelgänger.'

'Only you don't hand out presents.'

'Dropping hints, are we?' said Borgs. 'Be careful, son. I do give the odd gift now and then. It's just that the recipients don't usually notice.'

'I know, during the disciplinary proceedings, I know you—'

Borgs scythed off the end of the sentence with an energetic arm movement. 'They believe in Gruber over in the West. Maybe because they want to.'

'It'd certainly be nice, wouldn't it?' said Wegener. 'Takes the blame off the Stasi, the killers are as good as found and the consultations can take place. Kayser's sceptical. I haven't talked to Brendel yet.'

'And what do you think?'

'I think we have to check it out anyway. And as long as nothing's clear yet, we can carry on the same as before.'

Borgs stretched pleasurably in his too-small seat. 'If you had to make a bet on how the whole Hoffmann thing happened, could you decide what to put your money on?'

Wegener thought for a couple of seconds. 'No. It could be Gruber's telling the truth. Only, what are these papers the Brigade boys wanted from Hoffmann? Gruber claims not to know. Pretty sparse murder motive, if you ask me.'

'But the shoelaces suddenly make sense.'

'Or not at all. If I wanted to distract attention from myself I'd make damn sure all the clues point to me like flashing arrows.'

'Martin, Martin.' Borgs stared at the remains of his greens. 'You just don't like the State Security.'

'If the Stasi's not in on it I don't see why they have to hide the file from us.'

'Millard called Kallweit today.' Borgs was still stroking his belly.

'Yesterday, as well. They've got wind of the fact that Hoffmann had infiltrated the government quarter. And then the bomb. Suddenly things are happening here that used to be unthinkable. The gentlemen are getting scared. And those gentlemen's fear is the kind of fear that other people pay the bill for. I don't have to tell you that, but I'm telling you anyway.'

Mouse-face rammed two mugs of mulled wine down onto the table and held out her hand. Borgs counted coins into it. The waitress didn't move. There was a pale fuzz below her pointed nose and a ladder was nibbling its way into her grey tights. Borgs had finished paying, the money clinking into a leather purse.

Wegener waited until the girl was two tables away. 'Then maybe the gentlemen should ask their domestic intelligence service to provide the investigating officers with Albert Hoffmann's file.'

'And that's the trouble.' Borgs fished for his mug of mulled wine. 'These gentlemen want everything. The bull's already in the china shop but they want the porcelain to stay in one piece.'

'So we might as well forget about the file.'

Borgs took a sip and pulled a face.

'How's a man supposed to work if they hold back relevant information?' asked Wegener, picking up his mug and drinking a tiny mouthful. Lukewarm, sweetened paint-stripper with a clove dipped in it. 'We haven't made any mistakes so far. So I don't know . . .'

'What about Hoffmann's daughter?' Borgs' googly eyes floated above the brim of his mug.

'There was no indication that he had a daughter. It's only him registered at his Greifenhagener Strasse address, and only Fischer in Ludwig-Renn-Strasse. Before Blühdorn we didn't have a single witness who knew Hoffmann personally, we didn't find any documents. And this Marie's not called Hoffmann, she's called Schütz.'

'The photo of the girl on the beach,' said Borgs. 'Tights and tampons and so on in both flats.'

'And dildos and handcuffs. Everything said lover. Nothing said daughter.'

'Over fifty years younger, pretty as a picture. I'll guarantee he's got a will somewhere in his mountain of files with her name on it. He's got old insurance documents somewhere, her Minsk number, a photo album, a copy of the birth certificate, a child's drawing for Daddy. At some point in the past few years he'll have put money in her account or paid a bill for her.'

No reply from Wegener.

Borgs took a large glug of mulled wine, looking as if he wished he could spit it back into the mug. 'What I mean is, Martin – if the Stasi knew all that, the gentlemen from Wandlitz would prove you've made plenty of mistakes and oversights – lack of dedication, lack of criminalistic intelligence, lack of socialist sympathies. No matter how high the pile of material is that Frank Stein has to sort his way through with three overworked assistants, no matter if there's only one single clue to the girl's existence hidden between the pages of the nine-thousandth book on Hoffmann's shelves, the gentlemen would make you responsible for it if it suddenly turned out to be important.'

'And now?'

'Let's keep it to ourselves, you leave it off the file and keep working in that direction. If anything comes out of it we'll sort the paperwork out later.'

'OK.'

Borgs put the mug back on the table and dug a pack of cigarillos out of his inside pocket.

Behind him, the windowed wall had grown dark. There was barely any traffic on Karl-Marx-Allee. The silvery globe of the TV tower dangled in the void like an antiquated mirror ball, next to it the EastSide tower. Wegener tried to guess where he'd been standing half an hour ago, in which of the lit-up luxury cabins he'd been an onlooker for the length of two miniature bottles of sparkling wine, chomping, drinking, dreaming. Somewhere up there Kayser was lying on his bed right this moment in his underpants, ordering fillet steak, Warsteiner Pilsner and *Sachertorte* on room service, in the middle of the West in the East, flicking through the free porno channels, *Mascha Does Moscow, Playing Doctor with Zhivago, Busty Bolshevik Bitches, The Cum-munist Manifesto.*

'Kallweit went over to Werderscher Markt earlier,' said Borgs. 'The party leadership also believes Gruber's story, naturally enough, but they want to make sure it's absolutely watertight. No more humiliation in the West German press. So now it's all about substantiating Gruber's statement.'

'Or proving it wrong.'

'In the worst case, yes.'

'So it's all about finding the truth,' said Wegener.

'It's always been about the truth,' said Borgs, 'and not about compulsively pinning the blame on the State Security. That's why they've given us access to the witness Gruber named.'

'He did what?'

'He told the C5 boys about the witness he promised you. Why?'

'He told us he'd send a *TM* once he got to the other side.'

'He must have thought differently, then.'

Wegener felt a sudden jab of stomachache. He wasn't sure if it came from the mulled wine.

'Are you all right?'

'Who is this witness?' Wegener asked with some effort.

'Gruber seems to have worked as a helper in a specific cluster of the Brigade – that's what they call their subgroups. They're always three people and none of them know the big master plan, so they can't betray anyone if push comes to shove. Plus a couple of extras who don't know anything at all.'

'Just taking orders,' said Wegener. 'Sounds familiar.'

'Gruber's cluster was apparently responsible for Hoffmann and for the Palace. There were three people involved in planting the bomb – one was killed in the blast, one was arrested and one escaped.'

'That's what he told us at the junkyard.'

'So you know all that already.'

'You mean our witness is the arrested bomb-planter?'

'Precisely, my dear Watson.'

'And he was at the Müggelsee execution.'

'Gruber doesn't know that for sure. But the man was part of the core group.'

'Great. We'll talk to him then.'

Borgs swayed his round bulldog head. 'That's the sore point. The witness isn't just behind bars. He's looking at a charge of high treason, and also they're scared his people might break him out.'

'Where is he? In Bautzen?'

'Not even there.'

'I don't get it.'

'The GDR has a whole different type of prison. Compared to where he is, Bautzen is as cosy as the EastSide.'

'What are you trying to say, Walter?'

Borgs pushed his half-full plate of cabbage aside and heaved his stubby legs onto the wobbly table. 'When you violated the official rules a year ago, you wanted to find Josef Früchtl. But that wasn't all, Martin. You wanted to find out something about your country.

What goes on behind the scenes. How this state works in order to survive.'

Wegener put his cup down next to his seat. 'Maybe I did.'

Borgs nodded. 'Do you still want to?'

'What if I do?'

'That means dealing with what you see.'

Wegener didn't reply.

'And a bit more than that, Martin. It also means getting to know yourself. Not just your country. Your own, strange heart, that you can always be so sure of as long as your head's still buried in the sand. But what does that heart do if it finds out something big? How does it deal with the dilemmas that the system we're born into deposits outside our door every morning? What do we do with those half-dead, still-twitching mice?'

Wegener stared at Borgs. His bulldog eyes were closed. Only his mouth was moving. 'Do you stamp on it? Do you slam the door? Someone's forcing you to confront something that agonizes you. It wasn't you who caught the mouse and ripped its guts out. It was the cat. But the cat's gone. And it's your doorstop where the whole mess is starting to smell, thanks very much. Someone's got you into all this pain and doubt, and left you in the lurch with it. In the end you're always on your own in this land of boundless solidarity, aren't you? Alone with yourself and the tumour some people call your conscience. Whatever you do now there'll be something left behind. Metastases of that dirty conscience tumour that your body absorbs and can't excrete again, that it has to lug around with it until they trigger a cancer of their own, that needling conscience cancer that eats you up from the inside.

'You're not a spectator any more, you can't heckle the actors on stage from your padded box any more, Martin, you have to make your own decisions now and you know that you'll get the blame for every decision you make. From others, but above all from yourself. If you stamp on the mouse, it was you who killed it. If you let it bleed to death it's even worse. No matter what you do, that mouse's pain turns into your most private suffering. From the very moment you open the door.' Borgs opened his eyes. 'Do you want to open the door?'

Wegener tried to meet Borgs' bulldog glare, but that glare was too demanding, too amused, too knowing. Wegener stared at the floor. Scratched, red-brown parquet. Beneath the rusty radiators the wood was buckled, swollen and cracked, breaking apart bit by bit. That was what Früchtl meant, he thought, when he said I hadn't understood anything at all.

'And what if I don't open the door?'

Borgs folded his chubby hands in prayer. 'Then you'll instantly suffer from impaired vision, speech impediments, numbness, dizziness and headache, you'll be in the emergency department at the Charité within the hour, suspected stroke, they'll keep you in hospital four or five days for observation, and I'll take you off the special investigation for good at seven on the dot tomorrow morning. And I won't put you on any more special investigations in future.'

Coloured dots of light wandered across Borgs' motionless face. Wegener looked up at the ceiling. Huge chandeliers with chains of glass beads, between them mirror balls, silvery glittering miniature TV towers that had just started revolving and scattering blue, green and yellow stains around the room. The mousy-faced waitress skirted their table, scuttling on her skinny grey-tighted legs through the polka-dotted armchair obstacle course, balancing a tray of empty beer glasses. Wegener's eyes clung to her, scuttling along, suddenly seeing her spindly, gaunt body naked, the pointy ribcage under her white skin, the coloured dots wandering across her flat chest, her fleshy, blood-red nipples, the dense pubic wool between her little legs growing almost up to her navel.

And now the mouse stared at him out of her dark eyes, unexpectedly and directly, freezing in mid-turn, screening him for two, three, four seconds, photographing his spinal cord and his brain, his jaw, his heart, his fatty liver, capturing it all in black on white, and then she swept a pale tongue across her narrow lips.

Borgs turned his head and Mouse-face ducked away, almost running into a table. Two glasses slid off her tray and smashed to smithereens on the red-brown wooden floor, blinking gaily in the light of the mirror ball.

Wegener stood up.

The woman had thrown her tray on a seat and was now running through the room with a clatter of heels, past the Christmas tree and the bullet-hole stickers, guests and students staring agog, and then she was at the stairs down to the foyer, dived around the corner, almost slipped, arms flying, got her balance and was gone.

Borgs puffed at his cigarillo. 'Did you see any wires?'

'No. Maybe a directional microphone with a transmitter.'

'Or just another depressive nineteen-year-old who's missing her ex-boyfriend and loses her nerve when someone goggles at her non-existent tits.'

'You don't even believe that yourself.' Wegener sat back down again.

Borgs took another puff and tipped his head back. 'Believing, Martin . . . You can believe what you like. A lot of it might even be right. But our job's not about what you believe, I'm afraid.'

'So I have the choice between a stroke and a bullet in the head.'

Borgs smiled. 'A GDR citizen only ever has the choice between a stroke and a bullet in the head. Everything else is on wish-lists that'll never come true. Santa Claus is dead; as far as I know Antonia Hiegemann drags him by the feet behind his own sleigh in the hundred and twentieth minute.'

'I haven't noticed any signs of visual impairment,' said Wegener. 'Not at all. In the past few days I've had the feeling I'm seeing clearer and clearer.'

Borgs stubbed out his cigarillo in the greens. It hissed briefly. 'Then you'll be waiting outside your house at half past eight tomorrow morning.'

'Where am I going?'

'I don't know. And you'll never find out either.'

'And Kayser and Brendel?'

'Brendel's in on it, provided he dares to sign the necessary papers.'

Borgs got to his feet and put his coat on. He conjured up a large brown handkerchief and blew his nose.

'Just so you get what I'm talking about, Martin. Your ex-girlfriend, Karolina Enders. They indicated to Kallweit that she knew Hoffmann.' Borgs folded the handkerchief up fussily and put it away again. 'From now on anything's possible.'

Wegener felt like he was standing on the windowsill of Kayser's EastSide suite, the concrete maw of Alexanderplatz below the tips of his shoes. His stomach was Henry Maske's comeback punchbag, and Henry was on good form today, thrashing left and right hooks into him, wham, bam, bang. Wegener saw himself balancing up there on the 27th floor – dead people always live at the top – saw himself doubling over, tipping over, from now on anything's possible, his fingers squeaking down the illuminated EastSide glass, metre by metre, faster and faster, leaving ten greasy stripes in the sticky oil coating on the facade, in free fall, Karolina's pale blue toenails in the grass at Wannsee, her tight bikini bottoms that revealed the shape of her sex, the fabric half eaten by the camel toe, a slit can suddenly open up anywhere in the country and in you fall, says the tennis-ball-sized Vossian pubic bulge, and you're stuck tight in the meanest grotto of lies.

Everything was revolving, a wretched dizziness with Borgs inserting a regretful face into it, the first time in all the years that Borgs had managed a seriously regretful face. And then he patted Wegener on the back and turned himself and his regretful face away, stomped across the room like a puggish lone fighter, running straight into a train of movie people, in the midst of them Antonia Hiegemann in her bikini-like red combat suit. Borgs, who naturally managed to conjure up pen and paper, got her autograph, slow-motion poses, a photo on his Minsk: Hiegemann and Borgs the civilian St Nick at the discotheque, Borgs two heads shorter with three more chins.

Everybody laughed. Wegener gripped the arms of his seat to steady himself and felt like he needed to vomit again, so soon, a sequel to his previous nausea looming on the horizon, everything wanted out to make room for a martial pain that had only just fallen asleep and suddenly awoken again, even worse this time, even more frantic and even less prepared to be pacified by anything at all.

Women, said Früchtl, *women are grubby panes of frosted glass in a bricked-up darkroom, Martin – you can't see through them.*

His Minsk beeped. Ronny, thought Wegener. A *TM* ran across the screen:

Day after tomorrow, 12 o'clock, Boltenhagen pier. No microphones, no Stasi. Bring a pair of handcuffs. This is a one-off offer. Marie Schütz

Wegener automatically pressed Dial. They'd have to get someone out of bed for a trap-and-trace at this time of night and by then she'd have had her phone switched off long ago ... *of the number 0-1-8-2-3-5-6-6-6-2-4 is temporarily unavailable, but you can leave a message after the tone. Have you got our new Minsk M6 with national network function, 5.0-megapixel camera and automatic voice recognition? No? Then why not head straight to your nearest Telemedia POC branch! For every purchase of a new Minsk M6 on conclusion of a three-year contract, we'll credit you with a sensational 150 trust points! Make sure you get your personal trust points while the offer applies! Telemedia POC – Freedom of speech for all!*

TUESDAY 25 OCTOBER 2011

22

WINTER HAD GRIPPED BERLIN OVERNIGHT, a street-sweeper running
amok, tearing the last dead leaves from the sick trees, kicking at
rickety old windows, shoving rubbish across the crumbling pavements,
goggling under old women's plastic skirts and trying to blast the dull
pain out of Wegener's head, left behind by the toxic mulled wine, the
bottle of Goldkrone and a sleepless night. State trading organization
paper bags, crumpled *Public Eye* pages, dried leaves, tissues, empty
Club-Cola cans, chewing-gum wrappers – everything came flying past
him, swirling together on the potholed asphalt surface into a spineless
monster of mulch that turned in indecisive circles, was run over,
righted itself again and got blown away, further and further along
the road towards the West, all the way to the Wall, which caught all
the dirt in the whole GDR so that it grew into a rustling mountain
that would never be granted emigration status.

Wegener turned up his collar and took a step back into the doorway. He thought of his parents' grave, of the dark green ivy being

tousled by the wind that very moment, fourteen kilometres to the north, of the stubborn gravestone standing right now, while he thought of it, beneath a colourless sky, cold and unchanging, carved with the names of people who had used up their days and hours, their contingency of the present, and now had to be dead and gone for all time, people nobody but he could describe, who only lived on in the few seconds when he remembered them, and for a moment what Wegener most wanted was to go back upstairs into his mute flat where the rubbish didn't prance around but lay dead in the corners, and he'd have done nothing all day long but remember, no matter how tired he was, he'd have got out all the photos, reawakened every Christmas, every quarrel, every trip to Boltenhagen in Hannibal the Trabi, only to bring his parents back to life, to treat them to twenty-four hours in one go, their last chance at existence by coursing through their son's brain in the form of minimal electrical impulses, a mixture of chemistry, physics and illusion, and perhaps he'd have included Früchtl in his orgy of recollection too, secretly and silently and not meaning to say anything in particular.

Wegener wondered whether he'd have gone to his parents with his rampant loneliness, with the feeling of being alone that was suddenly getting louder and louder, if they didn't live in a four-square-metre patch of earth in Weissensee but were still ensconced in their carcinogenic old vault of a flat as the perfectly attuned couple, whether he'd have cried on Mama and Papa's shoulder at the age of fifty-six over this pasteboard life, this Potemkin village that was East Berlin, that spared you nothing and you obviously weren't allowed to spare anything either if you wanted to get on in life, or whether his parents would have disappointed him too, whether there'd be proof that they'd told lies, spied and murdered too.

Are you going to give Karolina the letter? asked Früchtl's voice.

I don't know.

Want to talk about it?

Anything but that.

Wegener leaned against the barred front door. Borgs was another confidant, another playmaker, just another Hoffmann, a further species of strategist, more cautious, less ideological, a man who even veiled his affiliations so you didn't know who he was loyal to and who he was whoring for. But Borgs was right in one respect: from now on there was no going back, now it was time to run, grab the bull by the horns, head West as fast as possible, find the light at the end of the tunnel and then get right on out of here. If you knew enough you might be able to force your way out, get yourself deported, an uncomfortable piece of shit expelled through some brick anus to the West. Just like Ronny Gruber.

You should sign up for the Suppressed Thoughts Olympics, said Früchtl. *You'd win a few nice shiny medals.*

I'll suppress you if you don't shut up.

What a comedian, laughed Früchtl. *I've got a lifelong residency right in your head, I'm part of the furniture, I am, a sitting tenant, there's no getting rid of me, your own voice, the bearer of uncomfortable truths. It doesn't matter one jot whether I'm a cloud of dust or a missing-in-action People's Policeman, what I am is your miserable remaining sense of what's right, of what does you good, and you know that very well. If you want to get shot of me you'll have to switch yourself off first – I'm staying put up here in your grey cells. Would the last one to leave please turn the lights off, Karo wipes Martin's smile off, someone always bumps that mouse off, I can't wait to see how you suppress me, you, yourself and thine!*

You've been drinking again.

Out of worry over you always falling for the wrong women, the

wrong friends, out of concern over what so much wrong stuff will
do to you, Martin, whether you and your crooked smile will end up
on a crooked path and you'll suddenly start making crooked assess-
ments. You know how much crooked stuff I had to get up to before
I became an upright citizen, before I could see straight, stand straight,
walk straight, how many people I – how long, how often, how
badly . . .

Wegener yawned.

Here they came again, the words of advice from the dark armchair
in the corner, raining down on him in that brandy-soaked barracks
tone, from the man who'd been a Nazi and a communist, who'd
made every mistake of the past century first and who had nothing
left but to gobble up variations of choice wisdom morning, noon and
night, a fatted German goose stuffed for fifty years with the knowledge of wars and defeats who could now lay big fat eggs of insight
every day, whose gavaged foie gras hoarded up the answers to all the
political questions in the universe.

Like the litter of Berlin, Früchtl's commands came flying around
him now: stand firm, don't descend to their level, don't play their
game . . . I know all this off by heart, Josef, thought Wegener, why
can't you just shut your trap? You're probably lying in your coffin
somewhere and you can't remember what it's like to be falling
between two stools with wobbly legs that someone's planted explosives underneath, you had to save up for your morals over two
dictatorships. I can't afford your morals – don't tell anyone, but to
be perfectly honest, I'm morally bankrupt.

That just got Früchtl all the more worked up, of course. He hadn't
shouldered all the suffering subscribed to his name for that – the
denazification, the getting spat on, the getting shot at, the always
coming too late – he hadn't played doormat for the marauding

Germanic character-crippling comrades for decades for that: for his quasi-son to not profit from it at least, to turn into his Quasimodo-son in the end, hunchbacked, turned out all wrong, unbearable; and if he made the same mistakes, didn't learn from his teacher's failings, then it was all in vain, then it'd all go on and on, a chain of detonations that couldn't be stopped. And so the ex-Nazi, ex-communist, ex-man waved his rattling skeleton hands about, crowed his rage out, shouted that it was no use in the end being insincere, being un-citizen-like, serving regimes that *had* to be transitory – no matter how long they lasted they were all just momentary snapshots, it'd still be over at some point because the extremes always decayed, because there was a festering, a mouldering, a rotting innate to them, overly strong concentrations of toxic juices, no balance of bases and alkalis, only acids that attacked everything and made it rot away from the inside, that successively broke down essential functions until the whole shoddy organism collapsed, burst, broke open and had to quit the field for its successor, which had the same identical death long since germinating within it. For the moment it might be beneficial, it might look like the only solution was assimilating to the system and copying it, but anyone who imitated the system had no other option but to imitate the system's end, and they'd perish along with the system.

And now Wegener had to laugh – Josef Früchtl, you oppressed apostle, you can tell that to your room-mates, the worms in your coffin home: copying the system – the very idea. Outdoing the system, Major Mort, is the only chance we have. If you're at level pegging you're struggling on behind; if you want to win you have to be a step ahead, or a piece of information ahead, but an important one, because information's everything: power, money, sex, survival, in this state even more than in any other, in this city more than in any other. Nowadays they leave their steel helmets in the cloakroom and their guns in the sock drawer – ah, now you're turning in your grave, I thought as much – nowadays we all listen along, listen in, make notes and play the game, we don't let anyone see our cards and we always have an ace up our sleeve, and if you gamble everything away like Hoffmann your neck gets longer and longer, but if you win then you might just end up sitting outside your holiday hut at the age of seventy, with the sun shining on your hairy back.

As a moral beggar and blackguard, said Früchtl.

But a moral beggar and blackguard who survives, said Wegener. That's the difference, dead man.

You're a dead man yourself, said Früchtl. *Or you soon will be.*

Soon, said Wegener, isn't now. The calendar of the living. I don't have any other.

Quite sure?

No.

A grey Barkas van drove slowly into sight, stopped, coasted five metres on and then stopped again. The engine was running. White lettering on the side: BADENHOOP FISH WHOLESALERS – OFFICIAL SUPPLIER TO THE STATE TRADING ASSOCIATION SUPERMARKETS, HESSESTRASSE 69.

The passenger door opened and a denim-jacketed man got out, the wind blow-drying his hair into a straw-blond bonnet. The man walked towards Wegener and stopped at a sufficient distance not to have to take his hands out of his pockets. 'Your taxi's here.'

'Let's hope there isn't a catch to this fish shop.'

The man pulled a face as if he'd disintegrate into a pile of ash at the slightest smile, turned away without a word, his hair bonnet now blown in the other direction, trudged back to the van, opened the back doors and waited.

Now Wegener was a dumb young dog expected to finally get the point of the back doors being opened.

The blond man looked past him. Another faceless example of the ten thousand crawlers in the state disguise division. Don't look at me, don't recognize me, just get in the van and keep your mouth shut.

Wegener took the letter to Karolina out of his pocket and tore it in two, tore the halves in two and then the quarters, until the scraps of paper were so small that the wind scattered them, mingling them with the dancing litter, carrying them underneath the cars, into the gutters, onto the rickety roofs, all the words forever separated, not a single sentence of his angry, vainglorious howl complete any more, a polemical jigsaw puzzle for all the points of the compass, which even the Stasi couldn't put together again, no matter how many agents they put on the job.

The denim-jacketed man stared after the scraps of paper as if the theory of everything had just been destroyed before his very eyes. Wegener walked past him, trying to look cheerful.

There were narrow benches on either side of the windowless back of the van. Out of the sweetshop-scented darkness came Brendel's voice: 'At last I know how it feels.'

'Looks like the Badenhoop wholesale company's caught a pretty big fish.'

'And they're not even allowed to fish for me – I'm West German property.'

Wegener clambered into the van. 'To be honest, I think these guys do their fishing without a licence. There's nothing they don't catch.'

The doors slammed behind him. No handle on the inside. A dim yellowish light came on in the ceiling.

Brendel gave a smile in the gloom. 'How are you, Martin?' The Barkas drove off.

'I've been better. I've got something for you.'

'Ronny Gruber's sad little fairytale?'

'That too. But that's not all. I've got a phone for you as an added bonus.' Wegener pulled a Minsk M6 out of his coat pocket and handed it to Brendel. 'With a prepaid card, it's still got seven marks on it.'

'Words fail me.'

'The phone won't be much use to you, then.'

Brendel beamed. 'What do I owe you?'

'I'll send you an order for chocolate once you get back home – it'll be a mighty big parcel.' Wegener leaned back against the metal wall.

'I've brought you something too.' Brendel reached into his briefcase and pulled out the new *Spiegel*, handing it over with both hands and an ironic, earnest look on his handsome face.

Wegener looked at the cover. A blood-smeared hammer and compasses, just like in the fax in the World Hall, and the headline and caption had stayed the same as well: *STASI MURDERING AGAIN. How an obstinate secret service is gambling away Europe's energy future.*

He flicked through to the article and counted fourteen pages, photos of the Müggelsee by day, by night, with Hoffmann hanging in the background, archive photos of Hoffmann and Moss, an interview with Jürgen Falter on Posteritatism, a pixellated photo of the source on a forest path, photos of Steinkühler, Brendel and Kallweit, a large picture of Lafontaine with the European stars resplendent above his head like a halo and next to him a Sony ad for Jan 'The Smooch' Hermann with his new hit single 'No Doubt, Time Hates Love'. Jan Hermann beamed at the camera in a burst of artificial jollity, his teeth as white as dental chewing gum.

'Kayser's got you up to date?' asked Brendel.

'From eleven-thirty last night till just before four in the morning.'

Wegener felt the Barkas slowing down. Now it turned left. Anemonenstrasse.

'A text message came in from Hoffmann's daughter,' said Wegener. 'She wants to meet us tomorrow in Boltenhagen, at the pier at noon. Nothing hi-tech to track her with but a pair of handcuffs.'

'Handcuffs?'

'Handcuffs.'

'Are you going to play along with that crap?'

'Sure. When did a twenty-year-old beauty last ask you for hand-cuffs? I was talking to Borgs last night at the Bar International. First the waitress got very interested, and when we gave her a bit of an eye she upped and ran away.'

The car took a right turn. Salvador-Allende-Strasse.

Brendel's dark face remained expressionless. 'State Security?'

'Presumably.'

'Did you go after her?'

Wegener shook his head. 'It'd only have meant weeks of fuss, and in the end it'd have been an observation error.'

'So they're on to you.'

'You spoke to Steinkühler yesterday. Did he say anything?'

'It was just about the signatures they needed for this little trip. The white Phobos at Hoffmann's holiday hut?'

'That looks like the Stasi too.'

'And we don't want to take any minders along to Boltenhagen.'

'I don't think we do. The comrades would only get in the way of our handcuff fun and games.'

The sound of the blond man laughing from the front. Or the driver. The laughter descended into coughing. Then there was a banging. The Barkas had taken up battle with the potholes on Bellevuestrasse. The laughter cut out. Broken stones exploded beneath the van second by second, the floor tray groaning like a Robotron robot in an OAP's home, all the suspension springs moaning in suspension-spring hell, and the dim ceiling light flickered. Brendel's face lit up in the rhythm of the lamp, his hard features now even more sharply contoured, face paint made of light and shadow, a Che-Guevara-style skull made up of a few pale scraps of skin.

'And at the Chancellery?' Wegener made an effort to sound casual. 'Did you tell Lafontaine that socialism's an ageing movie diva? So much more beautiful from a distance than close up.'

The potholes thinned out. A sharp brake. Left onto Seelenbinderstrasse.

Brendel gave a black-and-yellow smile. 'Lafontaine's on his way to the G8 summit. But Helga Ribbat was there.'

'Is she good-looking when you see her in person?'

'As good as an ageing movie diva.'

'So you shouldn't get too close up, then.'

'Presumably not. And apart from that you get the feeling she can't open her mouth without telling a lie.'

'At least she opens her mouth.'

'Believe me, you don't want to go there.'

'Reaction to Gruber?'

'Everyone's pleased.' Brendel crossed his legs, obviously found that uncomfortable and sat up straight again. 'They're not interested in Hoffmann himself or any underground brigades. All they want to know is one thing: will the consultations take place on the 19th and 20th of November or not? If the new transit agreements don't come about it'll be a historical debacle for Lafontaine. The whole Social Energy subject brought him key support, so he has to come up with the goods. Big business is breathing down his neck, and the working-class voters too. Everyone's counting on the State Security having nothing to do with the Hoffmann case and pulling a killer out of a hat so there's nothing in the way of the consultations.'

Right turn. Bahnhofstrasse.

'And now the killers are being pulled out of the hat,' said Wegener, 'and the Stasi really does have nothing to do with it.'

'Or at least it suddenly all looks quite clear.'

'A bit too clear if you ask me.'

Brendel nodded. 'They didn't send us over here to make major investigation progress. We're just a nice garnish for the European partners. And for the press, if push comes to shove. A chill pill. The Chancellery doesn't care how it turns out as long as the case gets solved swiftly. So Gruber's a godsend. Later they can stand up and say: Our people were there from the very beginning, monitoring the observation of the constitution and all that jazz.'

The car stopped. There was a clatter of rails. Köpenick station.

'That means if the Central Committee decided to go public with Gruber's statement, everyone in Bonn would be happy.'

'Assuming his story's watertight.' Brendel did cross his legs now. 'The EU's keeping a very close eye on it, not to mention the international press. There mustn't be any mud sticking to Germany – to either Germany. So much energy's got to come from Russia to Europe in the future, most of it via GDR territory. If the old rule-of-law and constitutionality discussion keeps flaring up that'll mean endless delays, price inflation, claims for damages, political debates and so on. Gruber's version of events has to be substantiated. Clear evidence, ascertained beyond doubt, not even the slightest mark on the clean slate that can't be wiped off. And that's our job. Ribbat made that clear enough.'

'Assuming what she says is true.'

'I think in this case she made an exception and told the truth.'

The car moved on again, bumping over new potholes. The wooden benches vibrated.

Wegener held onto a strut on the ceiling for balance. 'Let's just assume Gruber's lying. The Stasi did get rid of Hoffmann. We haven't got a suspect, we haven't even got a specific suspicion, we can't get the file, time's running out. But the consultations mustn't be called off under any circumstances. When exactly is the deadline?'

Brendel counted up: '10th of November. So another two weeks. If nothing's sorted by then it'll all be called off.'

'Then the Stasi have no other option but to give us what we're looking for so desperately. Killer, motive, statement. A nice fat package deal.'

Brendel kneaded his face with both hands. 'You mean they send us Gruber so that he pins the blame on this brigade on Stasi instructions?'

'Does it sound so unrealistic? What else can they do? They've suddenly got two West German cops on their heels, they can't just dictate the outcome as usual. So they construct a truth that everyone can believe with a clean conscience.'

Brendel stared at the groaning floor.

'Aren't you surprised at what's going on here right now? We're on our way to some bloody secret prison – why do you think they're letting us in there? Because they know exactly what information we'll take home with us, and because they want us to get that information.' Wegener tried to make eye contact with Brendel and failed. 'And the whole thing would have a useful side effect for the Stasi: the Brigade isn't just a protest gang with explosives any more, now they're suddenly cowardly murderers too. That's a big difference, even in this country.'

'All right, we ought to bear that possibility in mind, in principle,' said Brendel. 'But there's still the question of why the Stasi would want to kill Hoffmann. Why so close to the consultations? Why this modus operandi, which clearly points the finger at the Stasi?'

'Richard, the whole MO is such a clear finger pointing at the State Security that no one can seriously suspect the Stasi! If you turn up at the scene of the crime and find a business card from Manfred Murderer from Massacre Row, who do you think it can't possibly have been?'

'But what's the motive, Martin?' Brendel raised his eyes now and looked at Wegener. 'Why would the State Security kill an old man who worked for Moss more than twenty years ago? And right before the most important economic talks your country's had in the past decade, of all times?'

'It's not my country, it belongs to all the East Germans jointly. Great, eh?'

'Come on, tell me.'

'If you ask me, it's our job to find out just that.'

'If there is anything to find out.'

'You don't trust the Gruber thing either!'

Brendel looked unhappy. 'You know you have my full support, you can count on that. But we mustn't get caught up in a dead end. *You* mustn't get caught up in a dead end, Martin. If the Stasi did murder Hoffmann and we can prove it, we'll shout it from the rooftops in the West, that's a promise. But fanaticism won't get us anywhere. I won't say any more about it. Let's not look for Stasi killers, let's look for killers. Like we always do.'

Wegener nodded.

The van turned left, stopped, started again and took a sharp right turn, perhaps Wongrowitzer Steig and then Güldenauer Weg. Or the one after that. Certainly heading towards Wolfsgarten in any case.

Wegener tried not to think of Karolina again, not to end up in the
Karolina trap again but to keep his mind on the map of Berlin, counting the turns they made. Wongrowitzer Steig was the first on the left
off Mahlsdorfer Strasse, then came Kleinschewskystrasse, but there
was another road between them, one he could never remember –
when suddenly everything spun around, tyres screeched, Brendel
sailed across the smooth wooden bench and grabbed for the ceiling
struts with both hands, then the entire front left of the van sank into
a hole in the road the size of a construction ditch, drove as if into a
wall, broke through the wall. Everything seemed to fly up in the air,
Brendel bumped his head on the metal wall, the phenoplast bodywork
grating and wobbling, the *Spiegel* floating around the back of the
van.

An accident, thought Wegener. If these false chauffeurs crash
into a Yukos tanker you'll burn to death in a plastic cage, in a
sealed, mobile C5 jail on the way to nowhere, leaving behind an
unsolved state crisis, an unsolved murder case, an unsolved ex-
girlfriend, a traitor betrayed, and you'll kick the bucket in your
own little crematorium alongside Richard the Black-and-Yellow-
Faced. Maybe that's the whole point of the trip, they've got us in
a fish trap, maybe we're much closer to the truth than they want
us to be: Hoffmann's significance for Moss cleared up thanks to
Blühdorn, who knows what Marie Schütz has to tell us about the
days when her father was still pulling the strings; according to
Gruber, he had highly interesting documents – where are those
documents now? – and if you put it all together, sober and after a
good night's sleep, something might come out of it, maybe more
than Steinkühler & Co. would like, so they need bait, the interrogation in a secret prison, two C5 stuntmen drive their van
artistically into a hundred-year-old oak tree and jump out just in

time, the East and West detectives get a good roasting at 200 degrees, a tragic story . . .

The driver accelerated. A straight road with no holes in it.

'What are these idiots up to?' Brendel's former hairstyle was all over his face.

Wegener sat up. 'They're driving so we can't reconstruct the route.'

Brendel snorted.

'There's a good side to it.'

'Which is?'

'It looks likely they'll let us go again afterwards.'

23

THE BLOND MAN HAD GOT TALLER over the two-hour drive, grown broader shoulders, swapped his denim jacket for a dark parka and put on a black balaclava with different eyes staring out of it. The blond man wasn't the blond man any more, he'd never been here and he never would be, he doesn't even know where we are, because those bastards exchanged drivers along the way, a lightning swap at a traffic light somewhere, thought Wegener, having to shield his face with his hands after so much bumpy darkness.

Much too bright, unclouded East German sky, all around him the Stasi-coloured plaster of Normannenstrasse but not quite such tall buildings, only three storeys, a deserted yard with a puddle of wilted grass in the middle. Brendel leapt out of the Barkas behind him, his high-quality leather soles slamming onto the clean-swept concrete ground, the only sound for miles. The walls instantly rejected the noise, obviously loath to swallow the sound of West German soles. Nothing moved in the dark holes of windows.

The masked man went ahead, taking a few steps across the yard into a large, garage-like space without a door. On the right-hand wall two steps leading up to a wide set of bars, behind them a wooden door with ribbed glass panes. A black-gloved finger pressed a soundless bell.

Wegener and Brendel turned around as the Barkas started as if of its own accord, chugging off to the right. The fishmonger's lettering had disappeared from the exterior.

Silence that no one wanted to interrupt wrapped the entire scene in cotton wool, padding the moment, stuffing their mouths with swollen emptiness, pressing its unspoken commandment into their heads: there was to be no speaking on these premises, every syllable was to be weighed up. Language had always been an invitation to contradictions, so they didn't let language in here in the first place, and if it did get in somehow it died away in the blink of an eye, got lost, driven out, cut off. A gigantic warning sign floated before Wegener's mind's eye, with all the words in the German language crossed out and underneath the note: NO WORDS ALLOWED.

The wooden door opened with a low buzz, another masked man unlocking the bars from inside, swinging part of the barrier outwards, nodding Wegener, Brendel and his fellow mask-wearer into the building, locking up behind them and marching off. A kilometre-long semi-lit corridor, ancient PVC with a seventies flowery pattern on the floor, peeling adhesive wood veneer on the walls, behind it raw brickwork, on the right a dazzlingly bright stairwell glazed with ribbed windows, another row of bars going around the corner and blocking their way. The second masked man opened up, the first one remained behind them as sinister rear cover. Well-oiled hinges, not a squeak to be heard, the moving contorted shadow bars on the pale floor growing narrow and letting all four of them pass, then widening again and clanging shut.

Now heavy cell doors painted pale grey stood to attention on either side, nailed together out of ship's planks by beefy sailors, with ungainly metal bolts at the top and bottom, the drop-shaped covers over the peepholes a row of iron tears, narrow food hatches with handles – we're at the zoo, thought Wegener, in among the dangerous animals, the snappy beasts of the GDR. Whoever these beasts may be, whoever they may have snapped at, however they may have got here, in armoured cars or in fishy Barkas vans, now they're chained up, sitting tight, hunkering in solid stone dungeons behind boards as thick as a boat's hull, guarded by a horde of deaf-and-dumb bank robbers. The system's got them in a stranglehold.

He looked at Brendel. Brendel's gaze was darting about, a West German camera lens on holiday in the penal Middle Ages, somewhere between curiosity and complete bewilderment, between incredulity and confirmation. Brendel was tiptoeing. He couldn't keep up his confident stride in here; his strong sweetshop perfume had long gone from saccharine status symbol to olfactory cynicism, demonstrating an irremovable differential, an unfakeable scent-mark of class and origin, a sweet certificate of manufacture enabling withdrawal while the living dead vegetated behind grey security doors, each day the same as the next, the months interchangeable, no end in sight, not a gram of hope, but a sweetshop hint that freedom turned into a bad smell when it was put out of reach.

Wegener felt the Goldkrone headache awakening with a steady throb somewhere in his brain, feasting on his fatigue and set to grow from now on, intent to stay with him for the rest of the day.

Brendel looked at him. Wegener looked into Brendel's blue, blue eyes for a second or two. The black-clad men had them over a barrel, driving them deeper and deeper into this lightless place, through countless barred doors, past more masked guards leaning in doorways as if dead, skulking behind corners, suddenly popping up and then disappearing again, a monotonous ghost train with the same shockers again and again, branching out like a labyrinth you could wander until kingdom come.

Wegener tried and failed to keep track of the route in his head, just as he'd failed in the Barkas, up against the deliberate confusion of the permanent right and left turns, stairs up and down, up against the repetitive bare corridors, the alarm wire snaking along all the walls, linked by red and green jacks into an electronic spiderweb, connected up to the round, cherry-red lamps hanging from the ceilings like luminous boils.

They've built themselves a den, thought Wegener, a system of caves with enough space for an entire population, where only the initiated can find their way around, where they're at home, discreet and anonymous, no one knows anyone else, everyone has a task and a superior, written instructions, meetings only in emergencies, and all there is instead is tried and tested routine, cold administration of the anti-constitutional subjects in brick cocoons, decades of palliative care in this shabby palace of soundlessness.

But perhaps the entire cavernous labyrinth was just an illusion, much smaller in reality, much less fear-inducing, perhaps they'd been up and down the same corridor seven times now, past the same cell doors, merely following a precisely planned obstacle course designed to give visitors a dose of respect for the omnipotence of the State Security: nothing more than three masked extras acting as carbon copies of themselves over and over again, that good old Eastern European presentation trick, a game of thimblerig, a deception manoeuvre,

moving walls, a mouse dressed up as an elephant celebrating a communist carnival in its most artful form.

Wegener tried to take note of details but the cell doors weren't
numbered or named, the floors weren't lettered, all you could see
through the ribbed glass of the stairwell glazing was blurry brightness, the same flooring everywhere, the same peeling yellow grey on
the walls everywhere, the same strip lights, wire jacks, food hatches,
door handles, bars, balaclavas; the same black dress on the warders,
no differences, no details, nothing to hold on to.

Wegener noticed how dry his mouth had got, how his headache
was swelling and bringing the morning-after thirst along with it, those
two bastard twins conceived by men over the age of forty every
drunken night, and through the pain he suddenly realized what he'd
really got into here, what political quicksand he was already knee-
deep in, subsiding more and more with every movement, with no sign
of help on the horizon. As though he'd been daydreaming his way
through the past few days for all the stress and lack of success, and
had just come round in the museum-like wasteland of this endless
prison, woken up with a start, and now the knowledge came raining
down on him of how much power this country really possessed, of
what Borgs had meant yesterday that Bautzen was the EastSide of
the GDR jails, because Bautzen housed those who'd been sentenced,
perhaps unjustly sentenced but at least sentenced, people knew where
they were, could visit them or not visit them: they were under official
imprisonment and were thus present, in files and in cells.

But here on this Stasi planet, in this prefab fortress in the middle
of nowhere, secluded from all that was living, here you were no longer
existent, here you disappeared for ever, digested by the most dangerous of all state organs, a nameless, pulsing compost heap in a stone
waste bin, declared dead by family, friends and lovers, forgotten,

obliterated – it could happen to anyone, any individual, be they bomb-planters or captains or majors.

Früchtl, thought Wegener, perhaps Früchtl's squatting on the tiled floor behind one of these tree-thick doors, emaciated, hollow-cheeked, tortured, naked, with deadened eyes in a pale skull, only two or three metres away and yet still out of reach. Perhaps file number MW–B–1101–IV/2010 (PPB) was long since on some list or other, perhaps they'd set aside one of the concrete coffins for Hauptmann Martin Alfons Wegener. Of course the blond man still had to make his loops and detours so that the cargo didn't get nervous, would feel flattered by an exclusive visit to the secret service's most secret secret prison, would feel they had special investigation status, were bearers of state secrets. Those sons of bitches didn't drive anyone against a tree nowadays, they didn't even shoot you any more – why bother when they could just as well compost the dangerous elements, dematerialize them, dissolve them without the slightest bit of hydrochloric acid? No public attention, no questions, just an unsolved missing person's report.

Früchtl, thought Wegener, Major Mistrustful, did your last research job lead you here, with special dispensation to interrogate an inmate, did they hoodwink you after all in the end, did you fall for Borgs' mousetrap, end up on a hook for a Badenhoop fish? Suddenly Wegener saw as clear as day that the truth was an exhibit, on show on a well-lit plinth, something you could simply look at if only you declared yourself willing to open your eyes.

Of course Hoffmann had become a supporter of the Brigade, out of lust for revenge – his life's work betrayed by Moss and now it was time for the regime that had disappointed him to pay the price. Years of preparation, historic vengeance, worming his way into Wandlitz so that Hoffmann could give the Bürger boys important tips from

Emil Fischer: when, where and how best to get into the government quarter so as to take the entire Central Committee hostage or put them up against the wall and slice them into julienne strips with a Japanese knife or cure their chronic illusionitis with a nice cyanide enema. Of course the Stasi had hanged Hoffmann the traitor to give a clear signal and yet still divert suspicion from themselves, but then came the unforeseeable mistake: one of the killers got greedy, went back to the crime scene, took photos, sold the photos to the *Spiegel* to bolster his pension, and now there they were, the Stasi, Hoffmann dead but they'd still stepped in shit, a PR disaster on the bottom of their shoe that stank to high heaven and was gradually drying on, hard.

So they came up with Gruber, made him make a statement and an admission to paddle them out of shit creek – all the Brigade's fault, the consultations as good as saved. Except there was one detective still niggling away, not going gently, smelling that shitty shoe against the wind, he'd learned from Früchtl, hadn't he, so they pull the trick with the bomber interrogation again and off Martin Alfons Wegener was on the trail of the scent, voluntarily climbing into random Barkas vans, letting unknown men chauffeur him to unknown locations, not telling anyone where he was because he didn't know it himself, striding straight into the lions' den.

Steinkühler & Co. couldn't have wished for a better outcome, everyone in the picture all around him, everyone but Wegener, all in cahoots. Borgs was informed, Borgs knew what it meant when the Barkas came along, Borgs was one of them, Borgs had warned him, a small salve for his conscience by telling him Karolina had known Hoffmann, a warning shot that he'd refused to hear because the trail of shit smelled so tempting. Karolina was in on it too, one of the Judases, the woman he'd slept with far too long ago, who'd probably been spying on him back then, who'd told them which basement to find him in that night at Stasi HQ.

But there was one thing wrong and that was Brendel. They couldn't possibly put him away. Brendel was untouchable, he'd bang the press drum in the West to deafen all ears, he'd – and now there was an explosion in Wegener's throbbing Goldkrone-damaged brain like a People's Army hand grenade landing in a swimming pool full of Woltrow woodruff-flavoured jelly: Brendel wouldn't do anything at all, because they'd planned ahead, the playmakers at the Stasi, they'd been clever enough to plant their own man in the West, someone to protect them, someone to perfect the plan, someone who was now walking down the hundredth flight of stairs alongside him surrounded by his sweetshop scent, earning an Oscar for the role of the bewildered West Berlin chief investigator, visibly hesitant to follow these masked musclemen into the basement corridor, pulling an entirely credible concerned face, padding carefully through the musty gloom past more and more cell doors until it grew gradually brighter, until the corridor widened and led into a white-padded room without windows, a brightly lit rubber cell with white chairs and white tables, a perfect absence of colour in which the masked men looked like black holes on legs.

Two more masked men joined them, a thin man between them wearing orange prison uniform and a black hood over his head, which was now removed. And Wegener knew the face beneath it so well that he had to sit down on one of the white chairs immediately, while that face looked at him as if Wegener was Karl Liebknecht in Hitler uniform in a jacuzzi full of fizzing communists' blood, while that face composed itself with effort and said: 'Hauptmann. Now this really is a surprise.'

24

TORALF, THOUGHT WEGENER. TORALF OF ALL PEOPLE, and as usual he looks like he's jumped straight out of a West German music video, a pop singer who's just finished an ultra-camp dance routine and then been dragged off the soft-focus screen by the masked men. Even the orange prison overalls looked like a stage outfit, Toralf's blond waterfall of hair pouring onto narrow shoulders in shiny waves, the long, arrogant face on the fragile India-rubber body still telling a haggard tale of members of the ancient nobility who had had a little too much fun with their own relatives.

'You know each other,' Brendel stated.

The black-clad men went out, closing the white-padded safe door behind them. There was no sound of keys.

'Toralf Kleyer,' said Wegener, attempting to make a round of introductions. 'Richard Brendel, a colleague of mine.'

Toralf and Brendel shook hands half-heartedly.

'Toralf, you old beanpole, you must tell me how you do it,' Wegener said in faux-jollity. *They've got you,* murmured Früchtl, *but don't let them know you know, don't do them that favour. For once in your ridiculous life put a poker face on.* 'You're so incredibly thin. And I'm carrying all this fat around with me.'

'Because you probably still go out for meatloaf with your boss every day,' said Toralf with a slightly debilitated grin. 'Plus lipids and carbohydrates.'

I wish, said Früchtl, *and anyway it's called chips with mayonnaise, you camp biologist.*

'Those days are over now,' said Wegener.

'Is the old man retired?'

'You could call it that. What do you get to eat in here?'

'Only brown bread. Brown bread baked before Revitalization, if you ask me.'

'Jail's a tough place.'

'And I always thought Bautzen was the height of luxury.'

'You're not in Bautzen, Toralf.'

Toralf shrugged. 'No one talks to me in here. The last time was two days ago.'

'That's why we're here,' said Wegener. 'My colleague Brendel's come specially from West Berlin.'

Toralf's sleepy eyes shot open. 'West Berlin?'

'Yes.'

'Your ID, please.'

Brendel pressed a greenish plastic card into Toralf's hand. He gave it a sceptical look, turned it over and handed it back.

Wegener cleared his throat. 'Toralf, I don't think we have much time. The gentlemen who run this establishment presumably get a little nervous when they have visitors.'

'By visitors, I assume you don't mean me.'

'I'm afraid not.'

Toralf took a seat on one of the white chairs. His crooked face was tense. Cogs were turning behind his high brow.

'How's Juliane?' asked Wegener.

'Julia.'

'Right, Julia.'

'I don't know.'

'Because?'

'She went over to the West. Last year. On a Russian visa.'

'And you stayed behind. You'd prefer to bomb our country to pieces than go shopping for truffle pâté with Julia at the Kaufhaus des Westens.'

'Someone's got to do it, Hauptmann.'

'Of course.' Wegener nodded. 'Everything has to be done by somebody. But why you?'

Toralf's lips narrowed. 'First of all, you know that, and secondly I reckon you see it pretty much the same way at the end of the day. Or when's your next Caribbean holiday coming up?'

Wegener took off his coat, draped it over the back of a chair and sat down. 'Toralf, you've never been a socialist, and if it's up to me you'll never have to be one. But illegal publications, squatting houses, distributing fliers, insulting People's Policemen is one thing. Planting bombs is something else.'

Toralf combed his waterfall away from his face with one hand. 'And where did it get me, the fliers, the samizdat crap? Our country's been on its deathbed for sixty years and Revitalization was nothing but a life-prolonging measure instead of finally switching off the life-support machines. Even the dumb word tells you so! The patient must be long dead if you have to revitalize them, right?'

'Would you like to smoke?'

'Yes. Thanks.'

Without comment, Brendel took a cardboard box out of his coat pocket and extended it to Toralf, who fumbled three cigarillos out of it.

'If it hadn't been for Revitalization the whole thing would have been over years ago by now,' said Toralf, 'and we'd be sitting in a Munich beer garden with thirteen wheat beers inside us, laughing our heads off at all this bullshit. If a country's terminally ill it ought to be left to die in peace.'

'Are those Alexander Bürger's slogans?'

Toralf accepted a light from Brendel and sucked on the end of the cigarillo like a hungry baby at its mother's breast. A cloud of smoke blossomed around his head. It smelled of vanilla. 'They're the slogans of every thinking individual in this country, Hauptmann, and Alex put words into action. That's all.'

'You know what, Toralf, the question now is: What have you got to offer us?'

'Is that the question?'

'It is. You're sitting tight, and I don't think there's anywhere tighter to sit in this country than here. I'm even afraid there's nowhere tighter in the whole of the Socialist Union than here. And there's nothing I can do for you if you don't talk. Even I don't know where we are. They drove us here in a closed van, Toralf, via detours, even though we're policemen. This room, the chair you're sitting on, your brown bread – they don't even exist in the GDR. It's all thin air. And I don't think they'll let us come again, it's more likely Bodo Ramelow will open a branch of Goldman Sachs in Karl-Marx-Stadt. So it really is all about the question of what you've got to offer us.'

Toralf stared at the floor. 'What do you want from me? I've been

interrogated twenty-two times about Saturday's bombing and twenty-
two times I've kept shtum. I'm not a traitor.'

'We're not interested in the bombing.'

'So why are you here?'

Brendel held up a photo of Hoffmann.

Toralf looked uncomprehending. 'Who's that?'

'Come on, Toralf.'

'I've never seen him, Hauptmann. Who is he?'

'The victim of a brutal murder. His name's Albert Hoffmann.
Found hanged by the Müggelsee, as you can see. With his shoelaces
tied together. And guess who told us you had some more information
for us?'

'Santa?'

'Nearly right. Your good old Brigade buddy Ronny Gruber.'

'What?!'

'You heard me.'

Toralf looked frozen in shock. 'How did you find Ronny?'

'What do you know, Toralf?'

'Nothing! Ronny may think I had something to do with it, but I
didn't, it's not true!'

'Ronny was pretty sure you could help us.'

The inbred face didn't know where to look, furrows digging into
Toralf's pale skin and then smoothing out again, his mouth floating
between rage and fear, his long fingers grabbing at his blond hair, for
a moment looking as if they wanted to tear out the whole magnificent
lot of it. Genuine desperation, thought Wegener, but he's not a killer,
he hasn't got the nerve for that. He's got into something and now he's
sitting here and gradually starting to realize that the Brigade works
differently than he thought, that he's made a mistake that might cost
him his life. In the worst case without bringing his death.

Toralf looked at Wegener. 'Where do you think this is?'

'You're in the hands of the State Security. I don't know any more than that.'

'But the Stasi always looked different to this.'

'Because you were always in the visible part of the State Security. This is the invisible part.'

Toralf's hands burrowed in his waterfall of hair. 'Can you get me out of here?'

'Not if you don't help us.'

'That's blackmail.'

'That's an offer.'

'And if I do help you?'

'Then there's one possibility.'

'What is that possibility?'

'Bautzen.'

'Great.'

'Bautzen's better than this place, isn't it?'

'Anything's better than this place.'

'Those are the conditions,' said Wegener. 'What do you say?'

Toralf tipped his head back and looked at the padded ceiling; the blind sky of his new home, thought Wegener, a black hole in the land where he now lived, where you could hear insanity approaching on squeaking soles, creeping through the corridors hour by hour, not opening the cell doors, never saying a word you could shout out against, never asking questions or making demands, not threatening punishments, not taking shape, just deaf-and-dumb isolation, just your own voice that would one day start talking to you as if to a stranger, the soliloquy as interrogation, your own ego the most brutal truncheon, twenty-four hours a day of yourself and nothing else, just cruel grey silence.

'The conditions,' said Toralf with the voice of a man who knows the only way to get his head out of the noose is to saw away at it with a cheap blunt penknife made in China. 'Fuck the conditions.'

'Imagine I meet someone from the victim's family one of these days,' said Wegener. 'What am I supposed to tell them? That Hoffmann died because a group of young men decided to set up a really explosive club for bourgeois vigilantes?'

'The Brigade doesn't kill people.'

'I imagine Albert Hoffmann sees that differently.'

'I don't work with murderers, Hauptmann, I wanted to take a stand against this fucking country with all the fucking wankers on the Central Committee, but no one was supposed to get hurt! That was the top priority!'

'Maybe for the bombing, Toralf. But your people obviously had another operation going on. With different rules.'

'I don't know what happened there.' Toralf was still staring at the ceiling. 'There was some kind of operation, that's true, but it was only Sascha and our nexor who had anything to do with it. They kept me out of it.'

'Is Sascha the man who died during the bombing?' Toralf gave a mute nod. 'And what's a nexor?'

'The nexor is the leader of a cluster. He's the only one with a link to the next-higher level. You know all that yourself.'

'We don't know that. What was this leader's name?'

'Gabriel.'

'Gabriel what?'

'Opitz. Gabriel Opitz.'

'And why didn't you have anything to do with this mysterious operation? I was told a cluster always works as a team.'

'It was different this time.'

'Why?'

'It came from the very top.'

'From Alexander Bürger.'

'Presumably.'

Wegener sighed. 'Listen, Toralf, I believe you. But Ronny was pretty credible too when he told us you'd be able to help us. If you don't know anything and you weren't there, at least tell us where to find this Gabriel. If the thing they were keeping you out of was Hoffmann's murder, then your nexor geezer belongs in prison, because he's a murderer. So come on, Toralf, help us out here. Where is Gabriel Opitz hiding?'

Toralf's head slumped onto his chest, a blond curtain in front of his long face, the eyes behind it two freshly charged cigarette lighters.

Wegener held his silence.

Brendel cleared his throat.

Toralf gave a sudden smile, which wilted into a hard line. 'I'm sorry but I can't tell you where Gabriel is. The clusters are organized so that it's every man for himself after something goes wrong – we all have our own personal emergency plan. No one else knows that plan. There's no help from the Brigade. That makes it very hard for the individual and very easy for the movement. That's the way it works. It's the only chance.'

'The only chance for who?'

'For our fatherland.'

'You don't like the GDR very much, do you?'

'We might as well have stuck to the Third Reich, the way things work here.' Toralf took a puff at his cigarillo, spread his arms and stretched. A smoking, skinny saviour without a crucifix. 'Only Bürger and his closest circle know the operations, all the other information is graduated in hierarchies. The nexor is told what's necessary, the others are told nothing at all.'

'That makes sense,' said Wegener. 'But it's no use to us. Have you got any idea of what this murder might have to do with the Brigade?'

'No. I didn't even know anyone had died. I don't know this Hoffmann, I've never seen the man, I swear.'

'And what might make Bürger make exceptions to his rules? At what point is the struggle worth a human life?'

'I don't know.' Toralf stared into space. 'Maybe you ought to look for a man who got shot.'

'What do you mean?'

'Someone who got shot in the back of the head. Executed.'

'Albert Hoffmann wasn't shot.'

'I'm not talking about him.' Wegener stared at Toralf. Toralf stared at Wegener.

The cigarette-lighter eyes flashed in dark caverns, everything housed in that look: desperation, insanity, assurance, amusement. They're a gambling man's eyes, thought Wegener, the eyes of a gambler who has to put everything on a single card, because it's his last card and his last game, because the end is nigh and he knows he can never win again if he doesn't pull something out of his sleeve right now.

'I'm just thinking of where we always used to meet, Hauptmann,' Toralf said quietly. The right corner of his mouth twitched. 'At the Yeltsin.'

'They do good meatloaf,' said Wegener. 'Josef reckons it's the second best in town. After the Schusterjunge.'

If only they'd go easy on the caraway seeds, complained Früchtl.

'Do you remember the first time we talked, Hauptmann? The

Heiko Notter thing? That was twelve years ago now. On the 27th of October. 7 p.m.' Toralf's voice sounded almost sentimental by now. For a moment he looked like he was about to cry.

Wegener thought he could hear the cameras rotating their lenses, zooming in, closer and closer, onto Toralf's out-of-control face, which was rattling through emotions second by second: despair, ridicule, uncertainty, joy, satisfaction, disgust, the grimaces followed so quickly one after another that the black-clad men in the observation room must be sitting clueless in front of their monitors, presumably thinking it was a technical defect, a burnt-out cable in the system, a blown fuse in the high-security prison, a short circuit in Toralf's brainbox.

He's trying to give you a tip-off, said Früchtl.

I don't understand him, Josef, I just don't get it!

Give him time. Talk to him. Say something.

'You still remember that, Toralf? After all these years?'

'Crazy, eh?' Toralf tittered. 'I've always remembered that date – it's my sister's birthday. 27th of October.'

'I know the one,' said Wegener. 'Pretty girl.'

'Gorgeous!'

You're doing well, said Früchtl, *keep going.* 'That's a long time ago,' said Wegener.

'If you'd told me back then we'd be sitting here today, Hauptmann . . . '

'Then?'

' . . . then I might have run away. I might have had the courage then. Now I've got the courage and I can't run away any more.'

Keep going, said Früchtl.

'Where would you run to, Toralf? If you could?'

'To the West, Hauptmann. Like everyone else. To the West.'

'And then?'

Toralf smiled and shrugged. Silence.

The quiet here's not peace, thought Wegener, it's an artificial deathly hush. The impossibility of any sound. This must be what Andreas Jähn felt like, the son of the great German cosmonaut Sigmund, when his safety cable broke and he floated off into infinity, the unconditional forsakenness clear to see from the very first second, interned in his own skin, vacuum-packed, best before: see date of natural organ failure.

Toralf raised his right hand. 'Good luck, Inspector Brendel. Have a good journey home, when the time comes.'

Brendel looked as if he wanted to say something but held his tongue.

Toralf laughed a dry laugh, like rustling leaves on a forest floor, thought Wegener, an Odradek laugh.

Brendel got to his feet.

Toralf's laugh was still rustling in the silence.

Wegener got up too and put on his coat. He walked over to Toralf and heaved him half off the chair. Toralf swayed, drooping over Wegener like a marionette whose puppeteer had just been shot, his thin arms dangling over Wegener's shoulders.

'The conditions,' whispered Toralf, 'I've met them, Hauptmann, honest, I've fulfilled them, get me out of here, take me to Bautzen, please . . . '

'I lied to you,' whispered Wegener. 'I can't do anything for you, Toralf. Nothing at all. I'm sorry.'

Toralf gasped, coughed, gurgled, he sounded as if he was about to vomit, and Wegener held him close for twenty or thirty seconds, neither of them moving.

Brendel stood around indecisively and looked at the floor.

Wegener felt Toralf clinging to his jacket, grabbing hold of it as firmly as he could. We're an agonizing statue of Stasi victims, he thought, each of us in his own way, and he breathed in the scent of the waterfall of hair – they'd obviously let him keep his shampoo – and then Toralf's toothpick legs gave out on him, his grip loosened and his body sagged. Wegener let him slip slowly to the floor, took a step back, turned away and walked to the door.

Brendel followed with heavy footsteps.

Toralf lay rolled up on the white PVC, a blond bobtail, his face invisible under his mane, a groaning body who was now starting to give himself up and bury his last hopes but refused to do so, would keep believing he could make it, keep getting up again to fight, keep collapsing again, dragging himself to his feet only to lose every time, every day a funeral until one day nothing more stirred.

The door was opened before Wegener could knock. Two masked men were waiting, locking the white room from outside and escorting them as mutely as beforehand. The walk back through the building was either exactly the same as on the way in or a completely different route. Wegener thought of Wolfgang Lippert's game show, *Wanna bet I won't get lost in the world's largest secret service prison*, a wager for your own life – if you lose, you stay here.

'Maybe you ought to inform his sister,' said Brendel after they'd been sitting in the back of the Barkas for half an hour, as silent as the fishes of Badenhoop, staring into space on the way to Berlin, back to the grey that looked positively colourful when you'd seen that subterranean Stasiland. 'At least she won't waste time hoping he'll come back.'

Wegener shook his head. 'That'll be tricky.'

'Why tricky?'

'Toralf's an only child.'

25

WEGENER LOOKED AT HIS WATCH. Almost two hours had passed. They'd got the Barkas driver to drop them off in Greifenhagener Strasse, then broken the police seal on Hoffmann's door, called Frank Stein and searched the place again, not for DNA but for something to drink, until Brendel discovered two bottles of 1980 Claque-Pépin calvados, fetched three glasses from the kitchen and invited the others to a drink in the cotton-wool-sofa softness of the salon.

Silent and lost in thought, Wegener, Brendel and Stein had emptied the first bottle glass by glass, their eyes fixed on the darkening city sky above Berlin, the TV tower, the stoical light dome of the Palace. Pale blue had changed to yellowish pink and then dark blue, Brendel had cracked open the second bottle, lit candles and put his feet up on the coffee table. That Stasi silence steals your voice away for hours, thought Wegener, it sticks to you like the grease on the house fronts, it gives you a need to stay silent – talking's no use to anyone anyway, there's no point to it at all, inside or out, the situation's cemented, it's irreversible, impossible to grasp in words or in thoughts so no one even attempts it, we all fall silent as the grave.

'We're not getting it,' said Brendel at some point in a calvados-soaked voice.

Well, well, thought Wegener, the resigned super-detective, that Stasi hell's even got the better of him too. Of course we're not getting it, we've been thinking about nothing else for two hours and trying not to think too much of Toralf at the same time, that poor guy buried alive in there; the riddle's all that counts, the damned homework that we've got less than forty-eight hours left to do.

'Maybe he was lying to you back then,' said Brendel.

'He wasn't.' Wegener sipped at his glass. 'He didn't have to. Not only is there no sister, there wasn't a first informer meeting on the 27th of October at 7 p.m. at the Yeltsin. Like I told you, we first met in April 2000, one spring morning or other at Gendarmenmarkt.'

'So, let's go through it again. We've got the date,' said Stein. 'The 27th of October is the day after tomorrow. What's going to happen at 7 p.m. the day after tomorrow?'

'Maybe a second bomb. At the Yeltsin.' Brendel reached for the calvados, filled his glass to the brim and put it to his lips. A dark drinker's silhouette before the backdrop of the Berlin skyline. 'But he can't know the date of the next bombing, not with what he said. Unless his own cluster was going to carry it out.'

'And his cluster doesn't exist any more,' said Wegener. 'Gabriel's on the run, Sascha's in heaven, Ronny's in paradise. And I can't see any reason why he'd tell us the date of a second bombing, even if he did know it. He wished you a good journey home, Richard. *Good luck. Have a good journey home.*'

'Because he wishes he could come with me to the West. His girl-friend's over there. She is his girlfriend, this Julia girl?'

'She used to be, at least. In better days.'

'He didn't go over back then and now he regrets it. Julia's meeting plenty of men in the West and she's probably written him off for dead.'

'Which isn't far from the truth.' Wegener looked over at Brendel, who had half sunk into Hoffmann's cotton-wool couch. A drunken comic character, flattened by the inevitable steamroller, now a mere two-dimensional transfer flowing submissively down the contours of the sofa.

The comic character yawned. 'Do you think they noticed anything?'

'That's the million-mark question,' said Wegener. 'They'll listen to the tapes over and over, from beginning to end. If they notice anything I'll be the first to feel the pain, that much is for sure.'

Brendel sniffed at his glass. 'The Stasi snaps up Toralf, checks him over and finds out this Toralf used to be a police informer. And you were his liaison officer. So they get you in for an interrogation in the hope that he'll trust you and tell you something he wouldn't tell them. They can't force their barbiturates down his throat. Imagine the Hoffmann case comes to trial and it's monitored by the West. And they've been administering drugs to witnesses. You can forget that. So they thought they'd get some advantage out of the interrogation. But what?'

'Probably exactly what you two wanted to know,' said Stein. 'Where is this Gabriel Opitz character?'

'Only he can't give that away. Because he doesn't know. That's the point of the whole system, that they can't give anything away.'

'That's just it,' said Brendel. 'But he does give us a secret message, something about a sister, the day after tomorrow, Yeltsin and going home. What was he trying to tell us? I can't think straight any more.'

Wegener got up and walked across the creaking, shiny floorboards to the wardrobe-height arched windows. This was where Hoffmann had stood to view his playing field, a treacherous, scheming commander, the theoretical knowledge of the past century in his mind, a plan for this century in his mind's eye, with the aim of changing the city he'd once come to as a West German professor, the city that had given him power and taken it away again, that had proved obstinate, never easy to conquer and just as resistant this time around.

A city that perhaps, Wegener thought, demanded the death of the conqueror as the price for its conquest, and perhaps the Playmaker had even included that in his calculations, pledged his own death in return for the success of an unpredictable battle, or perhaps it was all completely different in the end and Hoffmann and Bürger were identical, one and the same strategist who was now posthumously carrying out his plan for the total destruction of the totally stubborn GDR, the failure of the gas consultations accompanied by bombings, economic bankruptcy and terrorism, as a plague on a land that had refused to take his advice.

Wegener downed the rest of his calvados. He realized he'd lost touch with his instinct, his mistrust had finally gained the upper hand, mistrust of everything and everyone, a mistrust that didn't allow any more insight, that made him Mistruster Number One with bells on top. The socialist sickness had him in its grip now, and suddenly he could imagine anyone and everyone in a black Stasi balaclava: Borgs, Brendel, Kayser, Lienecke, Hoffmann the double-triple-agent, the victim as perpetrator, everything was possible in this land of unlimited possibilities.

Wegener walked creakily into the next room, took his Minsk out of his trouser pocket and called Karolina.

The ringtone turned into a foghorn in his head, roaring six, seven, eight times, and Wegener was glad nobody picked up, because he basically had no idea of what to say to a woman you loved and hated, in professional and private life, a woman you admired and abhorred, abhorred with a sense of shame as you were afraid you only abhorred her because she'd learned to do without Martin Wegener, because you were no longer part of her life, you'd become a foreign body that she could betray with a light heart, a foreign body that had long since turned into a rapidly ageing object, unloved, eaten away by envy and jealousy and by your own bloody sense of powerlessness, that sat on your back like an unwashed dwarf with glowing-hot knitting needles, that stabbed you sixty times an hour and—

'Hello?'

'Karolina?'

'Martin! I tried to call you.'

'I know. I've been busy.'

'Still that murder case?' Karolina sounded uncertain.

'Yes, still the murder. That professor. Alfred Hoffmann.'

'Al*bert* Hoffmann.'

'Oh, Karolina.' Wegener felt something biting into his innards, a homicidal tapeworm just that instant breaking through the wall of his intestine and squeezing into his abdominal cavity and pissing all over everything with some kind of acidic secretion that instantly ate its way into all his soft parts. Wegener felt his guts burning while a foam hammer banged him on the head at two-second intervals and created a numbing dizziness, and on top of that he heard Karolina breathing directly into his ear, unnaturally loud and mechanical as if she was attached to an iron lung, and Wegener knew that she'd just closed her doe-brown eyes, that she was biting her painted lower lip in rage, that her sweet face had blushed bright red and would still be red in an hour's time, her hands two little clenched fists just about to be let loose on the tabletop.

'I'm so sorry, Martin.' Karolina made a sound as though the last breath of air was just escaping from her. 'When can we talk?'

Wegener hung up. Stood alone in the dark. In the dusty parchment air, the walls black with books, all these vellum-bound thoughts of dead writers, a gigantic repository for unrealized visions, abandoned social orders, forgotten philosophies, between which Hoffmann could seamlessly shelve his Posteritatism, another failed idea and another failed man, with nothing left of him but the documentation of his failure in book form, a few nice little thoughts about how lovely it could have been, what might have been possible: reading material for slaves to the subjunctive.

A library like this, thought Wegener, is really just another kind of purgatory. I've got mine and you've got yours, Albert, to each his own, an individual hell for every individual; tailor-made tortures – the non-existent creator was at his most creative when it came to that.

Wegener clicked into his phone's memory to the entry *MfS-W* and pressed Dial.

'Storck.'

'Wegener, Criminal Investigation Department. I'd like to speak to Franz Decker.'

'One moment, please.'

Crackling on the line.

'Decker. Who's speaking, please?'

'Martin Wegener.'

'What can I do for you, Mr Wegener?'

'Major-General Wischinsky was going to authorize me for surveillance permission.'

'That's correct, you're authorized.'

'Can I put in a request by telephone?'

'Of course. Right away, if you like.'

'Right, there's an address and a telephone number.'

'I'll note them down.'

'The address is Colombetstrasse, spelt with a C and B, E, T, and the number's 34. Third floor. Do you need any more information?'

'How many persons?'

'One woman. The inhabitant.'

'That's fine. Our surveillance includes a photographic protocol, a daily routine protocol and a list of contact persons.'

'OK. The telephone number is 113 20 23 34 53 190.'

'I'll repeat that: 113 20 23 34 53 190.'

'That's right.'

'The telephone surveillance team records all calls, and we also compile a contact list.'

'Thanks. How soon will the results be sent to me?'

'That depends on your requirements, Mr Wegener. We offer to inform you immediately of the target person's every movement. Or if you prefer you can come straight to Normannenstrasse and view the material here.'

'Can't you send me the stuff?'

'I'm afraid not. The material is not allowed to leave the premises.'

'Right. Goodbye.'

'Bye.'

Wegener hung up, leaned his head against a row of cool leather book spines and thought, now I'm Toralf Kleyer, alone in the dark, taken leave of my senses.

What would you do if they kleyered you away? asked Früchtl's voice. *What, Martin, what would you do?*

I don't know, Josef. I'm the drunk out of us two today.

But you still managed to call up the Stasi.

It's like dessert, there's always room for that.

Think about it: Just assume you've lost everything. And you know it.

I've lost everything and I know it.

Don't talk nonsense. What would you do?

Save Karolina, that bitch, that beautiful, unprincipled bitch.

You see, my nearly-son, you see, you see, that's the really crazy thing about people – the stronger the love, the weaker it makes them.

By the time Wegener shuffled back over the creaking floorboards into the salon fifteen minutes later, he knew what the homework was, he knew what the point must be to a riddle posed by a man who realized his fate was sealed but who still wanted to live on somehow, what ace he still had up his sleeve even though he was holed up in a concrete dungeon. That man sought his rescue in the rescue of another. That was his very last, final triumph. That man wanted to have the last word, to save a loved one who was much more important to his opponents than he was himself. If he managed that, they wouldn't have defeated him.

Darkness in the salon. Brendel and Stein were droopy shadows draped across their sofas, the candles nothing but two flickering stubs, a measly leftover of calvados in the slim green bottle.

'Richard.'

Brendel moved. 'Where've you been?'

'Toralf gave us a pointer to Gabriel Opitz.'

'What?'

'He wants us to save Opitz from the Stasi.'

Brendel was suddenly wide awake. 'Why do you think that?'

'Toralf's clever, he knows he'll never see daylight again. So now he's thinking about the only man in his cluster who's still free. He's Kleyer's last chance to live on. Through another man's freedom. I presume the two of them were quite close.'

'To be honest, that sounds like a bunch of esoteric nonsense,' said Stein. 'I thought this guy Toralf told you he didn't know where Gabriel was.'

Wegener shook his head. 'His exact words were: *"I can't tell you where Gabriel is."*'

Brendel struggled out of the couch. 'He couldn't say it because he knew we were being taped! That's what he meant! But he could drop a hint.'

'They must have arranged a meeting, just in case anything went wrong,' said Wegener. 'Against all the rules. The thing with the bomb was a much bigger deal than the stuff they usually do. And something did go wrong.'

'Assuming you're right,' Brendel tapped a cigarillo out of his box. 'They arrange a meeting place . . .'

Stein pulled a face. 'But not at seven at the Yeltsin the day after tomorrow, not in a million years! Half of Normannenstrasse will be sitting in there, eating solyanka soup and telling each other jokes they've picked up from their wiretaps!'

'What exactly did he say?' The doorbell buzzed.

Stein got up and left the room.

Brendel took a puff on his cigarillo. 'He quite clearly named this Yeltsin place. And the sister he apparently never had.'

'The imaginary sister was just a spontaneous pretext to give us the date. The 27th of October. 7 p.m. The day after tomorrow.'

'We ought to look for a second murder victim,' said Brendel. 'He mentioned that too. Someone shot in the head from behind. What was that all about?'

'No idea,' said Wegener.

Brendel dropped back onto the sofa. 'No one's been shot from behind. Not on our case, anyway.'

'You lot are drinking and I have to work.' Kayser came clomping in and dropped down onto Stein's armchair.

Stein sat down next to Brendel, who topped up his glass and pushed it across the table to Kayser: 'It's French.'

Kayser took off his jacket, reached for the glass and sipped at it. 'Excellent calvados. Very nice and cosy you lot have it here. We'll have to wait and see how long for.'

'Out with it then. What's up?'

'Ronny Gruber.' Kayser put the glass down. 'He's been an informer for State Security for nine years. Codename Hermes.'

Brendel's head dropped onto his chest. 'Says who?'

'Says the Federal Intelligence Service in Pullach, and they have several credible sources to back it up.'

Silence.

'A red herring,' said an incredulous Frankenstein: 'the whole Gruber Brigade thing's a gigantic red herring?'

Kayser nodded and looked at Wegener. 'Congratulations, Hauptmann. You've got a great nose for secret service shit.'

Wegener noticed he'd started to laugh, loudly and with abandon, so much abandon that his whole body was shaking, and he couldn't stop until he'd run out of breath.

WEDNESDAY 26 OCTOBER 2011

26

THE S-CLASS BONNET NOSED ITS WAY out of the police headquarters driveway like a black shark's muzzle. The rest of the car swam slowly out of its angular cavern, stopped for a moment, and then the shark glided out onto the road.

Wegener was behind the wheel of Christa Gerdes' old Wartburg, watching the Mercedes weave its way into the traffic in the rear-view mirror. He pressed himself into the narrow Wartburg seat and folded down the sunshade. A Mecklenburg Country Apple-scented air-freshener tree dangled beneath the plastic sky of the car's roof.

The usual gawkers stopped on the pavement, a young man taking pictures on his Minsk as the S-Class came closer and swished past. The outlines of the driver and the passenger behind the tinted windows, and the wide rear with its solid hunchback of boot got smaller, indicating left, then the Mercedes turned off towards the city centre.

A pale blue Phobos I left the row of parked cars, and a moment later a rusty red Phobos Universal started its ignition.

Wegener half ducked behind the passenger seat, stayed out of sight as he counted ten, fifteen, twenty seconds, and then popped up again.

The road was empty.

He started the engine. A craze of rattles and squeaks. The Mecklenburg Country Apple had no chance – there was an instant draught of chip-pan perfume wafting through all the rusty gaps and porous seals.

Your sweetshop scent'll be no use in here, thought Wegener as he put his foot down. We'll both have the same stench in Boltenhagen, Richard Brendel. The West German and his East German: two sardines in oil arriving in their own tin can.

The driveway to the EastSide was lined on both sides by terracotta pots planted with round box trees; a cordon of chopped-off green heads, Wegener concluded as he switched to the oxblood-red turn-off lane with five brass stars embedded in its surface. An asphalt-red carpet meant to make the Western fat cats feel at home. At the end of the curve of trees, two barriers blocked the way.

Wegener stopped.

A well-stuffed greyish-blue page's uniform with a double row of golden buttons appeared from nowhere and knocked at the greasy car window, visibly disgusted.

Wegener wound it down.

'Can I help you, sir?' The page spoke with an adenoidal twang, somewhere between boredom and annoyance. On top of his shaving-rashed neck perched a melon with a moustache and he clutched a can of sour cherry-flavour diet Club-Cola. The name tag on his uniform chest said in English: *You are talking to Sascha Günzow*.

'I'm picking up a colleague.'

Now Sascha Günzow felt sorry for him. 'But not at the EastSide Resort, I'm sure, sir.'

'Oh, I'm sure I am. The barrier please, if you don't mind.'

'You're not staying at the resort, am I right?' The page downed his cola in one large gulp and threw the empty can neatly into a public wastebin.

'I'm not staying at the resort and I don't intend ever to stay at the resort. But I do intend to collect my colleague, who is staying at the resort – right now.'

The contented smile of the part-time powerful spread across Günzow's melon mug. 'The VIP Car-Walk is reserved for our premium guests, sir, I'm afraid. I'll have to ask you to reverse your car carefully.'

Wegener slapped his police ID card open. 'Prick up your piggy ears, Sascha – in ten minutes' time I'll have let your boss know you've been spying on all the premium guests for the State Security.'

Wegener wound the window up again.

The melon had gone pale. In its watery fruit-pulp brain a duel was taking place between the two eternal alternatives for all Germans: bowing and scraping or yelling and shouting, bowing and scraping or yelling and shouting. Bowing and scraping won. The arms of the barriers folded upwards, soundlessly. Günzow stood next to them with clenched baby fists and fired off a hundred flashing glares per second, all of which bounced off the Wartburg's oily force field.

Wegener rattled along the terracotta cordon up to the white staircase and turned off the engine. Above the steel tent of the canopy the currency cock reared up in the air, a glass sausage growing slimmer and slimmer. The plasma mega-poster was lit up in yellow today, spelling out in black upper-case lettering:

THE DIFFICULTY LIES NOT SO MUCH IN DEVELOPING NEW IDEAS
AS IN ESCAPING FROM OLD ONES.

John Maynard Keynes

Brendel appeared below the canopy, donned a pair of black sunglasses, looked around, spotted the car and came casually down the
white steps, both hands in his trouser pockets, his pale trench coat
wafting around him – a brawny market-economy model on the show-
biz staircase of success, except that it wasn't the polished Mercedes
he was heading for but Christa Gerdes' mobile scrap metal collection:
greasy, rattly and smelly. The Scrap-Class.

How the mighty fall, thought Wegener.

Brendel tugged open the flimsy door, squeezed himself onto the
passenger seat and removed his shades. 'Good morning. So?'

'Morning. A Phobos and a Universal.'

'What do you reckon?'

Wegener started the engine. 'State Security, who else? We've got a
man posted just outside Pankow, so we'll know if they keep on our
tail that long.'

'OK. And that was it?'

'Well, I arrived at the VIP Car-Walk all on my own, at least.'

'The VIP Car-Walk.' Brendel smiled. 'Martin, could I have seen
your ex-girlfriend in the breakfast room this morning?'

Wegener taxied the Wartburg along the driveway and turned onto
the right-hand lane for Honecker-Allee.

'Could be. The Energy Ministry is across the square in the
Berolina-Haus.'

Brendel nodded. 'The photos in your file. You know.'

Vile photos, thought Wegener: it's funny, he says file but all I hear
is vile, I keep seeing her spreading her shaved legs for the Gazprom

boys' Zorki digicameras, that whore to success, that Berlin Mata Hari. They wouldn't have let her in through the staff entrance of the EastSide six years ago and now she struts around the place in her nice suit and plays at being West German, invited to spend the night with breakfast included, negotiating contracts, meeting Hoffmann, denying she's met him, celebrating contract conclusions with champagne binges and getting every last drop out of her business partners for the sake of the fatherland. After all, her qualifications are internationally recognized: doe eyes, freckles, fiery red hair and a smile to melt every Russian gas boy's frozen Fabergé eggs in split seconds, a Bunsen burner giggle that makes those syndicate stock bulls' mafiosi sperm boil, all for a bit more margin and profit – you opportunistic, money-grubbing, conscience-free rouble mattress, thought Wegener, having to force himself not to punch the rickety steering wheel.

Brendel was trying to take off his coat on the miniature seat. 'You're not surprised, then.'

'At some point you give up being surprised about anything.' Wegener stopped at a traffic light. The light instantly changed to green. He put his foot down so hard that Christa Gerdes' worn-down tyres screeched.

'Which one of you finished it?'

'She finished it.'

'Why?'

An interrogation, thought Wegener, and you're dumb enough to let yourself in for it. But it's just so good to get it off your chest, to a priest, a doctor or a cop, just as long as someone listens. 'Why do men tell lies, Richard?'

'Under socialism?'

'Anywhere.'

'Because of another woman,' Brendel said.

'Because of another woman,' Wegener confirmed, switching to fourth gear and suddenly up to almost 80 km/hr. The long, narrow apartment-house monsters of Honecker-Allee grew up into the sky on either side, barriers in front of the entrances, orange warning signs every fifty metres pronouncing *Danger!*, windows boarded up. All symbols of my relationship with Karolina, thought Wegener, crumbling ruins that there's no saving any more, but they still refuse to collapse.

'Was she beautiful, at least?'

'Much better than that: she was a beautiful Russian.'

'A policewoman?'

'Waitress at the Molotov Club.'

The Stangier monument came closer, iron Heinrich waving his accidental Hitler salute towards Mitte, fat pigeons perched on his horn-rimmed glasses, behind him the Jähn statue, Sigmund pulling at his steep bronze rope, a panicked tug of war in vain, his son Andreas drifting off with arms and legs outstretched, a flying X never to touch the ground again. Stangier turned his back on the father-and-son drama while the first of the apartment houses were being knocked down next to him. Excavators had eaten their way into the facades from one side and had suddenly lost their appetite, leaving a view of halves of living rooms and bedrooms, morbid doll's houses where sofas, chairs, tables and cupboards were still sticking it out, pictures hanging on the walls. In a halved bathroom, a pink toilet was balancing on the brink of demolition with its lid up.

'And she found out?'

'Everything gets found out some time.'

'You could be right.'

'I am right, believe me. Just look at Ronny Gruber. Even the Stasi got caught out. And they've got plenty of practice.'

'All right, let's just assume everything gets found out.' Brendel threw his coat onto the back seat. 'The question is, what does it mean? Does what's come out change anything? Or do you leave it at that? Do you take the consequences or is it enough to know the truth? Because you can tell the consequences would just make everything worse?'

'Karolina couldn't leave it at knowing the truth.'

Brendel nodded. 'She looks like that kind of woman.'

You idiot, thought Wegener and decelerated, you bloody idiot Martin Wegener, that rat Richard's lying through his teeth just like Karolina and you, stupid kolkhoz camel, lap up every word of it – saw her in the breakfast room! Saw her in the breakfast room this morning and all night long before that in his room, more like! And now he drops a chance meeting in the conversation; next time he'll say something to her – why not? That's a great way to make her official acquaintance, a great way to prepare the final revelation: Enders-Brendel, it sounds pretty crap but if you look that good you can put up with the world's dumbest double-barrelled name. So the two of them really are at it.

Now you really are losing it, said Früchtl's voice.

The birds and the bees.

The birds and the bees, Früchtl mocked him, *birds and bees!*

Two discreet informer turtle doves. And I'm Martin the plucked goose. The cooked goose. As usual.

My God, Martin the cooked goose, said Früchtl, *come back down to earth! You don't even believe this nonsense yourself!*

'And what would you decide?' Brendel's blue, blue eyes were still piercing him. 'If you were the one to find something out?'

'Decide about what?'

'For or against consequences. Do you have to take action on what you know, or can you accept things the way they are?'

Wegener changed down to third gear and tried to sound vaguely normal. 'I don't take action and I don't accept things. I remember things. If that qualifies as a consequence for you.'

Brendel nodded. He took his new Minsk out of his trouser pocket and dialled a number. 'Christian, it's me again. Who was that just now?'

Wegener looked in the rear-view mirror: Phoboses and Ladas floating along in the traffic, turning off, changing lanes, keeping to the speed limit. None of the cars looked familiar. Karolina in his head. Karolina naked, on top of and underneath other men. Andreas, thought Wegener, Andreas Jähn, you poor space sausage, you languishing lightweight, my brother in spirit. I may never have been up there but I'm right at rock bottom down here, I know exactly how abandoned you felt when you drifted off, how lonely you were on your way to Saturn, you world loneliness champion. And now poor Sigmund, the German Democratic Republic's first great cosmonaut, is all alone back home in Strausberg and mourning for his only son, just like I'm mourning for Major Meatloaf. It's only in the GDR that people disappear so radically, Andreas spinning through eternity in his airtight packaging, Josef vanished off the face of the earth, and at the end of the day the effect's the same: sometimes you think they never even existed.

Brendel listened at his telephone. 'OK. But be careful. I'll call you on our way back. I will, bye.'

'Kayser?'

'Yes.' Brendel put the Minsk back in his pocket. 'Someone called him fifteen minutes ago, said he'd been with GreenFAC for years. Wants to talk to him right away, apparently about incriminating evidence.'

'And?'

'It's pretty odd.'

'Why?'

'They called him on the hotel line. An external call, not via the reception. But nobody has that number.'

Wegener turned off towards the autobahn for the Baltic. 'What do you think?'

Brendel suddenly looked serious. 'I think we're getting somewhere.'

27

'HELLO?'

'Ms Schütz?'

'Yes.'

'We're here.'

'Where, exactly?'

'Fifty metres away from the pier.'

'Who's we? I told you to come alone!'

'I've got a colleague from the Federal Republic with me.'

'West German police? Rubbish.'

'We're cooperating on this case. As an exception. At the request of the Federal Chancellery.'

Silence.

'Ms Schütz?'

Silence.

'Ms Schütz, my colleague can show you his badge.'

'Just the two of you?'

'There's no one else here.'

'The State Security hasn't been informed?'

'No one's been informed. And no one followed us either.'

'Is your Minsk clean?'

'I don't know. I'm calling from a call box, though.'

'From the phone box at the roundabout?'

'That's the one.'

'Wait a moment.'

'OK.' A pause.

'You're wearing a brown coat and the other man has a pale one?'

'That's right.'

'I can see you.'

'And now?'

'You can leave right now if you're taking the piss.'

'I'm telling the truth, Ms Schütz.'

'No one's ever done that in this country.'

'That was just the first time, then.'

'Maybe. Maybe not.'

'Where do you want us to come to?' Silence.

'Ms Schütz, if I'd informed the State Security your telephone would have been pinpointed five minutes ago.'

'Go to the left-hand entrance. Act like you want to go for a swim and you've forgotten your towels.'

'Meaning?'

'Get a ticket for the spa and walk forwards to the white basket seat with the yellow sunshade, about 150 metres to your left. Can you see it?'

'Yes, but it's a nudist beach.'

'Well observed, detective. It's up to you – I'll be gone in five minutes' time.'

'Why don't we meet on the pier?'

'You'd like that, wouldn't you? Forget it, I know all your cops and robbers games. Have you brought the handcuffs?'

'Yes.'

'Take your clothes off and come over. The clothes stay at the ticket kiosk. All you bring with you is your police IDs and the handcuffs, nothing else. That is, if you want to talk to me.'

Now it was Wegener who was silent.

'Yes or no, Hauptmann Wegener – if that's really your name?'

'My name's Wegener.'

'How nice for you. What's it to be?'

'We're coming.' There was a click.

Wegener hung up the receiver and stepped out of the call box into the sea air. A surprisingly warm seaweed-scented wind hit him, blowing Brendel's coat up into a pale hunchback, tasting of salt and carrying screeching gulls towards the pier by an almost abandoned beach. The jagged screeches drifted above their heads, shrill, never-changing warning calls somewhere between pleasure and pain.

Silvery-haired senior citizens in white trousers and cardigans crept along the neatly swept promenade, huddled over as if they were searching the grey concrete paving stones for a meaning to their expired lives, for their biographies stuffed full of dictatorships, for the fact that they now had to take daily yard exercise in the uniforms of spa guests.

Mother's and Father's pathological utopia, thought Wegener, a spa lifestyle in pastel fabrics, keeping an eye on the deep blue horizon from the freshly whitewashed veranda and dreaming of everything that might wait for them beyond that marine border. If it has to be the GDR then at least as far as possible on the margin, at the northernmost edge, a box seat to keep a sharp eye on freedom for the rest of their dull days.

Brendel pulled a questioning face.

'She wants us to come to the beach.'

'Where?'

'Here.'

'The nudist beach?'

'That was her plan from the very beginning.'

'Why don't we meet on the pier? She'd have a much better over-view of the surroundings there.'

'Come on, before she buggers off again.' Wegener had taken off his coat and was walking straight across the circular plaza in front of the pier to the spa ticket kiosk. 'She's not bothered about the sur-roundings, it's about us, she's scared we'll be wired up to our ears or we'll knock her out with chloroform-soaked rags. What do I know? That's why she chose Boltenhagen, that's why it's this beach.'

Brendel was right behind him. 'She wants us to question her naked?'

'Exactly that.' Wegener stopped outside the open door to the wooden hut. Inside, an opened double page of the *Public Eye* was floating mid-air above a lumpy female body.

'Criminal Investigation Department,' said Wegener, holding his badge in front of him like a miniature shield. 'Would you mind look-ing after our things for half an hour or so?'

Brendel sat down on a bench, shaking his head, and started remov-ing his shoes.

The *Public Eye* lowered at the speed of an electric car window and a brown grandmotherly face emerged with alert eyes, which studied the plastic card for a couple of seconds. 'You can keep your togs on if you like, if you're here on business, Mr Hauptmann.'

'Not today, I'm afraid,' said Wegener, putting his card down on the windowsill in the hut and unbuttoning his shirt.

'If you say so. No one minds either way round here. You're in luck with the sunny weather and all, it's almost warm today, isn't it, eh?'

'But only almost.'

The grandmotherly face had vanished behind the newspaper again. 'You can put your things on the stool here and go through, no charge. I'm not seeing nothing today. And the bathing season's over in two days and all.'

Brendel had folded his clothes up into a parcel and was standing around nervously in a kind of black thong.

So that's what they wear over there, thought Wegener. He unfastened his belt, forced himself to look away, looked back again as Brendel was turning around and peeling off the tight black item. Two white arse-cheeks laughed at him. What on earth are you up to? thought Wegener: stop looking at the guy's backside, you'd better pull down your miracle cords and your underpants at the same time so he doesn't see that your country's still stuck in the underwear stone age.

'Have fun, gents,' said the newspaper as they were standing nude outside the hut, sunglasses on their noses, police IDs in their hands, grumpy stars of a second-class farce.

Brendel gave a sour look.

Wegener picked up the handcuffs.

Then they walked along the boardwalk to the water, side by side, eyes front. Now you're as naked as you've always felt, thought Wegener, but for once you're not the only one. The other guy's got nothing on either, the other guy's fully unprotected for the first time, undressed down to his police badge, and he may well be more athletic and muscled – that much was clear from the beginning, he hasn't got the slightest hint of a belly – but he still had to pull his pants down.

Wegener smiled.

The seaweed smell and the October sunshine sent a strangely intense feeling of happiness sloshing up inside him. This nakedness was a freedom he'd completely forgotten and now it came washing over him unexpectedly. It had been forced upon him but he found himself enjoying it again now, a childhood nudity he suddenly remembered, a perfectly natural feeling of letting go of everything that covered, hid, concealed. Back then he'd cast off the Trabant fustiness and the brown-coal dust alongside his parents, the damp of their old flat's walls and the boredom of the Free German Youth, and now it was the greasy Phobos exhaust fumes, the Karolina desolation, the festering uncertainty, the fear of one day ending up like Toralf Kleyer, officially missing, taken out of the game for ever, silenced and gagged for good.

For a few redemptory minutes all that didn't matter: the instant the cool sea air wafted everywhere, the instant it caressed his entire body and the Baltic Sea smelled as it had always smelled, not of the GDR but of ocean. At that instant everything seems possible, thought Wegener, even though you know that instant will be over in the next instant and then nothing will be possible any more, but for those few blinks of an eye even the most unrealistic things are conceivable, your own private Revitalization, all your fantastic dreams, an idyllically kitsch summer holiday with Father, Mother, Karolina and our three red-headed children, eternal non-loneliness, the only place of absolute trust, a just state, everything that could never happen because love and betrayal always take turns in this country: betrayal comes along, love goes on its way.

'Stop!' A friendly but firm commanding tone. Wegener and Brendel stopped moving in synch, turned around in synch and showed their amazement in synch.

'Handcuff yourselves together, then throw me the key and then your ID.' The young woman was naked but for a courier bag made of neoprene-like fabric, her head turning in all directions, a Stasi radar with green eyes and full lips, her fair hair hanging over her breasts in wet strands, one hand in her bag, holding a gun or perhaps not. 'Don't come any closer.'

Wegener pressed his right wrist into the handcuff, Brendel his left. The metal gave a click as the cuffs shut.

'Now the key and your ID cards.'

Wegener threw everything one after another with his left hand. The key was snapped out of the air in one swift motion, the two police cards landing on the sand. The woman squatted down, picked up the plastic cards and examined them closely, looking up at them alternately, finally eyeing Brendel's groin area uninhibitedly and getting up again. A derisive smile gradually appeared on her pretty face. 'I'd take your word for it that *he's* from the West without any ID, Martin Alfons Wegener.'

Wegener's eyes ignored the warning growl from his common sense, shifted their gaze downwards and got stuck. Brendel was totally shaved. Not one hair on his brown penis, which curved down like a circumcised banana and ended in a fat pale-pink head, not one hair on the full brown balls dangling beachward like two un-equally filled bags, stretched lengthways by their own weight, not even stubble where Marie Schütz had a deep black curly triangle, thinning out towards the sides and dripping water. She must have swum here, thought Wegener, and noticed even through his sun-glasses that Brendel's attractive face was communist-red. She's got everything she needs in her bag, some kind of watertight diving thing, and she'll leave the same way any minute now, while we're standing here as an indecently exposed involuntary reunification, East and West chained to each other by stainless steel, one of us hairy, the other bald, one of us hung like a horse on hormones, the other just about average.

'Ms Schütz, this is all a bit too much.' There was no need for Brendel to make a pretence of anger. 'Perhaps you find your father's death entertaining but we certainly don't.'

'You can call me Marie.' The derisive expression stayed on her face. 'I'll give you twenty minutes.'

'Could we perhaps take a seat?' Wegener raised his handcuffed hand and Brendel's arm went with it. 'That'd be a little more discreet.'

'The beach chairs are locked up. Or did you hire one?'

Wegener tried to sound casual. 'You make a suggestion, then.' He removed his sunglasses.

'Let's have a bit of a swim.' Marie smiled at him and took sideways steps to the water, a sauntering crabwalk, her eyes fixed on his face. Wegener was suddenly caught in her green eyes, two distant, circular ponds full of duckweed in the midst of a dense eyelash forest. That beardy old Hoffmann had produced a delicate, feline beauty, however and with whomever he'd managed it.

'It's a bit chilly but you get used to it.' The first wave rinsed the sand from Marie's toes. Black-painted toenails.

'Why are you in hiding, Ms Schütz?'

'Lots of reasons. Out of fear for one, since my father died. As you might imagine.'

Wegener gave a slight tug on the handcuffs and Brendel followed. The two of them ambled towards the water like a greying S&M couple, wading in immediately without showing the slightest emotion. Two humiliated men who didn't want to show any further sign of weakness.

'How did you find out about your father's death?' Brendel had found his polite questioning tone again.

'From a good friend.'

'A good friend by the name of Werner Blühdorn.'

Wegener had to get a grip on himself to stop his teeth from chattering. His feet were burning with the cold – later they'd be nothing but two blueish lumps that would fall off and shatter into a thousand pieces on the concrete promenade.

'You're right, it was Werner who told me. How do you know that?'

'East–West police collaboration,' said Brendel in a voice that didn't reveal the cold.

Wegener couldn't look away as Marie's nudity was swallowed up centimetre by centimetre by the Baltic, now licking at her thin thighs, now hitting the curly bush of pubic hair with a gentle wave, slapping it semi-transparent against her pale skin.

'Who do you think killed your father?'

'The West German newspapers are saying it was the Stasi. Werner sent me the latest *Spiegel*, it arrived this morning. I find it all fairly plausible, what they've written.' Marie put the handcuff key and the ID cards in her neoprene bag and closed the zip. Her pubic hair now disappeared for good in the frosty blue sea's ink. 'Have you found out what happened yet?'

'No,' said Wegener, 'not yet. That's why we want to talk to you. We now have reason to believe it really was the State Security that murdered your father.'

Marie stared at the water.

'But of course we have to ask ourselves one obvious question,' said Brendel. 'If it was the State Security, why did they tie your father's shoelaces together?'

'A cheap diversion tactic. You're not going to fall for that, are you?'

'But then it'd be a diversion tactic that backfired. It's because of the shoelaces that the *Spiegel*'s written about the case, and the consultations are at threat. That can't be in the Stasi's interest.'

Marie assumed a sulky look. 'How do I know what those maniacs think or why the whole thing ended up in the press?'

Wegener cleared his throat. 'Ms Schütz, I have to ask you this: Was your father with the Stasi?'

The sulkiness vanished and Marie gave a raw, hearty laugh. 'My father was never with the Stasi. Absolutely out of the question. Do you really think that?'

'No. But we've had a lot of surprises in this case, so we have to ask too many questions rather than too few.' Wegener's eyes searched Marie's torso for the slightest curves, instead finding two raspberry-sized nipples protruding fleshy and over-proportioned from between her wet strands of hair. God's dark-red, worthy replacement for the breasts He'd forgotten.

Marie smiled a tired smile. 'Have you heard of Martina Thal?'

'A former minister,' Wegener's teeth chattered, the icy sea now biting him in the arse, the hips, the back. 'I think, around about Revitalization.'

'Central Committee Special Representative on Internal Renewal and Restructuring of the State Security from '89 to '92.'

'Ah, right.'

'She was supposed to rejig the secret service for Moss, downsize it radically, adapt it to Western yardsticks and standards, and so on.' Marie kept walking deeper into the sea as she spoke, Wegener following her with Brendel in tow, the frozen feeling now coming up to his chest, his legs two tingling icicles, his cock a baby's thumb. Marie's nipples now submerged and got even larger in Wegener's mind, growing underwater into two rock-hard grapes that would never shrink back to size and would soon have to be entered in her identity papers by the People's Police, *Distinguishing features: the nicest nipples in the Socialist Union (SU)*.

'But that was all just an official scheme to get at the democratic hard currency, to tap into the emergency funds and pick up the EU's aid packages. Behind the scenes, everything was supposed to stay just the way it always was, a bit smaller of course but still the good old Stasi in the end, the same people, just that they now had huge budgets for their Research & Development departments, for secret service hi-tech gadgetry. All paid for with West German money that officially went into the Revitalization fund.'

'And back then Martina Thal fell in love with Albert Hoffmann,' said Brendel. 'Two fighters for socialist-democratic Posteritatism that nobody else wanted.'

Marie nodded.

'Tell us what happened.'

'My mother's maiden name was Schütz, her first husband was called Gerhard Thal – a literature professor from Leipzig.' Marie looked at Brendel. 'She met my father on the Standing Advisory Staff in 1989. No one was to know about the affair – the State Security and the National Strategic Control Council had contrary positions, they were supposed to keep each other in check and not jump into bed together.'

'And no one was to know about you either.'

Marie stroked her wet hair off her forehead. 'They kept everything a secret. They kept me a secret. My mother had me registered under her maiden name. She covered up the last few months of her pregnancy with sickness notes. Officially, I was the illegitimate child of a friend of Martina Thal's, who she helped to raise out of exemplary solidarity. It all got too much for her by the time I was seven. She threw herself in front of a train.'

Wegener looked at Brendel. With his tough sun-shaded face, he was standing as motionlessly in the Baltic Sea as if the Cosa Nostra had just chucked him in there with his feet embedded in a lump of concrete.

'And your father?'

Marie's hands were playing in the water, ladling it out of the sea and letting it slip back through her fingers. 'Later he became a friend I met in secret. Someone I trusted, someone who could only speak openly with me because he had nobody else.' Marie smiled. 'If they'd caught us we'd have said I was his whore.'

'Hence the condoms,' Wegener thought out loud, 'the dildos, the whip, the potency pills.'

'We laid a lot of clues that would have protected us.' Marie stared at the water. 'You're well informed.'

'Not well enough.' Brendel removed his sunglasses. 'Why would the State Security be interested in you? Your parents are dead. It's all over and done with. And you won't have had anything to do with your father's murder, I assume.'

'You can tell you're from the West.' Marie's delightful ridicule was back. 'My father spent hundreds of hours talking to me. Openly. Because we trusted each other. I know things about this country that you'd never believe. And I know how the Stasi works. My mother had to spend two years watching from the inside without being able to change it. That crap cost her her life. And I know the effect of thiopental and all that stuff.'

'Truth serums.'

'Yes, Mr Brendel, truth drugs. The East German way to get to the point quickly. If the Stasi has any idea that I exist they'll hunt me down until they find me. Think about it – the hidden daughter of two former members of the Standing Advisory Staff of the Chairman of the State Council, both security classification 1 for years, both quit their jobs out of protest, extremely conflict-relevant relationship structures plus serious emotional and ideological crisis, the most alarming combination there is, non-authorized passing on of highly sensitive information highly likely – that's how the socialist fascists put it in their secret-agent jargon. They have to make sure I don't know anything. That's their job. They'd put me on barbiturates until they'd heard everything my father ever told me, and then I'd never come out of there, I can promise you that.'

'But why . . . ?'

'He had to talk to someone.' Marie glared at Brendel as though he was the one who'd invented the State Security. 'It's as simple as that. He had to talk to someone he trusted.'

'Speaking of trust.' Wegener suppressed a shiver. 'Who would have a motive to kill him? Come on, help us out. And I promise you no one will find out that Albert Hoffmann and Martina Thal had a child.'

'And if I don't tell you anything?'

'No one will find out anything. I promise you.'

'A PP's promise.'

'The promise of a PP who'd be in deep shit if Uwe Speckmann knew who I'm taking a bracing dip with right now.'

There was a twitch in Marie's face. 'Dad never told me what he was planning or working on. His ideas were sacred to him, he kept his cards close to his chest. He didn't even share those things with me. And I didn't ask, either.'

'I thought he spent hundreds of hours talking to you!'

'He only ever talked about things that had already happened. Things he couldn't do anything to change. That really tormented him. He kept telling me about them.'

'Did you know your father had gained access to the government quarter in Wandlitz under a false name and worked there?' Brendel sounded impatient. 'For almost twelve years. As a gardener!'

Marie laughed. 'Pardon?'

'It's true.'

'No, I didn't know that.'

'He kept that from you for twelve years, Ms Schütz?'

Marie's laughter had subsided into a faint smile. 'We met once or twice a month, so there'll be a good few things he kept from me.' Marie looked back at the beach as if she'd heard something. 'His uncle in Heidelberg was a gardener, he worked for him as a student. He loved roses.'

'He loved roses.' Brendel puffed out his cheeks. 'Maybe he did, but it wasn't the roses that hanged him.'

Wegener looked Marie in the eye. 'Assuming your father wasn't with the Stasi but they still killed him – why? What secret would the State Security kill for, this close to the consultations?'

Marie held his eyes, looked over at Brendel briefly and swung back. Her lashes fluttered. 'I'm trusting you. And in return, no one finds out about my existence. Never, under any circumstances. Not at the police, not anywhere.'

Wegener couldn't answer, he was floating in the deeply sad duckweed eyes which were sucking him in with the force of a tide, paddling helplessly in Marie's lush green, noticing the blood flowing back into his penis, his penis stretching, enlarging, getting Karolina-warm out of admiration for that wet, open face.

'Have you ever heard of *Plan D*?'

'We have. A kind of energy supply concept.'

Marie looked amused. '*Plan D* was much more than an energy supply concept. It was a comprehensive strategy for democratizing and stabilizing the GDR.'

'What does that mean specifically?'

Marie looked Wegener in the eye. 'Stangier didn't take voluntary retirement as head of state in 1989.'

'What do you mean by that?'

'It was my father's idea. They chased the pig out of the farmyard. That's how he put it.'

'Moss staged a putsch?' Brendel's voice was almost turning somersaults.

'My father staged a putsch,' Marie said coolly. 'Without him, Revitalization would never have happened.'

Gulls shrieked somewhere high above them, at first not visible and suddenly there after all, gliding towards the pier, getting blown off course by the wind but just making it onto the white railings, lining up one alongside the next.

Marie's gaze had followed the seagulls and now came back. 'He worked on his plans for the coup from the early eighties onwards. Collected information, looked for weak points. Waited until he had almost the entire Politburo in the palm of his hand. When the time came they went through with it. It was against the constitution, but it was right. It was the last attempt to democratize this country. My father wanted socialism to live and breathe, not go to the dogs. Moss was his puppet. A pretty crap puppet, if you ask me.'

For a moment, Brendel's face had lost all authority. 'Hans-Walter Moss was never elected Chairman of the State Council by the People's Chamber?'

'No. Moss has been in power illegitimately for more than twenty years.' Marie's hands were playing with the water again. 'Blackmail, threats, pressure – that's how it went, all behind the scenes. Do you think anyone would have voted for that grinning loser? I've suspected for a while that my father wanted to go public with the story. Go to the press in the West.'

'Why wait till 2011? Twenty-two years?'

'That's obvious enough. He was waiting for the right moment, and that perfect moment is now. Moss on the ropes, the GDR under enormous pressure, the consultations coming up any day. There's never been more international attention on us. If Chairman M slips up now, Lafontaine will put the pressure on until they chuck him out. Lafontaine doesn't need Moss, all he needs is cheap gas.'

'So why on earth was your father working as a gardener in Wandlitz? For so many years?'

'I'd say you're thinking in the wrong direction. He just liked gardening. He always had. And he presumably thought it was funny to do it right in the middle of Wandlitz. Under the noses of the people who didn't want his political and strategic skills. So at least those fat cats couldn't get around his green fingers. That would be just like my father.'

'Did your father specifically tell you he wanted to take his information to the West German press?' Wegener asked.

'He said the party'd soon be over for the top cat.'

'When did he say that?'

'He kept saying it. The last time was two weeks ago. *Voilà*, there's your motive.' Marie pulled the strap of her bag tight. 'The biggest secret of all this country's dirty secrets. You didn't get it from me, though. Find yourselves a credible source or, better still, keep it to yourselves.'

'Thank you,' said Wegener.

'A sign of my trust.' Marie looked him in the eye. 'I presume you noticed the shoes?'

'What do you mean?'

'I mean the fact that my father didn't die in his own shoes.'

'What's that supposed to mean,' asked Brendel groggily, 'he didn't die in his own shoes?'

'Exactly what I said. Have you got the new *Spiegel*?'

'Yes, of course.'

'The photo. The close-up of the shoes with the laces tied together. My father would never have worn lace-up shoes. And certainly not such a worn old pair. He only ever wore horse-leather slip-ons. Werner Blühdorn used to get them for him. Don't tell me you did a post-mortem on the body and forgot the shoes?'

Brendel closed his eyes.

Marie nodded at Wegener. 'That's the GDR for you: Even West German cops go blind as a bat over here. You'll find the key to the handcuffs and your ID cards at the last jetty on the pier.' Then she turned around and launched herself into the water, disappearing towards the pier as if she never wanted to emerge again. After a few seconds she was nothing but a movement of the waves with two elbows burrowing out and digging back into the sea every second, burrowing out and digging in, rhythmic, powerful and absolutely determined.

Brendel watched her go. In his eyes was a mixture of dismay and lust.

If I ever need to look for her, thought Wegener, I'll start with the Penguin Clubs and move on to the swimming teams, ask for the best and most beautiful crawler, for a woman with duckweed in her eyes and raspberry nipples on a flat, soft, pale, magnificently absent chest. There was a time, thought Wegener, when you could have got to know that girl, when you could have won her over and stood by her, when her father was still alive, when you could have become part of her surreally tragic family, a fighter out of solidarity, rewarded with the

Eisenhüttenstadt-steel-hard affection of that beautiful, mocking, green-eyed, flat-chested, pubic-haired professor's daughter.

Wegener felt his penis tingling in the cold water and a debilitating melancholy worming its way into his mood at the thought that none of that had happened to him and never would happen to him, that his ability to love had been robbed of the chance of a historic examination, a test of his loyalty on existential terms rather than profane ones. But all that was left of Marie was a rippling crown of foam on the Baltic, long since out of reach in time that passed far too quickly. He could drown his Karolina sorrows with that woman, thought Wegener, with that woman like with no other.

He wished he could just stay in the water rather than scurry shivering to the pier with the naked West Berlin chief inspector, collecting up the key and ID cards from the jetty and clambering into his cold clothes while still wet. He wished he'd swum after Marie, taken her in his arms and told her that he understood her through and through, rather than rattling back to Berlin in Christa Gerdes' grease-exuding Wartburg, next to him Brendel, whose phone rang, whose face transformed into an expressionless wax mask while a nameless high-ranking FIS employee informed him in unadorned words that Dr Christian Kayser had been found dead in his suite at the EastSide that afternoon, half-naked on the bed, a hole in his head and his brains spread across eight square metres of saffron-yellow silk wallpaper.

THURSDAY 27 OCTOBER 2011

28

WEGENER OPENS HIS EYES, CLOSES THEM and then opens them again. The hypocrite of a ventilator is stuck to the ceiling above him like a round insect. The insect's legs are rotating. They shimmer in a circle, blurring into an almost invisible disc and driving cool wafts of air around the room, professionally fanned relief for everything that hurts. *Thanks,* says his hot brow in an exhausted Früchtl voice, *please don't stop, I'm in a fever of anticipation.*

Wegener stares at the fan. Its quietly buzzing rotors are a hypnotic whisk that whips the stuff of dreams, real life, wishes, fears, past and present into an inseparable mass, that stirs all perceptions into a creamy mayonnaise in which nothing must be found later on, no truths, no half-truths, no lies. Everything is mushed up into a homogeneous paste that has to be spooned up because that's just what's left over, even if nobody ordered the damn stuff, even if it has some kind of bitter aftertaste for everyone, too boring, too salty, unnecessarily spicy. If you want to be choosy now you'll go hungry, à la carte was yesterday: in the German Culinary Republic you get what you're given.

Blow boys, Früchtl speaks from the depths of the mattress, *bully boys, blow, no, those are the wrong words, oh my Hamburg years, Martin, man is an evil, talking animal, that's what I wanted to say, you always have known that, I say it almost daily, good's influence is minimal, I'm sure my life has shown that, you're breathing oh so gaily, what do you want to say?*

Wegener turns on his stomach.

All right, says Früchtl and gives a bit of a cough, *I'll stop the stupid rhymes, but you try lying in a churchyard day after day as an atheist and passing away eternity without West German TV, it's no fun, honest. Come on, don't expect answers from the dead; if the dead had had answers they wouldn't have died, I hope you see that. Maybe you should take a break, sometimes everything's perfectly simple: go to Dr Quellmann and get him to sign you off with paranoid paranoia, the persecutor suffering from delusions of persecution. Sounds funnier than it is – if you're constantly chasing after someone you have to turn around now and then, and then you come full circle, think about it, I do mean well. I've always warned you about this profession, detective and the GDR, that's a mixture where one of the two ends up kaput, and seeing as the GDR's already kaput it'll probably be the detective: don't I know it, I've tested it out on myself. All right, that's no use to you either, but you can guess for yourself what it is you need, you've got an inkling deep inside, it's easy enough, it's not truth you need, not justice, for God's sake, justice, take a look at me, or better not, my hips are much pointier than I found them when I was alive.*

What you need, Martin, is a woman, one who doesn't lie to you, who doesn't harm you, who doesn't cheat on you, one who doesn't

*run away and doesn't swim away, a confidante you can confide
everything in, from your willy to your weaknesses, just everything:
keep on shoving all those problem zones into the woman, if she's Miss
Right they'll all stay inside. I've set up a working group, you see, the
worms, maggots and cockroaches all share my opinion, only one
stinking mole was blind to human love and abstained from voting.
Our recommendation is clear, the case has fallen into other people's
hands anyway so you can just take your annual leave and conspire
against the conspiracies, rest and recuperate your soul, go to
su.proletarianpartners.gdr, exclusive bonus membership from only
twelve marks a month, set up a profile, a nice black-and-white photo,
lovely and serious, terribly respectable what with your job, meet
young, young girls and for God's sake get a little bit happy with one
of them, and make it snappy, that'd make us happy, believe you me
that's what you need.*

What I need, said Wegener, is answers.

*Oh, those never-ending answers, exclaimed Früchtl. At the end of
the day they're all on the table soliciting themselves, wanting nothing
but to be registered, vain harlots baring their pudendum to you
unasked-for.*

The shoes, Josef, what's the thing with the shoes about?

Three men went into the wood and two did the third one no good.

Tell me. I can't think any more.

*All right, my boy, it's only a minor matter, if you like I can show
you how the two baddies grab the old granddad and his feet come
unclad. They've planned it all well ahead, racked their conspirators'
brains and calculated down to the very last detail how they're going
to do it: one Hoffmann, one pipeline, one car roof, two shoelaces,
eight knots, one Stasi murder, no clues on the loose, so on your marks,
get set, go!*

Keep going.

Hoffmann gets away from them first of all, just to make it more interesting, gasps and rasps his way through the woods, stumbles, gets up again, hears the killers cursing, these guys aren't rehearsing, looking under trees and bushes, Hoffmann making his last wishes, thinking of his daughter, that pubic-haired beauty he'll never see ever again, for now a ray of rotten torchlight runs across the gardener in his den.

So they catch him again, and heave-ho onto the car roof, now quickly tie the hangman's knot, eight times round and round, the rope lies round his neck, the squirrels lie down to sleep, the wind lies in the treetops, the old man lays his head back, sees stars, he's a brave boy, doesn't move a muscle, doesn't pray, doesn't beg, a truly dignified prophet just about to snuff it, how proud and upright on his tuffet, even when one of the baddies gets in the Prius – my God, that sounds dumb, Martin, you know I can only stand pathos when I get the identical amount of irony on the side – but never mind, so they drive the car away and give Hoffmann a good hanging, wham says the Stasi rope and bam says the neck, and all that's missing is the shoes.

And?

Now the Müggelsee murderers learn a lesson for life: you never know beforehand how it's all going to end, you only know one thing – it's bound to end differently to the way you thought. Fate is a tubby fortune-teller at the Cottbus county fair, an esoteric madame who doesn't even have control over her own digestion, and providence is her midget brother, a mongoloid jester contemplating horoscopes under the influence of mescaline. The strategy and the plan are two rotten crutches riddled with woodworm, and God is an overworked meat-grinder fattened up with the dreams and hopes of the weak since the invention of fear.

*So, my friends, pay your respects to King Coincidence, the unpre-
dictable lord and master, the most moody, random, and consequently
most just of all monarchs, with an immortal dice in his brainbox
organizing lavish parties and turning every word on its head in the
mouth of coincidence, just to be on the safe side. Life is the only legal
game of chance in the GDR and murdering in the GDR is a game of
chance where every player carries a pistol for an extra round of Russian roulette, so keep your expectations in check, you can only win
if you don't bet on anything.*

The shoes, says Wegener. Hoffmann never wore shoelaces. Only
slip-on shoes.

*That's no use if you want to tie the victim's shoelaces together to
make a Gordian knot in the detective's brain.*

They had to lay the Stasi trail so they needed the shoes to tie, says
Wegener.

*The whole red herring only worked with tied-together shoelaces,
the well-laid plan wasn't allowed to go astray, the shoelaces are the
climax, the killer punchline, says Früchtl: it stinks to high heaven.
Why didn't anyone ask what shoes Hoffmann was going to wear on
his date with death? Why didn't anyone think he might be wearing
slip-ons? What kind of lousy execution preparations are these, what
bunglers think they're leading the inspector around the ring by his
nose? The whole clever scapegoat strategy's threatening to collapse
just because of this sloppy job!*

Where are you supposed to get shoes with laces in the middle of
the woods? says Wegener.

*Time to improvise, says Früchtl. If they don't want to put their
foot in it, there's no other way.*

So, says Wegener, the only way out – one of the murderers swaps
shoes with Hoffmann.

PLAN **D**

One of the killers kicks off his clogs, says Früchtl, and in return he gets genuine horse leather on his feet, two really smart slippers for the first time in his hangman's life, drummed up for silly money by Blühdorn in Heidelberg.

And now they can tie Hoffmann's shoelaces together, says Wegener.

Someone put himself in Hoffmann's shoes, says Früchtl. It was a close call but they'd do anything for a decent lie.

Thanks, Josef.

You're welcome. And what about your annual leave?

'Martin. Morning.'

'You sound like I feel.' Wegener sagged onto the kitchen chair with the broken back-rest. The back-rest made a cracking sound.

Frankenstein yawned into the telephone. 'What's the time?'

'Nearly three.'

'What time was it?' Frankenstein gave another yawn.

'Almost six.'

'My God. How did I get home?'

'Taxi.' Now Wegener yawned as well. 'We've got four hours left.'

'So?'

'5 p.m. in the Yeltsin,' said Wegener: 'meatloaf time.'

'What about Brendel?'

'I'll call him.'

'Right. See you there.'

Wegener got up, dragged himself over to the sink, knocked back two glasses of tap water in one, then another half in small sips. The usual vomit reflex rose up inside him, his skull was the Bautzen quarry, the political prisoners attempting to break the annual production record with their sledgehammers.

Sex, thought Wegener in the tile-green twilight of the shower, and turned up the hot water. You could have sex again some time and see how you react, if you can still do it, who ends up underneath you when push comes to shove. Whoever it is, you can bet it won't be anyone you're thinking of or wishing for now. You can bet it'll be someone you don't know or can't imagine right now. So who can you imagine least of all? Christa Gerdes.

Wegener shuddered, soaped himself up and for a moment felt like sliding down the tiles, squatting in the square shower tub and letting the water rain down on him for hours. But real men had to lean both arms against the wall, tense their muscles and act the desperate animal in the hopeless attempt to knock over walls with their bare hands, water on their stony faces, staring darkly at the grouting.

The bell buzzed.

Ten seconds of water-splashing.

The bell buzzed again, longer this time.

Why's the thing called a bell when it buzzes, thought Wegener, turning off the hot jet of water, climbing out of the shower and knotting a sexy towel miniskirt around his waist. He waddled down the hall, cursing, almost slipped over, opened the front door and suddenly every hint of headache was gone, his pulse eroded, because before him in a pale brown trench coat with a black skirt, black boots over her knees, black leather gloves, a dark polo neck and sad, doe-brown eyes in her freckled face stood Karo, my lifelong-life-sentence love Karo, thought Wegener, my enchanting chagrin.

'Come in,' he said and took a step aside. Karolina came in.

Wegener closed the door.

The shower dripped in the background.

Wegener was now a silent lollipop man in the sauna, pointing the way to the kitchen even though it hadn't changed position over the past few months, grabbing the two empty Goldkrone bottles off

the table and integrating them skilfully into the used-glass installation that was stinking away in the used-glass installation box by
the fridge.

'Do you want to put something on?' Karolina sounded timid.

No I don't, thought Wegener, and sat down on the kitchen chair
with the broken back-rest. The back-rest made a cracking sound.
'Don't you have to be in the ministry today?'

'I called in sick.' Karolina's eyes clambered over rubbish bags, dirty
plates and sticky glasses.

'Sit down,' said Wegener.

Karolina sat down. 'Are you on leave?'

Wegener shook his head. 'I was questioned for eight hours yesterday and then released from duties.'

'Questioned on the murder investigation?'

'Yes.'

Karolina stared a hole in the kitchen floor. 'Why?'

'Maybe you know that already.'

'No, I don't know.' Karolina looked at him. Her brown irises shim-
mered glassily behind a film of tears which was turning into fat drips
in the corners of her eyes. 'I met Hoffmann once, three months ago.
I was supposed to ask him if he'd work for us. He said maybe, later.
That's all. I don't know any more than that, Martin, really I don't.'
The drips had left two glinting trails on their way down to her chin.
'Why did they release you from duties?'

'An FIS man was shot dead yesterday. In the EastSide.'

Karolina gazed at him in amazement, her mouth agape.

'Christian Kayser, he was on the case with me. Now there's a delegation here from the Federal Intelligence Service, taking the whole
thing over from the start with C5. A mine-strewn, bilateral secret-
service and diplomatic battlefield. And I'm telling you all about it.

They could have me writing parking tickets in Pankow for the rest of my life for that, Karo, but you know that as well as I do.'

Karolina raised both hands and then dropped them again. 'The Hoffmann dossier was strictly confidential! That means not talking to anyone about it under threat of penalties, unless the information's authorized! What else could I have done?'

'Trusted me.'

Karolina sobbed so feebly that Wegener had to swallow.

'Please,' said Karolina. More tears dripped.

'And you wanted to send me to a doctor, Karo, you're the one who says I'm paranoid! What the hell were you thinking of?'

'That was about Josef, his disappearance!'

Wegener reached for a roll of kitchen paper and stood it up on the table. Karolina plucked two sheets off with trembling hands and blew her nose loudly.

'Is the information authorized now?'

'I don't know.'

'What was it about?' Wegener noticed the knot in his towel was coming loose and he pulled the fabric tighter with both hands.

'Does that matter now?' Wegener looked at Karolina. 'It was about a strategy paper,' said Karolina weakly, 'an energy supply concept to a great extent, something he drew up long before Revitalization. It was called *Plan D*.'

'I've heard the name.'

'I came across it about a year ago, while I was researching for the consultations. The plan's incredibly visionary; almost all the basic prognoses have more or less come true. Hoffmann was a quarter of a century ahead of his time, it's just that no one realized it.'

'Or no one wanted to realize it,' Wegener added. 'And you were curious as to whether he's still a quarter of a century ahead of his time.'

Karolina nodded. 'Yes of course, imagine he had a concept now that was as accurate as the old one. It's hard to imagine, I know.'

Wegener stood up, went to the sink and held his glass under the tap. 'So what was he like?'

'He was friendly.' Karolina looked as if she was surprised at her own words. 'Highly intelligent. We had a long talk. He was a brilliant strategist.'

'I've heard that before too. And?'

'He was working on his new concept. Not quite finished.'

'What does that mean?'

'That means he needed a few more months before he was prepared to discuss it with anyone.'

Wegener stared at Karolina. 'He said that? He said he was working on a new future energy concept for the GDR?'

'Not a future energy concept in the specific sense – more like a strategic vision, in which energy policy plays a major role. An updated *Plan D*. I've been thinking all along that was why they killed him.'

Wegener held himself upright by the sink. 'You knew of a possible motive for a murder case I'm investigating, and you didn't tell me? Even though I explicitly asked you about it?'

Karolina's gaze tipped onto the kitchen floor.

I could beat her up right now, thought Wegener, with the dirty soup ladle from the day before the day before yesterday, and she wouldn't fight back because she knows she's done the only thing she never should have done, and because she knows exactly that I can't possibly manage to whack her with the ladle.

'It was a huge mistake, Martin.'

'Who would it have been a motive for, do you think, this updated *Plan D*?'

Karolina wrung her hands together.

'Tell me what you think, Karo. No need to breach departmental secrecy, just tell me your own humble, personal departmental head's opinion.'

'Apart from the oil engine, we're well behind on regenerative energies, everyone knows that. If they'd listened to Albert Hoffmann back then . . . '

'But they didn't. Carry on.'

'The natural gas deposits in Russia are considered never-ending, but no one can predict the future price developments. Fifty to 60 per cent of the funding depends on the nuclear exit agreement between the SU and the EU. Brown coal's as dirty as it's always been. So the ministry's been negotiating with a West German consortium for almost two years now – they want to provide us with nationwide regenerative energy production technology.'

Wegener sat back down on his kitchen chair. 'What do you mean by provide?'

Karolina fiddled with one of her shiny, oversized trench-coat buttons. 'In this case, provide means leasing it out. They'd build geothermal power stations, wind parks, major solar installations in the GDR, and we'd pay rent for them.'

'So that we're not only dependent on Russia but also on the West.'

'You could see it like that.' Karolina reached for Wegener's water glass and took a gulp. 'Or you could see it the other way around: it's better to be dependent on two different sources than only one, we haven't got the money to buy in technology on a grand scale so our only option is renting; it creates jobs, we gain technical know-how in one fell swoop and polish up our image on the carbon-dioxide front.'

There was a clinking sound. A loud clattering right behind him.

Wegener jumped. An empty Goldkrone bottle rolled in front of Karolina's feet.

Karolina picked up the bottle and put it on the table, refraining from comment. 'The other option is: we put the money into research rather than rent, we're significantly slower and significantly worse at it but retain the theoretical possibility of energy independence. Some day.'

'And Hoffmann?'

'The ministry's split down the middle, the Politburo too; the process has been treading water for a year now. There was a preliminary decision in May that we draw up a contract with the West German investor. And then I happened to come across the first *Plan D*. And talked to Hoffmann. No one could overlook the fact that the man wrote down the future in 1975, down to the very last detail.'

Wegener tugged his towel skirt into place. 'And they all thought he'd pull it off again.'

'No.' Karolina shook her head. 'Nobody assumed he'd pull a paper out of his hat and we'd be the market leader for regenerative energies. All we wanted was a major impetus. A strategic course. And that's where Hoffmann – how shall I put it – he gave us hope. He encouraged us to think we could do it under our own steam. Confidence, perhaps that was it too. Confidence is a rare commodity around here. Like so many things. Whatever the case, there was a change of mood.'

'Well, well,' said Wegener, 'and suddenly GreenFAC had a very good reason not to like Albert Hoffmann. Because the whole windpark rental plan would be up the creek if they decided on Hoffmann's visions.'

Karolina stared at Wegener. 'How do you know it was GreenFAC?'

'And that's why you got your promotion,' said Wegener. 'For finding *Plan D* in the ministry basement.'

A stark blush crept up out of Karolina's polo neck and spread across her face. Two round patches glowed on her cheeks.

Now you're the girl I used to know, thought Wegener, the most vulnerable, the most feminine, because before you were the most brutal, the coldest and the hardest.

Then they sat silently opposite one another. Looking at each other.

They spent minutes reading amusing stories of cowardly lust in each other's eyes, fear of exposure long thought vanquished and rust-coated, stiff-moving good sense. But the damn thing does whatever it feels like, that's its job, thought Wegener as he felt the towel skirt slipping off his hips and onto the kitchen floor, and Karolina's eyes feeling up his erection, from top to bottom, curious, remembering, lovingly. He heard cardiac irregularities arriving, saw a skirt being pushed up, Karolina artfully spreading her legs like a Belarusian gymnast on a sure path to Olympic gold, a gymnast who couldn't afford underwear, presenting a small, rosy, childlike pussy, now minus the neatly shaved beard of copper wire, just the slit and nothing else. This is my day, thought Wegener: at last, after all the century-long nights my day has come again.

The bell buzzed.

Karolina pulled her bra up along with the polo neck, wanting to reveal her heavy, slightly pendulous breasts right now, the right one still bigger than the left one. Wegener noticed he'd like to react in some way but he had nothing left to take off, he didn't have anything new to offer her, he couldn't escalate in any way, he had to hold still and stay hard and watch, that was his role and it always would be.

The bell buzzed again, for four, five, six, seven, eight seconds, but Karolina simply ignored the idiotic buzzing and turned into a department head in the porno combine, sending the middle finger of her left hand diving from above like a Tupolev with double engine failure, a steep descent. But where every pilot would have been helpless, Karolina was in complete control, landing her finger gently on her mound of Venus, slipping a little further down, pushing her pale grey labia apart and showing a reddish opening shimmering with wetness, finding the fleshy knob of her clitoris.

There's none bigger, thought Wegener, there's none knobbier, there's none as hard to get going and then as hard to stop.

Karolina began her work. The telephone in the hall rang. The doorbell buzzed.

Wegener's skull spun around the kitchen, his pulse hammered against the cerebral membrane, his headache suddenly stabbed in again, sharp and mean, right where it hurt, the answer machine kicked in and he heard himself reciting an apologetic speech in the hall as Karolina pulled the finger out of her vagina as if out of a glass of milk and held that dripping finger out to him, her eyes wanting him to kneel down on the kitchen floor that instant and take the milky finger in his mouth. *Mr Wegener*, called an inappropriately tinny man's voice out of the answer machine: *State Security, open the door, we know you're at home!*

Karolina stared at him, so lamed with horror that her legs were still spread, that her wet labial mouth still formed its shocked O, a reflection of the upper shocked O-mouth, a miniature, eyeless, smooth-shaven twin in her crotch from which something white was running away towards her butt cheeks, Karolina's highly concentrated, creamy lust, not triggered by any contact, any touch, any approach; merely by the expectation of the stony detective, a tickly, undiluted anticipation of sex with her ex.

I will never, ever, ever forget that sight, thought Wegener as he fumbled his miniskirt towel together, staggered into the hallway, opened the front door a slit – slit, thought Wegener, slit, slit and slit again – and saw two grey coats with dark hats and invisible shadow faces, one of which growled: 'Your ID, please.'

Wegener hobbled to the coat stand, found his wallet and his police ID, went back to the door and held it out to the two hats.

'Major-General Wischinsky sends her regards,' said the one on the right, suddenly holding out an envelope and that was it, no goodbyes, not one more word, the two coats stomping down the old wooden staircase in unison. Every step gave a thud.

Wegener tore open the envelope. A visitor's pass plus appointment note for Normannenstrasse. Valid for four days. Under *Reason for Visit* it said in feminine ballpoint handwriting: *Inspection of strictly confidential documents on site in the surveillance matter Colombetstr., commissioned by Hauptmann Wegener, authorized by Major-General Renate Wischinsky.*

He turned around.

Karolina was standing in the hallway looking at him, huge shocked eyes that must have seen terrible things and now regretted bitterly.

Her hand reached out for the door handle.

'You're going?'

'I can't do it.'

'Stay. Please.'

'It won't work any more.' She was already outside, running after the Stasi men, her boots echoing downwards on the wood, second floor, first floor, ground floor.

The front door banged shut.

Wegener heard Früchtl's imbecilic giggle at the very back of his head. *Sorry,* gasped Früchtl, *sorry I have to laugh, I'm really sorry, Martin, don't be angry, excuse me, but it's so tragicomic, it's so sick. Martin has Karolina spied on, then Martin accuses Karolina of a major breach of confidence, and then the spies turn up to spoil Martin's Karolina-spying sex with their Karolina-spying report, come on, admit it – it's unbeatable, it could only happen to you, the extra-tragic hero, it's so incredibly hard, the only thing harder's your hard-on, muahaha. I can't take it any more, but you wouldn't listen to me, you had to let yourself in for their games where you don't know the rules, you had to make yourself a playmaker even though you know what playmakers have coming to them, and I'm not talking about their sexy blonde daughters.*

Wegener gripped his head with both hands. The towel slipped off. His ridiculous erection looked at him reproachfully and said: Brendel's is twice as big.

29

THE LOW-HANGING SUN HAD FOUND A GAP between the test-tube palaces that had once been the peak of Socialist Classicism, and was now slanting across the road into the floor-length windows of the Yeltsin, making the old cherry-wood panels glow the colour of Karolina's hair, glinting off the octopus arms of the brass chandeliers, displaying all the scratches and scuffs in the parquet floor simultaneously and submerging the whole room in a consoling warmth that seemed to Wegener as if someone had ordered it especially for him knowing full well that he'd become an invalid, a man with a sick heart, a sick head, a sick stomach, whose life was at risk if he kept seeing the ubiquitous grey, who had to avoid all hints of colourlessness if he didn't want to be scraped off the EastSide's VIP Car-Walk any day now, who could only recuperate in the soporific, snug cosiness of sun-drenched, red-brown wooden café surfaces, if at all.

Brendel lit up his third cigarillo in a row and sent out tiny jelly-fish of smoke, which seemed to float up in a light-filled swimming pool, drifting higher and higher as they gradually dispersed. His handsome face had been sucked dry by the events of the past twenty-four hours, like a Styrofoam pack of minced beef by a hungry Labrador.

Frankenstein was vegetating in a scuffed leather armchair, eyes closed and hands folded together. Perhaps he was asleep. Perhaps he was praying.

Shots in the head, thought Wegener, I could deal out shots in the head like a carnival princess blows kisses, I could just let loose and shoot at anything that moves, slip into the Robotron revolver-game role of Justin Justice out of *Fascism-Fighters III*. First I'd head for Colombetstrasse and wait until that lying bitch leaves the house, a swift double-kneecap job with two bullets, and only then make the most of her bleeding and motionless state by making one last speech, *radical thrusts in radical times*, put the cold metal to her temples and then take a last vain look inside her exploded head to see if there's a lousy explanation in there for so much betrayal and perfidy, one final Judas kiss on her cold nether lips, *do svidaniya,* Karolina, the only good gas whore's a dead gas whore, and then it'd be everyone else's turn, an exit for all, only Kayser got himself out of it by getting himself killed prematurely, but for the rest of the world it'd be the springtime of death, a sunny eradication.

Wegener saw Christa Gerdes slipping limply from her revolving desk chair, Jocicz running away and stumbling after three bullets in the back, falling to the ground and staying there, Borgs, Lienecke, Gruber, Blühdorn tipping over, Steinkühler slumping to the floor at Werderscher Markt, his blood spilling onto the grey flagstones and spelling out the words *I leave my bug collection to the Berlin Tiergarten*, Marie's bare feet with black-varnished toenails stepping in Steinkühler's blood and leaving red Amazon prints on the floor, which dried slowly as Wegener strolled off into the sunset arm in arm with the world's most enchanting feline beauty.

He looked at his Minsk. No envelope in the *TM* spot, no new mail, no missed call.

What are you thinking of right now? thought Wegener and drank a sip of coffee. If I knew what you were thinking right now I'd know everything. Everything I need to know. Then I'd never make another mistake. He'd sworn not to answer anything, not to react to anything that came from Karolina, to let her stew in the self-inflicted stock of her show of sensibility.

But Karolina, his future victim Karolina, refused to send a *TM* he could refuse to answer, did nothing he could ignore, made no apology, no accusation, no peace offering. That's the final proof of her superiority, thought Wegener, not even giving a poor bugger the chance to be passive, letting his attempts to show strength come to nothing until he weakens, robbing the secretly called-off attack of the surprise of capitulation. There was no topping that, every commander in world history was bound to fail up against that tactic, it would have stumped them all from Napoleon to Hitler. And only Karolina could do it.

The evening sun attempted to paint a little blusher onto Brendel's cheeks. Forget it, thought Wegener, that's the face of a finished man, marked by worst-case failure, by last night's long-haul interrogation, by the same accusations and questions over and over again. The men from the FIS were hard bastards, even better than the bastards from C5. Instead of crossing their streams of fire they interlocked perfectly, precision workers, internationally trained cogs that instantly assembled themselves into a well-oiled allegation machine, which ground any trace of collegiality beneath gigantic metal wheels. Anyone interrogated was culpable: West cops or East cops, they were all the same clots, and since when have they divided up losers by the points of the compass?

We might never be as equal as we were last night, thought Wegener as he looked at Brendel, a lying, hypocritical team that didn't mention a single word about Hoffmann's daughter, that merely served up a flimsy State Security conspiracy theory to the C5–FIS committee, unveiling Ronny Gruber's cameo role as a Brigade double agent and his main role as Codename Hermes, a timid finger pointed at Green-FAC and that was it. No concrete results, no evidence, no suspects, no idea in which East Berlin pub Hoffmann's murderers were ordering their beer right that moment.

Wegener felt his indifference to this defeat more clearly than ever before. Karolina and Hoffmann, the Stasi and the Brigade had left nothing behind, no wishes, no interest, just helpless hate that would soon fade into helpless emptiness. That emptiness might be the beginning of the end of wanting. The beginning of the end of lacking.

'Exactly one more hour.' Frankenstein had taken off his watch and put it down on the table, as if it would tell a more pleasant time there. 'Then it's 7 p.m.'

Brendel reached for the menu, opened it up and flicked through the pages. '7 p.m.,' Frankenstein repeated quietly.

The sun was now a dazzling orange that wouldn't hold out much longer, just about to lose its warm colour and dip beneath the horizon. You might as well give up, Gabriel, old terrorist friend, thought Wegener as he drank another sip of his coffee; don't run away, save your energy, they're bound to get you either way.

'When did you first meet Toralf?' Brendel had suddenly woken up. '2000?'

'Yes, 2000. In the spring. Like I said, on Gendarmenmarkt and not here.'

'So why did he say you met here?'

'We asked ourselves that the day before yesterday, Richard, and it was no use.'

Brendel held up the menu. 'The Yeltsin's only been called Yeltsin since 2004.'

'And before that?'

'It doesn't say here. Can't you two remember?'

'No idea,' said Wegener. Frankenstein shook his head.

For a minute no one said anything, all of them thinking, brooding over their cups until Frankenstein heaved himself up without a word and stomped off to the counter.

Wegener fumbled his Minsk out of his pocket, even though an inner voice yelped out loud and shouted at him, and opened a new text message to Karolina. The inner voice turned somersaults but he wanted to hear it from her and not on the grapevine, she ought to tell him herself, that must be allowed, it'd just accelerate the process of getting over her. But still the voice went on screaming inside him, an un-switch-offable warning system for grave and disastrous moments – in vain, for his fingers had already typed it in and sent it off: *Please tell me the truth. Have you got someone else?* That ancient, embarrassing, humiliating question that couldn't be put any more nicely, with which every ex-lover shrank instantly to a skinny school-boy, no matter how tall and wide and strong he might have been before.

The envelope fluttered off. The grand finale, thought Wegener. Don't you ever flutter again or I'll shoot you in the skull.

Frankenstein waved in the background. He and the Vietnamese waiter dragged a ladder out of the kitchen, carried it all the way across the smoke-filled room, transformed into two mis-matched firemen for a few seconds, followed by the gazes of the coffee-drinkers, beer-drinkers and vodka-drinkers, and then they were out of the door.

Wegener got up and Brendel followed him. Outside, the waiter had leaned the ladder against the facade and was holding it with both hands while Frankenstein was already at the top, picking at the shabby Yeltsin lettering. He found one end of the adhesive film and peeled it bit by bit off the illuminated sign.

Brendel grabbed the dangling end of the label and peeled along, carefully so as not to tear it.

Frankenstein climbed down the ladder.

Brendel left the peeled-off foil hanging in mid-air and took a few steps back.

The three of them stood in a line. Stared at the sign. The original lettering was faded, stained, pock-marked, but still legible:

CAFÉ RESTAURANT THÄLMANN'S

The Vietnamese waiter looked from one face to the next.

In the roar of traffic on Karl-Marx-Allee, the right-hand neon tube flickered briefly and the MANN'S flashed bright, then it returned to the original pale red glow.

'We've got him,' said Wegener.

'Who've ya got?' asked the waiter in a perfect Saxon accent.

'The man who got shot in the back.'

30

THE MERCEDES BRAKED AT THE SIDE OF THE ROAD with its warning lights flashing, the knobs of the central-locking system clicking up.

Frankenstein got in the front, Wegener at the back. 18:34.

Brendel put his foot down.

Twilight had descended upon Berlin, a semi-transparent, blue-grey blanket. We're all fighting under that blanket, all in bed together, thought Wegener, gambling addicts and former lovers, every one of whom ultimately says *what's best for my country* when asked about his motives at the end of all debates. *What's best for my country* was the lowest and highest common denominator, a five-word bible that always sounded right and always sounded meaningful, which could be used to justify any crusade. A line that fitted on every flag.

Wegener saw the dark streets rushing by, the high stone mountains of intimidating architecture, the glowing Nazi chandeliers, saw the glittering Mercedes symbol on the bonnet, speeding through the capital of the Third Reich directly to the domed Germania hall, and he understood in that second more clearly than ever before that he had lived in a dictatorship and still lived in a dictatorship and would one day die in it. How narrowly had this state scraped past its historical turning points? What would it be like if a few tiny things had gone differently? Who would he be if the world had taken a different turning somewhere in the past, instead of stumbling on and on straight ahead without a destination?

'We're being followed,' said Brendel.

By the inconsistent people, the selfish people, the opportunistic people, and maybe I'm one of those myself, hunting myself down, thought Wegener and he turned around to see twenty or thirty pairs of double headlights staring him down.

'A red Phobos and a white Universal.' Brendel turned off onto Greifswalder Strasse. Several indicators switched on, three or four cars staying behind them. The colours were indistinguishable.

'What now?' asked Frankenstein.

'We get him away from here to start with,' said Wegener, 'if we get him.'

'Meeting point in case we have to split up?'

'You suggest something.'

'If we don't get him, then the Molotov.' Frankenstein ran his tongue along his lips. 'Have you ever been there, Brendel?'

Brendel shook his head.

'The best place in all of East Berlin. In every respect.'

Brendel didn't react, staring tensely at the road ahead, his mouth a grim line.

They glided silently through the juddering rush hour, in which it was impossible to shake off a tailing car, Brendel's eyes on the mirror every five seconds and on the clock every thirty.

At some point the friendly woman's voice purred *Your destination is two hundred metres away*, took a short break and then announced joyously: *Your destination is on the right!*

The digital clock on the dashboard switched to 18:55.

Frankenstein smoothed his hair down with both hands. 'What do we do if it's the Stasi behind us?'

'I don't know that either.' Wegener looked at the black mass of treetops gliding past, from which lit-up prefab tower blocks protruded, high curves of street lamps pouring yellowish puddles of light on the asphalt, between them impenetrable bushes where whole football teams could hide, abandoned pavements, drifting traffic.

Brendel slowed down.

Wegener peered out of the rear window. No tails to be seen.

On the right began a broad, concrete semicircle, in the middle of which a high chunk of bronze rose proudly: Ernst Thälmann, staring determinedly at the nightly heavens where the communists assumed he'd been spending more than half a century. A clenched worker's fist grew out of his right shoulder, behind his back heavy flag fabric fluttered upwards like one cast-bronze wing. The plaza around the monument was empty.

'They stopped somewhere behind us.' Brendel switched off the engine and the lights, the Mercedes coasting a couple of metres between two lamps in the darkness and then stopping.

18:57

Wegener felt his Minsk vibrating and fumbled it out of his pocket. *You have received a TM from Karolina Enders.* And there it was again, that tiny dose of adrenalin that you couldn't turn off, a pure waste of energy for loveless text droppings, guaranteed miniature disappointments whose only surprise was the question of what combination of words she'd use to kick him in the balls from behind this time.

There's no one for me at the moment.

Hey, of course there's someone, thought Wegener, but you've bombarded him into emotional exile so you don't have to love him any more, because you couldn't stand the thought that you'd always keep on loving him, that's why you didn't feel, you *decided* you don't love him any more, just as soberly as you decide to send your incapable Siberian Gazprom intern back to his freezer a month early: ice-cold and irrevocable.

18:59

The S-Class windscreen was clouding over. Condensation amoebas were forming in the corners and growing gradually upwards.

Frankenstein suppressed a sneeze, searching his rustling jacket until he found a packet of tissues.

Brendel tapped his middle finger on the gearstick to the rhythm of the second hand, leaned his head back on the headrest, dropped it forward onto his chest.

Frankenstein blew his nose as quietly as possible.

19:00

How would you have decided, Ernst, if you'd known all this, if you'd survived all that German history? thought Wegener, watching Thälmann's stony face. It suddenly didn't look at all tough and heroic, but sad, uncertain, exhausted. That Nazi shot in the head saved you from the truth, plastinated you as a legend, as a canned communist with no best-before date. You should be glad you were spared all the later disappointments. You weren't forced to choose between faith and feasibility; all the others tripped up on that but you weren't given the opportunity, poor old Teddy. Give thanks and congratulations – you're the rightest of the wrong to this very day.

A shadow detached itself from the darkness of the bronze head.

Squatted down.

Straightened its legs and jumped.

For a moment it looked to Wegener as if an actual-size Ernst Thälmann were leaping out of his own skull, down from his pedestal, beaten down by the permanent glorification of a stance that was no longer his own, that had grown more and more alien to him with every year of stubborn stargazing. A couple of decades of thinking could do you good. You make your observations, you can hardly turn a blind eye when the bronze sculptor Kerbel has fixed them so wide.

The shadow was now standing motionless in the middle of the empty space, a gnome before a beheaded giant. No one else.

Frankenstein was a second faster, his hand already pushing the passenger door open as Wegener was still wondering where the black Phobos Datscha had come from. As if from nowhere, it suddenly swept across the concrete wasteland from the right and spat out two men who hit the ground running, after the limping shadow, which headed for the park behind the monument and vanished into a darkness that was no longer dark: a second six-eyed face lit up, making blurred silhouettes dance in a white fog of headlights, a stumbling Strip the Willow of grown men tugging at each other, which then got control of itself and finally, twitching, tense, bent-over, disappeared into the two cars.

Brendel swore and started the engine, Frankenstein pulled the passenger door closed, Thälmann still had his eyes on the night and ignored the screech of tyres, not seeing the two black jeeps flying across the plaza one after another, jumping the kerb, slamming onto Greifswalder Strasse and accelerating with a skid, didn't catch sight of the Mercedes roaring off, its xenon floodlights grabbing the Datschas' blueish-bright by their lacquered backsides as Brendel accelerated so hard they were all pressed into their seats. There were hooting horns all around them, swerving phenoplast boxes, the speedometer needle already at 70 km/h and rising.

Brendel bombed along the middle lane as if he was driving a tank, gripping the leather steering wheel with both hands, his right hand slipped off, tugged the car into fourth gear and was back on the wheel, Brendel's eyes in the mirror lit up from behind, caught by the light for half a second in which their blue shone out determinedly, adding it all up, calculating as if he'd predicted it all.

'The cars on our tail before – they're back.'

Wegener turned and saw two cars pushing their way through the interrupted traffic, a red Phobos and a white Universal, switching lanes, overtaking braking cars. Wegener turned back again – the Datschas had got bigger, Brendel was making ground.

The jeeps had no registration plates, tinted windows and two exhaust pipes, pimped-up models that enveloped the Mercedes in a stinking cloud of diluted diesel. Frankenstein fumbled at the switches between the seats to turn off the ventilators.

'They can't get away from us,' Brendel said through his teeth.

Frankenstein looked at him.

'AMG.'

'AM what?'

'We've got 450 horses in here.' Brendel pulled a lever and the Datschas were suddenly dangling in a cone of full-beam headlights, escaped convicts on the streets of New York City, the bounty in a spectacular helicopter chase without the copter, swaying across the lanes from right to left, dodging a Wartburg, a Barkas, a Lada, driving zigzags as if they had to manoeuvre themselves through a hail of bullets, and then suddenly both of them pulled into the right-hand lane and took the long curve towards Wedding.

Brendel squeezed past the Barkas van, wound the steering wheel to the right and landed in the turn-off lane behind them. Pressed against the cold side window, Wegener turned around and saw the Phoboses sticking to them, now also crossing the whole of Greifswalder Strasse to the Wedding exit. Brendel sped up even more, a succession of curved street lamps brushing past on either side of the rear window, forming endless chains of fairy lights that traced the outlines of Mittagstrasse, perfectly straight border markers along a political racetrack.

No one's going to lose anyone here, thought Wegener, the Datschas won't shake us off and we won't get rid of the Phoboses, we can shoot through Berlin in our crude convoy until someone runs out of juice and gets left behind, eliminated from an absurd race for the lost future of a lost country, and it's all in vain – the electrical nerve impulses between Brendel's brain and Brendel's retinas, the Datscha drivers' adrenalin kicks, the Phoboses' hammering pistons, Frankenstein's sweat-soaked shirt, the directly injected petrol in the S-Class's booming engine block, the oil, the blood coursing through the veins, the brake fluid pulsing in its tubes, the last mosquitoes, bugs and wasps hammered to a slimy yellow mush on five radiator grilles and dried to sticky stains in seconds by the air rushing past – all that had happened and might as well not have happened, everything was only going on and on because no one wanted to press the stop button, because every one of them lacked the necessary strength for resignation, because everything always had to be driven on until the ending lost patience and shouted: Enough!

Wegener saw the Datschas' brake lights illuminate as the two cars turned off one after another onto an industrial wasteland, *Renzinghain Slaughterhouse POC*. Brendel braked and skidded after them, the Phoboses following.

The jeeps were driving alongside each other now, sending up a double cloud of dust that robbed them of their orientation for moments, making them fear they might crash into rusty wire fences, skips and wrecked machines at any moment, and then warehouses appeared in the full beams, cranes, chimneys, long brick walls on either side. Instead of the dusty surface there was a road made of slabs of concrete, and one of the jeeps speeded up and took the lead.

Wegener noticed his hands clenched fast to the seat leather, the warehouse walls closing in on them, coming closer to the Mercedes on both sides, and they were hurtling head over heels into a V of brick at 130 km/h. Frankenstein's head flew to the right, to the left, a new section of building, built closer in, it's getting too tight, thought Wegener and felt himself slipping on the back seat, Brendel locking both arms straight as if that might dampen the thrust of his all-out braking – a red triangle button flashed next to the steering wheel, the Mercedes didn't break out, didn't turn a somersault, simply slid on towards the next tract of warehouse, two walls that left only a slim path between them, into which the Datschas were now feeling their way, hitting the brick, getting stuck, accelerating, breaking off their external mirrors, splintering paint, scraping along the walls with a screech of metal, while the Mercedes came to a stop, a much too-wide, mobile living room that couldn't tackle a brick warehouse complex even with 450 horsepower.

Brendel and Frankenstein were already out of the car, their guns drawn, vanishing into the brick corridor, running after the Datschas, which were scraping, rumbling, groaning their way through the slit between the walls, a minimalist escape route that would still be enough, which was just in the process of making marathon-man Richard Brendel the loser of a chase once again.

Wegener got out of the car.

The two Phoboses cruised towards him, slowed down, and the

Universal stopped while the other one drove a curve around the Mercedes and drilled its way between the walls, scraping after Brendel, Frankenstein and the Datschas.

The light of the four headlights dimmed. Car doors slammed. Two men, one young woman. No visible weapons.

Mouse-face, thought Wegener, Mouse-face from the Bar International, that damned waitress but with a different hairstyle. Cropped hair instead of the long, black wig.

'That mulled wine was awful,' said Wegener, knowing full well what was coming next: exit to Normannenstrasse, a bare room, two men and him, the biggest Stasi bollocking of his life, ruining a covert operation, disciplinary procedure, not just released from duties but suspended, suspended at long last. You never know beforehand how it's all going to end, Früchtl had said, and he'd been right all along, all the way to the deepest, darkest corner of Renzinghain Slaughterhouse POC. You always knew your career was a dead end, thought Wegener, and you could have guessed that the dead end was made of slaughterhouse walls – where else in this state can you get a faster, cleaner, conveyor-belt death sentence?

'Come with us please.' A male voice.

Wegener didn't know which of the two men had spoken, and he didn't care. 'Where to?'

'To a place where we can talk undisturbed.'

The white room, thought Wegener, that damned white room with the padded ceiling. Now they've got you, now they're going to marmalize you and wrap you in their web of silence. And you went and ruined our last goodbyes, Karolina, we could have done it in the rubbish, between empty Goldkrone bottles and mouldy mixed remains, I'd have licked your waterfall-wet pussy until you came, sucked at your pale grey labia, I'd have stroked your clitoris bud with the tip of my tongue until your juice dripped on the floor, and then I'd have licked the puddle off the floor, lapped at your feet, your arse, we'd have done everything, everything that fitted in there, like back then, spontaneous and senseless, hopeless and uninhibited, but your career fixation, your fear, your lies made us end up like all love's average losers: dried up, lonely, silent, gaunt, insignificant, misunderstood.

Shots echoed behind the factory hall.

'And who wants to talk to me undisturbed?' Wegener put the last of his strength into his voice. 'I'm a detective, I've got a nice little office at Köpenick police station. Get yourself an appointment.'

'We know who you are and where your office is.' One of the men opened the passenger door of the Phobos for Wegener. No registration plates on the car. 'But Alexander Bürger doesn't like police stations.'

31

HIS MOTHER WAS WEARING HER SLIGHTLY TOO TIGHT, lilac-coloured dress, standing outside the crooked half-timbered houses of a nameless town in Thuringia, a sausage in a bun in one hand, in the other a crocheted shopping bag revealing two bottles of Spreequell mineral water. White sandals, purple hair slide, on her face not the instant photographic joy of the usual pictures but a hesitant smile, a moment of honesty, captured by chance and from then on everlasting.

He himself eyed the camera expressionlessly, almost bored, a fifteen-year-old boy who wanted to please his mother by coming along to the Plänterwald pleasure park, his mother happy, her son practising gracious patience. A role reversal, the sad photographic proof that childhoods end with sharp edges, that their shrines become desecrated temples from one day to the next, cast-off skins which you never want to fit into again. Lives that have got too small.

In 1970 we were a family, thought Wegener, in 1970 I was part of a family; not being part of a family any more, never being part of a family any more, was inconceivable in 1970, it would have been tantamount to the human race dying out, the greatest possible abandonment, the loneliness of Andreas Jähn in the broad swathes of space. In 1970 Father and Mother stood for the life form of immortal beings, eternal parents without whom your own existence would collapse like the sheath of a hot-air balloon once the very last remaining air had escaped.

Wegener knew where his picture of that time was, where you could still find that timidly happy face, that hair slide, the sausage, the crocheted bag today: the middle section of the sideboard, bottom drawer, green artificial leather photo album, last page but one, top right, and beneath it in his mother's fountain-pen hand:

One last time.

In the place where she'd once smiled a lilac smile, weeds were now growing thigh-high. The model Thuringian town had long since reverted to a real-life town, complete with graffitied backdrop walls, rotten half-timbering and crumbling cheap plaster. Wegener realized he was staring at this fallen paradise as if the ruins were his parental home, as if he'd grown up in this theme park and not in their carcinogenic turn-of-the-century flat in Prenzlauer Berg. He tried to imagine what his mother would have thought and felt, had someone predicted to her that her son would one day return to the fenced-in fun zone of German socialism, not with his children on a summery Sunday, but in an atmosphere of twilight Armageddon, accompanied by enemies of the constitution, the park nothing more than a ruin of pleasures past, a bizarre artificial world with burnt-down huts and rotted railway carriages in semi-collapsed toy ghost stations.

There's nothing more scary than an evil clown, thought Wegener, and Plänterwald is the home of all the evil clowns in the Socialist Union. Here was where the Pennywises holed up in mouldy shooting stands and raffle kiosks, strangling eighteen homeless men a night on the chairoplanes, bathing in the kilometre-long, twisting tube-shaped pool in which the boats of the water ride had once floated past, and when they came up from the deeps they wore slimy seaweed hair, laughed out of toothless mouths and sang slippery dirges.

His guards stood mutely behind him, a silent trio that didn't push and shove, three polite young people who'd learned endurance, whose gaze followed his gaze: from the crumbling imitation Thuringia to spindly birches growing in the middle of the market square to the big wheel, which still rose majestically in the middle of the park, the deceased child king of the German Democratic Republic, a gigantic circular carcass visible for miles, a skeleton symbolic of the death of the Culture Park.

Wegener turned away. The three behind him kept walking slowly and he followed them around a curve to the right onto the Mesozoic Meadow and could now see himself, even earlier, in 1963, clinging fearfully to his mother's hand, above him the grey-green Tyranno-saurus rex, its hostile red eyes staring down at him from a height of three metres, its mouth open to present sharp white shark's teeth, a cruel colossus that came into his dreams for weeks, which ate up everything he loved night after night, and which was now defeated, lying on the grass with ridiculously stiff, folded-in little forearms, one-legged, the second rising out of the grass as a stump. Everything in the world could tip over, no strength lasts for ever; even the most dangerous of beasts finds itself biting the dust one day, thought Wegener, and he looked into the fierce three-horned face of the tri-ceratops, which was still standing, which time had treated mercifully, not a scratch on its plastic armour.

'The entire Politburo,' said a voice that didn't belong to any of his companions, a voice that was angrier, more dominant, more succinct, which spoke from some distance and was still easy to understand, a voice you could imagine listening to for a while because it sounded like it didn't beat about the bush.

Wegener tried to make something out in the dark. A short man came towards him between the herd of dinosaurs, briefly vanished behind a tailless whatever, reappeared and took the last few metres more slowly. The moon lit up his entrance with a pale semi-light: slim torso, slim face. Early forties. Straw-blond, neat hair. Dark suit jacket, yellow tank top over a white shirt. Pale scarf.

'How nice of you to come.' The man gave Wegener a warm hand and pressed for a moment. He smelled of cold pipe smoke. 'Let's take a little walk. I assume you're familiar with the park?'

'Every inch of it.'

'Good. Then we're both on home turf.' The man strolled lazily back towards the outer path.

Wegener kept pace with him. 'Is this about Albert Hoffmann?'

'Yes, of course. I hear you've been taken off the investigation.'

'Says who?'

'Your department, when someone calls and asks. But that doesn't particularly interest me. Do you know who killed Hoffmann, Mr Wegener?'

'Do you know?'

'Yes. I know.' The man turned onto the path around the park. To the left, not heading back to the entrance but deeper in.

'Are you Alexander Bürger?'

The man smiled. 'Let's just assume I am for the purpose of our conversation.'

'Are you or aren't you?'

'If I say yes you won't believe me, and if I say no you won't believe me either.'

Wegener turned around. The trio had disappeared. The black dinosaur silhouettes bowed and scraped before the blue evening sky. The brachiosaurus' long neck arched above the herd, and for a moment the entire prehistoric zoo came alive: grazing, stalking each other, staring over, every one of them just waiting for an unobserved moment to pounce on one another, tear each other to pieces, eat each other up, ram each other with grunts and shrieks.

'What do you want, Mr Bürger?' Wegener noticed he felt cold.

'I want to know if you've found out a certain fact in the course of your investigations, a fact that I'm interested in.'

The path curved to the left, becoming potholed and uneven. The roots of young birches pressed up beneath the cobblestones. On the right the Treptow Blitz came into view. The picket fence where the endless queue for the rollercoaster had once lined up had tipped over.

'What exactly are you after?'

'Just a minor detail.'

'Why are you interested in the case?'

'That's obvious enough. We're opposed to this state in its current political form. Albert Hoffmann was too.'

'You're wanted by the authorities,' said Wegener, 'and you ask a policeman to give you information. That's absurd.'

'This state is absurd, Mr Wegener. Everything that's going on right now is an emanation of a thoroughly absurd state.'

Wegener stopped and looked at the entrance to the rollercoaster tunnel: wild, wide-open tiger's jaws. The red-painted tracks curled out of the mouth as an endless concave tongue. 'Why should I tell Alexander Bürger, of all people, anything about a special investigation with strictly confidential status?'

'That's obvious too. Because you'll get the name of Hoffmann's killer in return.'

'Just the name, not the killer.'

'I'm not going to either threaten you or beg you. Either you opt for a deal or you don't. It's your decision.'

'Maybe I can't give you any information on your interesting fact. Then I've got nothing to offer in a deal.'

'Don't worry about that.' Bürger gave Wegener a friendly pat on the shoulder. 'No matter how you answer my question, it's still a valuable pointer for me. Assuming you're honest.'

Wegener could hear the rollercoaster. The never-changing children's screams. The metallic squeaks. The arms in the air. The girls' hair flying into his face. The tickly smell. His instantly stiff penis. The fear that someone would see the lump in his trousers. The tiger's maw, not painted on the other side, just wood screwed together, the tantalizingly threatening illusion of the front side suddenly destroyed, the banal background that was always disappointing but that you still wanted to see at any price, the mother by the picket fence, patient, leaning over, hands folded, the father walking back and forth with his camera, the same pictures every year. Only the child got older and older and older.

'If you're prepared to simply tell me the name of Hoffmann's killer,' said Wegener, 'in exchange for information I may or may not have, then I assume that name is going to be public in the near future anyway. Otherwise it'd be much more expensive.'

Bürger smiled. 'I was told people tend to underestimate you.'

'Sometimes I even underestimate myself.'

'I know the feeling. That happens to all the good people.'

'Interesting that someone who arranges terrorist bombings counts himself as one of the good guys.'

'I don't think we need to beat about the bush, Mr Wegener. Not all kinds of violence are the same. That may be the case in paradise, in simple morals as well, but not on our global terror planet. You can only fight an unjust state that locks its people in by deliberately violating its rules. Anyone who contents himself with the officially sanctioned methods wants to make a martyr of himself, not a victor.'

'You sound like you feel the need to justify your actions.'

'I sound like I feel the need to talk to people who lead the lives of loyal subjects, who haven't been able to develop any consciousness of a state's real privileges and duties. Fully grown children who've never been told what power they have.'

'That age-old dilemma of the subversive,' said Wegener. 'To meet the people's enemy on an equal footing, you have to take on its form. What comes out at the end is two enemies of the people.'

'You've forgotten one key difference. We're human, Mr Wegener, and the Stasi isn't.'

'You've only just started. Let's wait and see what your lot look like in sixty years' time.'

Bürger laughed. 'I hope our struggle won't take that long. Let me explain something. There are three types of people in countries like the GDR: the supporters of the system, the passive mass, and the resistance fighters. A resistance fighter will always make mistakes, there's no doubt about that, even major mistakes. But none of those mistakes will ever be as severe as the mistakes of the passive mass and the supporters.'

'Not even if the mistake's a murder?'

'Not even then.' Bürger looked Wegener in the eye. 'You're not a moralist in disguise, are you, Hauptmann?'

Wegener shook his head. 'Wrong. At worst I'm a pragmatist in disguise. It's up to the victims of your struggle to decide whether it's justified or not, Mr Bürger. But we can already tell what effect

terrorism has, both of us together if you like: always the exact opposite of what it aims to achieve.'

'And what's your conclusion?'

'My conclusion is that there's still fanatical vanity and heroes' wet
dreams for uneducated young men who need ideologies in the twenty-
first century.'

'Terrorism as masculine hormones gone astray – interesting.'

'Interesting because it's true.'

'It's never about the cause? Always only about getting in the lime-
light? And the resistance fighters in the Third Reich? Were they all
vain hooligans trying to grab a bit of admiration?'

'The legitimacy of violent resistance against a system is decided
by a very specific point, Mr Bürger: is that violence directed at the
guilty or the innocent? Is it directed at the leader or the people?'

'You consider a people that doesn't stand up to a leader innocent?'

'I consider the leader the definitive guilty party, so you ought to
have the balls to get at him personally instead of making it easy for
yourself with attacks on the general public. Stauffenberg still has the
support of the entire intelligent world today, but the Taliban won't
have it even in a thousand years' time.'

'You're right there.'

'Why don't you just put a bullet in Moss's head?'

Bürger laughed again. 'Maybe we're working on that right now.'

'Best of luck to you then.'

'Now we've found our common ground.' Bürger patted Wegener
on the shoulder again, harder this time. 'Now all we have to do is
reach an agreement on the information front.'

'Then don't just tell me the killer, tell me the background as well.
Tell me the whole truth about Hoffmann and his murderers.'

'I'm sorry, I can't do that.'

'Why not?'

'That's information we hope to gain a few more advantages from. I'm sure you understand.'

Wegener stopped walking.

Bürger stopped too.

'The truth about Albert Hoffmann,' said Wegener, 'and you'll get the truth about Ronny Gruber.'

Bürger's head jerked around. In the moonlight, his bent nose became a skimpy, slightly dented beak. Now he's an immobilized little pigeon, thought Wegener, that can't even flutter away in panic because he's so amazed.

'What do you say?'

Bürger's dark eyes were half closed. 'How do you know Ronny Gruber?'

'Are we going to reach an agreement?'

The pigeon put its head to one side and fixed its beady eyes on him. 'All right.'

'All right means yes?'

'Yes.'

'What detail of the investigations do you want to know?'

Bürger started walking slowly. 'Let's start with Ronny Gruber.'

'I thought there was one fact you had a burning interest in.'

'All right. Did you come across any controversial documents about Hoffmann's time on the advisory staff during your searches?'

'No.'

'That's what I wanted to know. Now what about Ronny Gruber?'

'Ronny Gruber came to the police to turn state evidence, accusing the Brigade of Hoffmann's murder. We had our doubts from the very beginning. Then it turned out that Gruber had been with the Stasi for years, codename Hermes. They had a double agent in your ranks all along, Mr Bürger. A double agent who wants to pin a murder on your people to take the blame off the Stasi.'

Bürger lowered his head, folded his arms behind his back and strolled on in silence, brooding minute after minute. He hadn't seen that coming, thought Wegener; anything but that.

The path opened out, turning into a round, overgrown space, the lonely full-moon eye glaring down at it like a confused Cyclops. Turning right would take them to the swan boats, left to the big wheel, straight ahead to the next miniature train station, the toilets, the merry-go-round, the ice-cream stall: vanilla, strawberry, chocolate, Baltic blueberry, 5 pfennigs per scoop. 1963.

'You probably know that Hoffmann was working in Wandlitz,' Bürger said finally in an unchanged voice. 'Undercover, if you like.'

'We know that.'

'But you don't know what he wanted there.'

'I'm afraid not.'

'Hoffmann had a regular client in Wandlitz. A man particularly fond of roses.'

Wegener nodded. 'Undersecretary of State Dr Gert Wanser. We checked him out.'

'Obviously not thoroughly enough. Otherwise you'd have noticed that Wanser studied law with Hermann Millard at the Humboldt University and later became his friend, his political confidant. And that Hoffmann's shifts in Wanser's rose garden almost always coincided with Millard's free afternoons in the government quarter.'

Wegener looked at Bürger. The moonlight was falling at an angle, transforming his slim face into a delicate, snow-white mask with dark holes for eyes.

'Hoffmann met Millard regularly?'

'Have you heard of the so-called *Plan D*, Mr Wegener?'

'An energy supply concept.'

'Right. And a great deal more than that. Do you know any more about *Plan D*?'

'I know that Hoffmann and Moss staged a putsch against Stangier.'

'You're a mine of information. That part of Hoffmann's plan worked, but what was supposed to come afterwards didn't go quite as well. And now I'm telling you that Hoffmann had regular meetings with Millard over the past few years, in the middle of Wandlitz but still in secret – in Wanser's cellar.'

Wegener realized he'd broken out in a sweat. Bürger smiled. 'You're thinking something. Am I right?'

'Yes.'

'Go ahead, say it out loud.'

'Hoffmann was planning another putsch?'

Bürger nodded. '*Voilà*, Mr Wegener. Hoffmann wanted to repeat what he'd done once before. A rerun of *Plan D*: with Moss against Stangier twenty years ago. And now with Millard against Moss. So that they could scatter the wonderful cornucopia of democratic socialism over the GDR after all. A good idea but it still went wrong. First he got found out, then he got strung up.'

Wegener sat down on one of the rotting benches that lined the square at five-metre intervals. The big wheel looked much smaller than it had used to. The rusty cars squeaked in the wind.

'The Stasi.' Wegener leaned back. He felt the bench's dampness through the fabric of his trousers. 'I knew from the very beginning that the Stasi killed Hoffmann. There was only one motive: we assumed Hoffmann wanted to go to the West German press with evidence of his first putsch against Stangier. To discredit Moss in the international media. But a second putsch is a whole different ball game.'

'Did you ever suspect anyone else? Apart from the Stasi?'

'A West German energy consortium. But there were a lot of loose ends.'

'Listen, Mr Wegener, we were both after the same person earlier on. Gabriel Opitz. And neither of us got him.'

'You haven't got him?' Wegener stared at Bürger. 'Your people kidnapped Opitz right in front of our noses, in two black Datschas!'

'The black Datschas weren't ours.' Bürger's voice sounded suddenly squashed. As if someone was squeezing his throat. He gave a cough. 'That was a State Security grab operation.'

There was a tingle. The tingle climbed up Wegener's oesophagus from his stomach into his mouth, slipped under his tongue and turned into a sherbet sparkle that refused to stop.

'They've got Gabriel now. And they'll kill him and present him as the killer. To take the blame for Hoffmann's murder away from themselves in the Western media.'

Wegener tipped his head back. The sky was dark and clear. Bright starry dots everywhere. 'That doesn't make sense.'

'Doesn't it?'

'We know the killers had to improvise,' said Wegener. 'Hoffmann never wore normal shoes, only ever slip-ons, including on the day he died. You can't tie shoelaces together without shoelaces. One of the killers swapped shoes with Hoffmann, and we'll get a flawless forensic match for him via the shoes. West Germany's looking over our shoulder on the investigation, and West Germany will have to answer to the whole of Europe afterwards. There's no cheating the press on this one.'

'There's no need to cheat.' Bürger pulled his scarf tight around his neck. Like a noose. 'Gabriel Opitz did kill Hoffmann. It wasn't the State Security, Mr Wegener, Ronny Gruber was telling the truth: it was us.'

You strange stars up there, you've seen everything before, thought Wegener, letting the bright spots in the night sky blur before his eyes. You've had millennia of lessons in global intrigues, there's no dirty trick that's passed you by, you don't get uptight as quick as we do down here, we aggravated ants with our built-in finite life-spans. You're smiling to yourselves up there at this ridiculous Hoffmann incident, at the crummy power fantasies of us chaotic fruit flies, at the whole childish game of hide-and-seek, at Martin the Ignorant, a forensic fool, one of the best the police have ever had. You're radiant with ridicule, the whole starry firmament mocks us anew night after night.

'We're fighting for democracy. Not for democratic socialism. Or Posteritatism.' Bürger spat out the word as if he'd bitten into some-thing sour. 'There's no such thing as democratic socialism. Socialism doesn't work. Because it doesn't work, the people are running out on it. Because they're running out on it they get locked up or shot. So you can't democratize socialism. It'd have to work in the first place to do that. Which it doesn't, and it never will. It's a vicious circle that anyone can see, as long as they're not too scared to open their eyes. It's about time humankind started putting their utopias back on the bookshelves.'

'Some people do put them on the shelf,' Wegener said weakly, 'and their children take them down again.'

'You're probably right. But it doesn't mean we have to stand by and watch.'

'And Hoffmann?'

'He'd have meant life-prolonging measures for the GDR instead of assisted suicide. He'd have sown new faith among the obstinate dreamers and pathological optimists. Millard would have been the new Moss, a bit more pro-Western, a bit more modern, on first-name terms with Chancellor Lafontaine.

'I can see them grinning side by side on the press photos, the Siamese twins of socialism, we stand for social justice, blah blah blah, those self-satisfied ignoramuses who get high on their supposedly great deeds for the precarious proletariat and would sacrifice two whole countries for their romantic pipe dreams, and when the writing's on the wall it'd mean everything stays the same here, another twenty or thirty years of the workers' and farmers' state, who knows how long Millard's got to go. This country can't afford that.'

Wegener looked at the ground.

'We've got influential helpers,' said Bürger. 'In the Socialist Union, the European Union, the USA. Helpers in governments, in global corporations, in the media.'

'At the *Spiegel*, for instance.'

'For instance. If a source turns up there with an execution story, with spectacular photos of knotted shoelaces and hangman's ropes on top, they listen very carefully.'

'Who is that source?'

'One of the many defectors that this country produces. And boom, it's the Stasi behind Hoffmann's death.'

'You wanted to incriminate the Stasi to prevent the consultations.'

Bürger nodded. 'We like to kill several birds with one stone. Hoffmann's dead, we've put an end to the Millard putsch, the consultations are off, the Stasi's denounced, the country will be bankrupt by next week. Moss will get chased out of office, democracy gets a chance. No ideological and no economic basis for continuing the GDR. Don't you agree that that prospect justifies Albert Hoffmann's death? One eighty-year-old hanged in exchange for 14.5 million people's freedom?'

'That's not for me to decide,' said Wegener, 'because it never ends the way you think.'

'You don't happen to have tickets to the premiere of *Red Revenge*, do you?'

'What?'

'*Red Revenge*, with Antonia Hiegemann. Are you going to the premiere?'

'No.'

'I wouldn't if I were you. It's not a good film. Goodbye then.'

Wegener stood up. His backside was wet. 'I do have a few more questions, Mr Bürger.'

The short man looked as if he enjoyed being called that, as if he was wondering what it was like to really be Alexander Bürger and not just pretend, for the length of dodgy talks in closed-down theme parks.

'What would they be?'

'I've been tailed over the past seven days.'

'There's no need for that as of now. Is that all?'

'Not quite.' Wegener took a step towards Bürger. 'When Gabriel Opitz and his helpers killed Hoffmann, why did it have to be at that spot?'

'What do you mean by that spot?'

'The murder scene. The pipeline.'

'Why's that important, Mr Wegener?'

'It's up to me what I think's important.'

The white face remained stiff. 'Gabriel's cluster was following Hoffmann on the 17th of October, they had been for several weeks.

We were waiting for an opportunity. That day he spent several hours at a retirement home in Heinersdorf, then he drove into the forest.'

'What retirement home in Heinersdorf?'

'Alpha Rest Home. A house for retired Socialist Unity Party people.'

'And then he drove himself to the Müggelsee.'

'I just said that. Gabriel called us from the forest. Hoffmann wanted to go for a walk. We couldn't have had a better moment.'

Wegener buttoned up his jacket. 'Who informed you so precisely of Hoffmann and Millard's putsch plans?'

'Ronny Gruber.'

'You're kidding.'

'No. And I think we can both answer the interesting question of where Ronny got his information from now.'

'From the Stasi.'

'Looks like it.'

The man who was or wasn't Alexander Bürger reached out a hand and Wegener took it, pressed it just as briefly as before, and then Bürger turned away and walked towards the big wheel until his delicate frame disappeared in the darkness.

For two minutes there was nothing to be seen or heard. Then footsteps approached. From three different directions.

'Time to go back to Mitte, Mr Wegener.' The male voice. The trio's speaker. 'Would you please hand us your Minsk battery for the length of the drive? There's no point in informing your colleagues anyway. There'll be nobody here by the time they get here.'

'Where are you dropping me off?'

'That's up to you.'

'Take me to the Molotov then.'

'I hope you've got enough money on you.' The trio laughed.

'And before that the bank.' Wegener breathed in. Breathed out.

For a few seconds, the park's silence pressed as heavily on his skull as the brutal quiet of the white room had; no squeaking of cars on the big wheel, no rustling of leaves on the trees, not a sound. A lone black bird winged across the square and disappeared behind the trees, now presumably above the River Spree, following the broad, glinting ribbon through Treptow, through the Osthafen loading port towards Mitte, flying on and on into the warm, hazy cloud of light pollution that floated above the city, hanging above tower blocks, prefabs, nineteenth-century tenements, church towers and domes like a dull halo, discharged by thousands of orange street lamps, a merciful light that flattered rather than illuminating the dirty-shimmering, misty nimbus of Berlin.

32

AND GOING DOWN, THOUGHT WEGENER, is always faster than going up, rule of life number 1 for mistruster number 1: on the way up you have to give it all you've got, getting up is a combat project, your teleological impulse, the great effort, but on the way down you slip, you fall, you ride, like on this never-ending escalator, lit up dull city-yellow by original street lamps screwed to the steep walls at five-metre intervals, stolen or organized via one of the top one thousand who regularly come down here, descend to the depths.

What are the Molotov people trying to tell us with this stairway to the underworld, the escalator illuminated like a Berlin street? So it's the official route to the abyss – tolerated, sanctioned, the one exception that makes it clear to everyone that there'll be no others. It's only here that they outdo the West in everything the West has to offer. They saved up every good idea for this cellar, every bizarre stroke of inspiration, every luxury: you can get more here of what you can't get anywhere else. Just stand perfectly still, it all happens automatically, it'll all turn out all right, it'll take you along on a journey, carry you through, build you up and knock you down, spit you out again at some point, into the backyard, through a lowered brick anus, and there's no electric lift waiting for you there, all that's waiting there are ancient, worn-down stone steps, the game's up, you have to walk the way back up, in life as it is in the Molotov.

The doormen, two Angolans imported specially for the job who granted the police ID a mere fleeting glance, handed Wegener on into a long corridor, also street-lamp-yellow, a glass cloakroom, more steps downwards.

Magdalena, thought Wegener as he got a payment chip-card and a welcome vodka and Bioneer soda pressed into his hand, rhubarb flavour – are you still around, Mussels Magdalena, Moon-eyed Magdalena, more, more, more Magdalena, are you still here, still prowling around this bunker full of lawless lumps of lust, down confusing corridors, through tiny rooms, great halls, landings, dead ends, are you still bringing the underground functionaries and civil servants and artists and combine directors and magicians and great white hopes and no-hopers their cylinders of seafood, their bacon chips, their chutney, their mascarpone mash, are you still pouring Red Riding Hood Superb into the flies of the *nomenklatura*, pointing the wrong way through this brick confusion? Far back, deep into the uncharted labyrinth, into the dark rooms, boudoirs and secret cabins with their safe doors, minibars, waterbeds, bathtubs, large-screen TVs, with their unassailable retreat spaces where you could disappear for hours, nights, days to scheme up spicy, dreamy, orgiastic plots, with their delicatessen hatches through which everything is handed in that the inmate wishes for, there where the world no longer matters, where only pleasure counts, cut off from the earth's surface for private recreation, delectation, celebration.

Wegener strolled over shining concrete floors through the entry lounge, past crooked walls pretending the entire Molotov had slipped into a rocky crevice, complicated, convoluted, Stalingrad sounds booming out from the speakers, old and new sounds, volleys of gunfire, ringtones, church bells, between them Budapest street noise, shouts of market traders, newspaper boys and injured soldiers, a few bars of Brahms.

The lounge was empty, the door area too. Seven gilded openings gaped in the walls, each a different shape, each leading in a different direction, to a different near future: a square, a triangle, a star, a trapezoid, a rhombus, a circle, a semicircle. If you dare to come in you have to find your own way, you don't get any answers, any directions, you're not allowed to ask anyone and if you do they lie to you. Wegener took the circular opening, *the round entrance, then right, right, right, left, right,* Frankenstein had written, *Tolstoy Cavern, the bounty's lost and so are we.*

Wegener sucked at his welcome vodka and Bioneer soda as he walked along the downward-sloping corridor, the walls coming closer and closer, leaving only half a door's width. Really fat men would have to turn around here, back through the circle for the next try, square or rhombus, but I can still make it, thought Wegener, I'll get through, I'll keep going somehow, I won't get stuck like the Mercedes in the slaughterhouse alley, I can still manage it but it'll be over in a few years. A window in the floor, beneath it barrooms, velvety seats, kidney-shaped tables, orangey light, drinkers and smokers who didn't see him – Wegener was standing behind their heads, watching but not recognizing anyone.

He carried on and took a right turn, the rear of a bar behind thick glass, on the windowpane the curving letters: *Vyacheslav Mikhailovich Bar*; the slim back of a dark-haired waitress – Magdalena, thought

Wegener – the waitress turned to the side, stood in semi-profile and wasn't Magdalena of course, but just as devastatingly Russian and pretty, looking at him now, smiling a good-naturedly frivolous smile, pointing at his empty glass and raising an eyebrow.

Wegener nodded. The girl reached behind her, opened a seaberry-flavour Bioneer soda, fetched vodka out of a fridge concealed somewhere, poured well over the measuring mark and winked, then placed the drink in a turntable and there it was with Wegener, who put his empty glass in the gap and added the payment token. The Russian beauty turned a handle, took everything out on her side, ran the token through a scanner, sent it back and turned around. Wiggled her small arse a little. Another glance over her slim shoulder, one last smile. Next, *pozhalusta*!

The Magdalena moments were now coming back to him little by little, appearing as he drank, as he strolled onwards, creeping out of a corner of his brain where they'd been well kept, and now they liberated themselves, not the slightest bit faded, no blackouts, no blind spots.

Magdalena outside the Molotov at the end of her shift, smoking, waiting in a tiny skirt, the image of a Hollywood whore, thought Wegener, which I found so incredibly sexy because she wasn't a Hollywood whore and certainly not a real one, but she still looked like one so you could imagine you had the guts for the red-light district, to do a dirty deal, pick up this brazen Russian girl from the street onto your back seat, like the hard-nuts from the vice squad did, and then off to lonely car parks.

The far too-small Wartburg, it's not much of an *Aktivist*, Magdalena had complained, wrenching and turning in all directions to give him what he lived for, what he'd been stuffing in protein for all night long, to give him a chance between rear windscreen and dashboard, but how's it supposed to work, one at the front, one at the back and seats in between, it's not as long as all that, so, *moyo solnyshko*, out with the seats! Magdalena had commanded and Wegener: Good job I got the Aktivist Omega, transport version, you can take it all out in three simple steps, well all right, it wasn't actually as quick as all that, but at some point it worked out, two little levers, one button, a good hard jerk and the passenger seat plonked out the door, a folded blanket over the rails on the floor, and still more complaining, still pretty damn tight in here!

You're tight yourself, *moyo sladkaya*, called Wegener, so stop complaining! *Moya!* came a moan from below, *moya* sladkaya! not *moyo* sladkaya!

Then instant peace on Magdalena's face, utter bliss, touched up by some street lamp, dunked in yellow, eyes closed, mouth half open, a sleeping beauty, a silent benefactress, not one who screamed, scratched, demanded, but a lethargic, a lackadaisical, a tired-out beauty, one with eight hours of fetching, carrying, clearing, smiling, cheeking behind her, a leading-lady minx who'd had enough of minxing now, slipped out of her role and her skirt, stripped off everything until her pale body lay naked, wanting to be served after eight hours of serving, ordering the same thing every single time: slow and steady, light and loving, make me happy, that was what Magdalena called it, make me happy, make yourself happy with me, make us happy, that's all there is to it, for everyone, so no messing around, no playing games, just in and out like a pump to inflate Magdalena with tenderness, to fill her with new strength, with new cheek, cheerfulness, with fresh chirpiness, up to the brim.

Her yellow face as if in a trance, as if switched off with the plug in the socket, no activity during recharging, enough done for today, it's time for the detective's turn and the detective should take his time, should imagine that every minute of in-and-out with Magdalena in this Wartburg would be credited to his account as a bonus on his lifetime, his personal life account set up by God himself.

So secure yourself a biblical age, it's so easy to shag your way into God's good books, a little bit of patience please, and don't you dare think of ejaculating, let's forget the quickie and learn the slowie, turn into a sex-slug, a copulating sloth, imagine you're defusing a bomb, Magdalena had said, and I'm the bomb, if you go too quickly the bomb will blow up.

I can't go any slower! Wegener had exclaimed, how's it supposed to stay hard! It's a question of friction, how am I supposed to get friction out of not moving!

But Magdalena was certain: It'll stay hard, and truly, it did stay hard, even without friction, because I'm sending my scents up to you, Magdalena had said, that's why your sweet East German dong's made of Görlitz granite, because my scents are sidling up your nose, I've worked hard for them, eight hours' work, all for you, every pore of my twenty-four-year-old body slogs away all day long so the old man doesn't have to take virility pills, a perfume from a thousand glands, a stone-age aphrodisiac, the guarantee of a good slowie after a tough shift, so remember: hard day, hard cock, Magdalena had said.

And Wegener had learned, learned to enjoy her silent face, the satisfied features, the childish, half-open cleft of her mouth with its two curious canines, learned to gently nudge the spaced-out girl, to pep her up from below, to extend his own lifetime, while Magdalena's fresh sweat got him high, battered his senses, lined the Wartburg, misted up the windows, against which she placed her feet, pushed herself off, a perfectly formed toe signature, while the detective was robbed of his sanity, not doing his job, not thinking, not calculating like a criminal, was even as speechlessly astounded as Karolina herself, who was driving to Thuringia on a rainy day and watching the vapour from their damp coats paint two naked ghost footprints on the windscreen, too late to turn on the ventilation and wipe out those telltale toes, too late because Karolina was already retching, zooming onto the hard shoulder, braking, screaming, punching the steering wheel.

And me, thought Wegener, what a child I was, what a horny little boy, my head full of pounding panic, excuses rotating in my skull, none of them good enough to even think through to the end, while Karolina's screaming made everything fact, created facts that could no longer be denied, so painful was her yelling, so full of knowledge, full of confirmed concerns, so bestially suffering. The biggest mistake of my life, Wegener noted and knew that he'd thought the very same thing back then, in the car, next to Karolina, at the moment she first began to shriek, when Magdalena's round heels, slim soles, long toes appeared out of nowhere like the jeering revenge of a huge arsehole of a God, who was now demanding he pay the price for the time he'd given him.

That was the mistake of your life that'll never be forgiven, least of all by yourself, thought Wegener. You gambled Karolina away, you managed to ruin one of those rare, natural loves, Magdalena's feet trampled everything to pieces and you couldn't do anything to stop it. There's no need for anyone to betray you, Martin, you do that yourself, you insane, horny, dumb idiot of a stallion, you're the one whose professional focus is on truth, you're the one chasing after it like a tribe of cannibals after Schalck-Golodkowski, you know the truth finds its own path, it can't be stopped, it creeps into the light of day at some point, through the tiniest fracture, for the truth, my friend, is a brutal, five-second sauerkraut fart in a teeny windowless cellar room, one second before the masterclass of the Académie du Sommelier comes in.

And the truth is also: Brendel, thought Wegener, if that's not Brendel behind that window talking to a dark-haired woman who looks nothing like Magdalena at first glance and so perhaps is Magdalena for that very reason. Shorter hair, less make-up, not the uniform but plain clothes.

It really is her, thought Wegener – that mole on her neck, those fur boots with the pale tops, that back-arching laugh while Brendel grins right at her. That charismatic joker, that stupid dog, first Karolina and now Magdalena, that can't be a coincidence, it can only be a plot, a plot by everyone against Martin Wegener, who's been wandering lonely through these convoluted corridors for the past half-hour like a threadless Theseus, who keeps taking the wrong turns, who's always standing in front of the wrong windows and never the right doors, a spectator to the drinking, smoking, face-stuffing of the elites, and right in the middle's the Magdalena–Brendel couple, flirting, chatting, getting closer, over in the corner's Frankenstein, fogged up in smoke but still unmistakable, that black Mephistopheles cap, that baggy jacket, a portion of steaming greens in front of him.

Now Frankenstein gesticulated, raised his beer mug as they once used to salute the Führer, touched glasses with two men sitting opposite him.

Wegener followed the corridor, suddenly realized he was running, but the green-lit hosepipe bent off to the right where he should have gone left, turned into a sinking curve, a spiral down to the next floor, a Karat tune throbbed out at him, dry ice rose towards him, lightning flashed from the ceiling: a retro disco. So he turned back, up the spiral, down the corridor, on the right a dim den in which men and women were bathing in broad brass bathtubs full of warm cream, spooning up pasta, scooping sauce onto their plates from their tubs, throwing mozzarella balls at each other, gorgonzola chunks piled up like blue-green marbled soap.

A woman of twenty at the most rose, cream flowed over her upright breasts, dripped from her sticky blonde pubes into the waiting mouth of a kneeling man who Wegener now spotted, smiling in artificial jollity: Jan 'The Smooch' Hermann, naked and plump, an inflated toffee of skin, and just then his concoction came out of hidden speakers, 'No Doubt Time Hates Love'.

Wegener forced himself back to the large window, Brendel's arm now around Magdalena's waist, a forceful occupier come to put things right, oh yes, who gave the sweetshop perfume a target person, a timid Cheers, a determined drink, Frankenstein stuffing his face, and Wegener walked along a twisting tube toward the entrance lounge, had to take every turn again, had to duck down, breathe in, decide on right or left, recognizing nothing and long since feeling as if he was in a mutated pipeline that could only mislead him.

Up a few steps then off to the right and that damn cavern must be somewhere on his right, but there were only doors on the other side, first a little Buletto branch crowded with fat men gobbling down grease-dripping cheese Wart-Burgers with rocket mayonnaise, in the midst of them the founder S. Seifer himself, opening his mouth wide and biting in, melted cheese hanging off his chin.

Wegener swayed – allegedly there are paths between the sections, secret doors that remain hidden, that no one had ever discovered, nothing but Molotov rumours – and he was running again, taking the wrong turning again, turning around, noticing the vodka and Bioneer sodas, getting hysterical, conjuring up ominous images: the big window and behind it Brendel–Magdalena arm in arm, Brendel looking almost like Früchtl but he still couldn't be Früchtl, after all

Frücht was sitting tight in his own head and wanted to hold one of his never-ending speeches, absolutely, there was no turning him off.

The sores stay with us for ever, Martin! exclaimed Früchtl, slurring his words: *anyone who raises hopes that humankind will one day learn from its past, that it won't learn from the history of its victors but from that of its losers, they haven't understood the principle of socialism, because socialism is the principle of hope, a childish and naïve hope of course, but that's precisely why it's a hope as strong as a bear, producing generation after generation of new hopefuls, magnificent idiots who fail to understand that utopias are only desirable because you can't ever have them, so they're guaranteed to fail, those real existing utopias, and the only people who refuse to listen are merciless imbeciles who think they'll find the antidote to one extreme in the other: they'd rather go so far left that they come out on the right again, unconvincible lemmings on the leash of ignorant ersatz religions, a complacent crock of junk that the human race presses out a million times over in every new generation.*

It's not about the GDR! Früchtl was shouting now, *what's the GDR anyway? A historical boil that's soon to burst, that might leave a bit of a stink but that's it. It's about all the GDRs in this world, everywhere, on every continent, blossoming over and over, sometimes for a long time, sometimes short, sometimes strong, sometimes weak, sometimes unrecognizable, sometimes perfectly clear, sometimes red scarves, sometimes brown shirts, alternating auspices producing identical injustices, murders, lies, hells, steered by the few, supported by the many, feared by all, provoked by the immeasurable arrogance of those who imagine themselves to be gods on the shoulders of giants, although they're born as cockroaches on piles of bones, mountains of skulls, heaps of rotting flesh, who look behind them, look down and secretly consider themselves immortal, cleverer than all those slaughtered before them, who storm cheering into the oldest ideologi-cal traps decade after decade anew, because the extremes promise them the only thing good sense can never offer: mortal enemies, a never-ending line of opponents and thus the entire anachronistic vanity package – faith, fights, fame, comrades, tradition, pride, honour, victories, defeats, the ridiculous illusion of achieving something mean-ingful, lasting, historical, carte blanche for every conceivable violation of humanity, of course all for sake of the cause, which has to be constantly praised as great so that no one notices how meagre it is, all concave mirrors wrought to reflect the saccharine-sulphurous spotlight for the upstarts' sunbathing sessions, vested interests over altruism, history-book entries over Weltgeist, it makes me want to puke, this whole, rarely understood, never cancelled inhuman comedy with its redundant plot: that many have always had to die only to persuade few of their alleged immortality.*

I was a Nazi, then I was a communist, gasped Früchtl, *I am Germany, the Teutonic twentieth century incarnate, tortured to intel-ligence, bullied into cleverness with great losses, and then that's all there is. Now that I can see clearly I have to step down to make way for the stupid: what a goddamned mess, the right-wingers, the left-wingers, all still standing, all still stinking the same – how are you supposed to leave when you're kept here? You do want to see them all out at sea, everything fermenting that once was your torment – all right, it doesn't quite rhyme, I'll admit, but is it so hard to get?*

No, Major Molotov, said Wegener, I get all of it, and I'm sorry but just shut up now, please, just shut up at long last, because one of the men's getting up from Frankenstein's table, going to the bar, past the window and it's suddenly Colonel-General Steinkühler, brushing his blond hair off his Stasi brow, waving at someone, displaying gold teeth, disappearing behind a wall while Brendel holds Magdalena's head in both hands like an ostrich egg, kisses her on the lips, sucks her mouth up to his, Magdalena on tiptoes, following Brendel's kiss, getting sucked up, holding his backside tight, pressing up to him. The brown banana penis suddenly flashed into Wegener's mind's eye, the pale pink nose of its glans, the plump, dangling giant scrotum, the toolbox from the tangas, with which Brendel had worked on Karolina and now was about to work on Magdalena, at last a slow screw without constraints, plenty of space on the Mercedes' leather, and Wegener's greasy hands helpless on the glass of the windowpane, even more prints, evidential smears: I was here.

He was swimming, drowning in vodka, before him Frankenstein's teeth, behind him an Angolan bouncer grabbing him under his arms, heaving him onto his strong black bouncer's back and dragging him off, disposing of him in a cauldron full of rhubarb juice, thought Wegener, in a toothpick forest full of tin dragons, in a white room with a carpet of dead leaves, in a rocket field full of mayonnaise, in all sorts of unfavourable lonelinesses where I have to hang around with myself, and then suddenly icy night air, a slamming door, the brick anus and the stone steps, steep, endlessly long, impossible to climb. In life as it is in the Molotov.

Rotten fish. Urine stench. A flat circle, long and reflecting. Puddle, thinks Wegener, with a yellow street-lamp head floating in it, reflected over from somewhere or other, actually belonging somewhere quite different, but then it is somewhere quite different too.

Grainy hardness pressing into your cheek, forest, no, asphalt, that's right, says Früchtl, *so that's the word that best describes the surface upon which they made your bed, and as they made your bed so you must sigh in it. At least you didn't puke this time, or perhaps it's long forgotten, perhaps you did, perhaps you spewed all over the bouncer's back at 160 bar, the vodka and Bioneer soda stomach acid foaming down to his tar-black crack, flooding out his really immense parts, tanning his hide – watch your step! Negative sexism cancels out positive racism! So perhaps you preferred to serenade the blackamoor,* 'Ten Little Nigger Boys' *to say thanks for making your bed between skips, crates, rubbish, dirt and puddles, new coordinates for your strictly confidential, lovingly kept collection of* 'favourite places I've lain me down to sleep'.

What now, Wegener? That question that ought to be your life's motto arises again, this time – a real innovation – for the sake of the nation, under threat of annihilation: What now, Wegener?

Josef, you're already incredibly annoying with your rhyming nonsense, says Wegener, but when your language chip goes wonky it's enough to kill a man, it really is.

Your defence does not constitute a response to my, that is, your question, especially considering I'm already dead, aren't I?

What now? says Wegener. I've come down to earth with a bump behind the elite disco, and *disco* is Latin, as we all know, for *I learn*, so that's what I'll do, there are things that have to be brought to an end at all costs, simply so that they don't have to be thought to an end at all times.

Correct answer, says Früchtl, but now let me play Big Borgs and tell you: Knowledge is a treasure, sure, mostly, often enough, but now and then, Martin, that treasure turns to torment, one thing to rule them all, then suddenly everything's an end in itself with a self-destruct button, the insight and the end of the world coincide, there's not even time to ask yourself whether one was worth the other, or perhaps in plain words for a change: Not knowing can also be a privilege. I was there at the time, and after the fabulous failure of the Third Reich all those in the know longed terribly not to know.

The question is always: Do you want to live ignorant or die clever?

I want to live clever, Josef, of course. I can guess you won't take that for an answer, but living clever is everyone's ineluctable attempt, the long run to the optimum, full risk and if it all goes wrong at least you get the good feeling of having tried, not a gnawing accusation, not a half-squashed mouse on the ground outside the door, squeaking in pain but you don't open up just to spare yourself the knowledge, battening down the hatches, locking out reality, because life's not like that, Josef.

If you hear that squeaking you open the door, you can't help it, *disco, discis, discit,* that's what we call human, *discimus, discitis, discunt.* And there's something gnawing in my jacket pocket, something squeaking, they're called a visitor's pass and an appointment slip, my personal entrance tickets to the heart of Stasi darkness, they're still valid and they promise insights, they bring certainties, final, lasting, reliable certainties. You can guess, my dear Josef, all I possessed was that little bit of trust, and if that trust's gone then all that's left is hope for knowledge.

Have you ever thought, says Früchtl, *that trust might mean tearing up the appointment slip and the pass, not taking the offering and thereby making trust possible in the first place?*

She lied to me, in the Hoffmann case.

And you cheated on her, in the Magdalena case, 1:1 I'd say, time to break off the game, a draw instead of dire revenge. Unhappiness isn't the same as immortality, happiness isn't the same as kitsch, secrets are more human than any bloody disco, discis, *and you, Inspector Karolina Investigator, now you want to go running to the Stasi and begging for a surveillance protocol. But what you forget is that making mistakes is more human than your pathological addiction to trust: you can only trust people who make mistakes in the first place, because only they know what they vote for and against, only those who make mistakes have retained their humanity,* errare humanissimum est, *and now I'm begging you absolutely, formulaically, short and sweet and alliterative: Trust over trumps!* Didicero, didiceris, didicerit.

Martin!

There's a squeaking outside the door, Josef, there's a gnawing in my jacket. And a buzzing in my pocket.

Wegener rolled onto one side, extracted his Minsk from his trousers and read the *TM* from Borgs' mobile that was running across the display, over and over, a redundant news ticker-tape: *Ronny Gruber liquidated last night. Killers escaped unrecognized. W. B.*

FRIDAY 28 OCTOBER 2011

33

'UNDERSTOOD.' BORGS LISTENED AT THE VIOLET RECEIVER as if it were a telephonic oracle in aubergine form, and blinked. The afternoon sun was a merciless interrogation lamp shining in his bulldog face and exposing the unflattering, stubbly truth: an old, jaded, wrinkled, overweight police dog who had too many dog days to look back on, who'd been yearning for his meagre state pension for too long and for a life without murderers, bureaucrats and phone calls to the State Security.

'Yes, that's what I said too. Fine. You too.' Borgs put the phone down and looked at Wegener. 'So, can you guess?'

'There aren't any grab commandos in black Datschas, there wasn't an operation in Prenzlauer Berg yesterday, Gabriel Opitz was never taken into custody.'

'You forgot one thing.'

'Which was?'

'Anyone who claims anything else is looking at a charge of

defamation of organs of the state, et cetera.' Borgs blinked. 'Would you mind . . . ?'

Wegener got up and pulled the dark brown curtain across the window.

'Let's talk straight, Martin.' Borgs was now sitting in the shade, looking just as unhappy as before. 'We can thank our lucky stars if they don't give you a real bollocking for what happened yesterday. You were totally off the case. It's all very well if you get smart ideas but you should have informed the Stasi immediately, they know that and you know that.'

Wegener laughed. 'They didn't need informing, they were there before we were!'

'They'll be coming to see you, about Bürger.'

'*They'll* be coming to see me,' said Wegener, 'and when *they* come *they* can take a long walk off a short plank.'

'You're taking a week's break from now on. Apart from the meeting with the Stasi, when they get in touch.' Borgs picked up the sketch of Bürger from his desk and stared at it as if the artist had drawn a naked, round, bulldog-faced little man who couldn't see his own dick over his huge beer belly. 'Martin, you spend an hour chatting to this babyface and all that comes out is an ideological debate?'

Wegener leaned against the windowsill. 'I wasn't in the Plänterwald because he wanted to give an interview.'

'Right, you were there because a terrorist asked the police for information! If I hadn't been your big fat boss for so long I'd say that's the craziest nonsense I've ever heard.'

'Nonsense is absolutely within my remit.'

'And why weren't you armed?'

'Walter, if I'd been armed I'd have handed over my gun on a velvet cushion – there were at least four of them, maybe even forty, what do I know?'

'And not a word about Gruber?'

'I wasn't going to hand over our informer to them.'

Borgs rested his head on his chubby hands. 'They might have found out some other way.'

'Or the Stasi did the job itself.'

'That's nonsense, Martin! Sick nonsense! The man was one of the Stasi's most valuable undercover informers and then he gets blown away in the hands of C5. The whole thing's driving me wild. The biggest disaster is the Kayser thing. And then this crap! Where are we here?'

'In a country where they call cows *roughage-consuming large live-stock units.*'

'I want you to write a final, conclusive, very last report.' Borgs levered himself up out of his desk chair. 'Brendel and Frank are just dictating what happened before into the FIS and C5 microphones, you can leave all that out. And, Martin, as soon as they want to talk to you, you make yourself absolutely available whenever it suits them! Lienecke's going over to the Plänterwald in a minute, although he won't find anything. And here comes the main point: Köpenick Police Station's not lifting a finger on the Hoffmann case any more. This case is a gay Pied Piper and we're the clever heterosexual rats who hold their pink ears shut, have you got that?'

'I assume we'll be signing something.'

'I assume so too.' Standing in front of his filing cabinet, Borgs rummaged through a drawer with a number of grunts until he'd found his cigarillo reserve, then pulled out a wooden box, opened it and took out a Corredo. 'What was this Bürger guy like? Is he off his rocker?'

'No. More like a man who's decided at some point that the ends justify the means.'

Borgs scraped a match alight, fired up the Corredo, waddled back to his desk while puffing at it and plonked himself down in his seat. 'They're the worst kind. We'd better be prepared for hard times. It looks as if they're being funded from abroad. Kallweit told me that, there must be a leak somewhere. It's going to be a blast.'

Wegener stood up and went to the door. 'Any news about Kayser?'

Borgs steamed in his window corner like a factory chimney. 'If there was we'd be the last to find out. And anyway, we wouldn't want to know, would we?'

'And GreenFAC? He was working on them all along, they can't just ignore that.'

'GreenFAC!' Borgs gave a dismissive wave. 'Absolute nonsense. An eco-energy supplier that goes round shooting secret-service men! Don't make me laugh. That crock of shit is stinking outside someone else's front door, just like the Hoffmann, Opitz and Gruber turds, and all the others. So at the risk of repeating myself: look forward to a week off work, write up your report and most of all keep your mouth shut. Then you'll be farting on my chair one fine day.'

'What a delightful dream of unbesmirched joy,' said Wegener, leaving the smokehouse and closing the door behind him.

Christa Gerdes wasn't at her desk. Antonia Hiegemann flickered across her Robotron screensaver in a bikini combat suit, a long wrapped present under her bare arm with the barrel of a machine gun poking out of the end. Hiegemann winked and gave a bold smile, and a flag popped out of the barrel: *Hiegemann avenges Santa's little helpers – in cinemas from 28.10!*

*   *   *

Wegener drifted through the rush-hour traffic in a brown Phobos II from the police car pool, changing gears automatically, braking automatically, in the midst of the mass, one among hundreds cruising around the Brandenburg ring road, embedded in a gasping, uniform convoy. Other men in other phenoplast casings protruded into his field of vision on either side, crept past and slid slowly back again, a tired tortoise race that would have no award ceremony. Brick chimneys, concrete chimneys, metal chimneys poked up out of the peripheral wastelands, tens of vertical sprouts of wasting-away industrial architecture, the last desperate shoots just before it withered and died for good. White and black smoke curled out of their thin ends into the sky and blurred together somewhere in the anteroom to the cosmos, into a boundless grey that stained everything its colour.

From the Moabit turn-off, timid rain threaded down. Wegener pressed and pulled at the plastic lever next to the steering wheel and two flimsy wipers squeaked across the greasy windscreen, like the gaunt arms of an ancient hag at a carnival procession, synchronized seesawing to the beat, to one side, to the other side, smearing the sodden film of rapeseed oil into an opaque layer, drawing clear lines, smearing the lines back, drawing lines, smearing them back.

Wegener slumped over the steering wheel, trying to make out the brake lights ahead of him, to assess the distance to the next cars, squirting soapy water out of the cleaning jets. Now the layer of grease on the windscreen foamed yellowish, turning into a viscous mush.

I'm flying blind, thought Wegener and braked, almost down to walking pace, I'm in chronic blind flight mode, whether I'm in the car or down at the station, whether I'm walking around out there or driving. You can't see five metres ahead here, you have no idea what's going on right in front of you here, you stay stupid behind walls of

mistrust and curtains of grease, an isolated, eyeless brain in a nutrient
solution made of a million possibilities.

Gruber dead, Kayser dead, the Stasi innocent, the whole Hoffmann
case as opaque as these sticky car windows, through which you had
to stare out at the dim, dawdling traffic while your left hand felt for
the visitor's pass and the appointment slip in your inside pocket, found
them both but still went on fiddling with them. The documents had
been issued and presented, so they were valid. If they hadn't registered
that he'd been taken off the investigation yet, if the Stasi's red tape
still took place in pen and paper for security reasons, via forms, stamps
and signatures rather than computers, then he was in with a chance.

And if I was to tell you, said Früchtl, *that you'll never again –* but
his words were drowned out by the sudden barrage of rain battering
at the plastic roof, sending streams flowing along the gaps between
the concrete slabs of the road, pattering down as if from a watering
can and washing down the rapeseed-oil-smearing system, releasing a
view of yet more chimneys, tower blocks, wastelands and ruined
factories, the wiper arms now leaping to and fro with abandon.

Wegener drove faster and faster again, grinning, saw himself grinning in the mirror, saw his contorted face grown old with his well-kept
row of teeth, his receding hairline, the wrinkles digging their way
deeper and deeper into his skin, the eyes staring at him as greeny-grey
as if they belonged to an unscrupulous clone that lived in his body,
that filled him out exactly, wearing the increasingly sluggish inspector's
body as a heavy coat, as a well-padded protective shield that stared
hostilely out of two holes in the head at a hostile world, an opponent,
a partner. Watch out for that guy, thought Wegener, he's had enough
of being fucked around, he's just about to strike back and stir up a
war he can't win. A war someone else will have to lose for him.

And that someone is you.

34

PARTS OF A LONG BRICK FACADE APPEARED behind shiny wet-black tree trunks: stained roof tiles, crow-stepped gables, bay windows, balconies, gradually converging into the front wall and the side wings of a stately home, three storeys of weather-beaten, dark violet bricks and rotting windows, crooked roofs and cramped towers.

Wegener drove the Phobos along the wide gravel driveway with a leisurely crunch. On either side of him were oversized, cracked amphorae with nothing growing in them; between them slim statues, their skulls eaten away to shapeless ovals by the acid rain, a whole collection of deleted faces, empty, coarse-pored spheres on top of mossy bodies.

The Phobos crept past them, up to the apex of the circular drive, and then stopped. Worn-down steps led up to a green-painted double door with club-shaped pillars on either side of it, holding up a more recently attached awning of rusty iron bars and corrugated aluminium. On the round lawn was a decommissioned fountain full of wet

leaves. Arm-thick vine tendrils had invested decades of work in climbing up the brickwork. Their large, jagged leaves glowed red as blood.

So this is where they dispose of them, thought Wegener, the functionaries and cadre. In the fat-cat final repository Alpha Rest Home.
He steered the car past the steps, stopped again twenty metres on,
parked on the lawn and got out.

A strong scent of autumn hit him in the face, nature's inimitable
aftershave, a much too obvious olfactory omen: mouldering fungus,
lush cushions of moss, moist earth, resinous bark, rotting apples.

The end is nigh, said Früchtl.

Wegener shuffled across the gravel, ascended the worn-down steps,
pressed down the golden handle on the right-hand door and entered
an overheated hall complete with a curving staircase to the upper
floor, black-and-white chequered floor tiles, antique grandfather
clock, antlers on the walls and a glazed cabin in which a gaunt,
middle-aged man sat behind a Nanotchev, flicking through a thin
book. The man put the book away and slid aside a small pane in the
cabin's glass.

'Can I help you?'

Wegener held his ID into the open gap. 'A man by the name of
Albert Hoffmann came to visit someone here on 17 October. I'd like
to know who he visited.'

The man's face grew friendlier. 'You mean Professor Hoffmann,
yes, he was here mid-month to visit Dr Frommann.'

'Dr Frommann.'

'That's right. Dr Gerda Frommann.'

Wegener put his ID away again. 'Right, then I'd like to pay her a
visit too, this Dr Frommann.'

'You haven't got an appointment?'

'Not at all.'

The man jammed a headset over his parting and clicked away at the Nanotchev keyboard. 'Hello, this is Hans-Walter from reception, how are you, Dr Frommann? Yes, thanks . . . yes, of course . . . well, if you say so!'

Wegener looked at the book on his desk and turned his head so that he could read the title. Christian Kreis, *Inputrescible Waste*. The perfect reading material for a Socialist Unity Party retirement home.

'Yes, there's a man here from the police who wants to talk to you. I'm afraid I don't know . . . Right! Good job you mentioned it! Yes of course. You too, Dr Frommann, bye bye, Dr Frommann!' The receptionist smiled at Wegener. 'Dr Frommann will see you now.'

'And where will the Doctor see me?'

'Apartment 26, second floor.'

'Thanks.'

'Just a moment! I almost forgot, I do apologize. Apartment 26 is being renovated!'

'That's all right.'

'I got muddled up there, sorry about that. Dr Frommann is staying in the guest room of the Ulbricht Suite for the moment. First floor!'

'These stairs here?'

'Yes, up here, then take a sharp left and keep going.'

'Up and left.'

'Sharp left.'

'Sharp left, OK.'

Wegener climbed creaking, polished steps to the first floor and took a sharp left turn along creaking, polished floorboards in the direction of *Apartments 1–5, Tea Salon, Ulbricht Suite*. Wall lamps with ruffled cream fabric shades lit up olive-green and gold paisley wallpaper; small crystal chandeliers grew out of stucco rosettes on the ceiling. There were brass signs mounted by the apartment doors:

MS ELFRIEDE BRÜNING, *MS LUC JOCHIMSEN*, *MS CHRISTA WOLF*. At the end of the corridor a man was sitting on a chair. As Wegener approached him the man stood up: froggy eyes, brown hair, ruddy skin and a coarse face.

'You can't go past this point.'

'That'd be a shame.'

'State Security.' Froggy suddenly had a Stasi badge in his hand. 'You haven't got an appointment.'

'But Dr Frommann's looking forward to seeing me.'

'Oh, you wanna see Mrs Frommann.' The coarse face switched from delighted condescension to mild arrogance. 'You're in luck.'

'Aren't I just?'

'Then face that way with your legs apart, please.' Wegener planted himself broad-legged beside the door with his hands on the wall. Fabric wallpaper. Patterns you could feel, raised ornaments. His eyes slipped down the olive green to a brass plaque: *MS MARGARETE STANGIER*, *MINISTER OF PUBLIC EDUCATION*, *GERMAN DEMOCRATIC REPUBLIC*, *RETD*.

Wegener felt his heart skip a beat. His pulse stumbled, lurched and ran wild. He broke out in a sweat as Froggy was feeling up his calves and thighs, practically grabbing at his crotch, fumbling at his backside and waist – a clumsy lover, ungainly but determined. Wegener tried to think, the entire Hoffmann case shooting through his brain like a blown-up balloon that's been let go without its knot being tied, farting around for seconds in unpredictable, crazy loops and then immediately going limp and falling from the sky.

'Come with me,' said Froggy, unlocking the door to the suite and entering a small reception room with six other doors off it. Walter Ulbricht simpered down from a golden frame on the opposite wall. The sound of guitar music came from somewhere, two voices singing a duet. A low male voice and a high female one. There was a smell of incense sticks and mothballs. Froggy squared up to the first door on the right, knocked, waited three seconds and poked his ruddy head into the room.

'A visitor for you, Dr Frommann.'

No answer. Dr Frommann obviously reacted with an encouraging gesture and silence.

Froggy opened the door as if he was a valet at Stasi HQ.

Wegener took a few steps in and was instantly transformed into a midget. The guest room of the Ulbricht Suite was a 70 to 80-square-metre ballroom with sprawling seating for more than fifteen people, a desk the size of a Phobos, a four-poster bed the size of a Mercedes, a grand piano and an en-suite conservatory. In a wheelchair for full-sized manatees, a pale heap of flesh was enthroned. The heap was wrapped in beige tents. Two pumpkin-shaped shoes protruded from beneath a plaid blanket, presumably left behind by Godzilla on his last trip to Berlin.

'So you're the police, are you?' the heap of flesh proclaimed in a remarkably nasal voice.

'Hauptmann Martin Wegener,' said Wegener, trying to close the door as quietly as possible.

'I still can't see you, though.'

'You can't see me?'

'It's nothing to do with you, it's to do with my eyes. But my ears work all the better to make up for it, unfortunately. Can you hear it?'

'The music?'

'Music? You call that music? Sit down!' A leg-sized arm folded out and indicated the floor next to the heap of flesh.

Wegener removed a delicate Biedermeier seat from the dining-table ensemble, crossed the creaking floorboards to the wheelchair and put the chair down. Dr Frommann was a mountain range with the head of a standardized old lady: white curls, pronounced features, a dark shadow of a moustache and bottle-bottomed glasses, behind which two boiled eggs stared out at nothing.

'Your flat's being renovated?' Wegener sat down.

'Since the day before yesterday. And now I have to put up with the arias that get sung here every day. Can you tell me why they have to paint a blind woman's apartment? There are plenty of deaf people here with terrible walls!'

'I'll have to pass on that one.'

'Me too.' Frommann's hands folded on the blanket – a ten-pack of sausages. 'Poor Margarete is a little damaged, I'm afraid. A tragic story. Old age is a mountaineering tour to the summit of impudence.'

'Dementia?' Wegener tried to sound sympathetic.

'Dementia, depression, schizophrenia, a little bit of everything.' Frommann smiled past him. 'She was such a bright, disciplined person. We admired her and feared her, admired her and feared her! But she's been going downhill for the past two years. She used to be so clear and now she's getting more confused every day. Human sanity is a cup of sour cream in a sanatorium for the obese.'

Wegener didn't know where to look. 'But she sings.'

'Biermann! She sings Wolf Biermann!' Her flesh trembled. 'All day long! Thinks she's an opposition activist against her own husband, would you believe it?'

Wegener wanted to say something but the heap of flesh was faster.

'No, you wouldn't. I can hardly believe it myself, and I'm the one who gets to hear it every day. *Throw Down Your Arms!* If anyone's throwing round here it'll be me, and throwing up, not down! And the psychiatrists talk about subliminal post-intellectual processing of

marital conflict structures via identification with political value pro-
jections. Here it comes again!'

Next door, the stereo was cranked up. Rhythmic guitar chords
hacked their way through the walls. Wolf Biermann embarked on a
song, but a gnomic voice instantly squealed him down. 'Don't let
yourself be broken' – someone beat a crutch against the floor in time
– 'in these days of wars and harms! The last words aren't yet spoken,'
tap, tap, tap, 'don't heed the generals' charms – and throw down your
arms! And throw down your arms!' Tap, tap, tap. The gnome-like
voice went head over heels, left the lyrics to their own devices and
began shouting out the tune, *Ta-damm-ta-da-damm, Ta-damm-ta-da
damm!*

'She was in a real tizzy the other day,' complained Frommann, 'she
started singing "From the Maas to the Memel". Life is a plummeting
paternoster at the tax office, Mr Policeman.'

'Dr Frommann . . .' Wegener pulled his seat up slightly closer to
her wheelchair. 'I'd like to talk to you about Albert Hoffmann's visit.
A week or so ago.'

'Oh, you know Professor Hoffmann?'

'Yes. Can you tell me why he came to see you?'

The ten sausages unfolded again. 'That's no secret. It was about
my last time capsule.'

'I'm afraid I don't understand.'

'You don't know what a time capsule is.'

'No. I've never heard of them.'

The heap of flesh heaved a sigh that came from unplumbed depths.
'It works like this: all the pupils at a school write down their wishes
and hopes for the future – for their personal future and for the future
of socialism. They're all collected up and put into a time capsule and
the time capsule is buried, in a place the pupils don't know.

Twenty-five years later you dig up the capsule, and the letter that every child wrote twenty-five years ago is handed back to them and by now they're fully grown, upright socialists. Are you following me?'

'Oh yes.'

'Right. And then every one of them can see exactly what they've made of themselves. What they've made of the GDR. An admonition in their own handwriting. Through their own dreams and resolutions. Do you understand?'

'You were a teacher?'

'Headmistress.' The heap of flesh puffed up a little more, the cliffs of her chest pressed a good bit upwards by a tectonic shift beneath her blouse. 'Three decades without a single day off sick, Mr . . . ?'

'Wegener.'

Next door, someone turned the volume up as far as it would go: 'So now we have awoken, in these times of desperate need!' Tap, tap, tap, 'don't let yourself be broken . . . '

' . . . Mr Wegener. At the Mielke Grammar School in Pankow. If only Margarete would be quiet for a change! Margarete!'

. . . *in desperate times indeed! In desperate times indeed! Ta-damm-ta-da-damm, Ta-damm-ta-da-damm*!

'And that's where Mr Hoffmann's daughter went to school.'

'Not his daughter!' Dr Frommann's teacherly head gave an angry wobble. 'The daughter of a colleague of Professor Hoffmann's. He was her godfather. Professor Hoffmann didn't have any children of his own. Luck is a Chinese condom factory, if you get my meaning.'

'Marie Schütz.'

'Yes, our dear little Marie . . . ' The sausages linked again, the boiled-egg eyes closed and the deep sigh returned.

Wegener tried to ignore the shrieking in the next room. 'And what does Professor Hoffmann have to do with the time capsule?'

The eyes snapped open again. 'He helped me to bury it back then. In May '91. I could do everything back then. See, walk, stand. Cynicism is Methuselah drowning in a fountain of youth.'

Wegener noticed his hands gripping each other nervously. 'You and Professor Hoffmann buried the capsule together. In the forest by the Müggelsee.'

'Of course. Did Professor Hoffmann tell you that?'

'And only the two of you knew where it was buried. No one else.'

'Professor Hoffmann was in charge of the cartography, with some kind of coordinates.' Mrs Frommann groaned as she attempted to sit more upright. 'Some kind of latitude and longitude meet there, don't ask me, I taught German and History. But Professor Hoffmann wanted it to be absolutely precise so that nothing could go wrong. Chance is a rusty bolt in the Greifswald nuclear power station!'

'And Professor Hoffmann came to collect those coordinates on the 17th of October.'

'Yes.'

'Did he say why?'

'Of course he did. They're building out by the Müggelsee, some kind of repair work on a pipeline. They're digging up half the forest. He had to rescue the time capsule.'

'And he didn't have the coordinates himself?'

'No one but me was allowed to know where the capsule is. Professor Hoffmann insisted we stick to the rules, he's a very strict person. The building work was an emergency, do you understand?'

'Absolutely.'

'The capsule's going to be recovered in five years' time. Who knows if I'll still be here to see it. It all passes so quickly, Mr Policeman. Time is a jet plane with diarrhoea, if you don't mind me saying so.'

'What did Professor Hoffmann want to do with the capsule?'

'Well, the professor wanted to bury the capsule somewhere else and bring me the new map. I'm sure he can't have forgotten it. Perhaps he's just been busy.'

The music and screeching next door had stopped suddenly. Now there was a short, forceful knock. At the same moment the door opened and a young Asian nurse came in, balancing a tray loaded with a teapot, teacup and a little teapot warmer holding a candle.

'Marilou?'

'Here comes your rosehip tea, Dr Frommann!' The nurse nodded at Wegener and put the tray down on a raised coffee table next to the seat. 'I asked Mrs Stangier to take half an hour's break.'

'Oh, thank you, dear! What did you tell her?'

'I said we had the State Security in the building. It wasn't a lie.'

'You're an oriental angel.'

Wegener waited until the nurse left.

'Dr Frommann, I need those coordinates.'

'You?' The heap of flesh felt for her steaming cup, lifted it to her mouth without a single tremble and took a slurp. 'Why?'

'For a police investigation.'

'You're pulling my leg.'

'I'm absolutely serious.' Wegener had to keep a grip on himself so as not to grab the tea-slurping, lethargic giant manatee by the shoulders and shake her. 'And it's urgent.'

'Young man, if you want to go to the Müggelsee then in Ulbricht's name go into that Transitnet thing, they know everything there! Don't think I was born yesterday! Learning is a brain-amputated octopus with—'

'It's about the time capsule, Dr Frommann!'

'What do the police want with our capsule?'

'There's an Energy Ministry no-go zone around the pipeline, no access for private individuals. Professor Hoffmann came to me to ask for my help in digging up a specific item. He wouldn't tell me what it was, he said I should come and ask you. If we don't act quickly the capsule will be dug up by the builders.'

Her tea sloshed over the brim. 'That mustn't happen! Do you hear me, under no circumstances!'

'Then I need the coordinates.'

'But Professor Hoffmann's already got them.'

'The professor had to go on a trip at short notice and I'm afraid he forgot to give me the note beforehand.'

The boiled-egg eyes narrowed behind the bottle-bottom lenses. 'All right then. But be careful! Don't you dare damage anything!'

'We'll be careful, I promise.'

Frommann put down her teacup, turned her wheelchair and rolled over to the desk at the speed of a gout-ridden sloth, took out a brass casket, opened the casket and removed a piece of paper. Then she unfolded a monstrous magnifying glass and spent three minutes drawing numbers on a notepad with a scratchy fountain pen. The piece of paper vanished back into the casket.

Wegener stood up.

Frommann tore the numbered sheet off the pad and handed it to him like a certificate. 'And bring me the new coordinates once you've moved the capsule, promise me that!'

'I promise you faithfully.'

'A faithful promise is a virgin at the registry office.'

Wegener put his chair back, went to the door and turned back. The doctor gave a silent salute with one leg-sized arm. Wegener waved back and then he was out.

Froggy was waiting outside the room.

'Finished already?'

Wegener nodded. 'Finished already.'

There was a banging from somewhere. The banging came closer. The door behind Froggy was jerked open and a half-naked old lady appeared, her chaotic blue-grey hair standing up in all directions. 'You Stasi swine!' The old woman stared at Wegener in absolute hate.

'Mrs Stangier, this man is Dr Frommann's guest!' Froggy had gone bright red in the face. 'A visitor! Could you please go back in your—'

'Visitor!' croaked the old woman, contorting her wrinkly face into a cruel grin. 'The Stasi swine are always right where you don't expect them! Right there's where they sit and wait for you to walk into their trap! But not me! Not the Queen of the Blue Rinse!'

Wegener fled past Froggy to the apartment door, tugged it open and hurried into the corridor, but her shrieks came after him, piercing doors and walls, echoing across every floor, relentless, hoarse, vitriolic: You miserable Stasi swine!

35

AN ACOUSTIC GUIDED WEAPON, the old woman's voice pursued Wegener down the creaking staircase, through the hall into the car and along the ring road all the way to Karl-Marx-Allee. He had the feeling that cruise missile of a voice was catching him up and about to hit him from behind as he turned onto Normannenstrasse – bull's eye, got that Stasi swine on the way to his Stasi swine mates! But he was only there to turn the tables, Margarete, quietly and unnoticed, because there was no other option, and you keep out of it, Josef, once and for all, the two of you are a great pair of guardian angels, the sedated sinner and the ex-commie-ex-Nazi skeleton, a dream disorientation duo. If you have to insult someone, take a look at each other. It'll be tough but it'll help matters.

I can see myself from above, thought Wegener, I can see myself walking across the deserted courtyard, past the spot where Kayser parked the Mercedes when he was still alive, not even a week ago. His murderer's walking the streets but even that killer will one day trip up over a coincidence, and now I'm alone here, no Kayser, no Brendel, no Mercedes, wrapped up in the cold and gloom of East Berlin, a black dot on a dark grey surface, a slow, steady motion towards an unmoving target.

Lonesome decisions entail lonesome paths, that much was clear from the beginning, and now he was seeing everything from the perspective of a man who'd just died and was looking down at himself for some incomprehensible reason, watching Martin Wegener walk his path, leisurely and unstoppably, with not the slightest regret, with not the slightest anticipation, with not the slightest fear, knowing that knowledge won't change anything, taking a walk in eighties computer-game mode: Steer the People's Police officer (PPo) as directly as possible across the square concrete space to the duty officer's cabin, then to the honeycomb entrance, through the glass doors into the lions' den. Into the dusty smell, floor-polish smell, citrus-cleaner smell, up to the counter, at which there's no red-haired lump of dough this evening but a not entirely unattractive ponytail-wearer, although perhaps a little too much make-up is visible when she cocks her head to check the documents and the ceiling light suddenly strikes her powdered face so hard it ought to give off clouds of skin-coloured dust.

Wegener stood motionless, breathing through his mouth so as not to smell anything while this State Security reception officer nodded at his appointment slip, stamped his visitor pass, pulled a list out of a drawer, wrote something down, telephoned for the accompanying officer, and even smiled as she gave back the slip and the pass. Like the women behind railway station counters. The ones who wish you a good trip, wherever you may be going.

Wegener made an effort to keep up with the accompanying officer, who seemed to be running away from him rather than accompanying him, on running duty along corridors that had no doors, passing guards and making gestures to leave his slip and his pass in his pockets; the company of an officer on running duty was enough.

Down one stairwell to the first basement level, where Wegener's eyes caught on rows of metal cabinets, LEDs flashing next to brightly coloured strands of cables behind glass doors. He'd seen it all before, by night and without company. Another corridor, another guard, behind him the reception desk of a library, a neatly dressed man in a suit with a name tag, *A. Butt*, who looked at the appointment slip, checked the stamp on the pass, added a second stamp alongside it, inserted both papers in a hanging file and filled in three short, pale green recycled paper forms in return, which he handed silently across the counter: *Permission to view State Security Surveillance Operation STÜ:1355/ha–A. T.2011, Permission to view State Security Surveillance Operation STÜ:1369/ha–A. F.2011, Permission to view State Security Surveillance Operation STÜ:1012/ha–A. F.2010.*

Three minutes later, Wegener was sitting on a wooden chair at a wooden table in a low-ceilinged room between dark blue carpeting and unshaded fluorescent strip lights. He'd sat exactly the same way on his search for the lost Josef, perhaps not on this chair but on a similar one, perhaps not in this room but a few doors down at the most.

He had kept getting up to take new piles of paper out of new filing cabinets, which contained everything but a clue to Früchtl's whereabouts. He'd been first nervous, then panicked, then insane, and finally he'd realized that there was nothing he could do here, he'd never find anything here, even if he spent his entire life in the basement of Stasi HQ – because this enormous collection of information, this meticulous rubbish tip of all East German biographies, this complete graveyard of everyday life in the GDR would need neither walls nor guards nor appointment stamps to protect itself from intruders.

All it took was to leave the searcher alone with the complete documentation of all existence in the state, without the key clue to where
to find a document in this galaxy of facts, the piece of paper on which
the key fact was written down for eternity.

And so every act of research was pointless, the insane meticulous-
ness of this apparatus was its own perfect protection. There was no
better way to do it, protecting power through the mass of crimes, the
hidden letter that is safest of all right where it's supposed to be.

Oh Hydra, you multi-headed scrooge, thought Wegener, you could
at least turn the heating on. November came through the cellar walls,
cool air grabbed him by the throat, trying to strangle him, giving him
goose pimples. The microphones were presumably concealed in the
ceiling. The cameras in the lamps. I can see myself from above again,
thought Wegener, on a monitor six rooms along, sitting here in black
and white and waiting for a priest from the information temple to
serve me the essential elixir to cure my chronic blindness. Down here
it didn't smell of floor polish, dust and citrus cleaning fluid, but of
damp plastic, of never-aired nylon carpeting, of ancient carpet
glue. The sour, sober scent of bureaucracy, which you got used to so
quickly that you didn't even notice it after half an hour.

The face to match the carpet fumes came in, balanced on the weedy
shoulders of a nameless officer from Central Reconnaissance Department. That face was a collection of anti-characteristics, components
of inconspicuousness category 1: an unspectacular nose, a boring
chin, pale blue average eyes beneath a mousy brown, dull haircut.
God must have really needed the toilet when he was making you on
his human press, thought Wegener.

'You applied for two surveillance operations as part of the bilateral
special investigation, file number B–ppk–88521(S) on 25.10,' said the
officer, with the robotic intonation of a Navodobro voice. 'Both

applications were granted by Major-General Wischinsky on the same date.'

Wegener nodded.

'The surveillance operation you commissioned did not yield any significant observation results. I'm presenting you with the report under the registration number *1369/ha–A. F.2011* – it's very short. For comparative purposes you're also receiving the target person's file from the years 2009 and 2010.'

'Just a moment.'

'Yes?'

'That means the person whose surveillance I commissioned has already been under observation for two years?'

'That's correct.'

Wegener's hands gripped the edge of the table.

The officer didn't speak. He was obviously accustomed to giving his visitors time to digest their shock.

It gets better and better, said Früchtl, *any minute now it'll turn out you've been having yourself watched, Martin, and then I'll laugh so hard I'll have to bite into this stinking carpet.*

You could have guessed that, Detective Clever-Clogs, thought Wegener, not letting go of the table. An application to the Energy Ministry leads to a routine check, and a routine check leads to permanent observation, because if there's no specific reason for an observation then there's no reason to stop it. Paragraph one of the Stasi logic rules, which had filled an underground vault with files to implement them, a second Berlin directly beneath the city. If only the Karolina observation meant that Karolina hadn't worked for the Stasi. Then he could get up and leave right now. But the Karolina observation didn't mean that at all.

Wegener nodded.

'Seeing as these surveillance operations are part of a bilateral special investigation,' the officer said, 'and the procedures therefore don't
fall under the administrative assistance agreement, all information
taken from the observation protocols is to be treated as strictly
confidential and is generally inadmissible as official police investigation findings or in court. It serves solely to provide new investigation
perspectives, which must be secured with standard evidence in line
with the relevant regulations. Do you understand that?'

Wegener nodded.

'You're only permitted to view the surveillance protocols on site.
You're not permitted to make notes or copy the documents, or to
take them away with you.'

'How much time have I got?'

'As much as you like.'

'Is this room under camera surveillance?'

'Yes, of course.' The man without a face placed two pale grey fold-
ers on the table, picked up the two pale green forms, compared the
registration numbers, whipped out a pen and signed the covers of
both files with a steep, illegible temperature curve. 'For the record:
the documents provided correspond with your order in terms of surveillance method and target person. Telephone surveillance of the
mobile number 1130 20 23 34 53 190 plus acoustic and visual observation of 34, Colombetstrasse, third floor, documentation medium:
photography.'

Wegener nodded.

'Then I wish you a productive working session, Comrade Hauptmann.' The officer left the room as if being pulled along on a string,
closing the door behind him.

There it is again – my old fear, thought Wegener, that the Last
Judgement has abolished purgatory sentences and the new maximum

penalty for human perfidy is eternal solitary confinement, never-ending vegetation in the Normannenstrasse basement or one of the white cells of Stasi City, an endless Phobos drive behind smeared windows, a daily, immobilized awakening beneath the same broken fan, a brain in a tank that can do nothing but observe itself, isolated for all time and having to subsist on a meagre diet of past experiences, possessing the memory of a handful of years and nothing else, insidious capital because the past has passed and finished for ever, unchangeable, because you never get a second chance and instead you spend a merciless future regretting, struggling fruitlessly with your own mistakes, with all that you missed, with the millions of paths life could have taken, a skip full of subjunctives, which you can drown in by the hour because you had to go and get the punishment you feared most of all from the very outset: sheer, bare, hermetically sealed isolation.

Whatever I do, thought Wegener, it'll turn out the same, the end of the game was fixed before it even started, it's kismet socialism, biographical planned economy, because the Stasi's always there before you call them in, because despite all your best-laid plans they always pick the right moment to find and exploit their target person's weaknesses, punish life's little negligences hard, are wide awake if the curtains are left open just once, in the heat of an all-numbing lust during which you can't think of footprints on windowpanes or of closing the curtains, which is why pictures are then taken showing Karolina lying in bed being undressed by a man with white hair, who's standing with his back to the window, who's holding her skirt, her tights, her bra in his hands, whose head's disappearing between her legs, with Karolina's face pained by lust, a moaning mouth, a fawning stare at the ceiling, while the old man burrows his skull into her, presses her legs apart, Karolina's feet in the air right and left, the photos so sharp that the folds on the cramped soles of her feet line up horizontally, the telephoto lenses so good that they see Karolina's toes splaying, see her mouth now an angry scream bridged by a thread of saliva, a lustful circle in the middle of her contorted face, a place of rage at her threatening to lose this duel, and then she does fight back, pushes the old man away with her feet so hard he falls off the bed, and now she's lying with her legs apart, no woman has ever spread them wider, playing with herself, then turns over and offers the white-haired man two fleshy cheeks, plunges her middle finger between them, inserts it deep into her opened arsehole, pulls it out, spits to wet it and inserts it again, widening, takes two fingers, three fingers, splays her fingers, stretching her arsehole, and now that hole's the softest, most inviting, wettest hole in the whole world, anything will fit in there, anything can be swallowed up by it, it's waiting patiently, it's open for the old man, who picks himself up again, spits a copious gob on his long, thin erection, shoos her fingers away, positions his erection, places it on the brink of the hole, supports himself with both hands and rams it so hard between the cheeks that Karolina's face explodes, sinking it down to the root in her arse and thrusting over and over so hard that Karolina's screams on the photos suddenly echo through the basement room, cast back by the walls with nowhere to go but into the head of Martin Wegener, who flicks over and over through the photos, a merciless flip-book, a Karolina Kama Sutra, in which the white-haired man slogs sweatily away, tackles every orifice he finds, going on and on, demonstrating all his skills, a record-breaking rogerer in a fever of fucking, until at some point he collapses, lying behind her on the bed, wiped out, then finally lights a cigarillo, smokes, presses up against Karolina, holds tight to her slightly pendulous breasts like a drowning man clutching at two buoys at high sea, kisses her shoulder and cries pitifully for joy, and this time it's on the record, thought Wegener, this time it's not a vodka and Bioneer soda high, not a Molotov fantasy, not a primeval fear turned delusion, not a projected complex or a masochistic daydream, this time it's perfectly focused truth, existing on countless prints, secretly organized, numbered, verified: the old man is crying with the brown, distinctive, suddenly youthful face of Josef Früchtl.

36

THE POLYPROPYLENE MOLECULES TOUCHED, grabbed, hooked into one another at their ends and became a twisted chain, producing a mesh along with other twisted polypropylene molecule chains, spreading out in all directions, growing upwards and downwards, building itself up on hundreds, thousands, tens of thousands of levels, becoming a thin layer on which numerous other layers rested, stuck to each other, pressed tightly together and thus formed the millimetre-thick, yellow and blue flower-patterned plastic tablecloth with white foam-rubber tassels that Wegener stared at until he raised his eyes, ran them over the collection of atoms making up the veneer surface, over the cells of the tulip in which the chlorophyll, the cytoplasm and the tonoplast vibrated, in which cell nuclei, vesicles, peroxisomes floated, billions of them alongside each other, on top of each other, producing structures, forming fibres, ground tissue, palisade mesophyll, made an epidermis and became a leaf, pale green and waxy and overlapping the edge of a vase, which was piled up out of mountains of silicon dioxide, aluminium oxide, boron trioxide and sodium oxide and held together an ocean of several billiards of water molecules, each of them one oxygen atom, two hydrogen atoms.

I see, thought Wegener, *video ergo sum*. For the very first time I'm seeing through the world I've been stumbling around blind as a bat for the past fifty-six years, getting an electron-microscopic X-ray of existence. Wherever I look I recognize structures, patterns, the mechanics of things, I see criminals, victims, eyewitnesses, principal witnesses, murder motives and puppet-masters. The detective's finally got a grip on things but he's not passing Go, not collecting 4,000 marks, no one's going to jail, the reward is the truth and nothing but the truth, so help me, good God.

Everything's spread out in front of me, thought Wegener, everything consists of clusters of identical items, of items easy to label, which relate to each other according to fixed laws, which react exactly the same way to each other for all eternity, with unavoidable chemical-emotional reactions such as meltdown, explosion, dissolution; in the end, with sealed decomposition. Nothing else has ever been possible since the beginning of the universe: the options are fixed, and only chance, which always trips you up, decides who meets whom and where, what comes together with which and when. All the rest has been arranged since time immemorial, every staring shot that falls for the nth time, on your marks, get set, never anything new, identical processes unreel, impossible to prevent, a field of perfectly placed domino gravestones that obey the laws of physics like the Germans obey their leaders, that is: they can be relied upon to tip over, one after another, and thereby produce an outcome that you could have calculated without even the slightest whiff of imagination:

$$(\omega\text{Wegener} \cup \text{Karolina}) <<< \varkappa\text{GDR} + \varkappa\text{chance} + \varkappa\text{sex})$$

The television pictures on the plasma mega-poster on the EastSide facade were repeating themselves. The woman with the blonde curls and the ragged golden cardboard wings on her back had shouted at the cameras ten minutes ago; now she was smudging her make-up with the back of her hand for the second time, her 36-square-metre tear-stained face shining again above Alexanderplatz. The mass of ants between the Berolina-Haus and the Kaufhaus des Ostens was still swelling, streaming into the empty space from four corners, pushing their way to the VIP Car-Walk, staring at the digital misery above their heads.

The cameraman was jogged again, the pictures wobbled again, showing Santas, angels and reindeer lying and sitting on the street, confused and distraught costumed faces, in the background the wall of flames, black smoke swallowed up by the dark, and beneath it all the never-ending ribbon of the news ticker-tape:

Explosives attack on Cinema International +++ *Numerous people injured at premiere of* Red Revenge +++ *Millard: 'They can't bomb socialism out of existence.' +++ Authorities investigating +++*

Wegener drank a sip of beer. His Minsk vibrated on the tabletop at intervals. Number withheld.

'Hello?'

'Mr Wegener?'

'Speaking.'

'Christian Nadrowski here, deputy director of the EastSide Resort. Can you hear me?'

'Perfectly well.'

'All hell's broken loose down here since we switched the screen to live pictures. Hold on a minute—'

There was a click. The connection was gone.

There was advertising running on the mega-poster now: a frustrated woman with a pudding-bowl haircut in a wind tunnel next to the new Phobos convertible, her hands stroking the plastic roof, painting an indecisive circle in the air, forming a rhombus in front of her white-coated belly. A text was superimposed: *Even greater efficiency thanks to even less wind resistance – Physics Nobel Prize winner Angela Kasner for the new Phobos II Flux*. The wind tunnel turbine turned on and blew the frustrated woman's thin hair into a tousled Mohican. The corners of her mouth stayed put.

The withheld number vibrated again.

'Mr Nadrowski?'

'Right, sorry about that, I'm in the hall now. Can you hear me?'

'Still perfectly well.'

'Head office informed me about your call. Mr Günzow has time for you now. He's waiting at the check-in desk.'

'To be honest, I'd rather not deal with it on your premises. It would be nice of Mr Günzow to come up to the TV tower restaurant for a moment. I'm sitting at table 4.'

'We'd be happy to provide you with a meeting room.'

'Thank you, Mr Nadrowski, but I prefer to deal with this kind of thing on neutral territory. The staff at the Fairview Terrace are in the picture, they'll let him in. He'll be back at his barrier in thirty minutes.'

'All right, OK, I'll tell him. But he hasn't got anything – I mean, don't get me wrong, Mr Wegener, but he hasn't got anything to do with the murder, has he? The man from the FIS, in our hotel? We're still very upset by the events, and Mr Günzow has always been one of our best and most reliable members of staff and—'

'I just need a witness statement.'

'Good, then . . . Do you know any more about the bomb at the

Cinema International, if you don't mind me asking while I've got you on the phone?'

'I don't mind, but at the moment all I know is what's showing on your screen. Sorry.'

'Let's hope for the best then. Goodbye.'

'Thanks for your help, Mr Nadrowski.'

Wegener ended the call, leaned back and let the restaurant floor's slow revolving mechanism carry him further eastwards, floating past the city on his seat, a former sex-slug drinking beer instead of drowning in it, seeing his head as a contorted puddle-reflection in the curved windowpanes and suddenly feeling very old indeed.

The luminous giant plasma screen, the Kaufhaus des Ostens, the Berolina-Haus disappeared metre by metre behind the curvature of the restaurant's sphere. Karl-Marx-Allee pushed its way slowly into view, its elongated, illuminated straight line nudging unstoppably to the fore, the Walter Ulbricht vista, the road to nowhere, the burning Cinema International a pfennig-sized bright dot with a weak corona of blueish light flickering around it, sirens still wailing mutedly from all the East Berlin districts, trying to force their way through the crowded streets in which the traffic was clogged between impromptu checkpoints.

Everything flashing, nothing moving. Berlin was standing still.

Perhaps I'm the only slug in the city making progress at this moment, thought Wegener, an exemplary example of my species: crawling in circles.

When Günzow appeared he slouched and padded with limp shoulders past the tables, counting off the numbers, spotted Wegener and froze for the length of a well-prepared penalty kick. Then he straightened his back, arched his uniformed belly even further forward and tried to play the confident page. The confident page came over to the table and sat down. His melon face was sweating.

'Mr Günzow, do you remember me?'

The melon's mouth curved down. Günzow made a face like the frustrated woman in the Phobos ad.

Wegener pushed his police ID across the table. 'Then you know I'm from the crime squad.'

An elderly waitress walked past the table, stopped and took three steps backwards.

'A large beer, please,' said Wegener, 'and my chubby friend here will have a sour-cherry diet Club-Cola.'

'Large or small?'

'Small, please. He's not staying long.'

The waitress looked embarrassed and set off again.

Günzow's googly eyes welled with tears.

'How do I know you drink sour-cherry diet Club-Cola?'

Wegener pulled his ID back across the table and put it away. 'Firstly, because you have a serious weight problem, and secondly because one of those cans is just being found, Mr Günzow.'

'What? What's being found?'

'An empty sour-cherry diet Club-Cola can. With your fingerprints on it. In the Cinema International.'

'Why?'

'Because I had it planted there. You ought to be more careful with your rubbish. Not just throw it in the public waste bin next to the VIP Car-Walk. Perhaps you should get yourself a VIP garbage can.'

Drips of sweat ran down Günzow's chubby brow towards his nose. His uniformed arm wiped them away. 'I've had enough of this, what's all this crap about?'

'All this crap can go really well for you,' said Wegener, 'or really badly. It's up to you.'

'Why badly?' Günzow raised his voice. Red patches on his chubby cheeks. 'What have I done? This is sick! What do you want from me?'

Wegener smiled. 'You're under suspicion of smuggling a bomb into the Cinema International. And unfortunately you dropped your cola can while you were at it. Pretty dumb thing to do, but I reckon people would buy it.'

Günzow's melon face was starting to look mushy. He rolled his eyes. Another drip of sweat set out, and this time no sleeve came to halt its journey; it made it all the way over the red-flecked cheek to the bottom of Günzow's chin and dangled there helplessly.

'At some point they'll realize you're innocent, Sascha, don't worry. But you won't be working at the EastSide any more by then.'

'What do you want from me, you arsehole?'

'That's Hauptmann Arsehole, to you. I want a phone call.'

'What phone call?'

Wegener took a sheet of paper out of his inside pocket, unfolded it and laid it on the table. 'You call this number here, from one of the hotel lines. You don't give your name, you just read out what it says here, word for word. Then you hang up, without waiting for an answer.'

Günzow stared at Wegener, then he stared at the piece of paper, pulled it closer and read it out under his breath, incredulously: 'Listen carefully. I'm going to say this only once. I know you killed Dr Christian Kayser from the Federal Intelligence Service. If you don't want me to go to the People's Police and make a statement, make sure you come at 2 p.m. tomorrow . . . ' Günzow broke off, stared at Wegener, then back at the sheet of paper, read silently to the end, sweating like a pig, his head spinning, cramming, on his last legs, fearful confusion and nervous hate chasing across the chubby coils of his brain, rinsing them clean and triggering a nervous wink on the melon face, a trembling bottom lip, even redder patches, even more dripping moisture. His googly eyes rose slowly from the paper, caught Wegener and darted to the left, to the EastSide tower, which was just coming back into view at a leisurely pace. The plasma mega-poster blew Kallweit's pale face up to bursting point, a hot-air-balloon-sized statesmanlike goat speaking into microphones and gesticulating with his hooves.

Antonia Hiegemann injured in bomb attack on Cinema International +++ At least one victim dead +++ Police: 'Clear leads found to bombers.' +++

'Why me?' Günzow had tears in his eyes.

'Maybe because you were such a smug bastard when I came to collect my colleague the other day. But maybe just because it makes sense for the FIS man's killer to have been seen by a page.'

The waitress placed a glass of beer and a glass of cola on the table.

Wegener reached for the beer, drank a large mouthful and wiped the foam off his upper lip. 'What do you say?'

The melon head nodded.

'If you do it right you'll never hear from me again.'

Günzow took the piece of paper, folded it up and put it in his trouser pocket. Then he downed the cola in one, half-heartedly suppressed a belch, got up and left without saying goodbye.

Wegener looked out of the window. You're lost, he thought, you're doomed, Berlin, my Sodom, my Gomorrah, my poor stroke victim. Paralysed on one side and thus incapable of living on either side. Incurably clogged with fat in every last nook and cranny. Obstructed by complicated structures of lies. How history has used you, how the rulers of all epochs have ravished you. One after another.

Unscrupulous swine, all men of course, the most depraved of all living creatures. And still they're queuing up. You're still lying helplessly on your back. You're still attractive enough to be humiliated a little bit more.

SATURDAY 29 OCTOBER 2011

37

Wegener spoke to the mirror, seeing his rounded face, the old familiar receding hairline, the cherished beakish nose. When you used to come to me in my dreams, Josef, you were a setter-righter, a patron saint, a circus weightlifter in a red-and-white striped one-piece suit, a dealer-outer, a strongman, someone who kept my fears in check, you the king, me his pawn. But last night you were a bug for the first time, a bug with three fat, flat shadows of legs, a bug that had knitted an all-encompassing web and was enthroned royally in the middle, so to be precise you were a mixture of a spider and a bug, a rare species that occurs solely in socialist scarcity states with Phobos traffic and notoriously fat-clogged air, that only finds its ideal habitat where there's plenty of grease, lots of greasing of palms so everything goes like greased lightning, where you can't catch anyone because everyone wears an oily skin that makes them smooth and slippery and fishy, that protects them from getting grabbed so that everyone slips through your fingers at any time.

That's the world you're at home in, Josef, the common scumbug, a parasite that likes parasites, a master of deception and disappointment, a patient knitter of threads who holds all the strings in all his hands and legs. And scumbugs grow old, Josef, they learn something new every day, so every minute makes them cleverer, the older the better, and their sex drive too, they say, rises and rises until kingdom come, grows further and further heavenwards to exponential potency, so that makes the common scumbug – let's not beat about the bush – an old pervert.

Früchtl's voice was silent in his head.

Of course you've gone now, said Wegener, perhaps you were done away with or perhaps you buggered off of your own accord, no one knows, it's the result that counts, in criminalistics and in amouristics – the guilty party eludes the punishment coming to him, whizz-bang and off through a trapdoor. There's always a bit of shrinkage, even the fattest of them all shrinks away and lives happily ever after at sustainable liberty, no one gets taken to account, everyone goes scot-free no matter what they've got to answer for.

If it was any different, if there was access to the main guilty party who's committed the worst of all possible crimes, worse than murder and manslaughter and fraud, namely betraying a friendship, then here's what I'd do with you, you outrageous gas-whore john: I'd hang you up by your thin penis, from the ceiling of a white room or a palm tree on Gondwana, Josef, by a thread around your bell end so your rod would stretch and stretch, longer and longer, get much thinner, like the cinnamon chewing gum from *Sweet Greetings Jena POC*, stretch unimaginably long under your Früchtl weight, and then it'd come unpeeled, come disjointed, come apart, a cheerful fountain of blood to give us deep red joy, the thoroughly deserved self-amputation snapping like a pompous crack of a whip through the secret-service cellar and bouncing from wall to wall to wall from now on, an acoustic permanent exhibition on the subject of historical perfidy.

Off with your cock, Josef, that's my last resort in the face of so much lack of imagination as to sleep with the only woman in East Berlin who was off limits for you, so the only woman in East Berlin who was attractive for you, that's for sure.

That principle too is an essential component of the human engine, I'll admit that much. But that mustn't be, because at some point every one of us reaches his own private cliff-edge, where he's a tragic Greek, where he has to decide by distinguishing right from wrong rightly or wrongly. At that moment you're yourself and nothing but yourself, unadulterated and pure, then you look down at the sheer home-made nitty-gritty, your personal heart-and-soul soufflé flashes past your mind's eye. And it might get nice and brown or it might collapse in an ugly heap, depending on what you represent in that moment, who you've become: friend or foe of the vain egotism that lodges lazily and rent-free in all of us, confident it'll get its next punctual delivery of truckloads of meaty mistakes.

But when everything's at stake everything's different, then it's a life that's decided, Josef, a human existence. In the face of red hair, brown eyes and a bizarrely desirable, slightly greying labia smile, you chose the most beautiful guilt, the woman to top all women, the showpiece of the species, a real trophy, the radiator ornament of her kind. I'm sure she enchanted you, like she enchanted me, and I know her miracle lasts for ever, outlasts even the longest periods without damage, gets only greater with distance. You love yourself to death with her, you concoct a punishing freeze-frame out of your memories, before which you humiliate yourself lustfully day after day, before which you wallow in viscose self-pity. You even grant Karolina power over your dreams and from then on she pillages her way through your nights, plundering whatever she can get, one nightmare after the next, and the sweetest of them all mutates into a burning threat that can never get enough of giving you her worst. In short: she's got you by the balls till your dying day.

But you won't get away without consequences either, Josef. Don't worry, if I don't want to choke on my own anger my only option for the time being is merciful forgiveness for the sake of postponed revenge, although I don't know if that'll ever take place because good stories are as open-ended as Karolina's pink anus in the Stasi photos.

So for the sake of this deferred vendetta I forgive you here and now and I'll get over that too out of pure drive to survive. Though I don't want to survive it at all, because I don't know the point of a life of survival, a life in which the last spark of hope has just been brutally stamped out, in which ego bankruptcy has been taken to the highest degree, but that too must be part of life: being condemned to existence if you find yourself too damned cowardly to reach for a rope. And now a little space for famous last words: More light, There's nothing to weep about, Put me back on my bike, I should never have switched from Scotch to Martinis, Precious I'm going in the bathroom to read, Treason! Treason! So this is loyalty.

Früchtl's voice was silent in his head.

Wegener took the bulletproof vest with the People's Police patch sewn onto it out of the wardrobe and put it on. The vest was tighter than usual, all eight Velcro strips pulling across his stomach, the seams pinching into the padding on his hips, but it'll just about do, thought Wegener, I'll just about do. Then he grabbed the salmon-pink deodorant spray can from the bathroom cabinet, threw it in the bin and listened to the bright clatter it made. And *action!* said his miserable face in the mirror before it closed its eyes.

38

WEGENER SLAMMED THE PHOBOS DOOR. Instead of the satisfied smack of the S-Class lips, all that came was the spare, thin plop that he'd have to get used to again now, the familiar charm of the victorious publicly owned plastic production for the mobilization of workers, farmers and detectives.

Puschkinallee was deserted.

A Lada and a Barkas were parked opposite, wearing thick hats of fallen leaves as a result of clearly spending days or weeks under the old plane trees. More wet leaves piled up at the sides of the road into brownish heaps that were gradually turning black. Dirty water filled the holes in the unpaved footpath. An opaque wall of bushes separated off the large space where the game was set to come to some kind of end, would have to come to some kind of end, because the full circle was almost turned, only a few degrees to go and then it'd reset to zero. Then everything could start over again at last.

Wegener walked along the sodden path towards the main entrance, dodging puddles, climbing over broken branches, trying to avoid splashing his cord trousers with mud. He looked around.

No one was behind him. No one was ahead of him.

Five hundred metres on, the wall of bushes withdrew slightly and the triumphal arch appeared, the right half hidden beneath dark green ivy, the left freshly cleaned, no moss, no cracks, just the remains of a graffito removed with such chemical fastidiousness that you could still read every letter, corroded pale grey into the dark grey: *Gas Gazprom.*

Wegener walked through the arch, automatically reverting to a strangely military stride and feeling like the Russian defence minister back in the old days, on the way to his annual wreath-laying ceremonies, which had flickered across the TV screen for the whole of Martin Wegener's youth, in the days of the superpowers when it was ideological monoliths that faced each other off and not their political remains.

Old Mother Homeland was still squatting sheepishly on her pedestal and bewailing the front square, hanging her heavy head, in which 80,000 Soviet soldiers were rumbling around, shot to death in the storm on Berlin, helpers in replacing one dictatorship with another, a football stadium full of betrayed men who nobody wanted in their head, thought Wegener, who wouldn't leave her in peace because they could find none themselves.

Now the monument's main axis opened up to the East, the broad Stalin Boulevard that you could stroll along at a leisurely pace, along flagstones that looked as if they were scrubbed with electric toothbrushes every morning by a thousand political prisoners – not a weed, not a speck of dirt, not a trace of vandalism. On either side were low-cropped weeping birches on mowed lawns, making the gradually rising boulevard into a gentle, framed ski jump, a ceremonial ramp that guided the eyes uphill.

Between the metre-high stylized red granite flags, motionless gate-posts that waved at each other at the end of the two rows of birches, the statue of the liberator rose to the foggy sky, towering above the entire monument with everything and everyone in view, despite the hazy weather – the heroic Red Army soldier crushing the swastika beneath his boots, clutching the requisite child of the future to his warrior's chest, holding a longsword battle-ready in the other hand, full of valour, optimistic that communism was still a spectre today, a vampire against which all the world's stakes were in vain, a system that might collapse at times, only to rise from the ashes all the more stubbornly elsewhere.

Wegener hesitated at the top of the ramp between two kneeling bronze soldiers with bronze machine guns, stopped and looked out across the deserted field. A broad staircase led down to the field of graves, the indecisive fog suspended above the tennis-court-sized square of lawn with its low hedges around it and pale stone sarcophagi flanking the area on either side.

1:24 p.m.

Go on, thought Wegener, you'll just have to force yourself. You have to. That's the way you learned your trade.

He undid his top coat button, strolled down the wet stairs, chose the path to the right of the lawn and walked slowly towards the liberator, across dark mosaic pieces with a wreath of pale stones inset in their midst, past the rows of sarcophagi, past Cyrillic inscriptions, pictures of battles and variations of death, past cloned Red Army soldiers marching westwards in a never-ending phalanx, past engraved Stalin quotes and hammers and sickles, while the liberator loomed larger and larger, looked more and more determined, a grim colossus on his kurgan, a black knight who had quashed the Berlin Nazis' dream of a thousand-year Reich with a Bolshevist bronze fist.

The burial mound staircase had thirty-nine steps, which Wegener counted as he climbed. At the top he turned and looked at the monument from the other side, from the liberator's perspective. Anyone who entered the monument area had to pass through the arch and take exactly the same path as he'd just walked, across the front square, along the ski jump, between the stone flags down the stairs onto the stage for sitting ducks. The liberator and I will see you three minutes before you arrive, thought Wegener. We two heroes are waiting patiently up here on our hill.

He leaned against the pale sandstone plinth, took his Minsk out of his jacket pocket, put the earphones in his ears and switched to the radio function.

1:30 p.m.

. . . Berlin People's Police this morning held a press conference, at which further details of yesterday's attack on the Cinema International were announced. According to the authorities, the fatality would appear to be one of the bombers, whose identity is not yet clear. Commissariat 5 apparently ordered an initial autopsy overnight. A DNA analysis of the man's shoes, however, identified him as the suspected killer in a murder case, on which no further details have been provided as yet. Rainer Kallweit, Deputy Police President of Berlin, assessed these findings as new proof of the anti-constitutional and unscrupulous attitude of the underground grouping claiming responsibility for the Berlin bombings. Mr Kallweit emphasized that the authorities have been investigating at full stretch for several days, but preferred not to make further statements on the content of a letter received from the bombers for tactical reasons. Meanwhile, security measures outside governmental institutions and in the inner city are being further tightened. We'll have more information during the programme, but first we'll go over to my colleague Michael Lünstroth,

who's waiting outside the Charité hospital for us and knows how the seventeen injured people are doing. Michael?

Yes, Bärbel, to clear things up straight away, none of the victims are in a life-threatening condition, so we can relax a little on that front. Most of them suffered from smoke inhalation but there seem to have been hardly any serious injuries, which is probably down to the fortunate fact that the explosives damaged mainly the cinema stage and not the auditorium. According to the authorities, the cowardly bombers wanted to prevent the premiere of the film Red Revenge, *a symbolic act, if you like, rather like the terrible attack on the Palace of the Republic a week ago. Nevertheless, lives were put at risk here too. The possible death of innocent people was taken into account, for the purpose, it is generally assumed, of articulating an anti-socialist attitude without arguments but with raw and reckless violence. One of the few victims who are more severely injured, as we've known since yesterday evening, is Antonia Hiegemann, the former Socialist Unity Party representative and the star of* Red Revenge.

According to the Charité hospital, she suffered a severe injury to her right leg and it looks like she'll remain marked by this terrible day for ever. Earlier today the doctors spoke of a permanent limp, and of course we're all very upset because we know Antonia Hiegemann as a striking and attractive young woman, as 'the only bomb our country doesn't want to do without', as Hermann Millard once joked. But Antonia Hiegemann's fans and supporters, who've been gathered here at the Charité since last night, have been holding vigils and have arranged candles into a machine-gun shape, in memory of the role of Laura Kraft that Hiegemann plays in the film. One of these young women told me earlier, in tears, that even if Antonia Hiegemann had to limp for the rest of her life it wouldn't change the love of her supporters, and that she'd also have more in common with her idol Rosa Luxemburg, who walked with a limp, as we all know. So it's not just a time of bitterness here but also a time of upright socialist solidarity . . .

Wegener pulled the buds out of his ears and switched off the radio function. He sat down on one of the iron bollards that secured the path around the monument with heavy chains, and waited.

The fog had got thicker.

39

WHEN A MOVING BODY EMERGED FROM THE MILKY AIR SOUP 150 metres away, taking shape step by step and gradually coming into focus, Wegener withdrew behind the curvature of the plinth. He was sweating, his breath came faster, and he laid his cheek against the cold sandstone. Mint-coloured liquid traces had eaten their way into the wide blocks, verdigris water that had been running down the liberator's bronze body for sixty years now and conjured an unpleasant metallic taste onto Wegener's tongue.

1:54 p.m.

A man in a dark hat, dark coat, dark trousers had appeared between the two granite flags, right at the spot where Wegener had been standing himself half an hour previously. He took his time to survey the field of graves, his hands in his coat pockets, and after a while went back down the stairs, took the left-hand mosaic path and came closer. A second black warrior, one without a child, without a damaged swastika, but with a fully automatic handgun, locked and loaded and used.

Wegener unbuttoned his coat, checked his bulletproof vest, buttoned the coat up again, mentally walked alongside the man along the mosaic path, past squares of lawn, trimmed hedges and sarcophagi, reached the staircase and had estimated correctly: footsteps were sounding out on the stairs, getting louder every second, leather soles that were in no hurry, that set about the unavoidable climb at their leisure, determined and under control, rhythmic and discreet, always concentrating on the next step, all the way to the top. The steps of a man with a plan.

There was a ten-second silence.

Then the footsteps started up again, coming towards him around the circular plinth from the left, and Wegener couldn't help thinking of Karolina. He'd never see her again to strangle her with his bare hands if he'd got his sums wrong now, like Hoffmann had got his sums wrong, like Christian Kayser and Ronny Gruber and Gabriel Opitz had got their sums wrong, in the unconditional belief that determination and cleverness turned to success if you simply wedded the two of them. He saw Karolina standing by the Wegener family grave, which he'd just been winched down into on a jerking rope. Perhaps she was even crying a few dutiful tears, out of pity or sentimentality at the memory of a past life, but the coffin had barely touched the ground before Karolina turned away, as expected, while Wegener could already hear the earth raining down shovel by shovel onto the pressboard coffin lid like huge hailstones.

By the time the muzzle of the gun appeared he already knew, he instantly understood what ought to have been clear to him from the very first moment – no loser smelled so beguiling, darkly sweet, intrusive, charming, so strong and lulling; that was how a victor smelled, someone who could only bear his own scent in the knowledge that he deserved it, because that scent had already announced his victory long before the battle began.

'Martin!'

Wegener forced a smile. 'You look surprised.'

'That's because I am.'

'I wasn't sure if I'd surprise you.'

'Well, here's your proof. I'm flabbergasted.'

'With a gun.'

'Sorry.' Brendel lowered the revolver. 'The man who called last night – that wasn't you.'

'No, it wasn't me. It was a Mr Günzow, a brainless page from the EastSide.'

There was a loud and sullen caw from somewhere; a raven, thought Wegener, the cheerful bearer of good tidings. Then its dark shape appeared in the fog, sailed across the central square towards the burial mound, suddenly bird-sized, beating its wings hard as it circled the statue in a wide curve, coming closer, drawing a tight spiral and disappearing from Wegener's view. It had landed on the liberator's head.

Brendel had watched the bird's trajectory too and now his eyes returned reluctantly. 'OK, so where do we go from here?'

'I ask, you answer.' Wegener sat down on his bollard again, took his Minsk out of his coat pocket and switched to vibration alarm mode. 'How long have you been working for the State Security?'

Brendel still had the revolver in his hand, the muzzle now pointing at the base of the plinth. He was thinking. For one long minute it looked as if the stubby barrel would be raised again at any moment, as if all it was about now was where to hide a dead People's Police Hauptmann in a Soviet memorial so that he'd only be found once the Mercedes had cruised back over the border. Back towards a neat and tidy life as an agent.

'Since I was twenty-nine. That's thirty years now.'

'Because?'

'This is the wrong place for political debates. But, Martin, nothing we do is without doubt.' Brendel nodded as if he had to confirm his own words. 'Nothing is the way it looks from the outside.'

'Tell me what happened, Richard.'

'You know most of it already.'

'Tell me anyway. I'll help you.'

'Do I have to?'

'Yes.'

Brendel gave a barely audible sigh. Then he closed his eyes. So that's what he'll look like when he's dead, thought Wegener, pale and feeble but still too handsome to be true, a male model of a spy who stays human despite it all, who clearly suffers from the suffering he's caused, and who'll still get a medal nonetheless because he did everything right. Richard, the star trickster. The greatest playmaker of them all.

'The Stasi originally planted Ronny Gruber in the Brigade to liquidate Bürger,' said Brendel. 'But that didn't work out. Bürger keeps his distance from anyone he doesn't know from the old days, that's his survival tactic.'

'Keep going.'

'So then they used Ronny Gruber in a different way. They came up with a lover for him who worked for the Stasi, and from then on he fed the Brigade allegedly hot information. He gave them a couple of old level-three stories and had them eating out of his hand. They treated him as a valuable source.'

'And then it turned out that Hoffmann wanted to stage a second putsch,' said Wegener. 'How did they find out?'

'I think it was Dr Wanser who talked, Hoffmann's rose buddy. Maybe they found some kind of dirty laundry in Wanser's basement and put a bit of pressure on him. Whatever the case, it emerged that Hoffmann was in close contact with Millard. It's just like Marie Schütz said: Hoffmann saw the gas consultations as the opportunity he'd been waiting for all along. He could prove that Moss was never voted in by the People's Chamber and he wanted to take his incriminating evidence to the West German press. The government was supposed to fall, Millard would be the new Chairman of the State Council, with Hoffmann as the powerful man in the background.'

'That's why he had to go,' said Wegener. 'But the Stasi didn't want to do it themselves, they were scared the consultations would fail if anything got out. Right?'

Brendel nodded.

'So they got Ronny Gruber to tell the Brigade about Hoffmann's plans. The Brigade had good reason to get rid of Hoffmann as well. Albeit the opposite reason.'

'The Brigade reacted more or less as planned. They bumped off Hoffmann so that he wouldn't save socialism by letting blood.'

'So you could say your boys got Bürger's boys to murder Albert Hoffmann.'

A hoarse screech sounded from the liberator's head, echoing back from somewhere on the River Spree behind the trees.

Brendel looked at his gun. He stroked his right thumb along the handle. 'The Stasi is under permanent observation by the FIS. It's highly likely that there are FIS people undercover at Normannenstrasse, who'd report every violation of the state-of-law agreements directly to Pullach. The risk attached to committing murder was just too great. The slightest hint of an illegal operation would have been enough to put the consultations at risk. But Hoffmann still had to go.'

'You could have locked him up in your secret prison instead of having him hanged.'

'They'd soon notice that in the West. If you put a West German in there, a former professor from Heidelberg and a political advisor to Moss during Revitalization, you can bet they'd notice straight away that something's up. And Hoffmann still could have gone public, even from the most secret jail in the world.'

'You mean West Germany knows about the secret prison and doesn't do anything about it?'

'Martin, the only difference between East and West Germany is that the citizens of the Federal Republic don't talk about the crap their state gets up to because they've got their mouths full of organic fillet steak. It's not until the stomach growls that man growls too, that's what Christian Kreis writes.'

'So Hoffmann had to be got rid of. Keep going.'

Brendel sat down on the next bollard and stared into the fog. 'He was the mastermind, nothing would work without him. And getting it done by Bürger's people had two advantages. First of all, Hoffmann's death was a clear signal to his fellow conspirators. And secondly, we could present the Brigade as a murderous gang of mercenaries. It's all over if the public starts sympathizing with terrorists.'

'And now I'm stuck,' said Wegener.

'Why?'

'Bürger asked me in the Plänterwald whether we'd found any state secrets at Hoffmann's place. How did they know there really are papers that could be used to topple Moss?'

'From Ronny. He told them the truth. Anything else wouldn't have been credible.'

'And where are the documents now?'

'Nobody knows. We haven't found them, Bürger obviously hasn't found them either. It looks like even Marie Schütz doesn't know where they are.'

'OK, and then?'

'And then something went wrong.' For a moment Brendel looked as if he was about to laugh. 'Gabriel Opitz was supposed to kill Hoffmann on Bürger's orders. It was Bürger who had the clever idea of making Hoffmann's death look like an ancient Stasi revenge killing, and to get the whole story in the West German press. To really land the Stasi in the shit.'

'And that backfired.'

Brendel nodded. 'Steinkühler and Co. thought of everything, just not that the enemy might think like they do. The *Spiegel* story turned into a worst-case scenario.'

Wegener looked over at the granite gate. Two men had appeared in the mist and were standing motionless between the bronze soldiers. That made four guards altogether.

'That's why you got Moss to suggest a bilateral investigation to Lafontaine,' said Wegener, not quite as coolly as he'd have liked to sound. 'A joint investigation with the incorruptible West German officer who can never be a threat to them because he's been on the GDR's payroll for thirty years.'

'I'm a well-kept secret.' Brendel smiled. For a moment he was back to the old likeable, correct Western Superman. You can't hold anything against him when he smiles, thought Wegener. As long as you're looking at him, the chief investigator of the West Berlin crime squad's not a socialist agent, he's Richard, the Upright. But if you look away you might end up with a bullet in your back before you can bat an eyelid.

'When the investigations got bogged down it was decided that

Gruber would turn himself in,' said Richard the Upright. 'To put us on the right track, all above board. But as it turned out we hit the jackpot. When the nonsense with the exchange of shoes came out we knew – as soon as we got Opitz the consultations would be back on. Then we could prove the State Security's innocence without a shadow of a doubt.'

'You killed Opitz and planted his body in the cinema after the bombing. And Gruber?'

'We've got nothing to do with Gruber's death. You'll have to ask Bürger about that.'

'Four people dead.' Or five, thought Wegener, including me.

Brendel's thumb was still stroking his gun. 'I'll spare you the lecture about what would happen to our two countries if the consultations fail because the Stasi gets fingered for a murder they didn't commit, and the Federal Republic can't sign a transit agreement under political pressure from the EU.'

'The Thälmann monument. Once we found out where Opitz was going to be, you must have called the Stasi. When was that? When you went to get the car?'

Brendel's eyes now drifted over to the granite flags as well, paused for a few seconds and returned sadly. 'You know the answer. So why are you asking?'

'And Kayser?'

Brendel breathed out audibly.

'Tell me.'

'You're addicted to the truth.'

'It looks like it.'

'Christian and I had that appointment with Steinkühler. On Monday, while you were meeting Borgs.'

'I know that. So?'

'Christian got to Steinkühler's office for our meeting a few minutes before me. I'd pretended I was late because of my flight back from Bonn.'

'But in fact you were back much earlier.'

'Yes, at one. I had a two-hour meeting with Steinkühler, just the two of us. Right before the official appointment with Christian.'

'And?'

'My scent.'

'What?'

'Fahrenheit.' Brendel gave a rather helpless shrug. 'Christian came into Steinkühler's office and from the smell knew that I must have been there a long while before him. On Wednesday morning, over breakfast in the EastSide, he suddenly realized what that must mean.' Brendel stood up. His voice was almost cheerful. 'As I said, everything gets found out at some point.'

Wegener noticed that his backside had gone ice cold resting on the metal bollard. 'He wanted to blow your cover.'

'No,' Brendel shook his head. 'That's not how it works, Martin. He wanted me to get rid of Granz for him. And then he'd have kept at me and kept demanding one thing after another from me.'

'Granz from GreenFAC?'

'Granz from GreenFAC. They're not particularly crucial at the moment, but they're preparing for the worst case. One day a pipeline will explode somewhere, a nuclear power station in Hamburg will go crazy or an oil platform will sink in the Gulf of Mexico. So the whole world will see how dangerous conventional energies are. The FIS knows all about their plans but they've got nothing to prove it, as usual.'

'So you had to stop Kayser from blackmailing you.'

'If you're susceptible to blackmail then you're as good as dead.'

Brendel's blue eyes looked straight through Wegener. 'It wasn't planned for me to shoot anyone, certainly not an intelligence service man. But then something unexpected happens and you have to make a decision. And the next time a problem comes up you think: I decided that way last time, if I don't do it again it'll all have been for nothing. And so on. It's a slippery slope.'

Wegener looked over at the granite flags. The two bodyguards were still standing motionless side by side. Two monument tourists as stiff as pillars of salt.

Brendel suddenly woke up. 'How did you work it out?'

'You read my file, so I thought it was only fair for me to tap your phone. I couldn't do it with the Siemens because of the West German net key. So I had to get you a Minsk.'

Brendel raised his eyebrows. 'I haven't used the Minsk, not once.'

'True. When we were on the way to Boltenhagen you pretended to call Kayser in his hotel room, from your Minsk. You alleged someone from GreenFAC had got in touch with him. But that telephone call never took place. The surveillance protocols don't list a single tapped conversation on that appliance. And Kayser couldn't have talked on the phone, he'd been dead on his bed for ten minutes by that point.'

Richard the Upright looked amused. 'You're a real one-man secret service, Martin. What a shame you haven't got a state you belong to.'

'Who knows about your double role? Only Steinkühler and Moss?'

'Not Moss. Steinkühler and two of his advisors.' Brendel's voice sounded suddenly confiding. 'And that's the way it has to stay, Martin.'

There was a cawing above them and the black bird plummeted into view, spun into the fog, sank lower and only beat its wings when it was almost touching the lawn, climbing again and vanishing into the murky white.

'So everything you've done in the past thirty years won't have been for nothing,' said Wegener.

'Yes.' Brendel put the gun in his coat pocket. 'And so the International Monetary Fund doesn't end up impounding your whole country any day now.'

Wegener attempted to muster a smile. He noticed that this was his moment of survival. You could watch moments like this like a wheel of fortune, turning more and more slowly, the small iron hand letting the round moustache of rubber nubs pass more and more reluctantly until one of the nubs does nothing but bend but doesn't get past, capitulates, springs back and the carousel stops, precisely one point before where it started.

'How did you lose your wife?' Wegener asked.

'Cancer. Lymph glands. That was in 1998. Why do you ask?'

'I was thinking that nothing shapes us as strongly as a loss.'

Brendel tapped his feet. He hesitated for a few seconds. 'And your Karolina? Is there still a chance . . . ?'

'No.'

'Not at all?'

'If you can't get closure you should at least acknowledge that you can't start things over from the beginning.'

Brendel nodded.

Wegener cleared his throat.

'I assume the Hoffmann case is closed for you?' Brendel's gaze was as friendly as it was pitiless.

'I know what I wanted to know.'

'So you've won.'

'More like I've lost everything, Richard. But even if I wanted to, I couldn't explain what that really means in detail to a man like you.'

'Try it.'

'For the most part, it means knowledge.'

'Knowledge is something you gain. So you can't have lost.'

'Let's just say I recognize my defeat.'

'And that's enough for you.'

'Looks like that's the way I wanted it.'

Brendel reached out his leather-gloved hand.

Wegener stood up and took it. 'When are you going back over?'

A strong, short handshake. The glove-leather was smooth and cool.

'This evening.'

'How was the cep?'

'What?'

'The cep mushroom you found in the forest.'

'Oh, that.' Brendel pulled a face. 'Full of maggots.'

They stood alongside each other for one minute, two minutes, contemplating the fog being wafted by a slight wind, trying to lift but not yet capable. Yet another kind of silence, thought Wegener, a peaceful silence, not ominous but a natural silence. And perhaps that was the big difference: inside silence and outside silence. Perhaps it could simply never be really silent outside because there was always some other creature in existence, a mole, a slow-worm, a slug, a raven, a rat named Richard – you were never really alone outside.

Then Wegener turned around, walked along the plinth's curve to the staircase, descended the thirty-nine steps, now clearly feeling the bulletproof vest pressing heavy on his shoulders, himself sweating underneath this thing that was watching his back for him but not his head. Ragged swathes of fog floated above the sarcophagi, trimmed hedges and soldier images, not a shot rang out, nothing happened, only the raven cawed listlessly from somewhere a few more times once Wegener had reached the stairs to the granite gateway, once the four guards had let him pass without a blink and his Minsk began to vibrate.

'Frank?'

'Martin, where are you?'

'I'm taking a walk in a soldiers' cemetery.'

'Whatever rocks your boat. I'm calling because a patrol car just reported they've seen a white Phobos with red racing stripes at the Müggelsee, but they couldn't keep on its tail. It's been on the vehicle alert list the whole time and now I was just wondering if I need to bother reporting it to C5 or . . . ' but Wegener heard nothing more, already running along Stalin Boulevard towards Mother Homeland, turning right for the exit, realizing he was too fast, had taken the corner too sharply and started skidding on the wet leaves so fast that nothing could stop him, his Minsk flying away as if it wanted to follow the raven, while he himself was suspended horizontally in mid-air for a moment, floating above the shiny asphalt, a pole-vaulter in mid-leap angry that he'd knocked off the bar, seeing his fall as if in slow motion, decelerated, enlarged, a clumsy affair full of mist and moisture, in front of Russian insignia and Cyrillic letters, hoping for a tiny instant that he could fly like ravens and telephones if he just beat his arms hard enough a few times, to rise into the hazy sky above the monument, float above the Culture Park, above the Spree and all of Berlin, until the second's dream burst abruptly, his telephone shattered on the flagstones in the background, until he himself hit the ground, slamming his hip onto the ice-hard stone and the pain tore him in two, as brutally as if a Cossack butcher were splitting his fattest pig: a sword thrust right down the middle.

40

THE PHOBOS ENGINE HAMMERED AGAINST the phenoplast bonnet from the inside, clamouring to get out of its cage, longing to blast away the trembling cover and arise, now suddenly Motoransky Man, the hero of countless idiotic Czechoslovakian 3-D movies, flexing his biceps, inflating his chest and shoulders, gathering momentum and propelling the entire vehicle so ruthlessly forwards that red veins popped out in his glowering headlamp eyes, that the first external components took their leave, trim, fenders, registration plates flew away and Pavel, the shy Balkan-faced driver in denim dungarees, crawled down in front of the seat in running-gag terror, while Motoransky simmered at the front, sprayed, glowed, just to squeeze out a few more km/h, just to flog the Skodamobil to the limit around a Technicolor Czechoslovakia, in which every trace of socialist decay had been animated out of the picture at the expense of the state film-funding board.

But I'm not Pavel and this tin can here hasn't got Motoransky Man under the bonnet, thought Wegener as he pressed the accelerator down to the floor, gripped the steering wheel with both hands, sweating even more, needing to pee even more urgently. I'm a pawn slipping off its chessboard, plagued by a stabbing pain in the hip and an enormous pressure on the bladder, equipped with a rattling police Phobos soapbox from the winter production season, screwed together by resigned proletarians from Trabant POC, who knock back their first round of schnapps at lunchtime and then install the radio in the boot and the sunroof in the oil sump. I'm the great rearguard, one step forward, two steps back, don't wait for me, just keep on going, I'll get left behind somewhere along the way.

He was still doing 150 when the Müggelsee hiking path network suddenly appeared on his screen, and he had to brake down abruptly, swerving, for a moment feeling that the back of the car was about to lose its grip on the wet, narrow road. He jerked the steering wheel around and sped out of control into the empty car park, slamming into potholes and splashing dirty water, which ran down the side windows and smeared the windscreen.

Wegener put the little wiper arms into action, drew a curve and pulled across the furthest corner of the car park onto the main forest road, and now he was racing through the forest, dark pillars of trunks rushing past. The golden carpet of leaves darkened here too into a dull brown that rose in gentle hills and flattened out again, the bare, monotonous autumn world, finally transformed from a shady summer thicket to an exposed collection of branches, visible from far and wide and at first glance harbouring no secrets. But only at first glance, thought Wegener, everything's always very different at second glance.

At the third path that crossed the main thoroughfare he stepped on the brake, turned onto the forest path and put his foot back on the accelerator. An earth-coloured wasteland in which the Phobos struggled onwards, burrowing in, crashing so hard over thick arms of roots that the dashboard crunched, the cigarette lighter leapt out of its holder, the Navodobro fell off the windscreen, the passenger-seat sun visor dangled like a lame wing, the door of the glove compartment jumped open, hung down beneath the seats and from then on slammed into the panels from below at every crossed root. This car's self-destructing, thought Wegener, and that's pretty much the best thing it can do.

Then the first warning sign appeared – MINISTRY OF ENERGY ECONOMY SECURITY ZONE – NO ENTRY – beneath it a no-cameras symbol and a no-hikers symbol. The path moved off to the right, heading downhill – the car slipped, Wegener braked and saw the silvery pipeline snaking ahead, curving towards him, coming closer and bending away again, saw a white Phobos with red racing stripes parked deep in the hollow between the trees, Wegener still slipping and sliding, getting faster, the brakes not helping matters, for the car had a will of its own now, had had more than enough of its inferiority and now wanted to put an end to it all, scraped along a tree trunk, tore off the right-hand mirror, skidded towards the second warning sign, steamrollered it and rammed its radiator into an oak trunk so hard that Wegener's head slammed against the steering wheel, bounced back again and slumped to his chest.

Even before the stinging pain in his forehead set in and made the pain in his hip feel like a pleasant sensation, he felt the blood running warm down his face, into his eyes and mouth, tasting of iron like the plinth of the liberator statue, seeping onto his coat, his trousers, the seat. The door was jammed, bent out of shape, so he had to hurl himself against it three, four, five times until it gave way and let his own momentum tip him out of the car onto the wet leaves, a heavy sack in a bulletproof vest that rolled a few metres downhill, picked itself up laboriously and staggered into the hollow.

Remains of the police tape fluttered in the brambles, the forest floor long since filled up with leaves again, a strong wind blew in his face and his bladder hurt. Under the mossy belly of the pipeline were several holes in the ground, just dug, the failed burrowing attempts of a haphazard treasure-seeker, and by the time Wegener heard the rustling behind him it was too late. Too late often comes very early, he thought as the shiny metal of the spade had long since been rushing towards him, then whacked him on the back of the head – ka-ching! – a dull ring and he was falling again, nothing new there then, watching the forest floor come towards him, everything moving in his direction, the root veins were the colour of the dent in Hoffmann's neck, and now he was pressing his bloodied face nice and firmly into the fresh earth, relieved and tired, a moist coolness, a clay feel-good feeling for which the fat cats had to shell out a fortune for mudbaths, and it all came for free here.

The first slap around the face slammed in from the left.

The second from the right. Then another from the left.

The person dispensing the blows was pretty slap-happy, that's for sure. Wegener tried to open his eyes. Water dripped onto his head. His forehead was burning. He tasted wet earth and blood.

'Wake up!'

'Difficult . . . '

'What?'

'Difficult if you keep knocking me out every time I come round . . . '

'Are you alone?'

'Yes.'

'Does anyone know where you are?'

'No.'

'Your phone?'

'Right pocket, but it's . . . '

'Can they locate you?'

' . . . broken.'

Contours began to crystallize: the trees, a pipeline stilt, long hair, someone searching his jacket, almost sitting on his lap, pressing against him. Their long hair was wet. It smelled slightly sweet. Of vanilla.

Wegener savoured the scent. Drew it in deeply. Felt warm breath on his face, on his ears, in his nose, noticed a tingling in his crotch, his trousers getting too tight from one second to the next, his erection throwing its weight around, making a fool of itself with not a thought for its owner.

'OK, got it. It really is broken.'

Marie's face appeared directly above him, a couple of blonde strands stuck to her sweaty brow, her mouth slightly open, her dark lashes fluttering.

For one extended, solemn moment they looked into each other's eyes. Wegener had the feeling those chapped lips were about to come closer. Never mind the slaps and the whack with the spade, ten centimetres was all that was missing for a little historical tenderness on the crime scene, for feelings beyond all political intent, for a moment of weakness full of passion that would instantly cut out all pain – hip, forehead, back of the head, bladder – that might chase away the taste of earth, blood and sweat, a kiss that perhaps tasted of vanilla, like everything about this gracefully dirty feline beauty must taste of vanilla, from the top of her head to the tips of her toes with their black toenails . . .

'Marie.'

The face jerked back. 'How do you know who I am?'

'Boltenhagen . . . '

Marie stared at him. Her mouth opened a little further before it closed, before she got up, turned in a circle and shook her head, one hand on her wet brow. 'It's you! But your face . . . '

'Had a bit of a hard time recently.' Wegener made an effort to sound like he wasn't in pain. 'What did you tie me up with?'

'With my tow-rope.'

'You just want me to tow the line, admit it.'

'I see your sense of humour's not damaged.'

'That's the main thing.'

'Sorry.'

'What for? For tying me up? For forcing me to get undressed on the beach? For handcuffing me naked to my colleague, a West German to boot? For hitting me with a spade? For slapping me round the face? Or for making me stand in the ice-cold sea so long that my parts almost froze off?'

Marie's scornful look inspected the lump in his cords. 'It looks like the relevant parts are still attached.'

That condescending smile got Wegener hot under the collar, whether he liked it or not. 'You lied to us. Your father told you everything. Absolutely everything. You were in the know from the very beginning.'

'That's almost true, Mr Martin Alfons Wegener. There was one thing he always kept to himself for security reasons: where the stuff is.'

'He didn't tell you about the time capsule?'

'Time capsule?' Marie was amazed. 'Perhaps it's a good thing you just showed up. Tell me more.'

Wegener looked at Marie. 'The documents are in the capsule your old headmistress buried here in the woods twenty years ago.'

'Mrs Frommann?!'

'Yes. Do you remember? You were only a child.'

'Another one of my father's tricks!' Marie laughed. 'Typical! And it always works!'

'You could say that.'

'I bet Mrs Frommann's the only person who knew the exact spot, am I right? And even he didn't know where she'd hidden the stuff.'

'That's right.' Wegener tried to move his hands but Marie had tied the tightest knot in the Socialist Union. 'When they caught on to your father he got hold of the coordinates from Mrs Frommann so he could dig up the capsule. But his killers got him before he could start digging.'

'That's more or less what I'd thought. Without the coordinates you'd need an excavating machine to find anything here.

'Why didn't your father call you when things got serious? You could have rescued the documents for him. You're his most important ally, his only child.'

'He wasn't stupid. Of course he assumed his phones were being tapped. Was he supposed to destroy twenty years' work with a single phone call and reveal my existence to the Stasi at the same time?'

'He had people following him too. He doesn't seem to have noticed that.'

'Maybe he didn't have time to worry about that any more. Maybe he had to go for broke.' Marie turned away and stared silently into the forest, running her hands through her hair. A minute's silence for Albert Hoffmann. Then she reached for the spade. 'I'd better carry on.'

'Ms Schütz, this is a forest!'

'You can call me Marie, Alfons.'

'Marie, this is a forest.'

'Very good observation skills, Alfons.'

'You're looking for a needle in a haystack.'

'I'm looking for documents that can bring down an unjust regime, so I'll keep on digging until I find them.'

Wegener tried to sort his various pains into categories. His forehead felt as if someone had slit it open with a razor blade. The back of his head was a football, which Michael Ballack was using to practise his free kicks, one every twenty seconds. His hip was burning. Cold water dripped down into the wound on his head, a reliable stabbing to nature's own rhythm.

Marie leaned forward. 'Everything OK with your head?'

'Very funny. What were you doing at the holiday hut?'

'What do you think? I looked everywhere for the papers. Including Dad's hut.'

'Marie. Let me give you some good advice: forget it.' Wegener felt the tormenting pressure of his bladder, a three-kilo water balloon that someone had sewn underneath his abdomen. 'You can't beat this state. Even your father didn't manage it, and he tried really hard.'

'He did. But sometimes children have to finish off their parents' wars. Just think of George Bush.'

Wegener smiled.

Marie smiled back. 'You know why you're unhappy, Alfons?'

'I can't wait to find out.'

Marie's delightful ridicule was back again. 'Because you use manoeuvres and tactics instead of following a straight path. You're like a bush warrior. Walking the beaten tracks snaking through the underbrush. You think secrecy protects you, so you can fiddle and cheat the system here and there as far as your modest capacity allows. But really you're no more invisible than a child holding his hands in front of his eyes. So you might as well just go straight ahead in the first place. Then you'll get where you're going quicker and you won't catch any ticks along the way – it's all much easier. Believe me, I've tried it.'

'You find mushrooms if you go through the underbrush.'

'And poison yourself.'

'Not if you know your fungi.'

'Mr Mycelium saves the world.'

'You could still be saved, Marie, if . . . '

'Wrong. The right answer is: This country can still be saved.'

' . . . you keep out of all this.'

'That's what you think.'

'I could help you.'

'He's lying tied up in the forest, bleeding like the sawn-up lady brigade leader in *Frontier Fear 3* and he wants to help me.'

Wegener grinned, despite the pain. 'That was one crap film, huh?'

'Not as bad as *The Thumbscrew Protocols*.'

'What are you going to do once you've got the documents?'

'Why should I tell you that, old man?'

'Maybe because we're on first-name terms now.'

Marie laughed. 'Sweetie, it's room-temperature butter and a hot frying pan that are on first-name terms here, in case you hadn't noticed.'

'You know how it is with opposites,' said Wegener. 'They're made to cancel each other out or attract each other. But in either case they have to come together.'

'He starts turning on the charm when he's stuck in a dead end.' Marie came closer. A trace of awakening interest was now inter-mingled with her ridicule. 'Can't you imagine what I'll do with the documents?'

'You'll give them to the West German press. Just like your father planned to do.'

'I must have been fibbing about that.'

'You tell a lot of fibs. How does your boyfriend put up with you?'

'That was a bit too obvious.'

'Tell me the truth.'

Marie squatted down and looked at Wegener. 'It's the future of socialism at stake and the future lies in Posteritatism, in a—'

'I've heard all this spiel.'

'Then you'll be prepared when the time comes.'

'Who do you want to give the documents to, Marie?'

'Lafontaine.'

Above them, the wind picked up speed, driving into the almost bare treetops and shaking a few last leaves out of them, which sailed to the ground as sluggish, yellow snowflakes.

Wegener felt himself getting dizzy. 'Why . . . ?'

'He's waiting for them.' Her duckweed eyes sparkled. 'Lafontaine and Millard. Two leaders, one goal. Do you understand, Alfonso? Do you finally understand now what *Plan D* really is?'

Wegener stared at Marie.

'Let me help you, you dummy. It's about reunification. About a united Germany under the roof of reformed socialism! A democratic, ecological, wealthy socialism, the likes of which the world has never seen. That was the goal from the very beginning.'

'But how . . . ?'

'Yes, but how? asks the butter, and the frying pan answers: It's perfectly easy, with the documents from the time capsule. Moss steps down, Millard takes over. Everything's prepared, Alfons, in the West and the East, everything's ready for battle, reunification under Posteritatism is my father's legacy, and no Stasi and no Hauptmann can do anything to stop it. Lafontaine's going to the press with the documents in a week's time, Millard will be interim Chairman of the State Council even before the consultations, they'll present a ten-point plan in a month to adapt the economic systems . . . '

'You'd better keep on digging, then.' Wegener gathered up the very last of his strength, the very last of his anger, and laughed a little.

'Maybe I don't have to.' Marie came closer, stood above him and then squatted down, accompanied by a cloud of vanilla and a casual smile. Marie knelt on his bladder, then on his hard-on, and Wegener groaned out loud. 'I bet you went to see Mrs Frommann, Alfons, didn't you?' Marie opened his jacket as she whispered, feeling in the inside pockets, 'I bet that old manatee couldn't resist your charm.' Wegener felt Marie's hands in his shirt pockets, so close to his skin, his nipples. 'I ought to have thought of the time capsule myself – one–nil to you, Alfons.'

Wegener heard himself yowling pathetically as Marie embraced him, he felt her soft, sweaty skin on his cheek, smelled her breath, it all smelled of Magdalena, of Karolina, Marie's fingers in the back pockets of his miracle cords, feeling up Wegener's arse, finding nothing, wandering into the front pockets of his coat. 'Where's that little note got to? You wouldn't have come here if you didn't have the coordinates, don't try lying to your favourite frying pan.'

Wegener heard his own whimpering, the sound of a wild forest animal being fried alive, as Marie shifted aside, her knee slipping down and ramming him in the testicles, a tank smashing into a china shop. Panoplies of stars were now riding the Treptow Blitz roller-coaster, the wide-open tiger's jaws from behind, the sad view of the backdrops that debases every secret as soon as you've seen it, no matter what, as soon as the truth's entered the room all you want to do is send it out again, like you send out a clumsy Polish whore whose blow-jobs massacre your penis with her incisors. Wegener coughed, retched, couldn't draw enough air to shout, Marie's wet hair in his face, Marie's knee a battering ram in his crotch, her hands in his trouser pockets, holding on to everything, the throbbing remains of his testicles, the pained penis, the note with the coordinates, which was now pulled out of his pocket and held up like a World Cup trophy. 'I didn't mean to hurt you, sweetie.'

Wegener had never seen such furious happiness on a woman's face, triumph and sweat and dirt simmering together into a militant grace that made him forget his own screams for seconds. So you can still make the girls happy after all, Martin, he said to himself, because no one else was going to. And then he tipped over onto his side, lay spent in the leaves and earth and vomited, of course, what else, saw Marie, who was holding her paper dream in one hand, tapping numbers into her Minsk and then walking right, and then left, until everything seemed to fit; who lifted the spade and began to dig like crazy, who kept jamming her heavy army boot onto the tread of the spade, driving it into the ground, cutting through roots, levering out lumps of earth, rubbing dirt across her wet face.

You're the real Laura Kraft, thought Wegener: that limping Hiegemann cripple can go home, if ever a heroine deserved a movie made about her then it's you, you hard-boiled defender of family honour and political delusion.

Marie dragged something pale pink out of the hole, unearthed a shell-shaped folding plastic sandpit, broke the shell open with a blow of her spade, opened the lid and rummaged around inside it, chucking painted sheets of paper, scrolls and letters behind her, finally tipping the whole clamshell out, and at last found what she was looking for, an astoundingly small brown envelope that looked like a letter from the tax office. She showered it with kisses before she shoved it into

her jacket and stood still for another moment in the midst of fluttering children's letters, in the soft-focus mild October sunlight, the
mud-encrusted heroine at the end of an incredible Babelsberg Studios
adventure.

Then she went over to her Phobos and came back instantly with
an umbrella in her hand, which she opened up and positioned above
Wegener's head between the concrete pillars of the pipeline stilts.

The dripping stopped.

'At last an umbrella organization for a poor East German,' said
Wegener and sighed his quietest sigh.

Marie squatted next to him. Her duckweed eyes were even more
bottomless than in Boltenhagen. It must be kilometres deep in there,
too much for me, thought Wegener, too dangerous, too determined.
Those eyes are miniature seas, dogged ocean trenches, anyone who
dives in there has to be prepared to stick his own brain in the Posteritatism washing machine or he'll end up floating face-down. This
girl's really something special, and you're the shoemaker playing the
detective at best, not even particularly well, just a mediocre actor.
Admit it, thought Wegener, if Martin Wegener was a match for this
girl he wouldn't have holes in his head or a tow-rope around his
wrists.

'Untie me. Please.'

Marie's duckweed eyes surveyed his face, looking pitying, and her
hand stroked across his cheek.

Wegener went woozy. He tried to stop himself from swallowing
but his larynx went ahead and did it anyway, with a loud smack. A
helpless, weak grunt.

'I'll call an ambulance in an hour.' Marie stood up. The vanilla
cloud vanished. 'You'll be all right until then.'

'I have to go.'

'Go where?'

'To the toilet.'

'You can manage that without me.' Marie had already turned away, and now she walked down the hill for the second time and disappeared between the trees for the second time. Then the Phobos started up, juddering, needing a good kick to get it going in this wet woodland, the engine rattled, chugged and was suddenly all there. The rear lights burned red, moved back a few metres and stopped. Then the car pushed past the steaming remnants of its invalid brother onto the forest path and juddered off.

The red dots vanished above the hollow. The juddering grew quieter. After a minute there was nothing more to be heard.

Wegener smelled the greasy cloud from Marie's exhaust, felt the cloud creeping up the hill and enveloping him, tasted the old, grimy oil on his tongue. The pipeline dripped onto his umbrella roof, a plop hitting the tightly stretched plastic skin every three seconds. The wind drove the contents of the time capsule across the forest floor, chasing letters, poems, photos and drawings around, scattering them in all directions, and blew a piece of paper between Wegener's legs, red handwriting on it, only two sentences:

> *Socialism is the future of the human race.*
> *I am the future of socialism.*

Then the paper was borne onwards, flipped from one side to the other, sticking on a bare bush, freeing itself, getting picked up and lifted into the air, spinning as a gust of wind took it along, carried it up to the treetops, way up, impossible to see exactly where. The umbrella roof blocked the view.

Wegener drew his legs in and tried to roll himself up a little despite his tied wrists. From a distance he thought he heard Jan 'The Smooch' Hermann breathing into his microphone, *No doubt, my darling, I hate time,* a quiet piano tinkling as the dried blood stretched into a hard crust on his forehead and at the corners of his mouth. He was freezing cold.

Then he let it flow. The urine thrust out of him in spurts, instantly spreading through his trousers, greedily sucked up by the cord, tickling down his thighs, giving him a pleasant warmth and the guilty childhood feeling of wetting the bed, both liberating and oppressive, lustful and forbidden, *Today we're still two turtle doves, but tomorrow that's not worth a dime, but tomorrow that's not worth a dime* . . . Wegener counted, for the tenth, the eleventh, the twelfth time a new gush of urine flooded into his trousers, then there were a few last drips. It only stopped once the Hauptmann had long since passed out and the leaves and the children's letters and the matchstick men were dancing around him with such abandon as if nothing had gone on. As though nothing had ever happened.

Acknowledgements

I'd like to take this opportunity to thank Josef Fitz, the literary magazine *am erker*, Matthias Schmidt from Scholz & Friends Hamburg, Susann Rehlein, Klaus Schöffling and – although I don't know him personally – Michael Chabon for their various kinds of help along the way.

Many thanks to Christoph Hoenings, Melanie Hölting-Eckert, Martin Korte, Christian Kreis, Ida Schöffling, Tim Tepaße, Anna Marie Urban and Hartmut Urban for their comments on the novel. Also to Alexander Rötterink for his hard work on the German book jacket.

I'm particularly grateful to Juli Zeh and Simone Miesner. Without their contributions, Martin Wegener would have had a considerably harder time closing his first case unsuccessfully.

Christian Kreis' wonderful book of poetry *Nichtverrottbare Abfälle* (which appears here as *Inputrescible Waste*) is thankfully not a fictitious invention. The book was published by Mitteldeutscher Verlag and is still available. If you read German, then I heartily recommend it.

S. U.

Simon Urban was born in Hagen in 1975. He studied German literature at the University of Munster, and creative writing at the Deutsches Literaturinstitut in Leipzig, and his short stories have earned him numerous prizes. He lives in Hamburg and Techau (East Holstein) and currently works as a copywriter for a leading German creative agency.

Katy Derbyshire is a London-born translator and blogger based in Berlin. She has translated contemporary writers including Helene Hegemann, Clemens Meyer, Inka Parei and Dorothee Elmiger.